The
Oceans
Between
Us

Gill Thompson is an English lecturer who completed an MA in Creative Writing at Chichester University. Her debut novel *The Oceans Between Us* was a No. 1 digital bestseller and has been highly acclaimed. She lives with her family in West Sussex and teaches English to college students.

Also by Gill Thompson

The Oceans Between Us
The Child on Platform One

The Oceans Between *Us*

GILL THOMPSON

REVIEW

First published in Great Britain in 2019 by HEADLINE REVIEW
An imprint of HEADLINE PUBLISHING GROUP

First published in paperback in 2019 by HEADLINE REVIEW

Cataloguing in Publication Data is available from the British Library

ISBN 978 1 4722 5796 3

Typeset in Garamond MT by
Palimpsest Book Production Ltd, Falkirk, Stirlingshire

Printed and bound in Great Britain by Clays Ltd, Elcograf S.p.A.

HEADLINE PUBLISHING GROUP
An Hachette UK Company
Carmelite House
50 Victoria Embankment
London EC4Y 0DZ

www.headline.co.uk
www.hachette.co.uk

To Paul –
For his unwavering belief and support.
And in loving memory of
James Albert John Marett, FIIP. FRPS
Otherwise known as
'Jack'

Prologue

Even after all these years he still dreads plane journeys. The take off is the worst: the rush of tyres on concrete, the scream of engines, a crescendo of pressure in his ears.

There's a light touch on his hand. He looks down. Her fingers on his white knuckles.

'All right?' she says.

He nods, then looks out of the window. The plane is climbing steeply, the runway already a biscuit-coloured blur. The landing gear folds itself in with a distant thump and the engine steadies to a low throb.

He wipes his forehead with the back of his sleeve and leans his head against the rest.

She squeezes his hand. 'Well done. You'll be fine now.'

Yes, he will be fine. He always is. But this time there is another anxiety. Not the journey but the destination.

He pats his jacket pocket and feels the firmness of the expensive cardboard against the warm wool. No need to take the invitation out again. He knows the words off by heart.

And suddenly he's a young boy once more, excited to be going on a long journey to a land full of hope and opportunity. How was his eager twelve-year-old self to know what was really waiting for him?

He glances at his companion. They are deep into a long marriage; her face as familiar to him now as his own, her hair shorter than when they'd first met. His breath still catches at the sight of her. He reaches out to stroke her cheek. 'I'm glad you're here with me.'

'Wouldn't have missed it. It's been a long time coming.'

He's suddenly too choked to speak. He swallows and runs a finger round his shirt collar. 'Forty years' he says. His voice sounds hoarse.

'Half a lifetime. But you got there in the end. Just as you said you would.'

The seat belt signs have gone off. She reaches under the seat, pulls a leather bag onto her lap, and reaches into it for her bottle of water. She passes it across to him.

He takes a long sip. She always knows the right thing to do.

'I just wish I'd got there sooner. It's too late for some people.'

'Those who can will come. And remember who you're doing this for.'

He nods, then turns to the window again. The horizon is striped with brilliant colours: turquoise, orange, green – all radiating from a fiery, sinking sun. They'll soon be hurtling through a dark sky in their metal tube, for miles and miles until they reach Canberra. And the ceremony they will attend.

This day is the one he's fought for. He closes his eyes and the faces of the past appear before him.

No one had listened to them then.

They would listen now.

2

Part One

1941–1947

1

They usually came at night. It was more frightening then.

From beyond the warm tangle of bedclothes, Molly heard a pulsing wail. She swung her legs out of the bed, wincing at the shock of cold linoleum, then tiptoed over to the window and tweaked the curtain. Should she risk looking out? She took a sharp breath, turned back the tiniest corner of the brown paper that covered the glass, and peered through. Beams of light criss-crossed the sky. They'd be searching for planes: bomb-heavy and approaching fast, no doubt. She'd have to wake Jack.

Flitting past the mirror, pewter-dull in the gloom, she caught her own ghost: white nightgown, dark hair frizzing round her face. Jack wouldn't be alarmed, though. He was too used to this routine.

'Mummy?' His voice slurred with sleep.

'Come on. Get up.' She hated to haul him from the snug nest fugged with thumb-suck breath and the faint smell of milk. Really she should wake him properly and make him walk down the stairs. But he needed his sleep, poor lamb, so she tipped him over her shoulder in a fireman's lift, his five-year-old body a dead weight, and staggered down. By the time she reached the kitchen table, she felt her back would break, and she thrust him underneath more roughly than she'd meant. He muttered, and curled himself into a ball.

Molly stumbled over to the cupboard and took out the basket of supplies she'd repacked after the last raid: a balaclava, a torch, Mick's flat cap and a greasy pack of playing cards with the two of hearts missing.

She shoved it under the table. Jack was still quiet and the noises outside hadn't increased. Dare she make some tea? She lit the ring, grateful for the sudden warmth, filled the kettle and put it on to boil while she searched for the flask. Perhaps some food, too? There was half a loaf in the bread bin. They'd have to eat it plain. She'd run out of butter, and jam was a distant memory. When she was a girl, her mother's larder had gleamed with jars of preserves: redcurrant jelly, marmalade, quince jam, tomato chutney. Mum would spend all autumn picking, boiling and stirring and the air would be sweet with the tang of fruit and sugar. No chance of that now. The war had robbed them of luxuries, even home-made ones. But it was pneumonia that had stolen her mum, just after Jack had been born. And the last war had claimed her dad.

The shriek from the stove competed with the siren outside. Molly lifted up the kettle and poured the boiled water into the teapot. Another swift release of heat. She stirred it while the steam curled round her face. No time to warm the pot. She strained the dark liquid, added a dash of milk from the jug in the larder, then ducked under the table, clutching the flask.

Jack had sat up. His hair was brush-like, as usual, and despite the darkness turning everything monochrome, Molly knew the red spots on his cheeks would be fading in the cold air of the kitchen. He always got so hot in bed, burrowing under the covers like a dormouse. She eased the balaclava over his head and rammed the cap onto hers. Jack needed to stay warm; besides, the splinters sticking out from the table's rough underbelly could hurt. She pulled him close and held him against her chest.

'Is it the nasties?' Jack asked, his words muffled by her nightgown.

'Yes, love. Bombers probably. We'll be all right under the table.' Molly looked round the shadowy room. How many hours had they spent here, night after night, while the Luftwaffe did its worst? Sometimes, if there was a daytime raid, the Clarks let them share their Anderson shelter. If they'd lived over Balham way, they could have gone to the station. But Molly didn't fancy the Underground. Or next door come to that. It was nice to be in their own house. She and Jack, safe in their den.

Jack didn't ask about Mick any more. She'd told him about Dunkirk. 'Daddy got on a boat to come home to us,' she'd said, 'but he never made it.'

'Did the nasties eat him?' Jack had asked once, halfway through a bedtime story.

'*Eat* him! Whatever gave you that idea?'

He snuggled against her. 'Bill said they eat babies.'

Molly winced. That Bill Clark was too old for his years. 'Of course not. Daddy tried very hard to come back, but the sea was too strong. He'll be looking after us from heaven now.' She blinked away the image of Mick flailing in the watery darkness. She untied her locket and showed the photo inside to Jack. Best he remembered his dad as happy and smiling beneath his head of dark hair, as dark and full as Jack's would be, though Mick's was hair-cream-slick in the picture. But the other memories she kept inside: Mick cupping her face as he kissed her; putting his arm round her as he lit a cigarette in the darkness; and singing. Always singing. Sometimes she'd wake up to his voice: *In Dublin's fair city, Where the girls are so pretty, I first set my eyes on sweet Molly Malone.* The words caressed her. And when, later on, she looked in the mirror, she'd still be smiling.

It was a rough old night. They barely slept for the noise: the banshee wail of the siren, the whistle and roar of the bombs, the crash and crack of falling masonry. The air was acrid. Once Molly was sure they'd taken a direct hit. There was the most almighty boom and the whole house shook. She put her hands over Jack's ears, every muscle clenched, and waited for the explosion to rip them from their hiding place. But nothing happened. Molly's heart was going like an ack-ack gun and her lips were paper-dry. She licked them with difficulty.

'Are you all right, Jack?' she whispered.

Jack's eyes were huge in the darkness. He gave a slight nod, then nestled against her again. She kissed his warm hair, inhaling the little-boy scent of him, and felt herself relax. The sounds grew fainter.

By the time the all-clear sounded, it was morning. The windows blocked out any light but Molly could hear the cheeky-chappy lilt of the blackbirds' song. A robin, too, chirping shyly. Probably the one she'd seen in the garden yesterday, digging for worms. Croydon would be springing to life again, as it did each time, no matter how badly it had been wounded during the night.

Sometimes she wondered if she should have sent Jack away. Every week, it seemed, a child from his class was packed off with a gas mask and a little brown case by a mother holding back tears as she waved from the platform. Jack would undoubtedly be safer in Hampshire or Dorset, the popular destinations for the evacuees, as the newspapers were calling them. But Molly couldn't bear to think of another woman bringing up her son, cuddling him, cooking for him. She'd already lost Mick; she couldn't lose Jack too. And who knew when this war might end? No, they'd stay together, come what may.

'Wake up, Jacky-boy.' He'd gone back to sleep eventually, foetus-like in the blanket, his light breaths a soft rhythm. He stirred and moaned. Molly crept out, her limbs stiff as wood in the chilly kitchen. She turned on the wireless and lit the ring under the kettle. The last dregs from the flask had been tepid. A hot cuppa would wake her up. That and a bit of music.

The wireless crackled, then issued a growling sound.

Winston Churchill was giving another of his rousing speeches. Jack said he was boring and Molly privately agreed with him. No amount of *blood, toil, tears and sweat* would bring Mick back. She twiddled one of the knobs, her ear close to the machine, alert for any snatches of music. At last: 'In the Mood'. That was better. She needed to shake down all this bile.

'Come on, let's dance.' She reached under the table and pulled a yawning Jack to his feet. He stumbled as she tried to swing him around, so she just held his hands instead and swayed to and fro. All the time she was humming, enjoying the feeling of lightness as the hem of her nightgown flew out.

When the song finished, Jack flopped onto the kitchen chair. 'I'm tired, Mummy.'

'Watch me, then.' It was the Andrews Sisters now: 'Don't Sit Under the Apple Tree'. Molly grabbed a wooden spoon and joined in, striking a silly pose to make Jack laugh. But instead of laughing, he frowned, reaching out to turn down the wireless, as if he'd heard something. Molly stopped. Jack was right. There was a series of bangs close by. She switched off the music altogether. The sounds were big in the silence: *boom-boom-boom.*

'Guns,' she whispered, gulping down the saliva that pooled in her mouth. 'Don't move.' Jack was already a statue, but just in case, Molly put her finger against her lips and tiptoed across the room. She held back the net and peered out of the window. Surely not again? Hadn't they been through enough? But it was just Mrs Clark, her head in a turban, wielding a carpet beater. A dusty orange and red rug hung from the washing line, and their neighbour was bashing it for all she was worth. Molly laughed. 'Mrs Clark must be doing her spring cleaning!'

Jack ran to look, then laughed too. Molly turned the music up again.

After Bill called for Jack to walk him to school, Molly stood on the doorstep watching the small figure in an overlarge blazer and carrying a brown gas mask case plodding down the road. 'Look at me, Mummy. I'm a schoolboy,' he'd said when he'd first tried on his uniform. It was a wrench to say goodbye after a night like that. Jack was briefly illuminated by watery sunlight before they disappeared round the corner. Something made Molly shiver as she turned to go inside.

Wearily she lit the copper in the kitchen, then trudged upstairs to collect the bundle of washing from the corner of her bedroom. Everything seemed to be covered in dust or soot these days. Whilst she waited for the water to boil, she made another pot of tea and sat at the kitchen table, thinking of Jack, as usual. It was a worry, the effect the war was having on him. She'd once caught him loading a catapult with some small metal balls he'd found in Mick's old toolbox. 'I can fight the nasties if they come,' he'd told her. 'That will teach them for getting my dad.'

'We've got soldiers to fight for us,' Molly had said, squatting down in front of him and pushing back a tuft of his hair. 'I need you to help me in other ways.'

'How?'

11

What do you say to a fatherless boy who is trying to be a man? 'Like dancing with me,' Molly had said finally, pulling him up and twirling him round.

The kitchen was thick with steam and the windows all foggy by the time she realised the copper had boiled. She stood up, rubbing her back, eased off her wedding ring and placed it on the windowsill. Then she started the washing routine: tip in the Lux, stir the water, add the clothes, boil, scrub the stains against the washboard, rinse. It was hard work, but at least it stopped her thinking. By the time she was ready to peg out the washing, her mind was lighter.

She opened the back door, balancing the basket of wet clothes on her hip.

And froze.

The garden was a scene of destruction: huge clumps of grass-encrusted earth lay everywhere. Flowerpots were shattered, plants strewn across what was left of the small lawn, the coal bunker in pieces, the washing line nowhere to be seen. And right in the middle was a deep gaping hole.

Like a sleepwalker, Molly put down the basket, inched over and peered down. Four blades of dirty metal in the shape of a cross, linked by thin rods. As though a huge monster had ploughed into the ground, head first, leaving only his tail visible.

Consciousness returned. 'Mick!' she screamed. No, not Mick. 'Mrs Clark. Help!' Silence from next door. Thank God Jack was at school. She ran into the house and stood in the kitchen panting, her hand against her chest. There'd been an unexploded bomb in Fairfield Road two weeks ago. It turned out to have a time delay on it. A Royal Navy unit had come over to defuse it, disaster averted. But this one could explode at any moment. She had to get help quickly or Jack would be robbed in one fell swoop of both his mother and his home. Where was the ARP warden? She sprinted into the house and out through the front door.

She was twenty yards down the road when the ground shook violently and a colossal explosion lifted her off her feet.

2

Kathleen glanced at her watch. Another hour and John would be home. She should be peeling potatoes, not looking out of the window. Just one more minute, then she must get on. It had poured earlier, but the sun was out now, heating the wet grass and releasing a fine mist from the lawn. She watched the raindrops dripping off the myrtle willows' spiky leaves. When the light hit them, they looked like diamonds.

The Carter children were playing in their back yard. Scott, bossy as usual, was telling Chrissie to hurry up and finish on the swing; he wanted his turn. He pushed her hard and Chrissie squawked indignantly. Kathleen knew Chrissie would hate that; she liked to go at her own pace. Scott wiggled the swing, trying to dislodge his sister. Suddenly there was a loud wail: Chrissie had landed with a thump on the balding grass and was holding up her arm. Kathleen started, wondering if she should alert Jenny Carter. She hated to see poor little Chrissie lying hurt on the ground. The child needed to be picked up and cuddled. If she were her daughter, Kathleen would scoop her up in her arms and whisper to her until she stopped sobbing.

But Jenny just hollered, 'Get up and don't be such a

cry-baby,' out of the window, her Kiwi accent contrasting with the kids' Aussie voices.

Kathleen put her hands against the glass. She wondered what she looked like from the other side, a sad face gazing out, like that of a child who'd been forbidden to play.

'Butt out of those kids' lives,' John had said to her once. 'You've got enough to do here without all that sticky-beaking.' But had she really? What else was there but endless housework?

The sun had exposed a minute insect, previously camou-flaged by the rain, creeping across the smooth surface of the window. Kathleen pulled her hanky from her pocket and bashed at the tiny dot. It crunched, and she gathered it into her handkerchief, breathed hard on the pane, then scrubbed at it. By the time she stood back, the window was blank again.

Five years of marriage had been time enough for the usual references to *sprogs* and *tin lids* to fade to an embarrassed silence. Friends left their children at home when they came to visit. Relatives stopped asking them to be godparents or even inviting them to christenings. No one wanted spectres at the feast.

Kathleen used the clean part of the hanky to dust their wedding photo. She carefully wiped the cloth over John's image: broad shoulders, thin lips stretched for the camera, a proprietorial hand round the waist of his gauche bride in ivory Shantung silk. Were they once so young and hopeful? The picture looked lonely on the sill, as if waiting for companions. But none had come.

She wouldn't have minded the sleepless nights or the sticky

15

fingers on the furniture if she could've had a child of her own. With each month came a soaring spiral of hope, followed, a few days later by plummeting grief and loss. The pain was almost unbearable.

The doctor had advised her to keep a diary of her fertile times. She also used it to record her feelings at each month's disappointment. Sometimes she wrote things in it about John.

John. Blast. Where had the last ten minutes gone? No time now to do the lamb in the oven as she'd intended; she'd have to fry it. She crouched down and reached inside the Coolgardie. The meat was at the back, two tiny chops wrapped in newspaper. They'd shrivel away to nothing in the pan. At least she'd managed to get a few old potatoes at the greengrocer's. She'd have to cut the green out, but a pile of mash would fill the plate up a bit. And there should be a bit of gravy browning left from when she'd stained her legs that morning. She unhooked her apron from the back of the door and tied it over her grey blouse and tweed skirt. Then she took the knife out of the drawer and started peeling.

Leaving the fried chops resting on a plate covered with a cloth, and the spuds boiling on the stove, she dashed upstairs. Just time to powder her face, shiny from the steamy kitchen, and check her hair, still thankfully in its lacquered waves. John liked the house immaculate but wanted his wife to look as though she'd never broken a sweat.

In the lounge room, two brown-checked cushions sat either end of the dark-green sofa. Kathleen plumped them, stepped back to inspect the arrangement, then, on impulse, darted forward and moved one of the cushions a little further from its neighbour. The balance was lost.

On the dot of six, she heard a car in the drive. She smoothed her hair, removed her apron and went to stand in the hall. John came in, bringing with him the damp, stale air from outside. He jabbed a kiss at her cheek and grunted a greeting. She darted off to the kitchen to serve up the meal while he wandered into the dining room to make himself a drink. Dishing up the lamb chops and mash by the hatch, Kathleen saw him frown at the sofa and move one of the cushions to restore the symmetry. She smiled to herself.

Later, they sat, as usual, at either end of the mahogany table that shone with elbow grease.

John shovelled in a mound of potato. Grimaced. Swallowed. 'Have you heard the latest?'

Kathleen shook her head. She rarely listened to the wireless these days. The news was seldom good.

'It's big.' John moved his mat a fraction so the edge lined up with the end of the table.

Kathleen suppressed the urge to push it askew before she answered. 'What's happened?'

'The bloody Nips have attacked again. Five midgets snuck into Sydney Harbour last night. We sank two of the shonky rats but they got a torpedo into the harbour wall.'

Kathleen inhaled sharply. 'First Darwin, now Sydney. It might be us next.'

'Perth's too far west. We're safe for now.'

'Is that official? Did you learn it at the department?'

John's face adopted its guarded look. 'Can't say.' He resumed chewing, a slightly martyred expression on his face.

It wasn't until she served pudding, an apple crumble made with windfalls from the Carters' tree, that John spoke again. He scraped his spoon across the bowl and cleared his throat in that self-important way he had.

'So, what did you do today?' He glanced around the room as if checking it was tidy.

An unbidden image flashed into Kathleen's mind: of outstretched arms and dancing feet. She snapped it off quickly. God forbid he should find her squandering her time on 'self-indulgence'.

'Shopping . . . cooking . . . cleaning,' she intoned.

John nodded his approval. 'The crumble's nice.' He moved the pepper pot fractionally closer to the salt cellar.

'Yes . . . I managed to get some sugar. There's enough to make a cake tomorrow.'

'Good on ya.'

Kathleen sniffed. 'Your mother overindulged that sweet tooth of yours!'

John chuckled. 'That's what mothers do, overindulge their kids. It's not like I ever get spoiled here.'

As Kathleen stood up to stack the crockery again she realised how stiff her legs were. The keep-fit class she'd been to at the Lacey Street hall was telling on her muscles already. It had been going for a year but today was the first time she'd plucked up courage to attend. She'd enjoyed the camaraderie of the other women and the opportunity to shed her tight clothes in favour of the loose-fitting shorts and Aertex blouse she'd bought and hidden from John. The class was fun too. Her body hadn't stretched and bent like that since she was a carefree girl. Instead of going straight home afterwards, she'd lingered in the park, breathing in the sweet, rain-soaked air. By the time she got back, the house had shrunk and she'd rushed to the window. Her trip out had reminded her how confined she was at home. She needed to reassure herself that the outside world still existed.

'Any chance of a cuppa in here?' John's voice drew her back. Tight-lipped, she put the kettle on to boil.

As she carried in John's tea, she realised she hadn't asked him about his day.

John smiled smugly. 'Not bad, darl. I spoke to the minister earlier. He enquired after you.'

He was looking at her; this was her cue, but she'd make him wait a little. She set down the china cup on the small table next to John's chair before walking over to her own seat. Then she sat down and crossed her legs slowly before she asked the question: 'Anything about that promotion?'

John reached out and straightened the spoon before picking up the cup and sipping the hot liquid. He leaned back slightly in his chair. Perhaps he too was playing games, or more likely just savouring the moment. 'Should be sewn up pretty soon,' he said.

'That's good. You've worked hard, John.' It wouldn't do to provoke him. If she made him wait too long for the compliment, he'd get tetchy. Better to endure his smugness than his temper.

'Yep.' John finished his tea and replaced the cup on its saucer. 'Said he liked the way I keep everything shipshape. Apparently I'm the full quid.'

Kathleen tilted her head at him. 'Give me your empties. I'll take them through.'

John passed the crockery up to her and she went back into the kitchen to finish the washing-up. She took her time standing by the sink, immersing her hands in the soapy water. The kitchen had been done to her taste: pale green cupboards, cream walls and a beige-and-green block print on the linoleum floor. Everything was perfect except . . . She frowned at the three flying ducks on the wall. John had put them up there, spending hours measuring and positioning them. They were the only things he'd insisted on in the kitchen. Every time she saw them, she thought of those poor creatures making their bid for freedom. And John nailing them down.

By ten o'clock, they were ready for bed. Kathleen smeared cold cream across her face, luxuriating in the moisture seeping into her skin as it removed the day's grime. The familiar scent took her back to her mother performing the same ritual. 'Vanishing cream', she'd called it. As a little girl, Kathleen had sat on her mother's bed watching to see if she would disappear.

'Try to be a good wife,' Mother had said to Kathleen the day before she married John. 'And a good mother too when the time comes.' She'd tried. She'd really tried. Listlessly, she picked up her hairbrush.

John had been a golfing friend of her father's, though younger than him. Father had engineered the marriage, as he engineered everything, eager to acquire an up-and-coming son-in-law. At first Kathleen had been flattered by the eager young civil servant keen to wine and dine her. She'd been surprised when he proposed so soon but had accepted without qualms. He seemed kind and appeared fond of her. And marriage would enable her to escape Father's strict discipline. Of course Father hadn't banked on them moving to Perth from Melbourne almost immediately after the wedding. What a shame the son he'd always wanted had disappeared from his life so soon. And Kathleen had realised too late that she'd merely gone from one domineering man to another.

It wasn't as though he'd ever laid a finger on her, thank God. Kathleen had worked with a woman once who wore foundation an inch thick to hide the bruises from where her husband had hit her the night before. No, John's methods were more subtle. A demeaning comment here, a disapproving look there. And that constant checking of the housework. She'd evened the score a bit earlier, though. She grinned at the memory of the repositioned cushion. Even though he'd moved it back, it had been a small victory.

She looked in the mirror. Without make-up, her face was the colour of the cake mix she'd whisk up tomorrow. Perhaps she should allow a little sun on her skin. A healthy glow would make her look more relaxed. She leaned forward and pinched her cheeks. Better than rouge. Her mother had taught her that trick. The redness spread and her face looked brighter.

A sound made her shift her gaze to John's reflection. He was lying down reading a book, flicking its pages impatiently.

The pink paisley cover looked familiar. She whipped round. He was studying her diary.

'Tonight looks promising.' The bedside lamp made hollows of his eyes.

She flushed, annoyed at the violation and embarrassed by his words. Unable to bring herself to speak out or criticise him, her anger turned towards herself, her stupidity. She was so careless. What other explanation was there for leaving the diary, with its telltale system of ticks and crosses, on the bedside table?

'Give me that,' she said, holding out her hand. John handed it over with a leer. Thank goodness he hadn't seen what she'd written about him. At least she didn't think so. She'd have surely known if he had. He'd have been furious. Fortunately it was only lust she saw on his face and not anger.

Intimacy was the last thing on her mind, but she couldn't put off joining him in bed any longer. There was no escape. She smoothed down her cotton nightdress, removed her slippers carefully and laid them beside the bed for the morning.

Then she climbed slowly in beside him.

3

She opens the bedside cabinet and reaches deep inside. The wood is rough; small splinters graze her hand. But there's nothing there. Why can she never find what she's lost?

She shakes her head to loosen the buzzing in her ears. The bees have crawled in again.

The woman from the next bed leans over. She has yellow teeth; cheesy breath. Her grey plaits swing. 'What's she doing, Matron?'

'Back to your bed, Annie. Leave Margaret alone. Margaret? There's nothing in there. I've told you before.'

'She's been doing it for hours, Matron. Running 'er hands around inside the bedside cabinet and mumbling about bees in 'er 'ead.' Annie picks at the scab on her nose. 'What yer looking for, duck? We've told you there's nothing there.'

She ignores the woman.

The war's in her head again. Crashing houses. Black smoke. Burnt timber. Charred dust. Stinking sewage. That was when the bees arrived.

Thinking hurts. Sometimes pictures come: a man, a child, a beach. A table with an orange oilcloth. But they don't last. And darkness returns.

The trolley clang-clang-clangs up the ward.

'Margaret. It's time for your breakfast,' says nice Nurse Sanders with her shiny yellow hair and bouncy walk.

She takes the tray from the nurse, eats the gluey porridge, drinks the tepid tea.

'D'yer want the *Sketch*?' Annie again. 'I've finished it. There's never any good news. The cartoons are the best thing about it.' A messy pile appears on the end of her bed.

What's the point of reading the paper? Always about the war. Photos of soldiers and aeroplanes; pictures of men in bowler hats. It never tells her anything she needs to know. Like what she's lost. And how to find it. She picks up the news sheets and drops them onto the floor.

'Now then, Margaret. Someone else might want that.' Dr Lee stoops to pick up the newspaper, folds the pages and puts them on the end of her bed. Then he sits down beside her.

'How are you today, Margaret?'

She shrugs.

'Matron tells me you've not been cooperating with your injections.'

She shrugs again.

'You need to have the insulin, Margaret. It'll help you put on weight.' Dr Lee circles her wrist with his fingers. 'You're still very thin.'

'Injections hurt.'

'But they'll make you better.'

There is something else. What is it? She hits her head with

24

her hand. Her head buzzes. That's it. 'I've still got those bees. Can you get them out?'

'Hmm.' Dr Lee picks up the chart at the end of her bed and writes something on it. 'It's not easy, my dear. We think your ears were damaged during the Blitz. The buzzing will wear off. We just have to give it time.'

She kicks at the bedclothes.

'Anything else?' He looks at her. He has dimples in his cheeks like thumbprints on dough.

'I still can't find it. I've looked and looked.'

'Yes. I've been thinking about that.' Dr Lee fiddles with his pen. 'I'd like to try some different treatment. ECT. It might help you to remember more.'

She sits up straighter in bed. 'Will it help me find what I've lost?'

'It might do, yes. It will feel a bit strange, but we think this treatment will improve your memory. We'll start tomorrow.' He pauses to write something else on the chart, then puts it back on the end of her bed. He moves on.

'Now, Annie, how are you today?'

Dr Lee gestures towards a wooden box sitting in the corner. Dials and leads come out of it. 'It looks a bit like a wireless set, doesn't it?'

'Are the Andrews Sisters in there?' she says.

He laughs. 'I'm afraid it doesn't play music.'

She lets her hands fall into her lap.

'I will be with you the whole time. I promise.' The doctor

rings a bell on his desk. 'Prepare the patient for intravenous, please, Nurse.'

'Margaret? I'm just going to give you an injection.' Nurse Sanders' hands are trembling.

'Don't like needles.'

'I know, dear, but this won't hurt much. Why don't you close your eyes?'

She feels pain, then cold.

'There we are. All done. You can look now.'

There is a rustling noise from the corner of the room. Nurse Sanders holds a black thing that looks like a small gas mask. Perhaps she's worried there'll be a bomb attack. Poor Nurse Sanders. She's very young.

Dr Lee's brown eyes are very close. He smells of tobacco. 'Can you count backwards from a hundred, Margaret? I'll start you off. Ninety-nine . . . ninety-eight . . .'

She's searching again. The smoke is back. Choking her. She can't breathe. Buildings are crashing around her.

Darkness.

4

As he strode down St George's Terrace on his way to Government House, John Sullivan listened to the satisfyingly clipped sound of his heels on the dusty pavement. In one of the few unboarded-up windows he noted the sharp cut of his brown suit, the precise angle of his trilby. He smiled approvingly at his reflection. The war had dragged on for five years now, but even in these God-awful times, he could still cut the mustard.

When the porter pulled open the large wooden door, John swept in without even looking at him. All his thoughts were on the meeting ahead. Inside, a thin girl sat at a desk in the cavernous reception area. As soon as she saw John, she stood up and led the way to the boardroom. John followed her, glancing down at her long legs, swathed in nylon. He wondered where she'd got the stockings. Kathleen hadn't been able to buy any for months.

'The minister is expecting you.' The girl wore a severe navy suit and her brown hair was pulled tightly back from her face, as if she wanted to look as masculine as possible. Perhaps the stockings were her one concession to femininity.

John nodded briefly in response.

The boardroom door was open. The girl addressed its occupant: 'Mr Sullivan is here, sir.' She hovered, indecisive. 'Should I stay and take minutes?'

'No,' was the terse reply. 'And no calls, mind. I don't want to be interrupted.' The mannish-looking girl left before John could give her his hat, and he had to juggle it awkwardly as the minister, a tall man in a light linen suit, came forward to shake hands. John always thought his mouth looked like a goldfish's.

'Sullivan. Good of you to join me.' The goldfish lips stretched.

'A pleasure, sir.' John looked round the boardroom: it was a relic from more affluent times. The thinning carpet remained a defiant shade of burgundy and the oak walls heaved with portraits of past governors. The room smelled of stale cigars and old leather.

'Do sit down.'

John lowered himself onto a worn leather chair a fraction after the minister himself sat down. His host poured them each some water from the cut-glass jug on the table.

'How are you? Not taken too many hits?'

John took a sip. 'A few on the coast, but we're all right inland.'

The minister inclined his head. 'And Kathleen. Is she well?'

'Not bad.' John set down his glass. He had a sudden memory of Kathleen's fingers, curled round the teacup she passed him that morning, her nails almost bitten to the quick. 'This war has taken a toll, though.' He looked up at the sound of a fly buzzing around the ceiling.

'Too much time on her hands,' said the minister. 'Get her pregnant, man! A brood of kids should sort her out. God knows, the population could use a boost.'

'Maybe.' John straightened a brown coaster on the table. He felt a muscle tighten in his jaw. When were these awkward pleasantries going to give way to the real business of the meeting?

The minister cleared his throat and motioned to a pile of papers in front of him. 'As you know, I've just returned from a trip to Europe. Officially I was there to view war damage and have some influence on European policy.'

John raised an eyebrow. 'And unofficially?'

The minister lowered his voice. 'Off the record, we can definitely swing this our way. There are vast numbers of displaced persons out there. Once the war's over, they'll jump at the chance of a new life here.'

So that was the deal. Importing aliens. But surely that would be scraping the barrel? John chose his next words carefully. It wouldn't do to be too negative. 'But what kind of state will they be in?'

'Well, not good, some of them,' the minister acknowledged. 'But we're not going to be inviting *them*. We choose who gets offered a passage. There'll be a clear brief – young, strong, healthy boys. And plenty of girls too. Decent-looking ones, preferably.' Another fleeting smile.

For a second John imagined the child he and Kathleen

could have had: Kathleen's dark-blonde hair, his athletic build. He switched the image off. No point going there. He needed to focus on the minister's plan. He cleared his throat. 'What about the cost of transporting them?'

'We'll ask the Brits for some ships. I think a lot will come from northern Europe – they're the ones hardest hit. But there's a way to get hold of a load of Poms too.'

John couldn't help his response: 'Let's just avoid the convicts this time.' The minister swatted at the fly, now buzzing around his head, his mouth a set line. Perhaps that was a little close to the bone. John tried again. 'How would you do that?'

A hard stare, then a relaxation of features. 'Put simply, the Poms have a problem: too many kids. Poor buggers whose dads were killed in the war and mothers lost in the Blitz – or else so busy dropping their knickers for the Yanks, they're not interested in looking after their own nippers any more.'

'But surely we need *vast* numbers if we're to ward off the yellow peril?' It still didn't stack up.

'Damn right we do! Populate or perish.' The minister pointed out of the window. 'There's three million square miles of land out there. If our nation's heart is to keep beating strongly, we need new lifeblood to feed it.' It sounded as if he was giving the speech already.

John nodded.

The minister put on his horn-rimmed glasses and picked up a handful of close-typed papers from the pile on his desk. 'This was the briefing document sent to Commonwealth leaders: "There are special and urgent reasons why a major effort should be made immediately in the field of child migration . . ." blah blah blah . . . "The peculiar circumstances of war have created in Europe a greater number of orphans, stray children, 'war babies', than ever before. This makes the present a time of potentially unparalleled opportunity for Australia to build up her population with child migrants who . . ." blah blah blah . . .' He looked up. 'You get the drift.'

John did get the drift. But he also saw the pitfalls. 'Will the Brits let these kids go?'

'They've got no choice! The orphanages are overflowing and the government's struggling to feed 'em. They're worried about the impact on the economy once the soldiers finally come back. It's a great chance for us. And it's simple – they have too many kids and we don't have enough.'

'So how many are we talking about here?'

The minister grinned. 'Fifty thousand!'

'*Fifty thousand?*' John whistled.

'We struck a deal.' The minister leaned towards him and John caught a rush of tobacco. 'The Brits want shot of these kids. There's no future for them in the homes. And no one will miss 'em, 'cos they're orphans. There's the beaut. We'll ship 'em across here – and get the Poms to pay for the passage.' He sat back in his chair, triumphant. The fly, perched on the table in front of him, rubbed its forelegs together.

'But will they come?' wondered John.

'Of course they'll come! Why wouldn't they? We'll lure them with sunshine, oranges, horseback rides. The kind of life they could only dream about.'

His enthusiasm was contagious. And there was clearly potential. This project would make a name for the minister. If John worked with him, it would make a name for him too. 'It's a great idea,' he said. 'The kids get a new start in life.'

'And we get good breeding stock from the old mother country. Seventeen thousand a year,' the minister consulted the paper again, '"during the first three years of peace in Europe, or as soon thereafter as practicable."'

John no longer had to feign enthusiasm. This was massive. 'Fifty thousand youngsters. Strong, strapping lads to work on the farms. Girls who know how to cook and clean.'

The minister grinned. 'You've got it, mate. Good white stock. We just need this bloody war to end and then we're in business.'

Now filled with optimism, John raised his glass in a toast. 'Here's to the end of the bloody war, then.'

'The end of the bloody war!' The minister chinked his glass against John's, knocked back its contents and upended the glass on the table, neatly trapping the fly.

5

He was back there again, running through the streets, trying to find his mum. Where was she? No one there. Who was the man? Uniform. ARP warden. 'Come on, young man. It's getting dark. I'll take you to the town 'all. They'll sort you out there.'

'Jack. Get up!'

Jack struggled to push back the fog in his head. Was there another air raid? But he couldn't hear the siren. Come to think of it, there'd been no alarms for a while. The dorm was quiet – just the usual snuffles and snores in the darkness.

'Come on.' He was being shaken. A shadowy figure leaned over him. Bert.

'All right. I'm coming.' Jack sat for a minute rubbing his eyes, then swung his legs off the bed, feeling for the stone floor with his bare feet.

Bert was already halfway down the dorm. He'd wrapped himself in one of the thin grey blankets. Jack wished he'd done the same. The ceilings at Melchet House were high and the windows didn't fit properly. It was always cold, even in summer. Sometimes it took him an age to get to sleep in the narrow metal bed. He'd think longingly of his old padded counterpane. It must have been destroyed with the house. Along with everything else.

'Wait for me.' Jack tried to run quietly. Bert was waiting at the end of the dorm, his arms folded and a scowl on his face.

'Honestly, I don't know why I bother with you. Do you *want* to wet the bed?'

Jack shivered. It was almost nice at first, when the warmth spread across the sheet and made him feel all cosy, but in the morning his sodden bedclothes would be clinging to him like an icy shroud and he'd be in for another punishment. Sister Angela had a round-ended stick, a good three feet long. You had to hold your arm straight and she'd whack you on one of your palms. If you were lucky, the bruise would heal before the next dose. Bert was trying to save him from that. As he followed his rescuer down the winding passage to the toilets, Jack heard howling. But he couldn't tell if it was the wind or a boy crying.

They were up at six as usual. Jack trudged downstairs with the Piccaninny paste and a scrap of old sheet, ready to clean the entrance hall. *Twice the shine in half the time*, it said on the tin. Underneath was a picture of a boy with a very black face, smiling. Jack prised off the lid with his thumb, releasing a sweet, waxy smell. He dipped in his cloth, knelt down and started to wipe the wood with wide circular strokes. Another boy was supposed to follow behind to shine up the floor, but he couldn't see anyone. Then he heard a muffled giggle. Bert

34

was staggering towards him, a cloth tied round his bottom like a huge nappy.

Jack stopped wiping. 'What on earth are you doing?'

'Quick.' Bert plonked his padded rear down in front of Jack. 'Pull me along.' He reached out a grubby hand. Jack grabbed it, but his fingers were slippery with paste. He wiped them down his trousers then tried again. Bert was heavy. Jack had to strain to pull him. He glanced round anxiously but couldn't see any of the nuns. Just another boy, Tom, walking down the corridor. He looked strong.

'Come and help!' Jack called to him. Tom sprinted over and grabbed Bert's other hand. Together they hauled Bert across the floor. Behind him followed a perfectly shined strip of wood, about the width of Bert's backside.

In Jack's dreams, *home* was a warm word. He could still remember kisses and kindness, whispered stories and soothing arms. But it didn't mean that at Melchet House. Here, *home* meant noise and orders and long polished corridors and endless singing and incomprehensible prayers. And everywhere women in black-and-white garments like huge flapping magpies.

There were forty boys altogether. At first Jack had been one of the youngest. Sister Beatrice used to sit him on her knee and sing 'Hail, Glorious St Patrick'. But she would still clout him if she thought he was being disobedient.

Mummy had never hit him, so it was a shock when Sister Beatrice had first boxed his ears. It wasn't particularly painful;

she wasn't even that angry, but he felt a burst of resentment nonetheless. He didn't belong to Sister Beatrice like he belonged to Mummy. How dare a nun do something like that? She hadn't even known him for long. Mummy had given him a right tongue-lashing that day he'd smashed her best teapot with the football he'd been told not to play with in the house. Then she'd sat at the table, put her face in her hands and cried and cried. That had hurt more than any smack.

It was the hugs he missed the most. Mummy's soft arms wrapped round him, pressing his face into her chest. Her blouses smelled all flowery, like a garden. Sister Beatrice smelled of peppermint and her knees were bony. Apart from Sister Beatrice, no one else at Melchet hugged him.

At first he looked out of the dorm window every day, standing on tiptoe to see if he could see Mummy marching down the drive in her good winter coat and the hat that made her look like Robin Hood. But she never came. He'd been told she'd gone missing in the explosion and never been found. But if she was alive, why hadn't she come to collect him?

'Melchet is your home now,' Sister Beatrice said. 'You have to stop thinking about your mother.' And Jack had tried. But was it wrong to think about Mummy? At night, when he lay on the hard mattress trying to get to sleep, he saw her dancing in the darkness. *Don't sit under the apple tree*, she sang. And he'd turn over and press his face against the pillow, replaying the scene again and again.

On Sundays they walked to church, two by two in a long line. The nuns went with them and the boys gave them names like the Hare, or the Tortoise, depending on how fast they moved. Jack pretended he was a soldier in the war. *Look at me, Mummy. I'm a man.* He swung his arms and stared straight ahead. That was how Dad would have marched. Jack was proud of his dad. Dad had been a soldier. But it was hard to remember him now. His face had faded. If he spent a long time thinking, Jack could bring back a few things: the scent of shoe polish and hair oil, and the rough feel of Dad's clothes. There was something else too: a raspy sound, a small jumping flame and a burning smell. Then his dad would be smoking and laughing and putting his arm round Mummy. And Mummy would laugh back.

After breakfast, they went to their classes. They had their lessons at the home. The nuns didn't want them mixing with the local children, and besides, there wasn't a Catholic school nearby. Bert was in a group with older boys but Jack and Tom were taught by Sister Immaculata. They sat at high wooden desks with the names of previous occupants scratched into them. Each had a dark-stained inkwell in the top right-hand corner. Once a week, a monitor would bring round a large bottle of Winsor & Newton's ultramarine, and carefully tip a small amount into each well. Another monitor passed along a box of pens. The boys at the front picked the best pens; if you sat at the back, you were left with the ones with scratchy nibs. If your pen leaked or you pressed too hard, there'd be blotches on the page and you'd be in for a thrashing. Jack was always very careful when he wrote. He'd had too many beatings to risk another.

That morning Sister Immaculata had an announcement. 'You'll all be sitting the eleven-plus this week. Tests will be administered in maths, English and problem-solving. The cleverest boys will go on to do Latin next year. The dunces will have woodwork with Mr Evans.' Mr Evans was the caretaker. He was old and bad-tempered and liked to tweak people's ears. Jack thought he'd prefer to do Latin, even though all that gobbledygook reminded him of church.

They filed into the hall to take the examination. Jack sat at his desk answering questions, trying to ignore the scratching of his neighbours' pens and the faint squeaking of shoes whenever a nun walked past to check they weren't cheating. He liked English best. He'd been looking forward to this paper. First of all they had to correct errors in sentences. There was a trick question about the apostrophe, but Jack remembered the rule: after the 's' if it's plural: *This is not an infants' school*, he wrote.

But he frowned at the next one: *The bishop and another fellow then entered the hall.* Did *bishop* have a capital letter? Jack didn't think so. What about the verb? No, *entered* was right. He tapped the wooden pen top against his teeth. It had bite marks on it where other boys had done the same, a bit more aggressively. He glanced at Tom next to him, writing furiously, his fringe flopping against his forehead. Somewhere in the room a clock ticked, like a pulse. Jack turned back to his paper. It must be the capital letter on *bishop*. He couldn't think of anything else. He wrote it down.

By the time they'd finished, Jack's shoulders were aching. He rubbed them as he walked out of the hall.

'D'you do all right?' asked Tom, who had followed him out.

'Think so. What did you put for that bishop one?'

'What?'

'Something about a *bishop and another fellow*.'

'Fellow!' Tom laughed. 'A bishop isn't a fellow. I changed it to *gentleman*.'

Jack thumped his forehead with his fist. 'Oh no! I didn't realise that.'

'Idiot.' Tom grinned. 'I expect you've done fine, Malloy. You usually do.'

Tom was right. When the results were announced, Sister Immaculata told him he'd be doing Latin next year.

Look at me, Mummy. I've passed the eleven-plus. You always said I was clever.

At first Jack didn't notice the change in the air. It was Bert who asked if he thought the nuns were behaving strangely. 'Always whispering or passing round newspapers.' Jack realised there'd been more excitement at the home lately.

They were called inside from the spring warmth, shepherded into the hall and told to sit down and be quiet. A large radiogram, never seen before, was wheeled onto the stage and Sister Perpetua adjusted it self-importantly. Suddenly Mr Churchill's voice boomed out. Jack couldn't understand all of the words but a few drifted down to him: 'unconditional surrender . . . brief period of rejoicing . . . Long live the cause of freedom . . . God save the King!'

Bert was sitting next to him and whooped loudly. 'The war's

over!' he said to Jack. Jack beamed back, but inside he felt strange. He'd heard other phrases too: '. . . the injury . . . inflicted . . . detestable cruelties . . . justice and retribution'. He wasn't sure what all the words meant but they made him think of Mummy telling him about Dad and how the nasties had got him. It wasn't long after that that the bomb had exploded. Jack's chest tightened.

But then he had another thought. Perhaps Mummy had stayed away because of the war. Maybe she'd had an important job to do, even helping Mr Churchill. That was why she couldn't get him. But now that the war was over, there was nothing to stop her. She *would* come down the drive. She *would* collect him. And then they could go back to Croydon and live together again. Not at the old house, obviously. But maybe a new one. Perhaps the government would build them one to thank her for all she had done for the war effort. And everything would be as it was.

6

Kathleen and John sat in Dr Myers' consulting room in silence. A large fan whirred from the ceiling, slicing the humid air and infusing it with a chilly blast. Kathleen was aware of John's clenched hands and rigid jaw. She stretched out her own fingers across her skirt, trying to relax. A clock ticked loudly on the wall behind them. She wondered if it'd been placed out of view so that patients couldn't easily calculate how much they were paying per minute. Dr Myers didn't come cheap, but he was reputed to be the best. It had taken her a long time to persuade John to come. He kept saying the consultation would be too expensive, but she suspected that embarrassment, not parsimony, was the real reason. She just hoped there'd be good news.

'Mr and Mrs Sullivan,' the doctor intoned. He had beaver-like front teeth and a grey moustache that did little to hide them. 'As you know, we have conducted a number of tests . . .' He paused to look down at a typed sheet of paper in front of him. My future is on that paper, thought Kathleen. This doctor knows whether or not I'll ever be a mother. Her chest was as tight as a drum.

Dr Myers was looking at her intently; she could see flecks

of amber in his brown eyes. 'Mrs Sullivan. Everything suggests you are fit and well. You should be able to conceive and carry a baby to term. We can't find anything obviously wrong with your reproductive system.'

Kathleen breathed out, then froze as John tensed beside her. The doctor transferred his gaze. 'Mr Sullivan. There appear to have been some irregularities in your sample . . .' He paused to clear his throat, but before he could continue, John stood up, shoved his chair back and strode out of the room.

As the door banged shut, Kathleen started to gather up her bag and gloves. 'Thank you, Doctor,' she mumbled. 'I must go after him.'

'Come back later when you have had a chance to talk. There might be things we can do to help.'

Kathleen ran out after John into the parking area, already dreading the journey home. It was obvious he blamed her. John went straight to his side of the car without opening her door or helping her in.

She stared out of the window as the car roared along. She didn't need to look at John to know his face would be flushed and his mouth clamped shut. Out of the corner of her eye she saw his hands gripping the steering wheel, knuckles white.

'Dr Myers might be able to help,' she said eventually, turning away from the blur of acacias and tuarts outside the window. 'You didn't stay to hear him, but he spoke as though the situation wasn't entirely hopeless. We could still have children.'

Silence.

'John. This isn't my fault.'

'It isn't mine either! I told you I didn't want to see a bloody doctor!'

'But what was the alternative? Waiting years and years without knowing?'

John slowed down and mangled a gear change. 'We're fine as we are.'

Kathleen glanced at his profile. His cheek was mottled red and white. For once she was sorry for him. If only the fault had been with her. She could have coped with the treatment, whatever it entailed. Anything to have a warm, milky weight in her arms or to smile at fat little limbs. John would have been all magnanimity and smug solicitude while privately revelling in his own fertility.

'I'm not giving up hope,' she said.

A cyclist ahead of them was taking up too much of the road. John swung the car wide to overtake, bashing his fist against the horn as he did so. The cyclist wobbled.

'Bloody idiot,' shouted John.

Kathleen opened her handbag, took out her compact and powdered her nose, trying to keep her hand steady.

She was putting on her blouse and skirt after a particularly strenuous exercise class at the Lacey Street hall when Kathleen heard a couple of the women talking. She didn't know their names. They were friendly enough with each other but they rarely spoke to her. They probably had children in common. Mothers were drawn to other mothers. There were so many things to talk about when you had children. And none of them related to her.

She'd tried to speak to John several times after the episode at the doctor's, but whenever she did so, he had an excuse: an urgent visit to the department, a favour for a friend, even a programme he wanted to listen to on the wireless. It seemed everyone could call on her husband's time except his wife. Everything was so hopeless. Infertility was like a deep wound, untreatable.

As it happened, the women weren't talking about their children.

'This'll be my last class,' said one. Her frizzy auburn hair floated around her head like a cloud. She dragged a brush through it, then bent down to retrieve a couple of hairgrips from her bag.

'How's that?' enquired the other, fanning her face with her hand. The air inside the cloakroom was thick with powdered chalk and perspiration.

'I've volunteered for victory work. Start tomorrow.' She put the grips into her mouth before coiling the now tamed hair behind her head.

Kathleen listened as she pretended to struggle with the buttons on her blouse. Lots of women were doing victory jobs now, filling the gaps left by men and doing their bit to help the war. She wondered if that was something she could do. She certainly had time on her hands. John was spending more and more hours at the ministry; she could easily have a part-time job. She flashed a smile at the women as she left the changing room and they automatically returned the gesture.

On the way home, she bought a copy of *The West Australian* and tucked it into her kitbag. She poured herself a glass of water, then sat at the table to read the paper, turning the pages until an advert caught her eye. It was topped by a picture of a soldier in an AIF helmet. He looked tired and dejected. *Won't you change your job for ME?* the advert said. Underneath was a picture of a woman. She wore a spotted apron and her hair was in a victory roll. She leaned over a small, stylish table with a duster in her hand. But she wasn't looking at the table. Her gaze was outward and upward as though listening to a far-off call. From the soldier, presumably. *What does it matter if the furniture does get a bit dusty . . . or the floors a bit dull? What does it matter — providing the man you love comes back sooner and alive?*

Kathleen took a sip of water. How would she feel if John was away fighting rather than in civvies pen-pushing at the department? What if she hadn't seen him for years? Would it make a difference to how she felt about him? It wasn't his fault he couldn't seem to father children. But she couldn't forgive him for not going back to the doctor.

She read on: *Come on, housewife. Take a victory job. You'll find it no harder than your house job. Easier perhaps. In fact, many war production factories, with their spic-and-span canteens, bright music and carefully planned rest breaks, are more fun to work in than any house.*

Kathleen stopped again. Was her work at home ever *fun*? The endless schedule of sweeping, polishing, washing, ironing?

But what else was there? Sometimes she fantasised about other men. Fathers for her children.

The advert drew her back. *But what does that matter providing you help to shorten these days of war . . . and get rid of that dark cloud of fear for him that's been hanging over you for so long?* Kathleen never had a fear *for* John. A fear *of* him, though . . . Perhaps that was what set her apart from the other wives. They were clearly anxious about their men away fighting. They were smug too: their husbands were doing their bit. Where did she belong among the proud mothers and perfect wives?

Come in and have a chat with another woman at your nearest National Service Office, the advert cajoled. *Every day she is finding jobs for women like you. Come on*, it finished. *Change your job for him – won't you?* At the end, the same soldier looked happy and relieved. The woman beside him had a spanner in one hand while the other was clutching the soldier's arm. Could that be me? Kathleen wondered, tracing her finger down the woman's body. She knew only too well what John's reaction would be. But what about something part-time that started after he left for work and ended before he returned? That was tempting. She tore the page from the paper and folded it thoughtfully. Then, at the sound of the front door opening, she shoved it into a drawer.

'Long day?' she asked, as John went straight into the lounge and slumped into an armchair. He hadn't even taken his coat off.

'It's all this planning to get the Pommy kids over. Taking an age.' He rubbed the space between his eyes. 'What's for dinner, darl?'

'Mutton stew. Won't be long.' Kathleen returned to the kitchen. The subject of children had been closed since the clinic appointment and she knew better than to bring it up. But John had seemed happier since the plan to bring the British children across.

'Might take forty winks,' he called. 'Let me know when it's ready.'

Kathleen took her time laying the table then mashing the potatoes. When she saw John stirring, she reached up to take the plates out of the cupboard before turning to the oven to remove the pot of steaming stew. She smiled to herself as she ladled out the meaty liquid. John thought he was the only one with work responsibilities. Of course he must never find out she was planning to get a job. He'd be forever accusing her of skimping on the housework or neglecting him. Probably make her life unbearable until she resigned out of sheer frustration. But now she had her own project. And what a great secret it would be. Her mouth twitched with the effort of suppressing a grin as she added the mash then carried the plates through.

On her first day, Kathleen found herself at a desk in the small finance office of the Sacred Heart Convent in Highgate. The suburb was only a short bus ride away; she didn't have to start until ten o'clock and could finish at two. It was a relief to know she could cope with the work. Her mental arithmetic was good – honed by years of shopping and housekeeping. She had always loved sums at school, the satisfaction of working out a solution to a problem, and the job suited her. When, at the end of the first week, she received her small wage, she put it away in a purse she kept at the bottom of her underwear drawer. John would never look there. After the diary incident, she had learned to be more secretive with her belongings.

She had to get up early to finish the housework before she left for the convent. It was cooler and easier then too. John questioned her about it once, but she told him she woke up sooner these days and there was no point lying in bed fretting. She didn't say what she fretted about. Let him figure that out for himself.

The office was cramped but friendly, run by Mr Brownlow, an ex-accountant who had come out of retirement when the previous manager was called up. Mr Brownlow was tall and stooping and spoke in a soft voice, so soft that sometimes Kathleen had to strain to hear him. He preferred poring over columns of figures to talking, but that suited her. When she left each afternoon, he would jump up and hold the door open for her. 'Goodbye, Mrs Sullivan, and thank you for your work today,' he said every time. He never called her by her first name. His neat moustache widened as he stretched his mouth to a smile, and he'd perform a little bobbing movement that was almost comical.

The other occupant, Mavis, was an ex nun. The rumour went that she'd had some sort of breakdown and left the order. Apparently the mother superior had found her a job in the convent finance office so she could keep an eye on her.

Mavis seemed so shy and miserable that Kathleen wondered if she wouldn't have been better off returning to the sisterhood. The nuns treated them all with deference but were chillier towards Mavis. Kathleen made a point of talking to her whenever Mr Brownlow was out.

Sometimes, when she had to leave the office to walk the long, smooth corridors in search of one sister or another, she'd hear snatches of unfamiliar hymns or mysterious chanting. As a child, her parents had taken her to the Anglican church at Forest Hill. She had a sketchy memory of light pouring across the picture of Jesus she was crayoning whilst the vicar droned. So different to the dark convent chapel. Once she tiptoed in when it was empty. It smelled of polish and incense. She looked around her. There were hard benches leading up to the altar at the front. A large cross was fixed to the wall behind, with an effigy of the crucified Jesus nailed to it. Kathleen shuddered. She was about to go out when she noticed a small statue of Mary to one side with several thin candles on the ground in front of it. One of them was still burning, its stem deformed with molten wax. She knelt down. Didn't people light these as prayers? Mary knew what it was like to be a mother. Perhaps she'd take pity on Kathleen, help her to have a baby. Her fingers scrabbled for a matchbox on the stone floor. She lit a candle and watched as the flame flickered and trembled. Then she left quickly. She didn't want to be there if the candle went out.

7

They were taken into Tisbury by bus for the victory party. Long tables, piled with food, were set up in the middle of the road, and red, white and blue flags danced between the lamp posts. The Melchet children all sat together. Jack was squashed in between Tom and Bert. It was hot, and the air smelled of the beef dripping oozing out of the sandwiches. Jack reached for a piece of cake.

'Not yet, please, Jack.' Sister Angela was hovering behind him with the other grown-ups. 'Have a potato scone first.' She motioned to a plate of pale yellow rocks. Jack took one and bit into it. It was dry and solid. A bit of potato lodged behind his front teeth. He eased it out with his finger, then swallowed hard. He glanced behind him. Sister Angela, her face shiny beneath her headdress, was chatting to Sister Immaculata. Jack swiped the cake and crammed it into his mouth before she noticed.

He glanced down the table. Beyond the line of Melchet children sat other boys and girls. A large lad in a red knitted pullover was tucking into a bowl of ice cream. A woman stood behind him smoothing down his hair and smiling. Jack swallowed again. Even the cake tasted dry. Next to the boy was a small girl with a paper crown on her head, cuddling a one-eared teddy bear. Her mother placed a bowl of ice cream in front of her. The girl turned round, beamed, and hugged her mother round the waist. Jack stood up.

A hand pressed down on his shoulder. Sister Angela again. Her face was all tight, as though she didn't have enough skin to fit around her body and it had to be stretched. 'No one's finished yet.'

'May I have some ice cream?'

Sister Angela pointed at the pieces of potato scone littering his plate. 'Not until you've eaten those.'

Jack sat down and took a slurp of the lemonade that had been poured for them in teacups. The only way he could eat that scone was if he washed it down. If Mummy had been here she'd have let him eat ice cream. If only he was amongst the children with parents, instead of sitting with fat Tom, the nuns lined up behind them. He shovelled in the last piece of scone. Sister Angela handed him a bowl of ice cream. As the cold sweetness slithered down his throat, Jack felt better. At least the war was over. Mummy must come soon.

Later came dancing and music. The village band played and a woman in a red turban sang that song about bluebirds. Jack just hoped she wouldn't sing anything by the Andrews Sisters. Those songs belonged to Mummy. He wondered if the nuns would join in the dancing, but they just sat on chairs vacated by some of the younger children, talking quietly and stealing little looks at small groups of men and women trying to do the Lambeth Walk.

They were given miniature Union Jacks on sticks to wave. When the National Anthem started up, they all stood and joined in. Afterwards Jack pressed the flag against his face, inhaling its smell. Maybe when he pulled it away he'd see his mother. 'Surprise!' she'd say. 'Sorry I couldn't come sooner, Jacky-boy. I've been to a victory dance.'

But after the party nothing changed at Melchet. There was still school and chores and punishments. The food was still bad, the home still cold, even in August. Now that Jack was older, Sister Beatrice sat a small boy called Stan on her lap, his head cushioned against her soft chest, comforted by the arms that had once held Jack close. It wasn't fair.

Lying in bed one night, trying not to hate Stan, Jack decided to run away to Winchester. They'd been there once with the nuns, to visit the shrine of some saint or other, and he remembered the way. If Mummy wasn't coming, he'd nothing to stay for. Melchet was only fifteen miles from the city. He could get a train to London, then try and find out what had happened to his mother.

He slid some bread into his pocket during tea, when Sister Constantia wasn't looking. He'd scrump for apples on the way and find a river from which to drink. He'd be fine. When the nuns were at vespers and the boys were supposed to be doing prep, he slipped out of the side door, skirted round the edge of the home, scrambled over the wall and ran down to the main road.

The first part of the journey was easy. As he sauntered

along, he filled his lungs with fresh air and watched the women in the fields digging up cabbages and carrots and throwing them into a cart. No one stopped him to ask what he was doing. He kept turning round, expecting to see a figure in a black habit running after him, but the road was deserted.

By the time he got to Ampfield, a fine drizzle was soaking his shirt and jumper. He hadn't thought to bring a coat; it was colder than he'd bargained for. Maybe he should have pinched some of the vegetables the women were collecting, but he'd been holding out for apples, expecting to find branches of them hanging over a wall or fence. If there were any, he didn't see them.

Although he chewed at the bread, which had turned into pulp in his pocket, his stomach still felt empty. Perhaps he'd have that drink from the river. Water might fill him up. Despite the fading daylight, he turned off the road towards a shiny strip meandering through the fields.

He squelched across the wet grass, wishing he'd worn a stout pair of boots rather than the leather sandals, which rubbed his feet. When he breathed in, the damp air hurt his chest. But he kept going until he reached the river.

He needed to drink quickly and be on his way if he was to make Winchester before nightfall. It was no use going over the bridge; he had to get down to the water's edge. But his path was blocked by dark reeds. He eased his feet over the marshy ground until he found a gap, then tentatively dipped one foot into the brown water. He nearly took it out straight away. The river was freezing. But he'd come too far to give up. He tried again, driving his sandal into the thick mud, then reaching out to scoop water into his cupped hands.

Suddenly his sandal shot out: he stumbled . . . flailed . . . and fell. Before he knew it, his whole body was thrashing about in the icy river. He clawed at the reeds and nettles, yelping from the stings and cuts and gasping from the cold.

As he floundered onto the bank, the howl that came from his own mouth sounded like an animal in pain. Slimy water was dripping down his face, running off his hair, his jumper, his shorts. His shoes were as heavy as lead. And his ankle hurt like hell.

There was nothing for it but to limp across the field, wiping the snot and tears from his face, his teeth chattering, his drenched clothes clinging to his body like frozen bandages.

After an eternity, he regained the road and stood, a block of ice, in the gathering darkness.

It would be so easy to submit to the cold and exhaustion, to sink onto the verge, to curl into a ball until he died of exposure.

But he couldn't give up that easily. It would break his mother's heart.

As he jumped up and down, trying to get warm, he saw a faint light coming from further down the road. He urged his body towards it.

Luck was finally on Jack's side. The light belonged to a small cottage, whose owner opened the door to his desperate knock, ushered him in, and made him hot tea as he stammered an explanation through numb lips.

'I'll phone the convent,' said the elderly woman, offering him a towel. And he sat on her soft settee, allowing the warmth of the room and the smell of roasting meat to ease through his body until he heard a car draw up outside.

Sister Angela briskly thanked the woman and ushered Jack onto the back seat. 'Do you realise how much trouble you've caused?' she barked. 'We've wasted a whole afternoon searching for you.'

Jack shook his head, mute with misery.

The nun didn't say another word for the whole journey.

Once they were back at Melchet, she marched him into the kitchen. 'Clothes off,' she ordered, dragging a tin bath across the floor. He peeled off his drenched garments, revealing blue-white skin. 'Now kneel there. Don't turn round.' He climbed inside the bath. Sister Angela banged the cupboard doors noisily, muttering to herself. What *was* she doing? Jack heard a clanging sound as she dropped something into the sink; the groan of the pipes as she turned the tap on and the spurt of water as it hit the bottom of something metal. Loud footsteps came across the stone floor towards him. Whatever she was carrying must be heavy. There was a splashing noise as water slurped over the side and he heard the loud wheeze of her breath. Jack braced himself, but he still gasped as the bucket of icy water was tipped over his head. 'That'll drive the devil out of you,' she said, going back for more. The bath was three-quarters full when she finished.

8

'Now, Margaret, we are going to try some basket work today.'
Lady Dawson is using her extra cheerful sing-songy voice. She
wears a purple tweed suit with a purple hat. With a feather in
it. 'Come and sit down, dear.'

She sits. In front of her is a brown oval mat. It looks as if
it is made of rushes. Straw prongs are dotted round it.

Lady Dawson hands her a pile of twigs. 'Let me show
you.' She takes one of the twigs from her hands and pushes
it through a gap between the prongs, bends it round the next
prong, then pushes it back again. 'See. In and out, in and
out. You keep going, building up the pattern until you've
made the sides of the basket. As long as you are gentle, the
twigs won't break. They bend quite nicely. Now your turn,
dear.'

She picks up a twig and snaps it between her fingers. It
breaks with a crack. Nice. She reaches for another.

'Now, Margaret. Please don't do that.' The sing-song voice
has sharpened. 'You know we need to make baskets for the
less fortunate. Yours might go to a needy family. Think how
good that would make you feel.'

She picks up another twig. Snap. And another. Crack. One

56

more. Snap. Crack. Snap. Her head is buzzing after Dr Lee's treatment.

'Margaret!' The voice is high-pitched now. 'Stop that.' A firm hand on hers.

She wriggles her fingers free. And picks up another twig.

'Matron! Can you come here quickly, please? I don't think Margaret is cut out for basket weaving.'

9

The war finally ended in August. A week earlier, two giant explosions had erupted out of Hiroshima and Nagasaki, and the Japanese surrendered at last. Australia celebrated in grateful relief.

John was still at the department when the news came, so Kathleen left work early and went into town by bus on her own. Her chest soaring with excitement, she joined the throngs in William Street, inhaling stale sweat and cheap scent as she watched people laugh and wave and shout. Two young women with linked arms had large pieces of cardboard strung round their necks with *Peace* in large black letters. In front of Kathleen a young man and a girl were openly kissing, their bodies intertwined. The girl's head was thrown back, her eyes closed, a look of bliss on her face. Kathleen swallowed and looked away.

She focused on an impromptu conga of young office workers threading through the crowds, laughing drunkenly. It was hard to understand such uncomplicated joy. Had they forgotten the loss and hardship? If they hadn't, Kathleen couldn't see it on their laughing faces.

In front of her, a small boy sat on his father's shoulders,

furiously waving a miniature Australian flag. Kathleen smiled at him and waved back. On the pavement beside her, a policeman blew a whistle, but the sound was muffled by the crowd. The officer shrugged at his own impotence. Above his head, thousands of pieces of paper, like autumn leaves, floated down from office windows.

Everywhere Kathleen looked, people were celebrating wildly. She watched as an open-topped tourer car drove slowly down the street showing off its occupants, all in fancy dress. Two young women with bright red lipstick wore large straw hats looped with ribbons; one of them had a paper flower garland round her neck. The driver was in a harlequin outfit. Kathleen stopped to admire them and a tall man bumped into her. He raised his hat in apology.

'Sorry – my fault,' said Kathleen. 'I couldn't take my eyes off them.' She gestured towards the car.

The man laughed. 'Crazy people!' He had a suntanned face and smile lines around his blue eyes.

'Where on earth did they get those costumes from?'

'I guess folk have been collecting stuff to celebrate with.' The man looked about John's age and Kathleen wondered why he wasn't in uniform. 'Have you seen the town hall?' he asked her.

Kathleen shook her head.

'Someone's hung a huge V for Victory sign from the tower.'

'I'd love to see that. I might go there now.' But she didn't move.

The man leaned forward and gently picked something out

of her hair. Kathleen caught a trace of cologne. She widened her eyes. A pulse beat deep in her body.

'Sorry. I couldn't resist it. You had a bit of paper lodged there.' He held up one of the pieces that had drifted down from the office window earlier, then cleared his throat.

'Actually, would you like to have a drink with me first? I believe there are some restaurants still open.'

He was standing very close. Kathleen could smell his warm breath, see the stippling of green in his blue eyes. She thought of the couple embracing earlier. They might have been strangers, yet they looked so intimate. How many affairs would start on this giddy, greedy night? How many babies would be conceived in its warm, dusky aftermath? Maybe she could slip away with this man who was smiling at her so invitingly. She didn't know anyone here. Perhaps there was a way to become a mother after all.

She smoothed down her dress. All those keep-fit classes had slimmed her hips and toned her waist. Her legs had always looked good. 'Nice pins, Kath,' John sometimes said when she wore her navy high-heeled shoes. He'd managed to get her some silk stockings recently, and she'd decided to wear them to the celebrations. They caressed her skin, and for a second she imagined the man softly drawing his fingers up her calves, her knees, her thighs . . . Desire coiled through her.

She was about to move closer when a woman jostled her roughly. Kathleen cried out.

'Are you all right?' the man asked.

Kathleen nodded, rubbing her arm. She took a step back. The street sounds rushed in again and the moment faded. This was madness. John could be difficult, but he didn't deserve infidelity. 'I'm sorry. I must go.' She smiled politely at the man, who raised his hat again.

It wasn't easy to turn away and make her way to Barrack Street. She felt the man watching her all the way down the road.

By the time Kathleen arrived at the town hall through the slowly moving crowd, it was getting dark and the victory sign had gone. She wondered if somebody had climbed up there and pulled it down. It was probably being held aloft by a group of revellers by now. Good luck to them. A shame she hadn't seen it, though. Perhaps it was worth the trip to admire the clock face, dimmed for most of the war but now allowed to shine in full splendour. The moon, just rising above it, looked pale in comparison. Kathleen realised the lights were on in the shop windows again. Despite their lack of wares, they still looked like sparkling Aladdin's caves. It's as though Christmas has arrived in August, she thought to herself. And a more extravagant Christmas than the city had seen for a long time.

Yet although Barrack Street was beautiful, it wasn't much compensation for the evening she could've had. Dejectedly, she caught the now empty bus back to Highgate.

When a tipsy John tried to make love to her that night, she felt the man's strong, warm hands on her body, saw his blue eyes, breathed his heady cologne. And afterwards she felt John grinning smugly in the darkness, as if congratulating himself that he could still ignite such passion in his wife.

The next day, Kathleen joined John at the official victory ceremony on the esplanade. She stood stiffly beside him with the party of dignitaries roped off from the crowd, in a pre-war blue suit that felt too big. The flags blew half-heartedly in the light breeze and Kathleen tilted her face so she could feel the warmth of the sun under her hat. This formal celebration seemed so rigid and solemn after the palpable excitement of the night before. She hated being on show after the blissful anonymity of William Street. How would John's ministerial colleagues have reacted if they'd seen her encounter with the man in the crowd? How would John have reacted, come to that?

The band started up. They all sang the National Anthem and 'Australia Marches On'. Kathleen watched John smiling benevolently, as if he'd won the war single-handed, his medal-less chest thrust forward. It was incredible how he assumed the role of victorious general despite having wielded nothing more dangerous than a fountain pen.

She wondered how this new peace would affect them. She might have to give up her job for starters. The government had warned that men returning from the war needed to be in work. Women had kept their posts warm for the duration but the decent thing would be to resign. At least John'd never found out. But the thought of spending all her time in the house again was depressing. No lying in bed early in the morning, plotting the day's deception. The innocent-sounding remarks about her plans to spend her time washing and ironing, whilst knowing she would drop the dirty laundry off at that discreet Mrs Markham's in Barlee Street on her way to the convent, and collect a clean, pressed bundle on her way home. By the time John came in, the laundry would be neatly stacked in the airing cupboard, as if she'd just finished slaving over the ironing all day. And John never seemed to notice that the clothes now smelled of Rinso rather than Lux.

John wouldn't need to work such long hours either. Although once the seas were safe, they'd start shipping the Pommy children, so he'd be busy for a while. Maybe even busier. Perhaps that would give her a reprieve.

Her thoughts flashed again to the man in William Street and she felt a shiver of pleasure as she remembered him standing in front of her, touching her hair. Perhaps he was in the crowd here. She started to look, then stopped herself. This was ridiculous; she'd decided yesterday to forget him. It was nothing, just flattery, the knowledge that another man found her attractive. She was married to John. She'd said her vows in St Mark's, the church she'd gone to as a child, in front of her parents, in front of God. And she'd meant them. She'd always believed she and John would have a family together. It would be wrong to give up on him now. To give up on all those future babies.

Dr Myers had said that stress sometimes made men temporarily infertile. Once the pressure of the war had eased, maybe she'd get pregnant. If she could have a baby, everything else would be bearable. Kathleen drove her nails into the palm of her hand. *Please God, let me become pregnant*, she pleaded, inside her head, as the band blared on.

10

Sister Perpetua ushered the visitor into the dining hall. Lunch had been the usual fatty lamb piled up with swedes and turnips, although they were given a bit more meat these days. Everyone put down their knives and forks with a clatter. An instant hush descended. The man, tall and thin with wispy hair and a nose like a beak, towered over the nun. His long black gown, and the flash of white at the neck, reminded Jack of Father O'Brian at church, although the priest never came to Melchet.

'This is Brother MacNeil,' said Sister Perpetua. This time she'd no need to raise her voice or clap her hands. 'He has come to talk to you children about a very exciting prospect.' Jack wondered what had made her so worked up. Sister Perpetua usually had only two expressions: devout and cross. She seemed to wear the latter in any dealings with him. Was it a good thing to see her so pleased? He couldn't remember her ever showing them kindness; he'd no confidence that this new mood might lead to anything worthwhile for them.

'I've come to invite you on an adventure,' Brother MacNeil announced. His voice sounded as though he had a cold, but the effect of his words was electric. Jack exchanged glances with Tom. His friend's face was flushed.

'In a few months' time, I am going to set sail for Australia.' He paused. Jack had a vision of the tall, beaky man standing on a sailing ship, holding the mast and shielding his eyes against the sun, a bit like Robinson Crusoe.

'I'd like some of you boys to come with me.' Jack added himself to the vision, shinning up a rope to the crow's nest, ready to go on lookout, Brother MacNeil gazing up admiringly at his strong brown torso and muscular arms.

'The Australians have invited us to live with them. They want strong boys and girls to share in a wonderful new life.' He stopped to survey the children. Next to him, Tom was eagerly thrusting out his chest. Did Australians want thin boys too? Jack wondered.

'Australia is a land full of sunshine, not rainy and cold like it always is here.' There was a billow of laughter. After all these years at Melchet, Jack had got used to the cold, but it would be exciting to live in a place where it was hot all the time.

'Those children who decide to come with me will live in the countryside on huge farms. You'll go to school during the day, but afterwards, and in the holidays, you'll learn to ride horses, shear sheep and drive tractors. It will be a great outdoor life. A much better life than here.'

Jack glanced at Sister Perpetua. Surely she would be offended by that? But no, she was smiling. She seemed keen for them to go.

'You will all become strong and brown in the fresh air,' continued Brother MacNeil. 'You'll grow your own food on the farm. You'll even be able to pick oranges and eat them fresh from the tree.' Jack couldn't imagine such a treat. He looked round. Every child in the room was staring at Brother MacNeil with bright eyes and a longing expression.

'Put your hand up if you'd like to come with me,' said the brother.

Tom's hand shot up. 'I can't wait!' he shouted. Everyone laughed. Jack wasn't sure. Would Mummy be able to find him in Australia? But she hadn't found him in five years. And besides, he could always come back. Australia couldn't be that far away, could it? They spoke English there. His mother would be so proud of him if he could ride a horse and drive a tractor. Australia would be like the film of *Snow White* they'd been allowed to watch at the American airbase – all bright colours.

He raised a tentative arm. Brother MacNeil saw him and smiled. 'Good man. You'll love Australia.' The brother paused briefly, surveying the eager faces in front of him. 'Anyone else want to have an adventure?'

The rest of the hands went up.

A few days later, Jack went to find Sister Beatrice. She was sitting by the window, sewing. Her fingers were knobbly and bent, green veins snaking across her hands. The light from the window exposed a haze of hairs on her top lip. When she saw Jack, she put down the sock she was darning and pulled him close. She smelled of gentian violet and mint imperials.

'Hello, young man. How is the world with you?' He could hear a mint clacking against her teeth.

'I'm going to Australia,' he replied.

Sister Beatrice inclined her head as though she knew already. 'You'll have a grand time there,' she said.

'I know,' said Jack, scratching at a patch of eczema on his elbow.

Sister Beatrice tucked a stray strand of hair into her black cap. A crunching sound came from her mouth.

Jack frowned. 'I'll miss you.'

'You'd better!' The nun creased up her eyes at him. 'But you'll get to know the fine Christian Brothers, and there'll be a cottage mother to look after you.'

Suddenly the truth welled up. 'But I want my own mother!'

'Now, Jack. You know she's gone.' Sister Beatrice paused and the arm around him tightened a fraction. 'If she was alive she'd have come for you by now, wouldn't she?' she said softly.

Jack wiped a hand across his eyes. 'I suppose so.' He'd known it deep down. Probably for years. He'd always hoped Mummy had survived, but these days he rarely looked out of the dormitory window to see if she was walking up the drive, and she was no longer dancing or singing in his head as he went to sleep. Now his dreams were sunlit. He was riding horses or driving a tractor. Surely his mother would be pleased for him. What was the point of waiting for her at Melchet with the horrible food and the cold and the chores? She was never going to come.

He leaned in towards Sister Beatrice and allowed his hair to be stroked. He squeezed his eyes tightly. A tiny bit of him was still worried he'd made the wrong decision. Perhaps he could leave a message.

'If Mummy ever does come, tell her I waited and waited for her. She'll need to come out to Australia to find me.'

Sister Beatrice blinked at him. 'Now off you go and finish your chores. They only want good lads in Australia, you know!'

*

She doesn't bother opening her eyes when she wakes up. The view is always the same: muddy cream walls, a polished wooden floor, twenty metal beds with white sheets and blue blankets, twelve sash windows with thirty-five panes of glass in each. She counts them every day: seven panes down, five panes across.

She breathes in deeply. The smells never change either: carbolic soap, surgical spirit and stale urine. The last one varies depending on whether Mary's sheets have been changed recently. Towards lunchtime, the odour of mince, fish or cabbage drifts in.

They tell her she's getting better, and some days she believes them. Dr Lee's treatment has ordered her thoughts and driven away some of the darkness. She's stopped searching for things. Whatever it was she's lost has never come to light. But she never feels whole. Something is always missing.

As the medical trolley rumbles its way up the ward, she grips the metal rails beside her. There was a time when she would have ducked under the bed and lain there trembling until Matron hauled her out. But not these days. The war is over. There won't be any more bombs.

Strange that she can't remember the things she needs to remember. Yet the things she tries to forget – the sound of explosions, the smell of burning, the black smoke – are always there.

11

Jack stood by the gunwale, looking out to sea. Although it was only just after breakfast, the sun was already hot. The sky reminded him of a marble he'd had years ago at the house in Croydon, with its layers of blue swirled with white. He was wearing the woollen jumper and shorts the orphanage had given each of them. The jumper was a size too small. Dampness spread under his arms and round his neck where the material clung to his skin. It was heavy and itchy but he wasn't allowed to take it off.

The engine hummed as the steamship sliced through the water, leaving behind a froth like crumpled parachute silk. Near the boat the sea was a seething mass of turquoise, dark blue and white. Further out it was calmer, a deep sculpted blue. And somewhere across that huge expanse lay Australia. It was waiting for him with its farms and horses and kangaroos and endless miles of freedom. The sun would be beating down there too, ripening the oranges on the trees so that they could reach up and pick them. He tried to imagine the citrus tang of their juice but all he could taste was the barley sugars the nuns had given them. They'd said it was to stop them from feeling seasick. Barley sugars were nice, but oranges would be nicer.

For a second Jack wondered what his mother would have thought about him being on a ship bound for Australia. He hoped she'd have been glad he was having an adventure.

They'd taken the boat train to Southampton. It was packed with people, who milled around the departure shed. Perhaps, like him, they were so brimming with excitement that they couldn't stand still. The SS *Asturias* was huge and had a chimney in the middle, which belched out black smoke like an angry dragon. They all walked up the gangplank wearing navy suits they'd been given at Melchet and carrying their cases. There were nuns with them, not ones he recognised, some other women called nannies and men in dark coats and hats. The quayside was packed with people, but there was no one for him to wave goodbye to, so he didn't turn round. Even at the last moment, he'd wondered if Sister Beatrice would turn up. But perhaps Stan needed her more. She'd given him a quick, fierce hug at Melchet, and Jack had heard a crack in her voice as she'd wished him a happy life. Would he ever be able to smell peppermints again without thinking of her? Feeling a strange tightness in his throat, and a prickling in his eyes, he concentrated on looking up at the ship.

Soon they'd left Southampton behind. More land loomed up ahead.

'It's Australia!' cried Nancy, one of the younger children.

'Don't be silly,' one of the nuns told her. 'That's the Isle of Wight.'

*

Jack was still looking dreamily out to sea when a metallic crash made him start. It was followed by a thundering drumming sound and a series of high-pitched screams. Saliva pooled in his mouth. He looked around for a hiding place. In the middle of the deck was a pile of lifeboats, stacked one on top of the other under a dirty-white tarpaulin. He ran towards the pile, skidding and sliding on the strangely slippery deck, plunged underneath the rubber material and collapsed panting beside one of the boats.

The outside world of glaring brightness vanished as though a light had been snapped off. Inside his gloomy hiding place the heat was intense, a stale odour coming from the tarpaulin's underside. Hearing a scampering sound, he peered under the pile of boats and saw a tiny mouse trembling at the back. Poor thing, Jack thought. He's just as trapped as I am.

He lay still. The blood pounding in his ears shut out every other sound. Had they been torpedoed like those children on the *City of Benares*? Jack had lain awake one night imagining their terrified cries as they fell into the icy water. And further back was another vision – of his father on a boat, trying in vain to stay afloat, struggling against the strong currents sucking him down. Jack had never been told exactly how his father died. But he knew one thing. He didn't want to share his fate.

Whenever he was frightened at Melchet, he tried to remember his mother holding him, his nose filled with her lily-of-the-valley scent. He did that now and the drumming in his chest slowed. The roaring faded and the screams outside quietened. Now he heard a new noise and knew it was a good sign. Laughter.

He pulled up a flap of tarpaulin and squinted against the bright light. He could only see a section of the deck but glimpsed a blur of bare feet and, in the background, great arcs of water, turned to rainbows by the sun. He scrambled out.

Children were running around the deck laughing and squealing under the jets, revelling in the delicious icy liquid. The boys had taken off their pullovers and left them, dark and sodden, on the wet boards. Baffled, Jack looked around and discovered the source of the water: several smiling crew members were standing against the rails holding out long hoses. They must have turned on the fire hydrants to cool the children down. Even the nuns, basking on deckchairs like stranded seals, were chuckling at the sight.

Jack hesitated for a second, remembering the time Sister Angela had tipped cold water over him as a punishment for running away. But this wasn't a punishment, it was a treat. And it was a lot hotter here than that miserable winter's day in England. He tugged off his jersey and ran towards the nearest jet of water. This was going to be fun. He shrieked and jumped with the others, trying to escape the freezing blasts but laughing when they caught him. The cold water ran down his skin, soothing the last bits of sunburn and puckering his arms with goose bumps. It washed off the dust and the grime. He didn't mind getting wet. Perhaps it could rinse away all the bad things that had happened to him.

An hour later, a neat row of grey jumpers hung over the railings, dripping onto the deck. Still flushed and with damp hair, and wearing their even hotter spare clothes, they trooped in for children's tea. Jack loved ship food. There were none of the miserable rations they'd had at the orphanage, which left him with a grinding hunger. If all this was just for children, he wondered, what on earth did the adults get? Today there were steaming bowls of Brown Windsor soup and heaped plates of cottage pie made with creamy mashed potato, accompanied by slippery cabbage. There were things like that on the menu at Melchet but they bore no resemblance to their description. There the meat was grey and gristly and the potatoes full of lumps.

Jack ignored the chatter around him; he just wanted to eat and eat. The boy next to him was matching him spoonful for spoonful. They finished at exactly the same time and grinned at each other in shared satisfaction.

'That was good,' said the boy. He was taller than Jack, not fat, but strong and healthy-looking, as though he'd been brought up on Yorkshire pudding and jam roly-poly, not dried bread and watery soup. Jack recognised him from the water fights earlier: Sam.

'Best dinner ever,' agreed Jack.

'Not as good as my mum's cooking, though,' said Sam. Jack stared at him. Did Sam have a mother who was alive?

'Where's your mum? Is she on board?' The orphanage children weren't allowed to sit with the families. Jack and the other boys from Melchet House sat on low benches alongside trestle tables at the back of the dining room. The lucky kids, the ones with mums and dads and summer clothes, sat in the middle of the dining room at tables with white covers and gleaming cutlery.

Sam fidgeted. 'My parents are back in England. I'm going to Australia to stay with my aunt and uncle.'

'Why?' Jack turned to face him. 'The war's over.'

'It's got nothing to do with the war.' Sam's tone was low, and Jack had to lean close to hear him. 'My mum and dad don't live together any more, so they can't look after me. My sister went to live with our grandparents in Kent, but they couldn't take me as well. I'm on my own on the ship so I've been told to sit with you lot.'

'Aren't you sad to leave them?'

'Of course not,' replied Sam, pushing the heel of a spoon into his palm. Jack noticed his eyes were glassy.

Jack couldn't think of anything else to say. Then bowls of syrupy rice pudding were placed in front of them and they were soon much too busy to talk.

Later, Jack took Sam back to his cabin. The three lads he shared it with, Bert, Tom and Mattie, were out on deck and the cabin was quiet. Jack pointed out the top bunk where he slept. There were grey scratchy blankets, like at the orphanage, but with lovely soft cotton sheets underneath. He showed

Sam the coin they'd all been presented with at the end of the war and the black-bound bible Sister Beatrice had given him. He didn't have much else. Sometimes he wondered what had become of the locket Mum had owned, the one with his dad's photo in.

Sam admired the coin and bible then invited Jack to see his cabin on the other side of the ship. The room was small but Sam had it all to himself. Jack looked at the neatly made bed, with a framed picture of the *Asturias* on her maiden voyage hanging above it, and the little wooden wardrobe in the corner with three dark-oak drawers underneath. He stood shyly in the doorway while Sam went in. Sam paused for a bit, then dived under his bed.

'Look at these.' He surfaced clutching some strange objects, then sat on the bed and patted the space beside him. Jack sat down.

Sam laid the objects in a line, then picked up one of them, long and thin and made of metal. About the same size as Sister Beatrice's glasses case, but much more ornate. It was a bright turquoise colour with gold patterns. Sam opened one end and drew out some thick yellow paper rolled into a scroll. The paper had strange black writing on that Jack couldn't read. Sam passed it to Jack, who held it carefully. 'What is it?'

'A *mezuzah*.' Jack just stared at him, so Sam went on. 'It's got the Shema Yisrael on.'

'The what?'

'The Shema Yisrael. It's a prayer.'

At last Jack understood. 'Ah, like the Hail Mary.'

Now Sam looked puzzled. 'I don't know what that is.'

Jack began to chant, *Hail Mary, full of grace* . . . The nuns had taught him well.

But Sam was chanting too, even louder, *Sh'ma Yisrael Adonai Eloheinu Adonai Ehad* . . .

Jack stopped. 'That isn't even English!'

'I know. It's Hebrew.'

'Hebrew?' Jack had never heard the word before.

Sam sighed as if Jack was stupid. 'I'm Jewish.'

Jack shrugged. 'I'm English.'

'I'm English too.' Sam seemed upset.

'Show me the other stuff,' suggested Jack.

Sam picked up a little white bowl. 'This is a *milchig*. It's for milk.'

Jack smiled, although he wasn't sure why. 'What about the other one?'

Sam picked it up. It was a pinky-red colour with a flower pattern at the bottom. 'This is called a *fleishig*,' he ventured. 'It's for meat.'

'Why don't you use them here at dinner?'

'I'll just keep them under my bed until I get to Australia. Then I can use them at my aunt and uncle's house.'

'But why hide them? Are you worried they'll get stolen?'

'No, not that.' Sam fiddled with the bedspread. 'Lots of people don't like Jews. I don't want other people seeing these things. Promise me you won't tell anyone.'

Jack nodded, although he wasn't sure what Sam meant. It

was nice that Sam trusted him, though. 'Let's go back on deck,' he said.

Later, back in his own gloomy cabin, Jack struggled into his pyjamas under the bedclothes. Bert was parading naked around the room like some great hairy ape. His face loomed.

'Got something to hide?'

'No.' Jack grabbed a book beside him. 'Just wanting to read.' It was an Enid Blyton he'd got from the ship's library. *The Mystery of the Burnt Cottage*.

Bert smirked, then stood back and beat his chest, drawing attention to its wires of dark hair. 'Tarza-a-a-an! Come on, Malloy, don't you want to play? I'll be Tarzan and you can be Jane. You certainly look like a girl.' He bent over, laughing.

Jack attempted to focus on the print, but it was hard to concentrate with Bert around. Why was he being so nasty? At Melchet he'd escorted Jack to the toilet in the night to stop him wetting the bed. But since Jack had met Sam, he'd changed: always pointing out his lack of chest hair to the other boys, or grabbing his balls when Jack reached up to his bunk to get his pyjamas.

A gust of hot air lifted the page. Jack looked up. Tom and Mattie had arrived. They weren't much cop, but Bert wouldn't take on the three of them. Jack put the book down on the blanket and let out a quiet breath.

Thank goodness he'd met Sam. He hoped they'd spend more time together. Best to avoid Bert as much as possible.

His mother would have been pleased he'd made a new friend.

They were leaning over the ship's rails looking for porpoises when a large shadow loomed over them, blocking the sun. They turned to see the captain with two nuns and one of the young nannies. He looked stern but didn't speak. One of the nuns put her arm on Sam's shoulder.

'Can you come with us, young man? We have something to tell you.' Her tone was gentle. Sam threw a worried glance at Jack before following the group down to the captain's office. Jack realised that the nanny hadn't gone with them. She seemed to be waiting for him. He'd noticed her before: young, short curly hair, shy eyes and a wide smile.

'Hello, Jack. I'm Joan.'

Jack tried to smile a greeting but his mouth had gone rigid. Joan looked out to sea, where Jack and Sam had been gazing earlier.

'What were you looking for?'

'Porpoises,' Jack said.

The nanny smiled but didn't comment. She pointed to two deckchairs behind them and they sat down.

Joan leaned forward and turned to look at Jack. 'You're good friends with Sam, aren't you?'

'Yes. He's my best friend, but only from the ship. He wasn't at the orphanage with me.'

'I know. He's travelling to Australia to stay with his aunt and uncle.'

80

'Yes. He said.'

'The thing is . . .' Joan's voice dropped to a low murmur. 'There's been a terrible accident. A car crash. Sam's aunt and uncle have been killed.'

Jack gasped. The ship tilted more than usual.

'Are you all right?'

His chest was tight. 'What's going to happen to him?'

'The captain has spoken to the authorities in Australia. Sam is to come to the farm with you and the other boys. That's what the nuns are talking to him about now. They asked me to tell you so that you can help him get used to things. He's going to be very upset. I know you will be a good friend to him.'

'Yes, of course.'

'Good lad.' Joan ruffled Jack's hair. 'I'll tell him you're waiting for him up here.'

The nanny walked away, treading softly on the wooden boards as though they were upset too. Jack was sorry for Sam, but part of him was pleased that he'd be coming to the farm with the rest of them now. They could still be friends.

When Sam appeared, he looked bewildered. He sat down in the deckchair Joan had left earlier, easing himself into the seat like an old man.

At first Jack didn't know what to say. Eventually he muttered, 'I'm sorry about your aunt and uncle.'

Sam shrugged. 'I'd only met them once. Mother will be upset but I'm not. Not really.' He pressed his knuckles together. 'You must have felt much worse when your mum died.'

Jack leaned back in the chair. If he just kept to the facts it might be all right. 'I came back from school and our house'd been bombed. I called and called for my mum.' He cleared his throat. 'But she never came. Instead a warden found me and took me to the town hall. I waited all night but no one could tell me where Mum was.' He paused, suddenly tired. 'I stayed there for a few days but they said I needed to go to the orphanage as there was no one to look after me. So I went to Melchet House.' It was no good. He wiped his hand across his eyes. They were starting to prickle. 'I thought Mum would find me there, but she never did. Then they told me she was dead. That's why I decided to go to Australia.' He took a steadying breath.

Sam lay back against the canvas of the deckchair. 'The nuns told me I can come to the farm with you,' he said.

'Don't you want to go back to England to be with your mum and dad?'

Sam chewed at some frayed skin near his thumbnail. 'They sent me to Australia in the first place. To be with Uncle George and Auntie Jean. I don't think I can go back to England now.'

Jack tried to smile. 'Well *I* want you! It'll be great. We'll learn to drive tractors and shear sheep. Maybe they'll let us share a dormitory.' He scratched at a fading patch of eczema. Another thought occurred to him: 'Will you have to be a Catholic now?'

'I'll have to pretend to be. The captain said I couldn't go to the farm if people knew I was Jewish.'

'Oh. What about your Jewish things?'

Sam frowned. 'I can't leave them behind.'

'You could hide them.'

'That's what I'll do.' Sam looked out to sea for a bit, blinking hard, then turned back to Jack. 'Who'll look after us?'

'The Christian Brothers. They run the farm. The cottage mother will cook us meals and do our washing.'

'Will we have to go to school?'

'Yes, but we'll ride there on horseback. And we'll pick oranges from the trees on the way home.'

'I expect there'll be lots of food too, in Australia.'

'Oh yes. Plenty. And at weekends we'll be out in the sunshine all day. We'll get brown and strong.' Jack paused to look at his own suntanned arm. 'We'll learn to hunt and shoot.'

Sam lay back in the chair and closed his eyes. He let out a long, low breath. 'It'll be good,' he murmured.

Jack closed his eyes too. In the amber glow behind his lids, he and Sam were riding horses in the sunshine, galloping through the fields after sheep.

The next day, Sam was told to go to mass. Sister Agnes insisted. 'You're one of us now.'

Jack was used to the knee-bending and chanting, the candles and rituals, but he could see Sam struggling.

'Do what I do,' Jack whispered. Sam baulked at the Hail Mary, though. 'Say your own prayer instead,' Jack suggested, and Sam muttered quietly in Hebrew.

When Sam and Jack left to go back to Sam's cabin, Bert was waiting. Mattie hovered anxiously behind him.

'Why won't he say prayers?' Bert asked Jack, nodding in Sam's direction.

'He's one of us now,' said Jack. 'He's coming to the farm, but he's not used to the way we do things yet.'

'His prick ain't right either. I saw it when he was pissing in the lav. He's a bloody Yid!'

Sam moved close to him. 'What did you say?'

'Go home, Jew-boy,' said Bert. 'They don't want your lot in Australia.'

Sam opened his mouth to answer, then turned and walked away.

'Don't turn your back on me, you bloody kike!' shouted Bert.

That was enough. Sam turned round, his fists already raised.

But it was Jack who threw the first punch.

Despite his obvious surprise, Bert got him back, right in the chest. Jack grunted but stood his ground. He lunged at Bert again, catching his shoulder with a hard jab from the right.

'Stop!' yelled Sam.

Jack took his eye off Bert and was caught on the jaw. The impact sent him flying backwards and he landed heavily. Bert was moving in to hit him again, but Sam caught his arm and pulled it hard. Bert roared and tried to shake Sam off, but he held on. 'Get help!' he shouted to Mattie, who sped off with rapid footsteps.

Within minutes a steward arrived, panting, and seized Bert's other arm. Bert struggled, but Sam and the steward overpowered him.

Sam went over to where Jack was doubled up holding his jaw. 'Are you all right?'

Jack nodded. He could hear the rasps in his own breaths.

'Shall I fetch the ship's doctor?'

'No, I'll live.' Jack shot an evil look at Bert. He'd had this coming for a long time.

The steward grunted and pushed Bert down the corridor. 'Right, young hooligan, 'oppit! And don't come back to this area again, d'you hear?'

'I'll go where I want,' yelled Bert, and stomped off. Mattie trailed disconsolately behind him.

The steward turned to Sam. 'I'm sorry, young sir. I don't know what that rascal was up to, but he shouldn't be in this part of the ship. I'll report him to the nuns.'

'Don't do that,' said Sam. 'I'm going to be joining them now. No one need know.'

'Very good, sir.' The steward looked relieved and moved on.

Jack slowly unclenched his fists. He was ashamed now at how satisfying it had been to hit Bert. And yet they'd been friends at Melchet. What on earth had got into him?

'I told you some people don't like Jews,' Sam said.

Jack nodded, although he wasn't sure that was the real reason. 'We're going to have to keep out of Bert's way at the farm.'

Sam smoothed down his shirt. 'It might be different in

85

Australia, though. We'll all get treated the same there. Come on, let's go up to lunch.'

On the last day, the captain announced a competition: a big bag of sweets for the child who spotted land first. They all leaned over the railings, squinting into the haze.

Eventually a small voice piped up. 'I can see it! I can see Australia!' It was Nancy, the girl who'd mistaken the Isle of Wight for Australia all those weeks ago. This time she was right.

Part Two

1947–1949

12

Kathleen stood with John on the dais as the briny wind tugged her straw hat and fussed at her linen skirt. Seagulls wheeled overhead, but the cheers of the crowd and the strident brass band playing 'Waltzing Matilda' muted their cries. The air was layered with different smells: the salty tang of the sea, the foul stench from the tannery, a fungal odour from the wheat bins and a whiff of smoke and diesel from the engines. Despite these, she could still detect a trace of perfume, persistent despite its airiness – Soir de Paris if she wasn't mistaken. John had bought her some once but she rarely wore it. She preferred the Chanel she'd inherited from her mother. John didn't know the difference.

Senator Josephine Langley was statuesque beside Kathleen. Perhaps she was the owner of the perfume. Next to Josephine was the Catholic archbishop, a proud robin in scarlet robes, and beyond him Gibson, the mayor. How John loved these occasions, thought Kathleen. A photographer approached and her husband beamed, stiff with self-importance, snaking an arm round Kathleen as he did so. She pulled her mouth into a grin as the bulb flashed, but kept her body rigid. She hated it when John was demonstrative in public.

She twisted round, pretending to look at the crowd roped off behind them, but really to release herself from John's grasp. Once free, she continued to stand out of line. It was more interesting to watch people than to scan a blank horizon for the *Asturias*. Fremantle was putting on its finest welcome. You wouldn't believe we've just come through a war, she thought. People looked thinner, and their clothes shabbier, but worry and grief were hardly visible. Instead she saw excitement and hope. These British children, travelling towards them across the ocean, had already made a difference.

At the front of the crowd was a small boy in a red hat, laughing as he bounced up and down on his father's shoulders. His mother was smiling up at him. She wore a sleeveless floral blouse over a flared skirt, not dissimilar to one Kathleen had. She'd been all set to wear it today until John had muttered about it being too casual. After that, she'd swapped it for the fitted linen suit, although it was less comfortable.

Elsewhere, a group of young girls in pastel clothes danced to the music – 'Star of the South' now. A toddler in a long vest and nothing else beat at a small drum, hopelessly out of time with the musicians. Kathleen mimed a clapping motion at him. But John's arm was on her shoulder again, pulling her back in line.

'Stand still, darl,' he muttered. 'Folk are staring.'

She glanced at the other dignitaries. As far as she could see, everyone was looking straight ahead, but she wouldn't let John down in public. It wasn't worth it.

Her white court shoes pinched horribly. John's brogues

gleamed beside them. He'd been up early, polishing them into submission. One of his shoes was positioned a little further forward than the other. Kathleen noticed him inch it back.

The cheers intensified. When Kathleen looked out to sea again, the *Asturias* was moving towards them in a huge rush of foam.

'At last,' Josephine Langley murmured. 'I thought I'd fall off the platform with boredom.'

Kathleen stifled a giggle. 'All the interesting stuff is going on behind us,' she whispered back.

'Yes. It's maddening that we can't see the crowd. Still . . .' Josephine put her hand to her forehead to shade her eyes, 'it won't be long now. Those big ships can certainly move.'

The *Asturias* was indeed getting larger. In the centre of the ship, grey plumes of smoke unfurled from a large funnel. There were little flags hanging from the ropes, contorted by the wind. Kathleen wondered where the children were. There were some tiny shapes on deck and she thought she saw faces in the portholes, but they might have been shadows.

The band was now playing 'There'll Always Be an England'.

Josephine snorted. 'Not for those sprogs there won't be. They're here to stay.'

Kathleen grimaced in response. She couldn't imagine what it must be like to leave your homeland and travel nine thousand miles across the sea. It had been bad enough leaving her parents in Melbourne to move to Perth with John. She hadn't been back often, but at least they were in the same country. These poor kids would never go home again.

While she waited for the ship to get closer, Kathleen listened to 'When the Saints Go Marching In' and 'Advance Australia Fair' with her eyes closed. Maybe the *Asturias* would move faster if she didn't keep checking on it.

She was right. She snapped her eyes open as a single stretched-out bass note penetrated the other sounds. The *Asturias* was steaming up to the quayside with its long-awaited cargo. The crowd roared. Now she could make out the children for certain. There were boys in shorts, shirts and jackets. Some of them even wore ties. They must be sweltering in the heat. The girls were in thick navy coats and berets. Most of the children were aged around ten or twelve, but Kathleen saw a little line of hats peeping out over the railings. Their owners must be very young. Men in dark clothes and black homburgs were dotted in amongst them, their stillness contrasting with the excitement of the children, who were jumping and waving beside the rails. A boy turned round as though to run across to the other side of the ship, but was restrained by one of the guardians.

Kathleen felt John nodding and smiling beside her. 'Wave back,' he whispered. When he raised a gloved hand towards the ship, Kathleen followed suit. She tried to pick out one child to wave to and chose a little girl with a pudding-basin haircut standing on her own near the back of the boat. The girl didn't return the greeting.

'How much longer?' she asked John.

'The captain has to dock the ship. Not an easy task with a boat this size.'

Josephine smiled across at her. 'There's a lot of waiting

around in this caper,' she said. 'My advice: fix that grin on your face but spend the time thinking of something else. Like the plot of a book you're reading. As long as your face looks right, your thoughts are your own.' She struck a saintly attitude. Kathleen went to laugh, then tensed as John glanced at her. She managed to make her face look more demure, and he returned to his waving.

At long last, a line of children appeared, marching down the gangplank, each with a small brown suitcase, the bright sun picking out glints in their hair. Kathleen watched the older boys saunter down, followed by about twelve young girls. Some of the girls fiddled with their clothes or twisted strands of hair round their fingers. Then came the little ones, each holding the hand of a young woman, clutching teddy bears or rag dolls, their small cases carried by the adults. Kathleen swallowed.

Photographers in shiny suits, wielding huge cameras, rushed forward. Flash bulbs popped, their brief intense lights creating haloes round the children's faces. Poor little orphaned mites, she thought.

When the Archbishop of Perth made his speech, Kathleen felt John puffing out his chest. This was his triumph: the culmination of years of work at the Department of Immigration. He'd schemed and laboured for this and at last here were the children – British stock to increase Australia's white population. Kathleen tried to ignore the way he beamed and waved, suitably imperious. She hoped he was satisfied now the children were here.

But she was shocked when the boys were led off to the wool sheds to be fingerprinted, like common criminals. Once again, she thought, Britain has shipped its unwanted goods. Now Australians were grateful – called them *white stock* and not *bloody cons* – but they still treated those lads like crooks.

'Do you know where they're going now?' Josephine asked as they walked over to where the other children were sitting at long tables drinking milk and eating oranges.

Kathleen pulled back her shoulders. 'To the Sacred Heart at Highgate for the night. We're bussing them there.' Was there a little too much emphasis on the 'we'? She wanted to confide to the senator that she'd secured the arrangements herself and suggested her plan to an unusually amenable John. But then she'd have to tell Josephine about once having worked there, and although a part of her wanted to impress the woman who'd achieved so much, she knew John would be furious if he found out about her job. Better to stay quiet. She'd got away with it so far.

'Where do they go from there?' Josephine asked.

'The girls will go up to Geraldton and the boys to Bindoon.'

'Bindoon?' Kathleen wasn't sure, but did Josephine's voice sound cagey?

'Yes. To the Boys Town. Run by the Christian Brothers.'

She watched Josephine's face for a further reaction, but her saintly look had descended again.

94

13

When the children filed into the convent, Kathleen gazed at them longingly. She'd expected them to have pale British complexions. But these children were brown and bonny. A girl with springy blonde hair was whispering to her neighbour and giggling. Behind her, a couple of boys were jostling each other. The smaller children, surely only five or six, didn't look upset by their new surroundings. The men with the homburg hats had disappeared, but four of the young women Kathleen had seen leaving the boat with the little kids were there. One of them spat at her hanky and wiped it across a girl's face, although it was scarcely grimy. Another was tying a little boy's shoelace. She had a smiling face and lively brown eyes, but looked uncomfortable in a tweed skirt and blue jumper. Did none of these Brits know about the weather at this time of year?

Kathleen watched as the mother superior, serene in her monochrome robes, welcomed the party, before the nuns showed them to the dormitories. The children followed obediently, looking around with careful glances. Their little brown suitcases looked old and cheap; they couldn't have held a lot. Not much to show for their lives so far.

She heard a sudden clatter. One of the boys had dropped his case.

A nun made a clicking sound with her tongue. 'Pick that up,' she commanded.

Kathleen rushed forward to help. Some items had spilled onto the floor: a pair of shorts, a few socks, two jumpers and a black leather book. The boy was scrabbling at the clothes, trying to stuff them back into the case as quickly as possible. Kathleen picked up the book. It was a bible. She handed it to the boy, who muttered his thanks. He looked about twelve, with a brush of dark-brown hair and bright, intelligent eyes. His cheeks were ruddy, as if he'd spent a long time outside, or maybe he'd simply flushed with embarrassment. He put the bible into the case and snapped it shut before walking on with the others to his dormitory. Kathleen stayed still, her eyes fixed on the door through which he'd disappeared.

The next morning at breakfast, Kathleen asked John if they might go back to the convent to see the children off.

'It'd look good for you to be there,' she said.

John scraped up the last mouthful of cornflakes and swallowed it, before speaking through a voice still clogged with cereal. 'Reckon you're right, Kath. I might make a short speech, send the kids on their way.'

Kathleen bent down to replace a jug of milk in the Coolgardie. She normally went to her keep-fit class on a Wednesday, but she could leave it this once. God knows she

96

was thin enough. The suitcase boy's face crept into her mind. She hoped she'd see him again.

John pushed his bowl away and took a slurp of tea. 'Better get ready, darl. Put on your navy dress. Reckon that'll do the job.'

Kathleen stood up and took off her apron. She'd hoped to stay in her old cotton skirt, but it was a small price to pay. She went upstairs to get changed.

By the time they reached the convent, the children were lined up outside, their cases in their hands. This time they seemed more subdued, and some of the girls were crying. Kathleen noticed the boy again. He was standing with another, taller lad and talking quietly. He didn't look at her.

She turned her head at a sudden scream: two girls were being wrenched apart by one of the nuns. She made to rush towards them, but John pulled her back.

'Butt out, darl,' he muttered. Kathleen bit her lip. It was so hard to do nothing.

'I'm sorry, but you're down for different places,' said the mother superior, striding over. She had a crisp sheet of paper with a typed list in front of her. 'Nancy,' she addressed a plump girl with short brown hair, 'you're to go to Geraldton, and Doreen,' she turned to Nancy's friend, 'you're down for St Joseph's.' A silver trail slid down Doreen's face. The child made no attempt to wipe it off. Nancy caught hold of Doreen's coat, but the nun prised her hand away. She pushed Nancy towards a short queue of girls and led Doreen to another line.

The two girls stared at each other, both shuddering with sobs. Kathleen turned away. If she watched any longer she'd cry too and John would be furious.

The mother superior held up her hand and the children became quiet. Kathleen listened to the nun's voice. It was low and warm.

'We have been pleased to welcome you to our convent,' she said. 'You will be in all of our prayers as you begin your new life in Australia.'

Kathleen looked at the lines of children. A tall, well-built lad at the front of the boys' queue opened and closed his hands constantly, making them into fists and then releasing them. One of the girls was plaiting the hair of the child in front of her.

'God has chosen you for a special life,' the mother superior continued, 'and will uphold you in His service.' The other nuns nodded. Two of them had their eyes closed.

Then it was John's turn. He squared his shoulders and raised his chin.

'The mother superior has extended her welcome on behalf of the Catholic Church in Australia,' he boomed. 'Now I would like to add my own welcome on behalf of the Australian government . . .'

Kathleen watched a small child with white-blonde frizzy hair sucking the thumb of one hand while stroking the sleeve of the girl in front with the other. The other girl didn't try to stop her.

'Your prime minister, Mr Attlee,' John was saying, 'has got

together with our prime minister, Mr Chifley, to bring you lucky children across to this beautiful country of ours.' He surveyed the little faces in front of him. 'You will be helping to make Australia a bigger and better place. You'll soon forget about England, and as most of you are orphans, you'll now be part of our big Australian family.' Kathleen looked for the boy she'd seen the night before. He was standing very straight, his eyes gleaming.

'Work hard at school,' continued John. 'Grow up big and strong, and when you are old enough, you'll be able to repay our kindness.'

Doreen was still crying. Her neighbour, a short, stout girl with round glasses, put an arm round her.

'You boys will work on the farms and the girls can help in the homes. It'll be a wonderful life, much better than you could have in rainy old England.'

Kathleen felt John chuckling at his own joke and laughed dutifully. When he had finished his speech, the nuns loaded the children onto the buses and waved them goodbye. Kathleen watched the faces at the windows: little ghosts against the dark interior of the vehicles.

'That all seemed to go very well,' said John. He strode up to the mother superior and pumped her hand. 'Thank you for your hospitality,' he said. 'You can be very pleased with the part you played in the White Australia project.'

Kathleen winced at the crass words. The mother superior smiled and bowed her head.

*

Jack and Sam sat together on the bus, breathing the hot air. The green plastic seats were sticky, and there was an unpleasant smell of sweat. Jack spent a long time gazing out of the window at the blur of spindly trees and scratchy-looking bushes, and caught glimpses of tobacco-coloured earth. He hadn't spotted any orange trees. Perhaps they only grew them at Bindoon. He imagined it would be jolly good to pick oranges and eat them for breakfast.

He hadn't realised Australia was so far away. They'd been three weeks on the ship. Despite Sister Beatrice's insistence that his mother was dead, a little part of him hadn't given up hope of her still being alive and coming out to Australia to find him. He'd be worried about her travelling so far on her own, though. But then she'd enjoy the dances. And she wouldn't have to cook any food. Maybe it would be all right.

There was a thump from somewhere behind him. Jack turned, but couldn't see anything through the mass of heads. Within seconds, the news travelled up the bus. Mark, a little lad with yellow hair and skin the colour of paper, had fainted. One of the brothers strode down the dusty aisle, picked him up and carried him back over his shoulder. Jack watched Mark's yellow hair flapping against the man's black robe. He couldn't see what happened to him, but a few moments later another brother ambled down, looking at each boy in turn. When he got to Jack and Sam, he made Sam move up, plonking himself next to him. Jack glanced sideways at the brother's face. A bubble of spit sat in the corner of the man's mouth.

'Seen any black boys, yet?' the brother asked Sam. The bubble deflated.

Sam raised his eyebrows. 'I don't think so, sir.'

The man stood up. 'A penny for the first person to spot a black boy!' he announced. Thirty heads turned to stare out of the window. Jack scanned the landscape for an African or an Indian child, perhaps standing by the side of the road or trudging through the undergrowth.

'There's one!' the brother shouted, pointing with a knobbly finger. The heads followed but Jack couldn't see a thing.

'And another!' The brother was chortling to himself. 'Can't you see it, boys?'

Heads were twisting and turning. Jack watched the brother, trying to latch onto his gaze. All he seemed to be pointing at were bushes.

'I don't know,' the man laughed. 'We're going to have to sort you lot out now you're in Uz-trailya.' He spoke in a funny way. As though he wasn't able to open his mouth very wide so had to talk through his teeth.

'D'you give up?' he asked.

Everyone nodded. The man was wiping his eyes. Jack thought his laughter sounded like a dog barking.

'Black boys aren't people! It's what we call a type of bush.' He stooped to peer out of the window again. 'See. Another one.'

Jack saw a furry-looking brown trunk with stuff like long grass splaying out of the top.

Sam rolled his eyes. 'He seems to be enjoying himself.'

Jack peeled his right leg off the seat. 'Bindoon can't be far now.'

No reception committee greeted them. Jack had been half expecting a brass band, or at least another archbishop, but they were just met by another brother, who marched them wordlessly towards a large stone building.

'I expect we'll see the horses soon,' said Sam. 'Hope mine is a good galloper.'

But Jack wasn't so sure. He'd thought Melchet would be fun, but it hadn't been. A line of sweat dribbled down the side of his face. He wiped it away with his sleeve.

'Park your stuff on the veranda and then come on down to the refectory,' the brother commanded. So he did have a voice.

'Where's our cottage mother?' asked Sam.

The brother turned. His short neck disappeared into his gown; Jack thought he looked like a boxer. 'There's no cottage mother,' he said. 'Not until we get the cottages.'

'When will that be, sir?' asked Sam.

The brother regarded him through close-set eyes. 'When you've built them!'

Jack placed his suitcase on the veranda as instructed. Best to show no reaction. It would only provoke the man. Sam's suitcase was much bigger. He'd dragged it all the way from the bus.

'Have you still got your Jewish things?' whispered Jack to divert Sam's attention.

Sam nodded. 'I'll have to find a good hiding place.' He moved closer to Jack as he yanked his suitcase along the stone floor. 'That brother doesn't look too friendly. What did he mean that we have to build the cottages? Surely there are workmen to do that.'

Jack didn't answer.

They trooped into the refectory and sat at low tables drinking tepid tea. An older boy passed round some grey hunks of bread. No butter or jam. And certainly no oranges. Jack tried not to think about the last meal on the ship, when he and Sam had devoured plates of corned beef hash. Even at the convent they'd had fish and potatoes.

'Maybe we'll have some supper later,' said Sam.

'Maybe,' Jack replied, scratching inside his elbow. His eczema had hardly bothered him on the ship. He looked round as a thin line of boys entered the room. Their clothes were scruffy and they had no shoes. They were deeply suntanned but their hair was dusty and they had dirty knees. Not one boy was smiling.

Despite the heat, Jack felt cold inch up his body. Like when he'd sat in the bath at Melchet and Sister Angela had tipped icy water over him. Sam was still looking around him hopefully, but Jack stared at his plate. This wasn't what Brother MacNeil had promised. There were no horses. No oranges. And the sunshine was so strong it burned you.

Suddenly he was five again. *Where are you, Mummy?* he pleaded inside his head. *And how are you ever going to find me here?*

*

Two months later, Kathleen and John travelled up to Bindoon. It was quite a journey to the Boys Town, inland along dirt tracks in sweltering heat. By the time they arrived, Kathleen's checked blouse was sticking to her back, her carefully styled hair a damp mess. She climbed out of the car into the fierce hot air.

John had got out already and stood by the edge of the road looking towards a sand-and-terracotta-coloured building surrounded by farmland. It's like an Italian mansion, thought Kathleen. Wherever she looked there were rounded arches and balustrades. Huge palm trees flanked the building and an immaculate lawn lay in front, a strange contrast to the scrubby land around it. A grand flight of steps led up to the entrance.

She must have gasped, as John said, 'Surprised?'

'Yes, I am,' she answered. 'I expected something much more ordinary. Who built it?'

'The boys,' said John, gazing out over the estate.

'*The boys?*' Kathleen turned to face him. A blowfly crawled over her arm but she didn't move.

'There've been shipments coming here for almost ten years.' John kicked at a piece of flint near his feet. 'A lot can be done in that time.'

'And will the boys we saw at the convent be helping?' She shielded her eyes against the sun and tried to make out any children in the distance, but she couldn't see a single one.

'Well, the main building is finished, as you see. They're working on the outbuildings now.'

'But surely that's too much for them? They're children!'

'Nah.' John tucked in the front of his shirt, which had escaped his suit trousers when he got out of the car. 'It's good for 'em. Build up their strength. Plenty of fresh air and healthy food from the farm.' He strode off down the track and Kathleen followed, the dust turning her beige sandals red.

As she stumbled over the rough ground, she heard a magpie screeching nearby, and in the distance, the sound of trucks and the scraping of spades on concrete. She expected to see children running around in the grounds or hear their voices through the open windows of classrooms. But there was only the relentless din of metal on stone and the occasional whirr of machinery. The noises grew louder as they approached and she thought she detected adults shouting. No excited schoolboy chatter or laughter, though. It was strange.

She and John walked across the courtyard and into a cool refectory, where around twenty men in black robes were sitting on low benches, eating toast and marmalade and drinking cups of tea. John greeted them and asked if he might see the boys. One of the brothers went outside and blew a shrill whistle. Kathleen looked round the dark-wood room. Portraits of men in black habits, Christian Brothers presumably, gazed back at her; stern faces staring out of inky backgrounds. A smell of toast and something less appealing – mutton, perhaps – filled the air.

A minute later, a group of dusty boys trudged in. Kathleen hardly recognised them from the tidy youths who'd come off the ship. These children had bare feet and their clothes were ill-fitting and dirty. They looked suntanned but weary. She wondered where their British outfits were and what had happened to the clothes in their suitcases.

The ruddy-cheeked boy was there, thinner than before. Although he glanced wearily at Kathleen, he showed no sign of recognition. There was a smudge of dirt on his face. Or was it a bruise? Kathleen started as a gust of hot wind slammed the door to the refectory shut.

'Well done, lads. Looks like you're doing a great job,' John was saying, even though he hadn't been beyond the building. He went up to one boy and straightened his collar. The boy flinched but John didn't seem to notice. He walked down the line, wearing his official smile and nodding importantly, and then went to talk to one of the brothers. Kathleen approached the ruddy-faced boy and quietly asked how he liked Bindoon. The boy shrugged in reply, then, noticing one of the brothers advancing, muttered, 'It's fine, miss, thank you.'

Kathleen turned to the brother, a bony man with thin sandy hair. 'Are the boys ever allowed out?'

'Of course, ma'am. We take them into the town or down to the river.'

'I mean away from here. To spend time with families.'

The brother hesitated. 'At Christmas, yes, some of the boys are invited to stay with people.'

Kathleen looked at the bedraggled group of children. She itched to comb their matted hair and wash their sad little faces. Give them each a cuddle and a hot meal.

The words were out of her mouth before she could retrieve them. 'Then may I extend an invitation?' Sweat prickled her skin. What on earth would John say? And how many children might she take back? She wanted to scoop the whole lot of them into a big bus and drive them somewhere large enough for her to care for them all. But what good was one person looking after so many? Maybe it was better they stayed where there were plenty of staff. But if she couldn't take them all, perhaps she could make a real difference for one child. That was all she'd ever wanted. One child. A son or daughter to call her Mother.

The brother bowed gravely. He pointed to a group of boys with amber hair and innumerable freckles. 'There're three brothers over there who've never been to a family.'

Kathleen glanced at them. They did look forlorn. But she mustn't let herself weaken. She'd agreed on one child. She pointed to the ruddy-cheeked boy. 'I'll take that one there.'

The brother followed the direction of her finger. 'Ah, you mean young Jack.'

'Yes, Jack!' she said. She was aware she was speaking as though the name was familiar.

'I will make enquiries,' replied the brother.

She mentioned the conversation to John on the way home.

'These boys aren't pets, Kathleen, to be taken out and spoiled. They're here to do a job for us.'

Kathleen knew the dangers. Getting too attached. Being unfair to the other children. The questions people would ask. But the yearning for a child came from deep within her, from her empty core. 'Please, John – just this one. He's called Jack.

We could have him over for Christmas.' She smiled encouragingly. 'We could collect him on Christmas Eve and return
him the day after Boxing Day. Maybe even get him a few
presents. Just as if he was our son.' She pictured the boy sitting
beside their Christmas tree, excitedly tearing the wrapping off
a rugby ball.

His frown lightened. 'Maybe.'

Kathleen felt bold enough to take the discussion further.
She'd been shocked by the state of the kids. 'I thought you
said the children would have a good life at Bindoon.'

John kept his eyes on the road. There wasn't another car
in sight. 'They do.'

Kathleen tried to keep her voice level. 'Then why were they
so thin and ragged? I thought they'd look better cared for.'
She turned to stare out of the window. An intersection loomed
up ahead. A motorbike was charging along the side road in a
spray of red dust.

John sped up to make the motorcyclist wait. 'I don't know.
Perhaps the brothers are on a strict budget.' He looked in his
rear-view mirror. Kathleen heard a distant roar; the motorbike
was far behind.

'The government paid for the kids to be shipped across.
Surely they're financing their board and lodging too?'

The guarded look descended. 'Yeah, well. Everything's tight
thanks to the war.'

'Even so, that's no excuse for hitting them.' That was a long
shot. The bruise she'd seen on that boy's face could just have
been dirt. She hadn't been close enough to tell. But none of

the kids had looked happy. And surely they needed to be fed well if they were doing manual labour? Bindoon was a farm, for God's sake. There should be plenty of meat and veggies.

John still hadn't looked at her. 'Boys need to be kept in check.'

'Kept in check maybe, but not hit across the face. Or dressed in rags. Or made to work in bare feet!'

'Stop talking rot, Kathleen.'

Kathleen clasped her hands together on her lap. She'd said enough. Best to placate him and bide her time. 'Sorry. My mistake. I'm sure you're right, darling.'

A smirk and a visible relaxation. 'That's my girl. I'll make enquiries about Jack coming as soon as we get back.'

Kathleen forced a smile. 'Thanks, John. That'd mean a lot.' She leaned her head back against the seat. They were approaching Bullsbrook. Not much further. Something was up with those kids. She'd sensed it when Josephine Langley had clammed up at the mention of Bindoon that day the *Asturias* had docked. She wouldn't push it now. Wait until Jack came to stay.

Then she'd get to the bottom of it.

She spent the next week getting the bedroom ready. Polishing the little bedside table and chest of drawers. Demanding John help her move the bed again and again until she was satisfied it was in just the right place for the morning sun to catch Jack's face. She pictured him, flushed and tranquil from sleep, allowing the warm rays pouring through the window to coax him into alertness. She bought a little lamp so he could read at night, and spent ages browsing in the boys' section of the William Street bookshop before buying the latest book by that Captain Johns. Beside the lamp was an alarm clock and a small brush and comb. If Jack let her, she'd make his thick dark hair gleam. She'd bought two model planes, too. John had hung them from the ceiling, smiling at Kathleen's instructions.

After another journey to Bindoon in the forty-degree heat, and a quick word with the brothers, who released a now smarter-looking Jack to their care, they returned home with him in tow. He sat in the back of the car, responding politely to Kathleen's string of questions: *Who's your best friend? What do you have to eat? What do you do on the farm? What about lessons?*

'Enough!' said John, and the questions stopped. Kathleen felt the heat and silence build up in the car. Every so often she threw a glance back at Jack, who was gazing out of the window. The last time she looked, he had his eyes closed.

The car swung into the drive. John jumped out and opened the door for Kathleen. Jack remained in the back, clearly uncertain what to do.

'Come on, sport!' yelled John, rapping on the window. Jack climbed out cautiously, clutching a small bag.

Kathleen smiled at him. 'Follow me, Jack. I'll show you to your room.'

Jack followed her into the hall, slipping slightly on the polished floor; dragged his little case up the immaculate stairs, across the landing and into the bedroom she'd spent ages preparing for him. It had been an empty space for so long. She'd almost given up hope that it would ever welcome a child.

14

They spent Christmas Day on Cottesloe Beach. Kathleen sat on a canvas deckchair beside the groyne, enjoying the sand under her feet and the sun on her body. She adjusted her straw hat, pushing its brim back to allow her to see Jack. Sweat had built up behind her dark glasses; she took them off and patted her face with the edge of the towel. She could feel the sun burning her shoulders. John had suggested she bring a book – he'd given her Agatha Christie's *Crooked House* for Christmas – but she preferred to watch. John's present to Jack, suggested by Kathleen, had been a rugby ball, and he was teaching the lad how to play. Jack had to race up the beach to practise his passing. He was a good runner, but he'd never thrown a ball backwards before and kept dropping it. Each time, John would gesture to him to retrieve it and throw it again. Twice he stood beside Jack, demonstrating how it was done. But even from a distance, Kathleen saw that Jack didn't seem to like John coming too close. He would back off or kick at the sand when John stood within a couple of yards of him. Strange. Maybe, as an orphan, he wasn't used to physical contact.

John's belly oozed over the top of his bathers. Too many

ministerial lunches, Kathleen thought. He could've done with going to her keep-fit classes.

Jack was deeply tanned and his muscles were taut. But he was too thin. Every rib stood out, even from a distance, and his stomach was concave. When he turned away from her to pick up the ball, his shoulder blades were sharp as chicken wings. And although he kept up with John's instructions, he seemed tired.

Despite the heat, he'd been reluctant to take off his clothes. Since he'd arrived, Kathleen had been careful of Jack's privacy. She'd put the khaki shorts she'd bought him in the chest of drawers. They looked a bit like army ones. She thought he might like those. Make him feel like a soldier. She had no idea where he'd been during the war. The Brits had had it bad in the towns. Perhaps he'd stayed in the country. Anyway, all boys loved to pretend they were soldiers, didn't they? There were some T-shirts, too, from Ahern's, in a variety of colours so he could choose which he liked best.

She'd never seen him bare-chested until now. There were some strange yellow marks on his skin. Were they fading bruises or some sort of rash? Should she take him to a doctor? But then he'd never have had hot sun on his skin in England. Perhaps he'd tanned a little unevenly. She must find a way to ask him about it later.

The beach was dotted with groups of people. Next to Kathleen was a young family: a mother with a small child asleep on her lap, and two other children digging in the sand with shiny spades. The father was supervising, wearing a striped shirt with the label still attached. One of the children prised up a clod of sand too forcefully and it sprang off towards Kathleen's basket. She tucked her tartan rug around the picnic to protect it from further onslaughts.

Further out was a large gathering: several adults playing a lethargic game of badminton, their makeshift court marked with empty beer bottles, and a group of teenagers rushing into the sea in a noisy pack. Behind her, an elderly couple, wrinkled hands entwined, sat snoozing in their deckchairs.

We look like any other family, thought Kathleen, seeking out John and Jack again. No one would suspect Jack wasn't theirs. She hugged her knees to her chest. Maybe he could be.

John's laugh cut through the other sounds. Jack had chased the ball into the sea and fallen over. He was covered in foam, his legs plastered with sand and a strand of seaweed hanging from the bottom of his trunks. John raced over to check he was all right.

Kathleen hadn't heard John laugh like that since they were first married. They'd been confident they'd have a family in those days. But the years of infertility had soured him. He hated not having a son to boast about at the rugby club. Maybe he thought he wasn't a proper man. It'd been hard for her too. She'd loathed the pitying glances of the mothers with their smug armoury of prams and pushchairs. She felt left out when friends spoke about their children. The photo frames they'd been given as wedding presents would never chart their offspring's milestones as other couples' did.

A child would have changed everything. Probably brought

her and John closer too. They'd limped on, John with his work and her with the keep-fit classes and her wartime job at the convent, although she'd given up the latter after VJ day. Nothing had ever assuaged the emptiness until now.

Other families were tucking into picnics. The man next to Kathleen had rigged up a Primus stove and was heating slices of turkey in a brown sea of gravy, while the mother ladled stewed sprouts out of a large checked thermos. The elderly couple were munching on what appeared to be herrings, and the large group had a huge cold buffet spread out on a rug. Kathleen glanced at her watch: one o'clock. John and Jack must be hungry. She removed the tartan rug from the basket and spread it out on the sand, anchoring it with pebbles. She took out a bottle of lemonade, another of beer and three sorts of sandwiches wrapped in greaseproof paper. She'd made some Christmas fancies from a recipe she'd found in a magazine and brought them along in a tin, as well as several apples and a jam tart. That should please them.

She stood up and called to them. Jack picked up the ball and looked at John, who grinned, and they jogged up the beach, sand spraying out behind them.

'Mind the picnic,' Kathleen said as they approached. She held out her hands to ward them off.

'Righto, darl.' John slowed his pace and Jack did the same. They squatted down near the rug. John's skin was already turning pink.

Kathleen handed him his shirt. 'Here, put this on or you'll fry.'

John took it and pulled it over his head, wincing as the material cut into his neck. 'Ouch, it must have been hotter than I thought out there.' He looked across at Jack's brown skin. 'Guess you're used to the heat, sport.'

Jack nodded and lay full length on the sand. He stared up at the sky, shielding his eyes. His knuckles were calloused, and one of his nails was black. Kathleen wondered what he was thinking. He'd been like this a few times since he'd arrived, as though he were trying to absent himself from them. It must be such a contrast being with a family after years in orphanages. John had found out that Jack had been in institutions since he was five. No wonder he found it hard to adapt. Kathleen picked up a bottle, wanting an excuse to bring him back.

'Like a drink?' she asked.

Jack dug a finger into the sand. 'Water?'

'I've only got lemonade,' she replied.

Jack sat up. '*Lemonade?*'

'Yep. As it's Christmas.' Kathleen passed him a cup.

Jack drank for several seconds, and when he stopped, his eyes were watering and he was out of breath.

Kathleen laughed. 'When did you last drink lemonade?'

Jack was silent for a while. 'At Tisbury when the war ended. The nuns took us to a party and we had ice cream as well as cake and lemonade.'

'The nuns?'

'Yeah. At the convent.'

'Oh yes, back in England.' John had told her a few sketchy details of Jack's life after the war.

John squatted down beside her as she knelt in front of the basket. She passed him a turkey sandwich and he put his arm round her to eat it. She didn't push him away.

As soon as they were back home, John insisted Kathleen dab his sunburnt areas with calamine lotion. He sat on the bed in just his trousers, while she patted the pink liquid over him, grunting whenever she hit a particularly sore bit. For a change, the flabby skin and the wiry hairs sprouting from his back didn't make her feel queasy; her mind was on the mottled patches of yellow on Jack's body. Something wasn't right.

Once John was on the veranda, a bottle of beer beside him, reading the new Raymond Chandler she'd given him for Christmas and grumbling at the way his long-sleeved shirt was sticking to the lotion on his skin, she tiptoed upstairs to see Jack.

As usual, she knocked on the door. The first day, Jack hadn't known what to do when she'd done that. He'd jumped up and opened it a fraction, looking at her suspiciously as though he'd been doing something wrong. Were all eleven-year-old boys this secretive? It was so difficult to know how to treat him. 'It's all right, Jack,' she'd said, clasping the clean towel she'd brought up for him. 'You just need to say "come in" if it's all right for me to enter. Otherwise you can ask me to wait if you're busy.'

Jack had looked alarmed, as though her instructions were too complicated to take in, but this time he called, 'Come in,' in a more confident voice. He was learning their ways. If she could keep him for longer, maybe even – her heart flickered – permanently, she was sure he could adapt completely. She just needed time, to ease the hurt of being an orphan, to soothe his bruises, to nourish . . . to cherish. Surely they both deserved that?

Jack was lying on the bed, his arms behind his head, looking up at the planes hanging from the ceiling. She knelt down on the rug. It was important she didn't come too close, even though she would have been more comfortable on the bed. He sat up, looking awkward.

'Jack. I'd like to ask you something.' She tried to make her voice low and sympathetic, but he reddened immediately. His Adam's apple shifted as he swallowed.

She pushed a stray hair off her face. 'I couldn't help noticing those yellow patches on your skin, when you took your shirt off at the beach.'

Jack looked away but said nothing.

'I just wondered whether they might be bruises.' Still no eye contact. He was biting his lip. 'Jack. Did someone hit you at Bindoon?'

No reply.

Kathleen smoothed a wrinkle from her skirt. Her knees were protesting on the thin rug. It was hard to handle this. All she had were her instincts. 'I can understand why you might not want to tell me. But I must know if you've been treated badly. You or any of the other children.'

Was that a sigh? Jack was still looking away.

'All right, you don't have to talk. I can see you want to be loyal to the folk at Bindoon.' Kathleen moved her right knee an inch to ease the pressure. 'If I ask you a question, can you just nod?'

Jack turned to look at her. She could see apprehension in his eyes.

'Are the brothers beating you?'

He turned away again. He'd grasped a fold of the counterpane and was squeezing and releasing it.

She waited.

Finally, an almost imperceptible dip of the head.

She stood up, stumbling slightly on her numb left leg. 'It's all right, Jack. You won't get into trouble, I promise. I just need to think about this. But I can assure you you're safe here. You've no need to worry.'

When she turned at the door to look back, Jack was leaning against the pillow, his eyes closed.

'I was right, John. The children *are* being badly treated. Jack's just admitted the brothers are hitting him. I *thought* they were bruises I'd seen earlier.'

John's book clattered to the floor. 'I'll go and talk to him.'

Kathleen stretched her arms across the entrance to the veranda. 'No, don't. It took me a long time to coax that out of him. You'll ruin any trust I've built up if you just go barging in.'

'Well, what do you want me to do?' He slumped back onto his chair.

Kathleen went out onto the veranda and stood beside John. She spoke quietly, hoping John would keep his voice down too. Jack's bedroom overlooked the front of the house but he still might hear them. 'I want you to make some enquiries. Speak to the minister.'

John scowled. 'Over my dead body.'

Damn. She shouldn't have said that. John was too keen on his promotion to risk any implied criticism of his boss's methods.

'Then I'll phone him myself. He's always liked me.'

John was on his feet again, his face white. 'Don't you dare!'

'Why are the brothers mistreating the boys? I thought we'd imported the *white stock* . . .' she said the words as mockingly as she dared, 'to build a healthy Australia. Damaging the goods won't help.'

John sat down. 'That wasn't part of the plan,' he muttered. 'But we've handed the kids over to these institutions. I guess it's up to the brothers how they discipline them.'

'*Discipline* them? Bloody torture them more like.'

'Kathleen.' John's face was red now. 'You've only got Jack's word for it. Of course he wants us to keep him. Nice life here. He's probably exaggerating to get our sympathy.'

'I don't think so. I think he's telling the truth.'

John's words were iron. 'Butt out, Kath. I'm not taking this further and nor will you.'

Kathleen pressed the back of her hand to her face to soak up the moisture. It needed powdering. She patted her hair too. Make him wait a little. She had an idea. 'All right, John, I'll

119

keep quiet. I won't take this further, even though I've a strong suspicion there's something badly wrong at Bindoon.'

The red returned to pink.

'But you've got to swing it so that we keep Jack.'

John reached out to pick up his second beer, now perched on the veranda ledge. He took a long, slow draught, draining the bottle. Perhaps he was making her wait too. Or maybe he was thinking. 'Okay,' he said. He placed the empty bottle on the ground beside him, lining it up against the first. 'I'll talk to the brothers. Might take time, though. Paperwork.' He closed his eyes and tilted his face to the evening sun.

Kathleen wanted to pour water over his smug expression. But what would be the point? Something was wrong with those kids, but riling John wouldn't help them one bit. She wouldn't think about the others. She'd put all the guilt and worry in a box and keep it shut. Anything to keep Jack. John liked him. They'd got on so well on the beach, playing rugby. It was as much in his interest as hers to keep him. She drew in her breath as she turned to go into the kitchen. Perhaps she'd be holding it until Jack became hers.

15

Jack lay in his narrow metal bed not daring to move. In the long dormitory only the lightest sighs pierced the darkness. It seemed the other boys were trying to breathe as quietly as him. A slow intake of air through the nose, mouth clamped shut, hold it for four or five counts then release it just as quietly. Yawns had to be silent. An itch had to wait. Sometimes Jack made such a tight fist of his hand, determined not to give in and scratch, that the crescent indents of his nails were still there the next morning.

No one wanted Brother Cartwright to visit their bed. Jack wished with all his might that his mother was there to protect him.

A muffled click had announced the brother's arrival several minutes earlier. At once the dark air of the dormitory turned thick and stale, everyone on alert. Sometimes Jack wished Brother Cartwright would be noisier. It was the stealth that scared him.

And he still hadn't heard from those Sullivan people. That Kathleen had been nice. She wasn't Mum, of course, but she was kind. He could tell she was doing her best for him. And John was good, too. He'd a temper, mind, Jack had heard him shout at Kathleen. But the rugby practice had been fun. He'd been hoping for more.

Why hadn't they called for him? One of the older boys had gone to stay with a family for Christmas and never returned. Jack had thought if he was good, trying to keep out of the Sullivans' way and not asking for anything, then they'd have him back. Maybe even to stay permanently. It might be easier for Mum to contact him there, if she ever went to Melchet and got the message from Sister Beatrice. But there'd been no word from anyone. Was it because Kathleen had found out that the brothers hit them? But she'd promised he'd be safe.

Sam, in the next bed, wasn't making a sound. Jack could just make out his motionless body under the grey blanket. Sam was the best thing about Bindoon. Jack hated being back here, but he would have missed him if he'd gone to live with the Sullivans. Thank God for Sam. And thank God Brother Cartwright had left them both alone so far.

A groan from a bed spring. A muffled gasp. An eternity of waiting. Then the sound of footprints receding.

Jack had had another escape.

But someone else hadn't.

*

Kathleen tiptoed into Jack's bedroom. Really, it was ridiculous to be so quiet when he was no longer there, curled up under her white counterpane, only his tousled hair visible, his breaths a light rhythm in the still room. Instead, he'd be fast asleep in a dormitory with other boys his age.

She folded the cotton pyjamas she'd spent ages choosing, pressing them to her face to inhale the scent of him, then tucked them under his pillow. She wouldn't wash them. Wouldn't that be an admission he might never be coming back? He'd only worn them for three nights. She couldn't imagine ever having another child who could wear them. Not now.

The planes were still hanging from the ceiling. Perhaps she'd get John to take them down. In a week or two.

She brushed some creases out of the counterpane. It looked as though someone had sat on it, although she was sure she'd smoothed it straight earlier. The little brush and comb on the bedside table had been moved too. Lined up, not at an angle where she'd left them.

Kathleen glanced round the room. Everything else was as it'd been before, almost as though it had never housed a child. A bright young boy whose future she thought she had planned. In her mind, she'd even filled the photo frames: Jack in his school uniform. Jack with his degree certificate. Maybe even Jack on his wedding day. And she and John smiling proudly beside him.

A family at last.

Damn John. And damn Bindoon. Why was it taking so long?

She closed the door behind her, then trudged down the stairs to start preparing some fish for John's supper. Another meal they would eat at separate ends of the table.

16

There's a new orderly on the ward, with a shiny brown face, brown eyes, and a thin black moustache.

He smiles at her as he cleans and whistles.

'What's his name?' she asks Matron.

'Reggie.'

'Where did he come from?'

Matron sniffs. 'Jamaica, I believe.'

'What's he doing here?'

'Too many questions, Margaret. He has work to do – he mustn't fraternise with the patients.' Matron strides away on her clip-clop shoes.

She watches Reggie as he sweeps up a pile of dust. He bows to her. 'Princess Ma-a-argaret,' he says.

'That's not my name,' she tells him, through her laughter.

The sun wakes her; it's warm on her face. The rays make golden shafts, the dust motes dance. She needs to get up. The nurses put out her clothes: jumpers aren't scary any more. The woolly darkness doesn't last. She pushes her head through and there's the sun again. She steps into a flared cotton skirt. Paisley. She puts on her wooden clogs. There's no need for stockings. The suspenders never fit. There are no mirrors. 'Too dangerous, Margaret.'

'Margaret is not my name!' she screams, inside her head.

She runs her hands through her hair, trying not to disturb the bees. The curls loosen. She sets off for breakfast.

She opens *The Daily Sketch* and tries to read. But Reggie is there, in the corner of her eye. He beams at her and taps his broom to a beat. Someone laughs. Jane? Jane doesn't usually laugh; she just combs her long white hair and sucks on her dentures. But she chuckles at Reggie. Reggie pretends to dance with his broom. It *is* funny. But then comes Dr Lee, ready to do his ward round.

Reggie sweeps a bit of rubbish under the bed. Dr Lee walks on past.

She picks up the newspaper again. The words are difficult and dull. She looks at the photos instead: men in suits; people's faces; a new building; a football team. A young boy in shorts and a sleeveless pullover. Dark hair. Smiling. Why is her heart bumping? She doesn't know him. Or did she? Before the thief came.

The thief who stole her memories.

Reggie is always singing. Nat King Cole . . . Bing Crosby . . . Ella Fitzgerald. One day he sings an old song as he's polishing. What is it? Someone else sang it to her a long time ago. She doesn't know who.

Sing it again. A few words float down. *Dublin* . . . Something about pretty girls. She puts down her knitting and picks up a cloudy-looking glass from her bedside cabinet. She wanders down the ward with it, pretending she needs a refill. Reggie gives her a wink when she comes near, but she ignores him. After she passes him, he starts singing again, and then she hears it. Even the bees listen.

I first set my eyes on sweet Molly Malone.

She turns round. 'Who's Molly?'

Reggie stares. 'It's just somethin' I heard on the ship. The sailors used to sing it.'

'When was that?'

'When I came over from Jamaica.'

Who cares about the ship? Who's Molly? Is that what she's lost? She grabs his arm. 'I need to know who Molly is.'

Reggie says nothing. But he lifts his chin and begins to sing. *In Dublin's fair city, Where the girls are so pretty . . .* His voice is all smoke.

The hospital ward, with its beds and trolleys and chipped cabinets and constant smell of disinfectant, fades. Instead she's in a small garden with dusty hollyhocks by the fence and the scent of soot in the air. A deep cockney voice joins Reggie's: *I first set my eyes on sweet Molly Malone.*

Suddenly, she knows.

'Molly,' she whispers. 'That's me.'

*

Jack and Sam tramped through the wet grass to the cowsheds. A fine mist still clung to the trees and the sunlight filtering through their branches was watery. Despite the effort of getting up early, this was the best time of day. Before the sun grew really hot. Before Brother Cartwright came looking for them.

Jack pulled on the sliding door of the shed and it juddered across, releasing the stink of stale manure. The cows greeted them with low groans. He and Sam grabbed their pails from beside the door and squelched over to the far end of the barn, where the first cow stood, swinging its tail and chewing. Sam unwound a length of twine from his pocket and handed it to Jack. Then he held one of the cow's back legs while Jack tied it to the post. Hobbling, it was called. Stopped the cow from kicking them. Sam squatted down by the cow, spat on his hands, wiped them together, reached for two diagonal teats and squeezed. The cow turned her head, flicked a glance at Sam, then carried on chomping. Milk spurted into the bucket.

Jack envied how easy Sam made it look, pulling on the teats in a steady rhythm as the milk hissed and frothed. After a few minutes, he changed teats fluidly. The level in the bucket rose; when it was full, he stood up, arched his back and handed it to Jack to tip into the churn. 'Your turn.'

Jack went over to hobble the next cow. He'd decided that morning that if he approached the task briskly, like Sam did, he'd have more luck. Perhaps he'd squeezed too gently last time, or the cow had smelled his fear. Whatever it was, she wouldn't yield her milk, no matter how hard he tried.

He sat down, grabbed the teats and pulled. Nothing. Tried again. Still nothing. He rested his head against the cow's warm flank. 'Come on, girl.' He spat on his hands as he'd seen Sam do, then rubbed them together to warm them.

He turned round at a sudden noise from the back of the barn. Bugger. Brother Cartwright. Already.

'No milk, lad?' The brother was stomping towards him, glaring at the empty pail.

Jack grasped the teats in his hands again, tightening against them with his fists. Still no milk. Come on. Come on.

'Let me help.' Brother Cartwright pulled up another stool, grunting as he sat down close behind Jack and encircled Jack's body with his arms. He held Jack's hands as he pulled on the teats. 'There you are, slow and gentle, slow and gentle,' he said, his fat fingers guiding the action. Brother Cartwright's breath was hot on Jack's neck, his arms transferring their heat to his. He pressed so close his crucifix bored into Jack's back, as though branding him with the hot metal.

Brother Cartwright seemed to be everywhere these days: yellow teeth protruding at him as Jack spooned in his porridge; dusty black boots peering round the door when he was in the shower; fat hands smoothing down the blanket when he climbed into bed.

Eventually the milk came. Brother Cartwright released his grasp. But he didn't stand up. Jack focused on the cow's udder as he pulled and squeezed. *One . . . two*, he counted in his head as the milk streamed. He tried to ignore the sound of heavy breathing behind him.

Brother Cartwright's hands stroked Jack's back, a slow circling motion. Then they were at his waist, kneading Jack's skin, slipping across to his stomach, then down, down until they were pressing on his prick through the stiff material of his shorts.

Jack let go of the teats. The milk stopped.

'Damn,' muttered Brother Cartwright, close to Jack's neck. He took Jack's hands in his own again, curled his fingers round the cow's teats and resumed guiding. The milk flowed.

At last Brother Cartwright stood up, his clammy shirt peeling off Jack's back. The sensation of cool lightness was instant.

'You can manage on your own now, lad. I'll see you later,' he said loudly. Then, a rasping hiss in Jack's ear, 'And I'll finish what I started then.'

Jack tried to stay still to stop his body convulsing. He wanted to throw himself around to shake off even the memory of Brother Cartwright's hot breath, his paunch, his threatening voice, his fat fingers. He glanced across at Sam, but Sam was hidden by the curve of his cow's belly, only his legs visible. He couldn't have seen a thing.

The milk continued to stream. Jack pressed his forehead against the cow's hide. What did Brother Cartwright mean, *I'll finish what I started*? Was it Jack he'd be visiting tonight instead of some other unlucky boy? Would the others all breathe a sigh of relief when the brother climbed onto his bed and not theirs?

He changed teats easily but his success barely registered. He was wondering what Mum would say if she knew what he'd allowed Brother Cartwright to do. But he must stop thinking about his mother. She was never going to come for him. Probably the Sullivans weren't either now. He'd been abandoned to Brother Cartwright and his fat, hot fingers. Jack swallowed down the saliva that pooled in his mouth and tried to focus on the cow. At least the milk was still flowing.

Eventually the other boys arrived, bleary-eyed and yawning, and by eight they were done. It was a Saturday, so after weak tea and porridge, they set off to the building site.

Brother McBride had already taken up position. He looked like a boxer at the beginning of a fight. In his right hand he carried a strap consisting of four pieces of leather stitched together and a metal weight. Jack had seen him using it a few times. He'd seen the wounds too, on the boys' backs, after he'd finished.

Jack and Sam picked up their shovels. The foundations were three feet deep now. They wrapped their blistered hands round the handles and set to work whilst Brother McBride barked at the boys heaving stones from the lorry.

'What are those piddly rocks for? If I wanted gravel I'd have asked for it . . . Put your back into it, boy, or you'll feel my strap . . .' He turned to glare at Sam, who'd paused to draw breath. 'Head down, Becker. I don't want to see your ugly mug.'

The heat had become intense. The boys had taken off their shirts and the sun pounded at them, scorching their backs and searing their arms. A rivulet of perspiration trickled down the side of Jack's face and he wiped it away. The air smelled of sweat and dust.

I'll finish what I started.

Jack carried on. Drove the shovel into the hard ground, levered up some earth, twisted round and tipped it onto the surface. Dig, raise, twist. Dig . . . raise . . . twist . . . Dig . . . The heat sucked at his insides until his body was dry and weak, his arms and legs hollow tubes. *I'll finish what I started* . . . The horror that lay in wait for him at bedtime.

He stood up, staggering a few paces. The sky whirled around his head. Flashes of blue. Brother McBride's scowl. Brother Cartwright's fingers. Sam's anxious face. Keep going. Pick up the shovel. Raise . . . Blinding sunlight. The earth rushing to meet him. The shovel clattering. Twist . . .

The pounding of blood in his ears.

The galloping beat of his heart.

Then, 'Jack. You're wanted.'

He looked up. It was Brother McBride. The brother held out a rough hand to Jack, and Jack grasped it, relieved to encounter strong, thin fingers and not Brother Cartwright's fleshy ones. His body felt flimsy. He stumbled up on straw-like legs, his head still spinning. Mattie stood behind Brother McBride. It must have been him that brought the message.

'Mattie will take you to the refectory. Off you go, lad, you're off duty for the day.'

Jack didn't dare glance at Sam, although the regular thuds suggested he was still digging. He trudged after Mattie back to the main building. Even walking was an effort. Who wanted him? Not Brother Cartwright this soon. Surely he'd wait until night-time. Until the other boys were asleep, or pretending to be, in the crowded dormitory.

131

I'll finish what I started . . .

The refectory was cool and dark after the blinding heat outside. Normally Jack would have been glad of it. But not today. His heart drummed as he scanned the room for Brother Cartwright. He wiped his hands down his shorts, trying to stop them shaking, then stared at the ground. In the distance was a pair of polished black shoes and some beige sandals.

'Jack.' A voice spoke from the shadows. Not Brother Cartwright's rasp but a woman's tone. Light. Posh.

He looked up.

It was Mr and Mrs Sullivan.

*

'That will be threepence ha'penny.'

Molly handed over the coins to the shopkeeper carefully and received a bar of Sunlight soap in return. It wasn't really a shopkeeper, though. Just Madge, smiling at her encouragingly. And she wasn't really in a grocer's, just in her Preparation for Life class at the hospital. They'd spent weeks playing shops. Just like children. At first Molly had been cross and refused to cooperate, but the thought of the outside world was so scary, and Madge was so nice, that eventually she'd given in.

'Try again,' Madge said. 'A packet of Bisto this time.'

Molly dug in her purse for more coins. Only a shilling left. She handed it over.

'That's sevenpence ha'penny. How much change should I give you?'

Molly rolled her eyes. 'You're the shopkeeper.'

'Yes, and out to diddle you if you're not careful. Always check your change, Molly.'

'Fourpence ha'penny,' Molly said, holding out her hand.

Madge smiled. 'Well done. I think you'll do just fine.'

Molly rubbed her ear. Preparation for Life. It was all very well, but how could she really prepare when she didn't know if she even had a life?

Or whether she would ever have one in the future?

17

These days Kathleen felt relieved she no longer had the job
at the convent, even though it was two years since she'd worked
there. At first she'd missed Mavis and even that strange Mr
Brownlow – in fact more than she expected. But now she was
glad she could devote her time to Jack. She had to do everything
possible to help him settle in. Like today.

A little flutter of happiness rose inside her throat as she
walked along Grosvenor Road. Jack would've gone this route.
She'd arranged for Scott Carter from next door to collect him,
and she'd watched the two boys as they plodded down the
street, their satchels slung round their chests. She'd been
pleased to see Scott talking to Jack and Jack nodding cautiously.
She so hoped it would work out at school. That he'd do well
in lessons, make friends, play sport . . . that good experiences
would push out the memories of Bindoon.

She'd taken care getting ready that morning. Put on her
flowery cotton dress. The dog-leash belt accented her slim
waist and she liked the way the wide skirt flared out as she
walked. Was a hat too much? She'd no idea what the fashion
code was for school mothers. In the end, she wore her navy
straw. She could always take it off and hold it if the other

women were hatless. She'd managed to track down some pink Elizabeth Arden lipstick too. It said in *The West Australian* that cosmetics were paler these days. She glanced down at her polished fingers. The lacquer was in the same shade. Her nails caught the sun as she walked. Jack would surely be proud of her. At least her figure hadn't sagged like those poor women who'd had babies every year. She'd had her hair tinted, too. Even John had commented on it. If she said it herself, she looked a picture.

Already a small group of mothers had congregated at the high-school gates. Some of them were clutching baskets, as though they'd done some shopping on the way. A couple of women had prams. Kathleen smoothed down her dress as she approached. She decided to keep her hat on, even though most of the women were bare-headed. It made her stand out – and shielded her from the sun.

She stood next to a blonde woman in a green dress. The woman half smiled at her, then turned away and spoke to someone on her right. Everyone else seemed involved in the low buzz of conversation. Kathleen swallowed. She'd waited for this day for so long, when she could finally join the ranks of mothers outside the school gates. Yet even now she didn't fit in. Of course, they'd have known each other for years. They'd have been coming here since their children had started kindergarten. Her hands were sweaty inside her navy gloves. At least the cotton hadn't stained yet.

Dead on four, the school bell clanged, and within seconds children were spilling out of the door. A leggy boy of about seven jogged over to his mother, the green-dressed woman, and hugged her. One of the pram bearers held her arms out to a little girl with her hair in pink ribbons, who threw herself into her mother's embrace. Everywhere Kathleen looked, children were approaching with varying degrees of enthusiasm. Some of the women had left the gates and were walking back along the road holding a child's hand.

She adjusted the brim of her hat. These children were all much younger than Jack. Had she got the time wrong for his class? Eventually all the mothers dispersed. Kathleen looked round anxiously, conscious of how conspicuous she was standing on her own. What should she do?

At 4.15, another bell sounded. The children who exited now were more like eleven or twelve, Jack's age. And they were coming out of the upper-school entrance. Not the lower-school one where Kathleen was standing. She walked to the other side of the building. There didn't seem to be any other mothers waiting. At last Jack emerged, walking beside Scott Carter, grinning shyly, with another boy to his left.

Kathleen waved. 'Ja-ack!'

Jack froze. After a moment, he approached her unsmilingly while Scott and the other boy waited. Were those smirks on their faces?

'Hello, Jack. I thought I'd come and walk you home.'

'Hello.' A flush spread up Jack's neck. He swallowed. The flush reached his cheeks. 'It's all right, thanks. Scott and Tim are going my way. I said I'd walk with them.'

Kathleen stretched her lips into a smile. 'Oh yes, of course.

I've a little shopping to do anyway. I'll see you at home. The key is under the flowerpot, where we showed you.' She'd waited years for this moment. And now that it had finally come, it was too late. Her heart plummeted. She bit her lip and blinked rapidly.

Then turned on her heel and walked away from the school before anyone could notice.

After supper, when Jack had disappeared upstairs to do his homework, she spoke to John about it as they sat drinking tea in the lounge room. 'It's all right for you. You can play rugby with him. Take him to watch matches. Teach him to like beer when he's old enough. What can I do?'

'Dunno, darl. Perhaps you should have picked a girl.' John took a slurp from his cup.

Kathleen hadn't touched her tea. 'There *are* no girls at Bindoon!'

'Perhaps we were too hasty. Should have gone to Geraldton instead.'

'Well we didn't. We went to Bindoon. And *picked* Jack. We can't swap him! We've got to make a go of this.' How could John be so indifferent? He'd wanted Jack too. In fact Kathleen had a shrewd suspicion he used to visit Jack's room after they'd taken him back to Bindoon. She wouldn't let him know she'd guessed, though.

John picked up a copy of the newspaper from the table in front of him. 'Course we have. It'll be fine.' He shook out the sheets, then disappeared behind them.

Kathleen fumed as she took the cups into the kitchen to wash up. She tipped the brown liquid from hers down the sink, then immersed both cups in soapy water. Jack was nearly twelve. She couldn't dandle him on her knee, or feed him from a spoon; she couldn't blow raspberries on his neck to make him squeal. She'd become a mother from a standing start. The ache in her arms had been for a baby. Flesh of her flesh. Flesh of John's, too, although that was less appealing.

She reached for a tea towel. Jack wasn't naughty. That would almost be a relief. No, he was always polite. But too often he disappeared into those silences of his. Was he still thinking of his mother? John had told her she'd been killed in the Blitz. She wondered what Jack had witnessed; what horrors had imprinted themselves on his child's brain.

She reached up to replace the clean cups in the cupboard and hung the tea towel on its hook beside the oven. Perhaps she'd make him some cocoa. It would be an excuse to go upstairs and see how he was getting on. She put a pan of milk on to boil, then searched for a cup that he'd really like. Eventually she located a bright red one John had bought her years ago. She'd hidden it away as it didn't match her set, but perhaps Jack would prefer it to the flowery teacups she usually favoured.

That was the way. The more contact she had with him, the more he'd forget his own mother.

*

Molly lingered on the porch, peering through the fog of the late-October afternoon. She'd been out of the hospital before, of course, for short outings with some of the other patients, but always accompanied by one of the hospital staff and always to return to the safety of the ward. This was different. It was hard to know how she felt. A new start was exciting. In some ways her life was just beginning. But it was scary to think she'd be coping on her own from now on.

In the shadowy air, the bare trees were skeletons lining the path. The gnarled roses in the beds stretched out to her like claws. Everything seemed out of kilter. Like when she'd tried for hours to do a jigsaw here at Warlingham, only to realise half the pieces came from another set.

Nurse Sanders touched her shoulder. 'Ready?' She wore a red coat with a dark blue hood over her nurse's uniform and carried an old brown suitcase. She'd helped Molly pack it earlier. It didn't contain much: a few garments she'd been given from the hospital store, and a little bottle of eau de cologne from Annie. She'd suspected Annie had used some of it already, as the packaging was crumpled and the level of perfume looked slightly low.

Molly had said goodbye to everyone else inside, even though she was coming back the next day. Nurse Sanders was going to take her to her lodgings and help her settle in. Even so, it was an effort to walk down the drive. Her feet were spongy and she wondered whether her legs would carry her all the way. Nurse Sanders held out her arm and Molly took it gratefully, pleased to be with the nice nurse with her bouncy yellow hair and kind voice.

As they made their way slowly out of the hospital grounds and down to the Limpsfield Road, Molly looked around her. How run-down the houses were. Some of them still had bomb damage, though their owners had tried to disguise it. She pointed out a patched roof on one house, like a darned garment, and a boarded-up window on another.

'Everything looks so tired,' she said.

Nurse Sanders nodded. She probably saw this every day.

A large bus lumbered down the road. Molly flinched and tightened her grip on the nurse's arm.

'Well, what shall we do, Molly? A quick trip to the cinema and a fish-and-chip supper? Or maybe a cocktail or two?'

Molly looked at her in horror.

'Only joking, dear.'

Molly tried to laugh. She knew Nurse Sanders was trying to make light of the situation. It was all right for her. She walked backwards and forwards to the hospital each day. It wouldn't take her long to put on her uniform each morning, apply a bit of lipstick, gulp down some tea. Probably did it without thinking. Did she really know how much of an ordeal it would be for Molly even to get ready by herself?

It was getting dark. Street lamps drizzled yellow light on the pavements, turning their shoes a lemon colour as they walked past. The air was damp, and Molly felt a drop of water slide down her nose. She sniffed. Her hair would be frizzing from this moisture. Perhaps Nurse Sanders would brush it for her later.

They walked past closed shops, their wares only shadows in the half-light. Molly wondered if she'd ever have the courage to visit them on her own. What would she buy anyway? She was to have breakfast provided for her at her lodgings and then she'd be at Warlingham for the rest of the day, at least for a while. If she needed more clothes, Matron would give them to her from the store. No need to buy any yet.

Mr Travers in the office had given her ten shillings' worth of change to keep in an old handbag. 'Here's your Welfare money, love. Your board is paid, but this is for you, for any bits you need.' She wondered where the handbag had come from. Probably donated by one of those earnest women who came to visit them, like that horrible Lady Dawson. The 'do-gooders' she'd once heard Nurse Sanders call them. They would bustle into the afternoon therapy sessions and help with the pottery classes, or sit and read to the patients who didn't get out of bed. Sometimes Molly thought the visits were more for the visitors than the patients, they looked so pleased with themselves.

'Not far now,' said Nurse Sanders. 'This is Park Street.' Her face was all pink and white, like ice cream. They turned into a narrow road full of tall, squashed houses with windows that looked down at her with disapproving eyes. Molly couldn't see a park.

'Number twenty-three. Here we are.' Nurse Sanders stopped outside a beige building with a scuffed front door. Molly trudged up the broken concrete steps behind her and waited while she knocked.

After a few seconds, a large woman with a flowery apron tied round her stout figure opened the door. Molly noticed thin red veins on the woman's cheeks.

'Mrs Croft?' asked Nurse Sanders.

The woman inclined her head.

'This is Molly.' She stepped to one side so the woman could see her new guest.

'I'm not expecting no Molly,' said Mrs Croft, peering at her.

Nurse Sanders frowned. 'Oh dear. Perhaps the hospital's got it wrong.' She looked tired suddenly. Molly wondered if they'd have to walk all the way back. Perhaps that would be for the best.

'It said *Margaret* on my letter,' the woman offered.

'Oh, of course.' Molly heard the relief in Nurse Sanders' voice. 'Margaret is her official name. It will be on all the hospital documents. But we know her as Molly now.'

'Didn't know I was putting up hoity-toity. Does she have an official birthday, like the King?'

For a second, Molly thought of Reggie calling her 'Princess Ma-a-argaret'. Maybe she *was* royalty.

Nurse Sanders laughed. 'Well, in a manner of speaking, she does. She came to us without any details, you see. Didn't you, Molly? After the Blitz. We know very little about her. Her name . . . her birth date.'

Mrs Croft sniffed. 'All right, love. As long as I get paid, I don't need to ask no questions.' She widened the door behind her by kicking at it with her foot.

'I'll just come in briefly to get Molly settled,' said Nurse Sanders. Mrs Croft shrugged. They followed her into the narrow hall, smelling of old fish and Woodbines, then up a threadbare staircase with a dark-brown handrail. Mrs Croft paused at the top, then turned right and walked down a short corridor. Molly saw a door at the end covered in peeling paint. The landlady pushed it to let them in.

'Breakfast between six and eight,' she said. 'No visitors or food in your room. Bathroom's along the corridor. Baths are sixpence extra. Let me know in advance if you want one. And no more than two a week.'

'Thank you,' said Molly, and the woman ambled off.

Nurse Sanders dropped the suitcase on the bed, releasing a slight puff of dust.

'I'll help you unpack.' She clicked open the case and drew out a series of garments: two ancient girdles, four knitted bloomers, two skirts, some blouses and a couple of cardigans. Everything seemed to be brown, green or grey. 'Now, where's the wardrobe?' She looked round the room before advancing on a dark-oak cupboard in the corner with a brass key sticking out halfway down. 'Won't budge,' she said, tugging at the handle. 'I'll try the key.' This time the door burst open, almost knocking Nurse Sanders over. 'Hmm. I can see why it's locked. It won't stay shut otherwise. You'll have to turn the key each time, Molly.'

Molly nodded. Another thing to remember.

'Now, I'll line your clothes up like they do at the hospital: skirts at the bottom, cardies and blouses on top.' As she talked, she was dragging hangers from the rails, sliding the clothes onto them, then repositioning them in the wardrobe.

'What shall I wear tomorrow?' asked Molly.

'Do you want me to put something out for you, like we do at Warlingham?'

'Yes please.'

Nurse Sanders chose a plain grey skirt, dark green blouse and brown cardigan. 'There we are. I'll leave them on the chair.'

'What do I wear underneath?'

Molly thought she heard a sharp breath. 'Here.' Nurse Sanders pulled open a drawer underneath the wardrobe. 'This is where I've put your smalls.' She drew out a girdle and some lisle stockings and tossed them onto the end of the bed.

Molly felt better. That was what she wore at the hospital. If the button went on your suspenders, you could ask for a threepenny bit to hold them up. If that happened here, perhaps Mrs Croft would help.

'Now,' said Nurse Sanders, looking round the room, 'I think we're shipshape. I'll just slide the case under your bed.'

'What do I do now?'

Nurse Sanders looked at her watch. 'It's nearly nine,' she said. 'You could read your book for a bit.' She motioned to the paperback on the bedside locker.

'Lights out at ten?'

Was Nurse Sanders laughing at her? 'Well, it's up to you.

You make your own decisions now. But probably best to keep to hospital times on the first night. Now,' she stood up and smoothed down her coat, 'are you sure you'll know your way back in the morning?'

'Left out the front door. Down Park Street. Right into the high street, then Limpsfield Road, then the hospital.'

'Well done.' Nurse Sanders gave her a hug. Molly held onto the warm coat, breathing in the smell of lavender and cigarette smoke. She wanted to stay like that, where she felt safe, but Nurse Sanders prised her gently away.

'Ta-ta then, Molly. I'll see you tomorrow.'

'Yes.' Molly heard the wobble in her own voice. 'Thank you.'

Nurse Sanders blew her a kiss, then there was a clattering sound, a brief 'goodbye' from somewhere below, and the bang of the front door being shut.

Alone for the first time in years, Molly smoothed the cream candlewick bedspread, willing the buzzing in her ears to subside. It seemed to be the only noise in the room. Warlingham's hectic wards had grated on her nerves but now she'd have been glad of the clatter of bedpans or even the incessant wail of a disturbed patient. The silence outside her ears scared her.

To distract herself, she ran her hand down the wall. It was covered in burgundy flock wallpaper, fading to brown in places. She sensed she'd seen the design before somewhere. Maybe somewhere she'd lived. She closed her eyes and allowed herself to drift off. It was something she'd learned at Warlingham. If you shut out the real world, you could allow your thoughts to wander. And as usual, she tried to remember the past. What had her old home looked like? She willed her mind to take her there. Was that music she could hear? It made her want to dance. Then she felt something hard and rough on her head, like the underneath of a table. Was there someone with her? She stretched out her arms in the darkness, trying to connect. There it was. The sensation of smooth, short hair under her fingers. But who was it?

The sound of a church bell brought her back to the room. And the fact that she was alone in it. Had she always been alone? Had she been married? Or had she lived with aged parents, the spinster daughter kept on to manage the home when the other siblings flew the nest? Molly knew a patient who'd been in that situation. All Lucy knew was keeping house and nursing her elderly mother and father. And when they'd died, she couldn't face life on her own and had a breakdown. She was still at Warlingham, a slight, bewildered figure who no longer knew where she fitted into the world. But at least she *had* a place in the world. Do I belong anywhere? Molly wondered.

She stood up and stretched, then wandered over to look out of the small window, surrounded by dingy curtains, that faced onto the street. It was pitch dark now, too dark to see. She moved into the corner of the room and ran her hands over the chest of drawers. The wardrobe door was made of the same wood. Probably cheap, but nicer than her bedside cabinet at the hospital. She'd never found what she was searching for at Warlingham. Maybe it was here, at Mrs Croft's. She could look in the morning. The beige linoleum was cold under her stockinged feet, so she returned to the bed, where the floor was covered by a small rug of indeterminate colour.

She didn't know what to do next. No one came to tell her to get ready for bed, or to put out the light. Perhaps she should use the bathroom. She crept down the corridor and opened the door at the end. The room was dark and smelled of damp. Plaster had peeled off the wall above the bath, in the shape of a tear. She took off her jumper to have a quick wash, then realised she'd left her things in her room. A cracked block of coal tar soap congealed on the washbasin and a threadbare pink towel hung on a nail. She used those, soaping under her arms with the scant lather and inhaling the familiar antiseptic smell, then blotting the moisture as best she could, before replacing them carefully so Mrs Croft wouldn't find out. She'd decided against a bath: too complicated and expensive.

Once back in the room, shivering a little, she tried to draw her bedroom curtains but couldn't hide the gap in the middle. She attempted to force them but they wouldn't stretch. Wasn't that dangerous? She didn't want the warden to fine her. It was only when she was putting on the flannel pyjamas Nurse Sanders had tucked under her pillow that she remembered the war was over. It didn't matter about blackouts any more. Strange that she'd thought that, though. She climbed into bed, then curled up on her side and waited for sleep to come.

But her mind stayed busy. It was so quiet in the room. She even missed Mary snoring. Occasionally a car drove by, and once she heard footsteps from the other end of the house. But otherwise nothing. Her ears started to buzz. Would she ever learn to cope here? Dr Lee had told her that some of her memories might come back but there were no guarantees. Some people never recalled their past. She might be one of those. She'd been so excited when Reggie had sung and she'd remembered her name. But she'd had no moments like that since. Maybe she should be content with the improvements she *had* made. Since Reggie had joined the ward, her recovery had come on in leaps and bounds. Maybe Dr Lee's ECT had made a difference, but it was Reggie who made her feel alive. He was the best medicine.

And what about the future? Eventually she'd have to find a job to earn her keep. Perhaps shop work, or waitressing. The hospital would help. Once she knew what she wanted to do, Madge would help her practise. Madge said she was a quick learner; she'd get there.

The buzzing slowly eased. It'll be all right, Molly told herself, again and again, as she drifted off to sleep.

She woke to a pale beam that striped the lino and a clip-clopping sound echoing down the street, accompanied by the clanking of bottles. Was that the milk horse? It must be – she heard Mrs Croft open the front door and rattle something.

She looked round the room. In a minute, she'd get dressed in the clothes Nurse Sanders had put out for her last night, then go down to breakfast. Then she'd walk over to Warlingham and tell them how well she'd done.

Mrs Croft's voice drifted up to her. 'Go away. I'm not having the likes of you hanging around her. Be off with you.'

'But excuse me, ma'am . . .' Molly sat up sharply. Was that Reggie? She strained to hear. '. . . I've come to call on Molly. I work at the hospital. I thought I'd escort her in on her first morning.'

'Well I don't know where you got that idea from.' Mrs Croft's voice was full of indignation. 'I'm sure the hospital didn't send you. This is a respectable neighbourhood.'

Silence. Molly rushed to the window. Reggie was walking down the road, his shoulders hunched. Poor Reggie. It had been such a kind thought. She'd seek him out when she got to Warlingham and tell him so. Hurriedly, she clambered into her clothes. Some mornings at Warlingham she'd wanted to stay in her pyjamas, but Matron had insisted on her getting dressed.

'We'll have no lazing around here,' she'd say, consulting the fob watch pinned to her immaculate uniform. 'Up and dressed, then you're set for the day.'

Molly had no idea where the outfits had come from. The staff handled her clothing rations. For years she hadn't cared what she looked like. Wartime clothes were boring anyway: just square-shouldered jackets that made you look as though you were a soldier, or baggy cardigans, itchy blouses and straight skirts that stopped at your kneecaps.

She glanced in the mirror. Nurse Sanders had chosen well.

The blouse matched the colour of her eyes. Maybe later she'd buy some lipstick and powder. Even a small bottle of lily-of-the-valley perfume. Make herself look really nice.

After tea and porridge in Mrs Croft's poky dining room, she set off for Warlingham, retracing the route she'd taken with Nurse Sanders.

She found Reggie in the garden, propped up against the wall, a packet of Luckies in his hand and one of the cigarettes in his mouth. He must be on a break. His eyes crinkled at the corners when he saw her.

'Hello, princess.'

'Thanks for calling for me this morning, Reggie. I'm sorry Mrs Croft was so horrid.'

Reggie shrugged. 'She had her reasons.'

'Well I don't know what those reasons were. I can't think of any that would make someone behave so rudely.'

'Folk are a lot more judgin' outside than in here. Jamaicans can work in their hospitals but not walk their streets.' Reggie smiled grimly at Molly. 'Anyway, perhaps I can escort you home instead.'

Molly smiled. 'Yes please.'

Reggie looked at his watch. 'I've got another ten minutes of my break. Let's stroll round the garden.'

They traipsed through the long grass, still heavy with dew. A few tardy chrysanthemums lingered in the flower beds, tingeing the air with their musty scent.

They reached the edge of the park. Only one set of railings

remained now. Molly ran her hand along the black wrought metal. 'Dr Lee had the rest taken down.'

Reggie held the rail too. His hand was inches away from hers. 'A prison to a sanctuary.'

Molly smiled up at him. The air between their fingers vibrated. It would be so easy to take hers further, to slide them under Reggie's strong palm.

A wasp, drowsy from the late-autumn sun, was crawling along the rail.

Finding its way blocked, it buzzed in sudden irritation.

Reggie flapped at it. 'We'd better go back,' he said.

Molly spent the rest of the day doing the usual Warlingham things: therapy, lunch, a meeting with Dr Lee. By the time she was ready to go back to Park Road, Reggie was waiting for her outside the hospital.

'Fish and chips suit my lady?'

'I'm supposed to go straight to my lodgings,' she said.

'Nah. Celebrate your freedom first.'

'Is it something to celebrate?'

'Yes. A new life!' Reggie put his hand on her elbow. It felt nice. As they walked into town, Molly noticed again the way many of the buildings seemed patched up. As though they'd suffered an injury that was healing; new skin growing over old scars. Like me, she thought.

Reggie led her to a small café. 'Here we are.'

'Lovely,' she said, trying to smile. Their table by the window was dark brown, white rings seared into it. Molly imagined all the hot plates that would've been slapped down on it, leaving their mark. The window was covered in condensation, transformed to a pearly glow by a street lamp outside. It swaddled them in the damp, warm air of the room.

A weary-eyed waitress appeared at Reggie's shoulder, a pad in her hand. 'Yes please?'

'Two plates of cod and chips and a round of bread and butter,' Reggie said.

'And a pot of tea,' added Molly.

'You and your tea!'

The waitress shuffled off to the kitchen. Molly cleared a circle on the wet window. A man in a dark suit, holding a black umbrella, hurried by. Where was he going? What did people do that made them so busy? Another bus was rumbling along, packed with people in raincoats. Was the bus taking them home? Would each one go to a different house, to the lives they shared with other people? She shook her head to loosen the chaos that was building up inside it.

'You all right, Molly?'

She swivelled to look into Reggie's eyes. They were still and brown.

'It's so difficult to deal with everything,' she said. 'I can't remember the rules any more.'

'There's no need to remember. The war broke all the rules.'

Molly twisted her fingers together. She felt like crying.

'It's like these buildings,' Reggie continued. 'They'll be as good as new one day.' He placed his hand over hers. 'And so will you.'

The waitress appeared and slapped down two cups of tepid tea. She scowled at Reggie. He ignored her. 'After this, I'll walk you to your lodgings,' he said. He took a sip of the warm liquid and shuddered. He wiped his thin moustache; it followed the shape of his lips, as though painted on by a brush.

'Then what?' asked Molly.

'Then your time's your own.'

That was what Nurse Sanders had said yesterday, more or less. But how to fill it? Molly glanced at the waitress trudging back with two plates of battered fish and pale yellow chips. Could I do her job? she wondered. Wait on tables all day long? It was a possibility. She had no idea what she'd done before the war. They'd tried to get her doing a bit of typing at the hospital, but if she'd been a secretary, she had no memory of it. Her fingers ached as they clattered the black keys and she would rush ahead, typing increasingly fast to create a frantic rhythm, only to read back her work and realise she'd made mistake after mistake. She glanced down at her plate. Whatever was she going to do?

The café was filling up. A middle-aged man was seated at a table in the corner, slurping tea and eating bread and butter, a scruffy-looking newspaper unfurled on the table in front of him. As Molly watched him, he took out a stubby pencil, sniffed, and started circling sections of the paper. Perhaps he was looking for a job too.

Behind them, a young mother sat with a small boy. He was perched on a wooden chair, his chin level with the table, sturdy legs swinging below as his mother fed him chips from her plate. He churned them round his mouth, emitting little sounds of enjoyment. Molly smiled. A faint memory stirred her mind but slithered away before she could grasp it.

Reggie finished his mouthful. 'Eat up,' he said. She picked up her knife and fork and did as she was told.

He walked her through the darkening streets to her lodgings. A few people were out, hurrying home after work, and they darted curious glances at Reggie and Molly. One woman, in a greasy white mackintosh with a scarf tied under her chin, stopped in her tracks and stared at them, clutching her handbag tightly before tut-tutting loudly and sweeping off down the road.

Reggie's smile turned into a grimace. 'Seems people around here don' like to see a white lady with a coloured gentleman.'

Molly faltered, then slipped her arm through his. His muscles were rigid, even through two layers of material.

'I'd understand if you'd rather not be seen with me. You dun want to start your new life on a bad foot,' Reggie murmured.

Molly stopped. She withdrew her arm and turned to face him.

'I won't pretend I don't know you. You're my friend.'

Reggie stared at her. Molly couldn't tell what he was thinking. 'Thank you,' he said.

They walked on until they reached Mrs Croft's. Molly had forgotten to ask for a key, so she knocked at the door. Reggie waited with her on the step.

'Thank you so much,' she said to him. 'I've had a nice time.'

She gave him a quick peck on the cheek. Just as she did so, the door flew open. The landlady stood there, her mouth open in amazement.

'Well!' she said, staring at Reggie. 'Is he pestering you?'

'Of course not. He's my friend.'

The landlady sniffed loudly. 'I don't like darkies hanging around here. And if you think he's coming in, you've got another think coming.'

Reggie bowed. 'I was just makin' sure this young lady got here safely.'

Mrs Croft's expression didn't change.

Reggie angled his body towards Molly, away from the landlady. 'Is there anythin' else you need?' he asked.

Molly shook her head anxiously. 'See you tomorrow, Reggie?'

'Of course. Sleep well.' Reggie tipped his hat to both women, then sauntered off down the road, whistling.

The next day, Dr Lee called her out of the art room. 'A word, please, Molly.'

She followed him into his office, inhaling the familiar medicine-and-tobacco smell.

He fiddled with his glasses for a bit, then straightened a sheet of handwritten notes in front of him.

'I'll come straight to the point. I've had a call from a Mrs . . . er . . . Croft.'

'She's my landlady.'

'Yes. Quite so. Apparently she's concerned because you

turned up last night with . . .' Dr Lee looked down at his notes, 'a *coloured gentleman*.' He regarded her over the top of his glasses. 'Reggie, I assume?'

Molly's face grew hot. 'He took me out for a meal. Nothing more. We're good friends.'

Dr Lee raised an eyebrow. 'And he's not forcing his attentions on you?'

'*No!*'

Dr Lee made a calming gesture with his hands. 'I have to ask the question.'

'Reggie's a perfect gentleman. He would never do anything like that.'

Silence.

'And besides, I can look after myself.'

The calming gesture again. 'I know that. And I know you get on well with each other. It hasn't concerned me until now. But I needed to check.' He shuffled his notes again. There was something else. 'Molly. The outside world doesn't operate like Warlingham. It judges people differently. And *unfortunately*, most people don't like to see white women with black men. Or indeed the other way round.'

'Reggie told me much the same thing.'

'Yes. I would imagine he's experienced quite a bit of prejudice since coming here.'

Molly shook her head, thinking back to the woman in the white mac staring at them disapprovingly. Once, Reggie had told her, a little boy had come up to him in the street and rubbed at his hand to 'see if he could get the dirt off'. Reggie

156

had reacted politely, as he always did, but it must have hurt and puzzled him.

'The problem is, how do we deal with it?'

Molly placed her hands firmly on the table. 'People keep telling me I've got to be independent now. Make my own choices.'

'Ye-es.' Dr Lee paused, as though he knew where the conversation was heading and wished he didn't.

'Reggie looks after me. He makes me laugh. I really like him.'

Dr Lee cleared his throat. 'You've done very well in the last few months. But you are still recovering. We don't want to undo all the good work we've – *you've* – done.'

Molly stared at him. 'How would *we* do that?'

'Well, you are still very vulnerable, my dear. It's hard enough for you to deal with this new world you find yourself in. You need people on your side, not being hostile towards you.'

Molly thought of Mrs Croft again, and the lady in the white mac. 'Surely not everyone is like that?'

'I wish I could reassure you.'

She stood up. 'I have to make my own decisions. Reggie has helped me more than anyone I know.' She was aware of an intake of breath. 'Don't get me wrong. You've been wonderful. But you look after me here. Reggie will look after me outside as well.'

Dr Lee was silent for a moment, tapping a pen against his teeth. Then he stood up too. 'Just be careful, my dear. We want you to flourish. Remember that.'

She patted his arm as she left the room. 'I know,' she said.

18

At first Kathleen didn't touch Jack at all, and he preferred it that way. Then there was the lightest brush of his shoulder when he said goodnight or a brief sweep over his hair when she checked he was tidy for school in the morning. He didn't duck his head or move away. He just stayed still and tried to smile. But the last person to touch him had been Brother Cartwright, and Jack still had nightmares about that day in the barn. Would he ever have human contact again without wanting to flinch at the memory of Brother Cartwright's fat fingers?'

In some ways, John was simpler to deal with than Kathleen. He called Jack 'sport' as though he couldn't remember his name. He tweaked his ear or clapped him hard on the back, but the gestures weren't cruel like Brother McBride's. 'Stop mothering him, woman,' he'd say to Kathleen if she laid a concerned hand on Jack's forehead when he had a cold, or allowed him to leave the table before he'd finished his dinner – a rare event admittedly. Occasionally he caught John looking at him speculatively, as if sizing him up. This would usually be followed by a comment such as 'Shooting up, boy – you're taller than Kathleen now', or 'Don't stay outside too long, don't want you turning the colour of Abos.'

There'd been a debate about the names Jack should use for the Sullivans.

'I think you should call us Mum and Dad,' said Kathleen. She was making jam in the kitchen, stirring the bubbling red liquid in a huge saucepan. A warm, syrupy smell oozed through the room. Jack hovered near the door, wondering if he dared dip in a finger if Kathleen happened to turn away. It would be worth the pain of a burn. They were never allowed jam at Bindoon. The promised oranges hadn't appeared either. All they'd eaten was porridge, dried bread, and gristly meat, slippery with grease.

Kathleen didn't look like his mum. Her hair was fair where he thought his mother's had been brown; it was pinned up close to her head where he sensed Mum's curls had hung down the side of her face. Mum was younger too. But maybe they were both the same shape.

Jack wasn't sure how to answer. If he turned down Kathleen's suggestion, she might send him back to Bindoon and replace him with another boy, one more eager to please. If he accepted, it would be as if his own parents hadn't existed. It was hard to remember much about them now, though. He'd been too young when his father had died to recall anything of Mick Malloy other than his name. And all he had of his mother were some increasingly blurred memories of her dancing and singing. Although whenever he caught the scent of lily of the valley, Mum came to mind.

For once, John came to the rescue. 'He only had one mum and dad and they're dead,' he said, laying out sheets of newspaper

159

on the floor ready to polish his shoes. 'What about Mr and Mrs Sullivan?'

Kathleen baulked at that one. 'Too formal.'

'All right.' John dipped a brush into a flat tin of soot-coloured paste. 'John and Kathleen, then. What do you think, sport?'

Jack nodded with relief. John and Kathleen suited him fine. He could still tell himself he'd only had one mother.

Jack had never wanted to go back to Bindoon after he'd left. Each time Kathleen suggested a visit, he'd found an excuse not to go. But she seemed determined that he keep in touch with his old friends. 'Would you like someone to come and stay with us?' she asked, more than once.

Jack hesitated. The obvious answer was Sam. He'd liked him from the first day on the ship. Facing Bindoon together had only made them better friends. But Jack still had night-mares about the place, despite only spending two months there. If he were to meet Sam again, it might stir up memo-ries of Brother Cartwright. And he'd feel guilty. What should he do to help the boys he'd left behind? He certainly didn't want to see Bert again. Too much of a bully. He rubbed his chin at the memory of Bert's punch when they'd had that fight on the ship. And he'd never really warmed to Tom and Mattie. If he saw anyone, it ought to be Sam. He certainly owed him something after he'd rescued him from Bert that day. Maybe things had got better at Bindoon and Sam would be able to reassure him. Perhaps he could give Sam food to take back. Kathleen wouldn't mind. Sam could share it with the others. That would be a way of helping.

'Sam,' Jack said, scratching at a patch of eczema on his arm. It was still sore despite Kathleen's best efforts to treat it with cold cream.

'Okay,' replied Kathleen, putting a hand on his arm to remind him not to scratch. 'I'll get in touch with the Boys Town.'

*

Molly sat in Mrs Croft's front parlour, staring out into the street at a small poodle relieving itself against the trunk of a plane tree. Two girls, in grey cardigans and plaits, were playing hopscotch on a clumsily drawn chalk grid.

Molly wore her dark green suit. She'd bought a little make-up recently; her face was carefully powdered and there was a smear of pink on her lips. She'd even tracked down some lily-of-the-valley perfume to dab on her handkerchief.

'You off out?' Mrs Croft paused in her dusting, wheezing audibly.

'Yes, thought I might do a bit of shopping.'

'*Very* nice.' Mrs Croft sniffed, a little self-pityingly, Molly thought. In actual fact Mrs C could easily afford to go shopping herself. It was Molly who was on tight Welfare rations. She really needed to get a job. Perhaps today she'd find the courage to go for something.

Reggie was coming round soon. It was his day off and they

were going into town. Not that Mrs Croft would know that. They'd long since decided he wouldn't call for her at the house. Now they had a different strategy.

There it was. Molly's attention sharpened as the faint strains of 'Molly Malone' drifted through the window. Reggie would be standing next door, away from Mrs Croft's eagle eyes, whistling tunefully: their secret signal.

She stood up. 'Must be off,' she said, putting on her hat and gloves.

'Right you are, love.' Mrs Croft polished the sideboard with exaggerated energy. 'Have a pleasant day.'

'Thanks. I will.' Molly opened the front door, walked down the steps, and onto the street.

There was Reggie, smart as you like in a brown suit and a trilby. When they'd first stepped out, she'd found it strange, wanting him to be in his familiar orderly's uniform with a broom in his hand, not this curious smart figure. But she rather liked it now; it was nice he went to so much trouble for her. She noticed a small cut on his chin. He must've shaved in a hurry.

She couldn't have got through the last few months without Reggie. His strength rubbed off on her; it made her feel she could do anything. When they were apart, she became fragile, nervous. She needed him, in spite of what Dr Lee had said. Who cared if people stared and sniggered? If Reggie could cope with it, so could she.

She smiled as he greeted her with his usual bow. Best to enjoy the day for now and leave the worries for later.

They took the 403 into Croydon. The bus rattled up the Brighton Road. Once it hit a bump and she was jolted towards Reggie. She tried to keep her body rigid so that she didn't make contact, but he didn't seem to notice. He was telling her about his attempts to find lodgings. He'd got weary of the Clapham shelter he'd first been assigned to after docking at Tilbury, despite the friendships he'd made there. But his search hadn't been easy.

'Had another door slam on me last week,' he said. 'She made up her mind the minute she saw the colour of my skin, even though I couldn't have been more polite, called her ma'am and everythin'. . .' He tailed off.

'Oh Reggie, I'm sorry.'

'Hey, don' worry.' Reggie patted her hand. 'Somethin' will come up. I was talking to Nurse Betty at the hospital.' Nurse Betty had lost her husband during the war. She was a lovely, friendly woman but obviously lonely. 'She's thinking of taking in lodgers and might be able to offer me something.'

'That's nice. I like Nurse Betty.'

'So do I. I just need to make sure she knows what she'll be takin' on.' Reggie winked ruefully at her.

Molly wondered if Nurse Betty had a thick skin. She'd need it when people started to make comments about her black lodger. 'I really hope it works out,' she said, trying to make her voice sound more optimistic than she felt. To her surprise, she even felt a bit jealous of Nurse Betty.

Over Reggie's shoulder, through the window, a woman with a tight perm was pointing up at them from the street. A muscle

163

tensed in Reggie's cheek. Molly stared straight ahead at another bus in front with an advert for *Wild Woodbine Cigarettes* pasted on the back. The advert came closer: *W. D. and H. O. Wills*, it said. *Bristol and London*. Their own bus stopped with a jerk, and she knocked into Reggie again. This time she let her body relax until their shoulders touched.

They got out at the high street and walked up to the junction between North End and George Street, where Molly's favourite shops were.

'Where would madam like to go?' asked Reggie, making a wide sweeping gesture with his arm.

Molly looked around. 'I need to pop to Kennards for a pair of gloves. Perhaps a quick look at Allders' sale, then maybe I'll do some window shopping at Grants.'

'And tea there afterwards?'

She frowned. 'Better make it Lyons. Cheaper.'

They wandered along the road, Molly peering into shop windows and Reggie smoking his way through a packet of Luckies.

'Look!' Molly drew in a long breath. She'd stopped in front of a small dress shop and was regarding a snooty mannequin modelling a tight-waisted blue polka-dot dress with a voluminous skirt. 'How much d'you reckon that'd cost? All that material.' She peered closer, trying to see a price.

Reggie shrugged and took another drag on his cigarette.

'I'd love to have a dress like that.'

Reggie laughed. 'And I'd love to buy it for you!'

Molly stepped back. 'I was just dreaming.' The model had

a little blue scarf tied round her neck. Perhaps she could find one in Kennards and do something similar.

Reggie threw his stub onto the pavement and ground it in with his heel. Then he moved closer to the window. 'See that, Molly?' He pointed to a small card in the corner: *Sales Assistant Wanted. Please Enquire Within.*

Molly straightened her skirt. 'D'you think I could? I haven't had much luck with jobs lately.'

'Of course. You always look nice.' He pressed his hand into the small of her back, gently propelling her forward, then turned away. Molly took a deep breath and opened the door.

The shop smelled of perfume and expensive cloth. She noticed a rail of silk dresses in pastel shades, shimmering in the light, and several shelves of hats and shoes. She'd have preferred to wander around, running her fingers over the rich material and trying on a couple of the hats in the mirror, but the manageress was watching her. The woman had a pale powdered face, bright red lipstick and matching nails. She wore a little black jacket over a red swirly skirt. Molly had seen something similar in a magazine. *New Look.*

'May I help you, madam?' the woman asked, smiling brightly. Some of the lipstick had made a mark on her teeth.

'I'd like to apply for the sales assistant job,' replied Molly. She tried to breathe naturally. Her breakfast bacon felt uneasy in her stomach. As the manageress scrutinised her, Molly was conscious of the old green suit. So straight and dull. She hoped her hat was still in place. Pulling her shoulders back a little, she smiled at the woman.

'Do you have any experience?' asked the manageress.

'No, but I'm willing to learn and I'm a hard worker.'

'References?'

'*References?*' Molly's hands became clammy.

'I won't consider anyone without references.' The smile was haughty now.

'Of course.' Molly wiped her palms surreptitiously on the back of her skirt. 'May I collect them and bring them in tomorrow?'

'Yes, very well,' the manageress said, 'but don't take too long. There'll be quite a few people after a job this good.'

'Of course.' Molly turned and walked out of the door towards Reggie, her pulse thrumming.

Reggie winked at her. 'Definitely Grants,' he said.

She'd been due to see Dr Lee the next day so mentioned the references then.

'I'll see what I can do, but I am duty-bound to mention your stay here.'

Molly chewed at her lower lip. 'Could you pretend I wasn't here long?'

'*Molly!*'

'I know.' The buzzing sound was back again. She placed a hand close to one ear. It muffled it slightly. 'I probably wouldn't be good enough anyway.'

Dr Lee looked over his glasses at her. 'I think the job might suit you. Leave it with me.'

By the time she'd returned from sharing a cigarette with

Reggie in the garden and chatting to two of the patients she'd been friendly with, a crisp envelope was lying on his desk with *To whom it may concern* typed across it.

The next day she took it to the manageress, who sniffed and said she had her reservations, seeing as Molly had been at Warlingham Park, but she was willing to engage her on a trial basis. 'Any nonsense, mind, and you'll be out the door.'

Molly smiled meekly, although inside she fizzed with excitement. She was going to be a shop assistant! She had to let Reggie know as soon as possible.

19

They all went to the bus stop to greet Sam. As he climbed down and limped towards them, Jack saw bony ankles below the hem of his trousers. The cuffs of his short-sleeved shirt cut into his arms as though they were elastic bands.

Jack grinned and waved at his old friend, and Sam raised a hand in return. But his eyes were wary.

The two of them sat in the back as John drove them from the city centre to Highgate. Jack imagined the scene through Sam's eyes. Highgate was so busy in comparison to the remote farm at Bindoon, where all you saw were paddocks and cattle. The road was full of traffic: there were several Holdens like the one John drove, plus the usual Chevys and utes. A dusty green bus, packed with people going into town, lumbered along the other side of the road. The noise filtered in through the car's closed windows: horns tooting, people shouting, engines rumbling – the sounds of a busy city. In the country, the sounds were natural: the screech of a magpie; the whirring of crickets; the occasional kookaburra's laugh.

He turned to Sam. 'A bit different from Bindoon, eh?'

Sam didn't reply. He seemed much quieter now. He hardly looked Jack in the eye.

'What do you want to do when we get back?' Jack asked.

'Don't we need to do chores?' Sam didn't turn from the window.

'Nah. We're free till dinner. We can chuck a ball in the back yard, or there's two boys up the road will play cricket with us.'

Sam chewed his lip. 'Just us.'

'Okay, just us then.'

They went straight up to Jack's room. It was like on the ship, but now it was Jack who had the nice things.

'D'you like my model planes?' he said.

Sam looked up at the ceiling where the black *Lutana* and another DC-3 were rocking in the warm air. He nodded.

Jack pulled out his new Biggles, the one about him becoming a big-game hunter, from the bookshelf. 'I've just read this one. Do you want to borrow it?'

Sam shook his head. 'There's no time.'

'Oh yes. Sorry.' Jack had a sudden memory of standing at the sink at Bindoon, the hot, greasy water stinging the cuts he'd got on his hands from heaving stones all day, hearing Brother McBride bark, 'Hurry up, Malloy, it'll be bedtime soon,' and knowing there'd only be a few short hours before it all started up again. No, there was no time to yourself at Bindoon.

Sam sat on Jack's bed, kneading the soft counterpane. He stared at the bedside table with its low lamp, alarm clock and smart brush and comb. It was hard to know what he was thinking.

Jack tried to get him talking. 'How are Bert, Tom and Mattie?'

Sam shrugged. 'Mattie has a bad cough.'

'Have the brothers given him any medicine?'

'He was in sick bay for a bit, but as soon as they said he was better, he had to go back to work. But he wasn't better. Not really.'

'Kathleen gave me cough medicine when I was crook last winter,' said Jack. 'I could see if there's any left for you to give Mattie.' Jack liked the word *crook*. He'd picked up a bit of Aussie slang at school. Australians had odd names for things. He'd learned *dinkum* meant true and a *dinkum bloke* was a real man and a *dinkie* girl was pretty. He knew what *yakka* was too – hard work. There'd been plenty of that at Bindoon.

'Thanks. I'd have to hide it, though,' said Sam.

'What about your Jewish stuff? Do you still have it?'

Sam glanced round as though Brother McBride were in the room, eavesdropping. 'I've hidden the *mezuzah*,' he said. 'But the brothers confiscated the *milchig* and the *fleischig*.'

'I'm sorry,' said Jack.

Sam chewed on a fingernail.

Jack looked out. The sun was glinting off the myrtle willows in the yard, and a pair of pipits darted their beaks at the ground, probably hoping to prise out insects. He turned back to Sam.

'Are you Jewish or Catholic now?'

'I have to pretend to be Catholic. But I'm still a Jew. Always will be.'

170

Jack picked up his brush from the table and ran the bristles over his fingers. He felt bad that his life was so much better than Sam's. And there was something else too. 'We heard what happened in the war,' he murmured. 'I didn't know about it when I was in England. The nuns didn't have wirelesses and no one said anything on the ship. It wasn't until I got to Australia that I found out.'

Sam didn't speak.

'Did any of your family get sent to the camps?'

'I don't know. Mum and Dad never talked to me about things.'

Jack wondered how Sam must feel knowing his parents had sent him away. At least *his* mother had wanted him.

The room was quiet except for the steady tick of Jack's alarm clock. Jack wanted to ask Sam about the brothers. What they'd done to him. Brother Cartwright in particular. But he couldn't find the words.

'Let's go outside,' said Sam.

'Okay,' said Jack, filled with relief. They raced down the stairs.

The garden was fresh after the stuffiness of the house. Jack felt a cool breeze cuff his neck and lift strands of his hair. *The Fremantle Doctor*, John called it. It came every afternoon, slicing the warm air with crisp strokes and sending everyone running for jerseys and cardigans. Sam rubbed his arms where goose bumps had appeared.

'Just run around,' said Jack. 'You'll soon warm up.'

But Sam stayed still, his hands under his armpits, his chin tucked into his chest.

Jack disappeared indoors and returned with a jersey Kathleen had knitted him. As he lifted his arm to throw it, Sam flinched, then grabbed its sleeve as it flew past. He pulled it over his head.

A large bird bath lay in the middle of the garden. Kathleen loved to watch the honeyeaters drinking and splashing in the early evening. But it was right in the middle of the pitch. Jack gripped the sides of the bath, squatted down and heaved. It was far too heavy. He looked over towards Sam, but Sam seemed to have turned into one of those religious statues the brothers made them build.

'Can you give me a hand?' Jack called.

Sam's body unravelled slowly. He trudged over to the bath and picked it up in one movement.

'Thanks,' said Jack as Sam stood with the bath in his hands. 'Put it under that willow over there.'

Sam deposited the bath where Jack indicated. Like at Bindoon, Jack thought: when we prised the rocks from the quarry, loaded them onto trucks and unloaded them at the building site. He could still hear Brother McBride barking orders.

He retrieved the oval leather ball from the hedge. 'Now we can play. I'll sprint down the wing and throw it back to you. Start running.'

Sam jogged slowly down the pitch, wincing.

'Faster, Sam.'

Sam frowned. He bent down, took off his shoes and placed them by the fence. Then he ran. Jack lobbed the ball back to him and Sam caught it.

'Well done. Now you try.'

Sam sprinted towards the end of the garden, and hurled the ball at Jack. He seemed to run much better now he'd taken his shoes off.

'And again.'

Sam repeated the manoeuvre. A stripe of sweat appeared on his hair. He pulled his jersey off impatiently and took the ball from Jack again. Then, while Jack moved into position, Sam spun the ball in the air and caught it a few times. He grinned.

Jack was pleased. This was much more like a game now: throwing, catching, running, passing. Dodging and diving in the evening sun. Sam was almost as good as John.

When Kathleen called them in for dinner, Jack was surprised to see the shadows from the boundary fence halfway up the lawn. He realised he was starving. They left their shoes at the kitchen door. Jack glanced at Sam's Oxfords. They looked quite small next to his sneakers. Jack wondered whether they were the pair Sam had worn on the ship. Kathleen had replaced Jack's old shoes long ago. He'd forgotten how much the stones hurt at Bindoon, where the brothers made you work in bare feet.

They washed their hands at Kathleen's insistence, then sat at the cream kitchen table, demolishing the slices of rabbit pie she'd put out for them. She tightened her mouth at the sight of Sam eating with his fingers, but didn't comment. Jack was glad. At Bindoon, the hunger gouged your gut; any food had to be eaten quickly to stop someone else pouncing on it. They all ate fast, and often with their fingers when the brothers weren't looking. But here in Kathleen's tidy kitchen, Sam seemed like an animal. Jack realised how much his own manners had improved at the Sullivans'. Neither John nor Kathleen would tolerate him eating like that. He was relieved when Kathleen left the room.

He tried to slow Sam down. 'Sorry you've got to go back tomorrow.'

Sam kept eating.

'I'll ask Kathleen if she'll pack up some of this pie for you. And the jam tarts you liked. I'm sure she won't mind putting in some for the others too.'

Sam took a sip of water and swallowed.

Jack stood up and put his plate in the sink. Sam had changed since they'd become friends on the ship. He was sorry for him having to go back to Bindoon. But their lives were different now. Perhaps it hadn't been fair on Sam either, bringing him to the Sullivans'. He wondered if he ought to ask Kathleen if he could give Sam some of his shoes. But sometimes it didn't do to stand out at Bindoon. And besides, it wouldn't be fair on all the other children. Jack didn't have enough shoes to go round.

A few weeks later, Kathleen asked if Jack wanted another friend to stay at half term. Jack was torn. Should he invite

Sam? They could play rugby again, maybe with some boys from the street. And Kathleen would bake more jam tarts for him. Jack smiled to himself at the thought of how Sam's eyes would light up at the food. But then Bindoon would be even worse for him when he got back. Perhaps it was best not to raise his hopes.

Jack scratched at a patch of dry skin on his arm. Ignoring the guilt that chilled his stomach, he told himself he was only thinking of Sam. But the truth was he didn't want to be reminded of Bindoon again. The memories were still too strong. And the nightmares too vivid. Kathleen and John had given him a chance; he had to make the most of it. Though he hated to acknowledge it, being with Sam had made him feel uncomfortable. It would be easier to pretend Bindoon hadn't happened if he were to cut contact with his old friend. And maybe someone would rescue Sam too. He'd been well brought up before he went to Bindoon. Perhaps someone would take him on. Yes, that would be sure to happen. Jack knew it.

So he suggested a boy from his class at school. And blinked away the memory of Sam's too-small shoes lined up by the back door.

Jack didn't mind school. At Bindoon, he and Sam had been put in a School Certificate class with several of the local children. But Bert, Tom and Mattie, who'd not done so well on the test they'd been given when they arrived, were put in the 'Opportunity Class' with mostly Bindoon kids. Bert said there weren't many opportunities there.

Now Jack went to the high school in Highgate. He'd been a bit behind the others at first, but John had helped him and he'd soon caught up. The teachers were kinder than the brothers, although they still hit people they considered lazy or talkative. But in some ways he didn't mind the teachers. They didn't take it personally, like John and Kathleen did, if he did badly in a test or failed to come up to scratch with a piece of homework. The Sullivans were always checking up on his schoolwork. Jack wanted to do well but he sometimes wondered if John and Kathleen expected too much.

He was doing algebra, sprawled on the living room rug, when the phone rang. Kathleen put down a grey sock she'd been darning and went into the hall to answer it. Jack didn't listen to the conversation. He was wrestling with a sum. *Calculate the value of* x. He stared at the equation. If he moved x across, he'd have to divide, rather than multiply. That would just leave numbers on the other side, no more wretched letters. Good. That was the way. But it was hard to calculate because of the odd noises Kathleen was making. What was going on? Jack put down his pencil.

'How terrible,' she kept saying. 'Yes, of course I'll tell him straight away.'

Jack looked up as Kathleen returned. She was fussing with her apron, tying and untying the bow at the back. For once she didn't comment on his homework.

'That was John.'

'What did he want?'

Kathleen knelt down beside him. Her face was blotchy.

'The police in Bindoon have just called him.' She pulled at a thread from the rug, then smoothed it again. 'It's Sam. He's had an accident.'

'What kind of accident?' Jack picked up his pencil and ran it between his fingers. It was cool and solid.

'He fell off a roof.'

Jack sat up. 'A roof?' He laughed. 'Did he break anything?'

'No, Jack, you don't understand.' Kathleen's voice sounded very odd. She placed a hand on Jack's shoulder. 'I'm afraid Sam's dead.'

20

Molly and the manageress, Mrs Cooper, were at the back of the shop unloading a new delivery. Molly couldn't afford much on dress shop wages, but each week she added an item to her wardrobe – a scarf, a ribbon for her hair, a pair of gloves. A parcel had arrived from Paris and Mrs Cooper held it reverently. She spoke in a different voice when they were out of the shop.

'Can't wait to open this one,' she said. 'I've ordered half a dozen silk blouses from a designer called Balmain. Stuff from abroad is coming through a bit quicker now. This lot'll go straight in the window.' She passed the package to Molly and paused. 'I'm going to have to get rid of old stock. I can let you have it at discount.'

'But I'm not really on the staff yet, am I?'

Mrs Cooper examined the bright red nails of her right hand. 'You've been here a month and you haven't done anything terrible, I suppose.'

Molly knew she'd made some good sales. She went to thank Mrs Cooper but was stopped by the jingle of the shop door. 'I'll go,' she said. She threw a grateful glance at the manageress then walked into the shop, where an elegantly dressed woman was holding a young boy's hand.

'May I help you?' asked Molly, pronouncing the words as Mrs Cooper had instructed her.

The woman nodded. 'I'm looking for a suit to wear to a wedding.'

'Oh yes. These are our wedding ensembles.' Molly led her over to a rail at the side with a line of bright garments in luxurious fabrics. She pulled one out, disturbing the careful arrangement, shook her head, then selected another. It was in amethyst wool with a large black collar, a tiny waist and an exaggerated peplum. The skirt was gathered and full. One of Molly's favourites.

'I think this would suit you, madam,' she murmured.

'Maybe.' The woman glanced round for her son, who was looking across the road and yawning. 'Jack, Mummy's going to try this on. Wait here. And mind you behave.'

Jack. A bus was driving over Molly's chest, crushing her heart and lungs. Her ears roared. She tried to remember how to breathe.

It had happened. Just like before.

Molly looked at the boy. About eight. Light tan. Earnest green eyes. Dark hair. Bored.

He gave a wary smile in response to hers.

She became an automaton: compliment woman (the suit *did* look good), wrap garment (careful, mind), count the notes (nice and crisp), put them in the till, hold the door for them (force a smile.) But afterwards her legs were too fragile to stand; she grabbed a chair and slumped onto it.

Jack. Who was he? Why was that name having such an

impact on her? Little electrical pulses ran up and down her body. She felt sick and sweaty. The buzzing was back in her ears but she barely noticed. The thoughts crashing through her brain drowned out everything else.

She was still sitting there when Mrs Cooper came back from visiting the bank.

'Are you all right? You look like you've seen a ghost.'

Molly wondered if she had.

Reggie picked her up from the shop later. They'd intended to have a bite of supper at Lyons then to see *Sunset Boulevard* at the Odeon. Molly had been looking forward to it but the incident earlier had pushed everything else out of her mind. The waitress brought them plates of tiny lamb chops and peas, dwarfed by mounds of boiled potatoes.

Molly wasn't sure how Reggie would react to her news. She pushed the potato across her plate. 'I heard another name today,' she said.

'What name?' Did he sound a bit guarded? Maybe he'd just forgotten.

'Do you remember that time at Warlingham when you were singing and I remembered I was called Molly?'

'Ye-e-s.'

'Well, it's happened again. I was in the shop when a lady and her son came in. She called him Jack and I came over all funny.'

Reggie cut into his lamb chop and put a piece in his mouth. 'Go on.'

Molly's brain couldn't seem to find the right words. She

swallowed. 'Reggie . . . do you think Jack might be the name of someone important in my life?'

A long pause. What was Reggie thinking? 'Such as your husban'?' he said at last.

'No.' So that was what was worrying him. She screwed up her eyes, shutting out the murky interior of the café, and willed herself back onto the ward at Warlingham. A memory sidled in. Reggie sweeping. Her reading the *Sketch*, rustling the pages. Bored. Then the quickening of interest: that photo. The dark hair. A shy smile. She snapped her eyes open. 'I think the name belongs to a boy. Like when I saw that picture of a young lad in the newspaper. I felt strange then too.'

Reggie carried on eating.

'Could he have been my son?' Molly cupped her left ear to muffle the buzzing.

Reggie put down his knife and fork. He gently prised her hand away and held it in his. 'If you did have a child, I'm not so sure he'd be alive now.'

'Why do you say that?'

'Well . . .' Reggie's clasp tightened. 'I imagine lots of children were killed in the war.'

Molly pulled her hand free and stood up. 'I'm sorry about the film,' she said. 'You go. I couldn't concentrate now. I'm going over to Warlingham to ask Dr Lee.'

Reggie stood up too. 'At least let me escort you to the hospital. I can go to my digs from there.' He followed her into the chilly street.

*

It was warm inside the doctor's office, with the usual smell of tobacco mixed with something medical; surgical spirit perhaps. Normally Molly found it comforting. But not today.

'You *knew*?'

Dr Lee fiddled with his pen, removing and replacing the lid. He didn't look at her. 'Soon after you came in, during a routine examination, we found evidence of an earlier pregnancy.'

Something came through to Molly from those hellish early days. The bitter taste of phenobarbital . . . the snap of gloves . . . a cold, gouging instrument.

Her ears hurt. 'Was it a boy?'

'My dear. We'd no way of knowing. All I can confirm is that at some point, several years before you came to us, you gave birth.'

'Then why didn't you tell me?' She put her hands to her head to muffle the buzzing.

'We thought it for the best. You'd lost your memory. It would have been too traumatic to discover you were a mother. You might never have recovered.' Dr Lee smoothed the yellowing page of notes in front of him. 'And besides, you didn't have a wedding ring. It may well have been that the child was illegitimate; another stigma to deal with. And if it had been born out of wedlock, you might have given it up. That was another reason not to mention it.' He folded his hands and leaned back in his chair. 'No one has ever come forward. We had to draw our own conclusions.'

'But I have to know what happened! Even if it's bad news.' Molly rammed her fists against her ears.

'We don't know what happened.' It sounded as though he was speaking to a child.

'Why not?' Molly said.

'You were in here for most of the war. It was chaos. People went missing. Records were destroyed. Croydon was very badly bombed.' The pen lid was off again.

Molly blinked. Was that a child hovering on the edge of her memory? Could she make out ruddy cheeks and troubled brown eyes? 'But he might still be alive,' she shouted. Then, more quietly, 'Mightn't he?'

The doctor took off his glasses. 'I told you. We made enquiries when you were first admitted but drew a blank.'

'What enquiries?' Molly rubbed her eyes. The picture was coming in and out of focus.

Dr Lee glanced down at his notes. 'We did all we could, but we had no paperwork from the hospital to say who you were or where you'd lived. Apparently you'd been found a long way from any residential areas. You must have wandered a distance from home. No one had come forward to identify you, so we had to conclude that you had no family. We called you Margaret after the royal princess, as you looked a bit like her.'

'But what about my child?'

'Molly, you were very lucky to survive the bomb blast on your home. Anyone else with you would probably have died instantly.' His voice softened. 'Your child would not have suffered.'

The indents in Dr Lee's cheeks, the ones Molly once thought resembled thumbprints on dough, now looked like small gashes. But in her head the child smiled encouragingly.

'And if, by a miracle, he did survive?' she asked.

'Look, Molly, we've got no record of this. And I don't think we should give you false hope.'

The child retreated into the shadows. 'Then if he did die, what would have happened to his body?' she whispered.

Dr Lee paused. His voice quietened. 'I'm afraid there often aren't any remains.'

Molly stood up. She gripped the back of her chair with both hands. 'How am I supposed to cope with this?'

Dr Lee walked round the desk, gently sat her down and squatted beside her. 'We don't know where you lived, Molly, and you can't remember. Why don't I get the care-taker, Fred, to put a wooden cross in the cemetery here? In honour of your child? You could visit it every time you came to Warlingham. Maybe bring flowers. Tell you what, I'll put him onto it tomorrow.' He stood up, rubbing his back, then reached for her notes and stacked them neatly.

Molly knew who Fred was. The poor man's brain had been so damaged by the war that he stood watch outside the cemetery each night, thinking he was guarding the graves. The nurses used to laugh about the fact that in his broken mind, he was convinced that he'd prevented the dead from escaping. But Fred never deserted his post. Molly knew he'd look after her son.

She wiped her hand across her eyes. 'His name's Jack,' she said.

Reggie collected her from Mrs Croft's on Saturday. 'Where would you like to go?' he asked, tucking her arm through his.

'Can we go to the park? I need to pick some flowers.'

They often went to the park in the evening. They were less likely to encounter curious stares and comments once it was dark. In the late-afternoon sun, the lime trees glowed yellow and the red maple leaves were translucent. Molly looked around. The flower beds were almost empty. Just thickly turned earth, with fat worms threading through the surface. All she saw was a clump of old Michaelmas daisies in the corner. She rushed over to them and snapped a few stems off, holding up a ragged bunch.

Reggie raised an eyebrow. 'Isn't that stealing?'

'They're for Jack,' she murmured. 'They'd only go to waste if no one picked them. We can take them over to Warlingham later.' Reggie squeezed her hand.

They crossed the park, making for the main road on the other side. No time to go home and get a sheet of newspaper for the flowers. She would just have to carry them as they were. She didn't care if people stared. They stared anyway when she was with Reggie. Might as well give them something else to look at.

She glanced at her watch. 'If we get a move on we should be at Warlingham by four.'

Reggie didn't reply. Three young men were strutting towards them, their jackets swinging loose.

As they drew near, something whistled through the air. Molly ducked and a small stone landed near Reggie's foot. He kicked it out of his way and walked on. The men were a few feet away now. She reckoned they were in their early twenties, if that. Reggie placed a firm hand on the small of her back.

Another sound. Slime trickled down Reggie's cheek. He wiped it with his cuff: spit. He folded his arms and stared fixedly at the men.

As the youths sauntered past, Molly heard a low voice: 'Nigger lover!'

She hollered after them. 'Leave him alone, he's worth ten of you!' Without thinking, she shook the flowers at them.

'Molly!' Reggie pushed his hand deeper into her back. 'You're mad. Don' antagonise them.'

One of the men looked over his shoulder. 'Stick with your own kind, lady.'

Molly's ears shrieked. 'He is my kind!' she shouted.

Reggie steered her firmly away. 'That was a crazy thing you dun,' he said.

'Why didn't you retaliate?'

A pause. 'I didn't wan' trouble, Moll.'

'You *are* worth ten of them.'

Reggie winked at her. But when Molly looked down, Jack's flowers were nothing more than a bunch of stalks, and the path was strewn with petals.

*

It was twilight by the time they got to Warlingham. Clouds bruised the horizon, and a yellow glow lingered over the turrets of the hospital. They skirted the main building, through the garden and across to the cemetery. Fred was standing to attention at the gate, still guarding the graves. He showed no sign of recognising them.

Tall yew trees stencilled the surface of the moon with their spiky leaves. Molly heard an owl in the distance; nearby, something pattered in the undergrowth. They made their way to the far side of the burial ground, where Dr Lee had told them the cross would be, past the little tombstones and simple grave markers. Finally Reggie pointed out two bits of wood, nailed together at right angles. Molly knelt down, examining the crude lettering chiselled into the cross. She peered closer. *Jack* was all it said. She couldn't even bring him flowers now. Instead she kissed her hand and pressed it to the rough grooves. Reggie stood behind her, his head bowed. She was faintly aware of birdsong, rising and falling in the gloom.

When she was ready, Reggie led Molly towards a bench and sat her down. Then he put his arm round her and she leaned against him, pressing her face into the rough wool of his coat. She smelled night air, cigarettes and cologne on the thick fabric. Reggie stroked her hair, smoothing and releasing the curls until she wanted to creep into his coat, shutting out every bit of the outside world, and live in the sleepy warmth.

'I'm so glad you came with me,' she murmured.

She felt him smile in the darkness. The cologne scent became stronger. It mingled with the musky sweetness of his mouth as he leaned towards her. He tasted of hope and peace and new beginnings. She snuggled closer.

Reggie had wanted to ask Molly to marry him that evening. She'd been so vulnerable at Jack's grave, leaning into him on the bench, her fragile body pressed against his. When he'd put his arms around her, drawing her even nearer, his heart had heaved with love for her. They were so close they were almost one person, their breath combined, their heartbeats a single pulse. When he'd kissed her, her mouth had yielded warmly and he'd wanted to caress every part of her, to tenderly remove her coat, her blouse, her skirt . . . to adore her body under the moonlight.

It had taken every ounce of willpower to draw back. She'd have let him go further, he knew. She'd already had a child; she must understand a man's needs. But the place belonged to Jack. Molly was here to mourn him and Reggie couldn't take advantage of that.

Later, as he smoked his way through a packet of cigarettes, propped on a lumpy pillow in Nurse Betty's spare room, he told himself he'd done the right thing. Back home in Jamaica, many a young girl had succumbed to his advances, and to his shame he realised he'd given them little thought afterwards. But Molly was different. Fragile, dependent. And far from irritating him, as the other clinging girls had, her vulnerability made him want to protect her even more. She had taken over his mind as much as the English cold had taken over his body.

*

188

But the next time Reggie was alone with Molly at Warlingham, he beckoned her into the garden. It was a breezy November day, full of scudding clouds and rustling leaves. He sank to one knee in the damp grass, took Molly's hands in his and proposed. At first she looked startled, then a smile softened the anxious line of her mouth and Reggie saw relief, joy and hope in her eyes. 'You'll be safe now, Moll,' he said. 'I'm going to look after you for the rest of your life.' And Molly wrapped her thin arms around him and buried her face in his shoulder. It was only later that he realised it was her tears that had seeped into his uniform, not the autumn mist.

On his next day off, Reggie went to the town hall to fill in the paperwork for their marriage. The entrance hall had a high, ornate ceiling that made echoes of the distant voices and the tapping of high-heeled shoes. Everywhere he looked was dark, gleaming wood. The colour of skin, he thought. That morning he'd put on his suit, the one he'd had on when the *Windrush* had docked back in June, hoping it would impress the registrar. This meeting was so important. It had to go well, for Molly's sake as well as his own.

He clattered up the steps in his co-respondent shoes and knocked on a door with 'Register Office' engraved on a brass plate.

'Come in,' replied a stern voice.

Reggie entered. Inside was a short man with a balding head and a white handlebar moustache that was oddly luxuriant, as though to make up for the sparseness elsewhere. He shook

Reggie's hand. 'Good morning, Mr Edwardes. I understand you are here about a marriage licence.'

'Yes, sir,' replied Reggie, beaming. 'I am desirous of marrying as soon as possible. Please.' He'd been surprised how quickly his and Molly's friendship had turned to love. Sure, he wanted to protect her, although he admired her too. Each day more strength emerged. She'd coped so well with leaving Warlingham, with the job. With him. But it was more than that. He couldn't stop looking at her. At those green eyes that could plead, and question, and invite, and promise. How could he resist them? How could he resist her?

He never told Molly he had an open return to Jamaica. He'd booked his passage on the *Windrush* on a whim, whipped up by the spirit of adventure and pioneering zeal that had spread through all the young men on the island. The Caribbean had suddenly seemed remote and boring; England was the place to be. He thought he'd give it a go for a while; he could always return if things didn't work out. But he'd hated England from the start: the cramped conditions at Clapham; the way he was bossed around at the hospital; the ignorant stares and muttered comments wherever he went. And most of all the cold that penetrated his very bones. He'd been on the verge of quitting when he'd met Molly, and for a long time he still didn't know if she was enough to make him stay. But whenever he saw her, he wanted to hug her narrow shoulders, stroke her wild hair, kiss her trusting face. Make her laugh. Leaving her would be like wrenching out his heart. Impossible.

The registrar leaned forward, regarding him from under snowy eyebrows.

'I'm afraid we have a problem, Mr Edwardes.'

Reggie sat down. 'Problem? I don' understand, sir. Is it because I'm Jamaican? I've got all my documents right here, you know.' He patted the pocket of his suit jacket.

'No, the problem isn't with you. It is with your fiancée.'

'Molly? But she dun need papers. She's a British citizen.'

'That may be the case.' The man pressed slender fingertips together to make a steeple, 'But you don't give me any evidence for this.' He motioned to a form in front of him, ran his finger down it to locate the place and intoned: 'Surname – blank. Place of birth – blank. Previously married – blank.' He looked at Reggie. 'You can't seem to supply any information about this woman other than her Christian name. And even that seems debatable.'

'But sir – eh-hem.' Something unpleasant clogged his throat. Reggie cleared it hastily. 'Excuse me, sir. I'll begin again – I have already informed you people that Molly has lost her memory. She been in the hospital for a long time – Warlingham Park. The staff there called her Margaret to start with but later she realise her real name was Molly. She under the care of Dr Lee. You can hask him if you don' believe me . . .' He knew his careful command of English was slipping. The man had unnerved him with his picky-picky ways.

'I'm sorry,' the registrar said from behind his steeple. 'But for all we know she might be married already. That would make her a bigamist, Mr Edwardes, and you an accessory.'

191

'I've explain' to you, sir. Molly been in the hospital for several years now. There is no husband.'

'At least give me her surname. We can check to see whether there is anything in our record of marriages.'

Reggie placed his palms down on the desk. 'Surname? We don't know a surname.'

'Does she have a birth certificate?'

'She came to Warlingham Park with nothing but the clothes she wore.'

'Well, has anyone reported her missing or claimed to be a relative?'

Reggie ran his hands over his head. 'Look, sir. If anyone came looking for Molly, I surely would have ask' for information about her.'

The registrar stood up and held out a hand to conclude the interview.

'I'm sorry, Mr Edwardes, but unless you can confirm Molly is not already married, and until she produces her birth certificate, I cannot proceed with this application.'

Reggie rose too. He ached to pick the man up by his lapels and shout at him. He wanted to hammer his fist on the wooden table until it hurt. Anything to marry Molly. But he'd been long enough in England to know how it would end.

So he took the man's cold hand in his, squeezed it lightly, then left the room without even slamming the door.

*

When Jack put his head on the pillow that night, all he could see was Sam. The last time he was with him at Bindoon, they'd been allowed down to Moore River one hot evening and had jumped and splashed in the cool water. Sam had ducked his head to wash out the dust, then lain on his back squinting into the still-bright sky, his wet hair slick as an otter's. Jack tried not to imagine Sam's smashed head as he lay on the ground. Or the crumpled body as the boys picked up and laid him in the truck. How on earth had Sam fallen off the scaffolding? He was so careful not to take risks. Unless his death hadn't been an accident. The brothers had made no secret of their contempt for him. Perhaps they knew that Sam had never given up being a Jew, despite pretending to be a Catholic like them.

Jack lifted his head and punched his fist into the pillow. Why hadn't he asked Sam back to stay? Or begged the Sullivans to keep him? Jack had known what things were like at Bindoon. Seen how quiet Sam had been. Noticed his too-small clothes, his scratches, his bruises. But said nothing. Done nothing. Sam had gone back to the Boys Town, to his death, and Jack had stayed with John and Kathleen in their safe, comfortable house, reading the new books, eating the good food. Would the hideous guilt ever go away?

Kathleen had been wonderful that evening, assuring him again and again that it wasn't his fault, holding him whilst he sobbed, listening to his stories about Sam. But it was no good talking to John, or trying to get back to Bindoon to find out what'd happened. No one would listen to him. He'd be branded a troublemaker. And besides, they might try and keep him at Bindoon. Prevent him from coming back; tell John and Kathleen to pick another boy. It was too risky.

He was doing well at school. The teachers said he was clever. Maybe if he worked really hard he could get to be a policeman. Then he could launch a raid on Bindoon and arrest all the brothers. He wouldn't rest until he'd avenged Sam's death. Or the brothers' cruelty.

He turned over in the darkness, imagining Brother McBride and Brother Cartwright sharing a miserable cell together. And him in a policeman's uniform, locking the door.

Part Three

1950 –1954

21

When Jack came in from school one autumn day, he found John and Kathleen sitting on the armchairs in the lounge room waiting for him. It was strange. John was usually at work and Kathleen busy in the kitchen. The air was heavy with tension.

'Come and sit down, sport,' said John, gesturing to the sofa. 'We've got something to tell you.'

Jack deposited his satchel reluctantly. Oh no, it wasn't *that* talk, was it? Sam had told him how uncomfortable it'd been when his parents told him about 'the birds and the bees', even though he'd found out months before from the boys at school. Jack's own sex education had been piecemeal. The nuns had been very clear that you weren't to touch yourself 'down there', whereas Brother Cartwright seemed to think 'down there' was his prerogative. The rest of Jack's information came from Bert's smutty jokes and an old Biology textbook he'd found in the school library. He sat down.

Kathleen fiddled with a cushion. 'You're happy here with us, Jack, aren't you?' That was an odd opener.

Jack scratched the inside of his elbow. 'Yes.'

John leaned forward, smiling. 'And you know we want you to be our son?' For a second Jack had a bizarre vision of himself getting smaller and smaller until he fitted inside Kathleen's tummy. This was going to be stranger than he thought.

'Yes.'

'Well.' Kathleen put the cushion down. 'What we would like to do is to adopt you properly.'

'Adopt?'

John cleared his throat. 'It's a legal thing. Lots of paperwork. Make you into a Sullivan for real.'

Jack knew what adopt meant. He just hadn't expected the announcement.

'Is that all right, Jack? You're looking a little unsure.'

Jack scratched his arm again. Surely they weren't allowed to adopt him if there was the faintest chance that Mum was alive. Wasn't that illegal, like having two wives or two husbands?

'Jack?' Kathleen again.

Jack couldn't look at her face. All that hope in her eyes. 'What about my mother?' he asked. Now the vision was of Mum. Dancing with him in the kitchen. Singing along to the Andrews Sisters. Making him cocoa.

John shifted in his chair. 'Your mother's dead. You know that.'

The vision flickered.

Kathleen got up and sat next to Jack. She put her hand on his knee and Jack tried not to flinch. 'Were you still hoping deep down that she might be alive?'

Sister Beatrice had told him Mum hadn't survived the bomb. Mum hadn't come to Melchet. Hadn't even sent a letter. Yet she still felt alive in his heart. He nodded his head slowly.

John got to his feet and marched off to the study. There were some rattling and scraping sounds, then he returned with a piece of paper. 'Look at this, Jack.' He plonked himself down on the other side of him.

Jack stared at the thin sheet of typed paper. It was headed *Commonwealth of Australia*. Underneath was his name, *Jack Malloy*. His full postal address was listed as *Melchet House*, and then his age: *11 years*, with the date and place of birth as *12 April 1936* in the *London Borough of Croydon*. 'Religion' was followed by the letters *RC*. The next line stated: 'Furnish name and address of parent, guardian or next of kin (if father is living his name must be given)'. Under this were written two words:

Parents dead.

'No!' Jack shouted. 'It's a lie!'

'Sorry, sport.' John shrugged. 'You can't argue with this.' He flicked his hand at the paper. 'It's an official document.'

Jack stood up, grabbed the sheet from John, screwed it up and hurled it across the room. Then, ignoring John's shout of protest, he staggered to the door and stumbled upstairs.

At first Kathleen wanted to follow him, but John persuaded her to stay. 'Give him time, Kath. Lad's had a big shock.'

'Which is why I need to comfort him.' She picked up the cushion again and hugged it to her chest.

'You don't know boys.' Another jibe. Kathleen was all too aware that she was the wrong gender where Jack was concerned.

And as an only child, she hadn't grown up with brothers and sisters to practise on. Her lack of experience showed all the time.

John stood up to return the paper to his drawer in the study and Kathleen departed for the kitchen. She took a couple of carrots and some potatoes out of the fridge, ran water into the sink and dropped in the vegetables. Then she rummaged around in her cutlery drawer until she located the sharp knife she liked and started to peel the potatoes. Usually she preferred to remove the potato skin in one continuous spiral. It was a challenge she set herself, like cutting the carrots into identical cubes or peeling a whole onion without crying, anything to make chores interesting. But today she didn't bother; she just shaved the spuds roughly, thinking about Jack as she did so. Her heart heaved for him. He must have always believed his mother would come back for him. Perhaps that explained the strange silences when he seemed to disappear into himself. They should have been more careful with the way they brought up the adoption issue. She just hoped his reaction was more to do with being finally confronted with his mother's death, rather than the prospect of being legally bound to her and John.

She shook the vegetables and laid them on the wooden board she kept behind the bread bin. Then she hacked them into pieces, grabbed a saucepan from the rail over the cooker, tipped them in, ducked the pan under the tap and released a stream of water. She put the full saucepan on the stove. There. Those were ready to boil later. A cold joint of lamb lay in the fridge; she'd get John to carve it just before the meal. She glanced at her watch. Twenty minutes and not a sound from upstairs.

She poked her head around the door to John's study. 'I'm going up to Jack now.'

'Righto.' John thrust some papers hastily back into the drawer and locked it.

Kathleen pushed aside a loose strand of hair. 'That document you showed Jack. Where did you get it from?'

'Bindoon. When they handed over the rest of his file. School reports, health records and such.'

'Was it genuine?'

'Of course it was bloody genuine. Why wouldn't it be?'

'Well, is there any proof of his mother's death? Death certificate or something?'

John stood up. 'Haven't a clue. And I'm certainly not going to go looking. If the immigration papers are good enough for the authorities, then they're good enough for me. Go and tell the kid we're putting the adoption in motion.'

Kathleen backed out of the room and went upstairs.

She knocked softly on Jack's door.

'Come in.'

Jack was sitting on the bed, but the counterpane was ruffled as though he'd been lying down. His eyes were puffy and his face flushed.

'Jack, I'm sorry.' Kathleen sat down on the bed next to him.

Jack looked away.

'It must have been brutal, seeing that document. Up until

201

now, I guess there's always been hope that your mum survived, but this confirms that she didn't.'

A sound escaped from Jack's mouth, midway between a groan and a howl.

Kathleen reached across to gather him into her arms. At first he tensed, but then she felt his body slump against hers. The sounds increased until his shoulders were shuddering and he was sobbing and keening. All Kathleen could do was stroke his back and whisper, 'It'll be all right, it'll be all right,' again and again.

She wanted to cry with him. Her body ached in sympathy.

But a tiny part of her mind was telling her that at last he was hers.

Afterwards, Jack never referred to the episode again, but in time Kathleen found him being less withdrawn in her company. He no longer flinched when she touched him and didn't pull away if she put an arm round him. Sometimes he even kissed her goodnight. She was so glad she and John had adopted him. Perhaps one day he would really believe he was their son.

22

Lord knows, a trip to the record office was the last thing Reggie needed after a long day at Warlingham. Today the rain was glistening on the tarmac and the newly lit street lights picked out a steady drizzle against the darkening, smoggy air.

One of the nurses had lent him a bike. It was a lady's one, of course. He wouldn't have ridden it had it not been nearly night-time. And if he hadn't been desperate. He was tired already. Every time a car passed him, his trousers got a soaking. His gloveless hands kept slipping on the wet handlebars and the backs of his legs ached as he pedalled up Selsdon Road. Another two or three hours slumped at a desk would do nothing to relieve his weariness. He often returned home with a pounding head and smarting eyes. Several times he'd been tempted to give up. It was such hard work, especially for something that might all be pointless anyway. But every time he saw Molly's pale face first thing in the morning, or glimpsed the sadness in her green eyes if they walked past a young lad in the street, he knew he had to keep going. Molly could have come with him to the record office, but he didn't want her worn out after a long day working in the shop. This was something he could do for her.

He padlocked the bike to the metal railings at the front of the building and trudged up the steps. At least it was light and warm inside and the smog couldn't penetrate there. The usual smell of old paper and cleaning fluid greeted him as he approached the record clerk's desk. Mrs Harper today, hair in a bun, pink cardigan, and those spectacles women wore that gave them cat's eyes. She pushed them down her nose to look at him.

'Mr Edwardes. Here again?'

Reggie was tempted to reply, 'Obviously.' But it wouldn't help. So he just nodded as he removed his raincoat and smoothed his hair.

'And how can I help you?'

'I'm up to 1936 now.'

'Very well.' Mrs Harper disappeared into the office behind her. Reggie drummed his fingers on the desk and sniffed. The rain had even gone up his nostrils.

She returned with a long brown box of yellowing cards. 'January to March. Bring them back when you've finished and I'll give you the next lot.'

'Thanks, ma'am.' Reggie picked up the box and made his way to a desk, his sodden raincoat under his arm. He hung it over the back of his chair, wiped his palms on his trousers and got to work.

He'd developed a rhythm now. Each time he picked up a card he clicked his fingers; each time he replaced one he tapped his feet. It was the only way he knew how to work. He did all his chores at the hospital to tunes inside his head: everything was a musical instrument – a broom, a dustpan and brush. You could even tap out a rhythm on a bedpan as long as you didn't spill its contents.

But a shadow on the desk caused him to stop. Mrs Harper was standing beside him, her face pinched with disapproval.

'Mr Edwardes. I can't have you making that noise in here.'

He turned to her in surprise. 'What noise, ma'am?'

'All that clicking and stamping. It's disturbing.'

Reggie looked round the room. Apart from the clerk, he was the sole occupant. He beamed up at her. 'I do crave your pardon.'

She tutted and made her way back to the desk. Obviously not one to succumb to his charm.

Reggie resumed his task in silence. He was only doing this for Molly. He didn't know how Mrs Harper could stand working here. Shouldn't she be at home with Mr Harper of an evening – if he existed? She must have the most boring job in the world. At least at the hospital there were people to talk to and every day brought its drama: a patient who'd wandered off, a fight over possessions, a nurse whose boyfriend had jilted her. But here was just monotony and silence.

It reminded him of school: old Mr Cairns marching up and down the rows of desks, barking, 'Nothin' comes free, boys, remember that, nothin' comes free.' And they'd lowered their heads, muttering the names of English counties or the list of British monarchs over and over until the information was indelibly etched on their brains. Sometimes he thought he knew more about the motherland than most of its inhabitants.

Mrs Harper was moving paper around her desk in an officious manner. She probably thought he was uneducated or that he couldn't stick to a task because he hadn't the backbone. He squared his shoulders and shook the box firmly. He'd show Mrs Fussyknickers.

It was nearly seven. Reggie could hear the jangle of the caretaker's keys out in the corridor. He rubbed his tired eyes, determined to finish the month he was checking before Mrs Harper made him leave. Suddenly he sat up straight and pounded out a loud drum roll on the desk with his hands. Da, da, da, dah! There it was, in fading type, Jack's birth record:

Jack Malloy, b. 12 April 1936 in the London Borough of Croydon. To Mick and Molly Malloy, née Agnew.

He'd found other Jacks born to women called Molly, of course. But the details had never quite stacked up. Dr Lee thought Molly was in her late thirties. That would put her as being born between 1911 and 1914. Molly had remembered that her dad had been killed in the First World War, which fitted. She'd been admitted to Warlingham in 1941. She'd not been wearing a wedding ring, and as no one had come searching for her, Dr Lee assumed the father of her child had either disappeared off the scene or died in the war.

Reggie stood up stiffly and returned the box to the desk.

'Any luck?' Mrs Harper was putting on her coat.

'Yes – I think I've found what I'm looking for. Are you able to check a mother's birth and marriage for me, if I have her child's birth record?' He showed her the relevant details.

206

She firmed her lips. 'We'll have to apply to Somerset House for that. And it will cost you. Come back tomorrow and we'll fill in the form.'

Reggie had been hoping he could get this sorted straight away. But it *was* getting late and he needed to keep Mrs Harper sweet. So he smiled his thanks, and retrieved his bike ready for the long ride back to Harrow Road.

Once the paperwork had been completed and the fee paid, thanks to a timely stint of overtime for Reggie at the hospital, it was a matter of waiting for results. Eventually Molly received a letter with a Somerset House postmark: it transpired that she'd been born in Bath on 10 January 1913 to Edith and Raymond Agnew and had married Mick Malloy in 1934.

'Mick,' she said wonderingly as she showed Reggie the letter. A song was playing in her head. But this time it wasn't Reggie's smoky voice delivering it, but an Irish brogue. 'Mick grew up in Dublin. He used to sing "Molly Malone" to me. Just like you.' Other fragments filtered through . . . mahogany hair gleaming with Brylcreem, yellow stripes on a khaki uniform, curling cigarette smoke, shoes that shone like mirrors, the smell of Craven 'A's.

'Do you think he's still alive?' Reggie's face was anxious.

'I'm not sure,' she whispered. 'I think I have a memory of a letter.' She rubbed at her ear, disturbed by a distant wail of grief, and her knees remembered the sudden rush of the carpet as her body had buckled.

'Let's find out.' He had been too long at this game to take

any chances. They both needed to be sure Molly could really be his.

Another trip to the office, another set of forms – military records this time. Then finally some news. Mick had been killed at Dunkirk in 1940. He'd been dead for over ten years. So, nothing to stop them getting married. Molly could hear Reggie whistling wherever they went. But her own reaction was more complicated. Much as she wanted to pledge herself to Reggie, the discovery of Mick's death certificate had shocked her, triggering more memories. When she cut through the park on her way to work at the dress shop, she remembered Mick blowing smoke rings in the garden of the Croydon house. Fastening her sandals in Mrs Croft's hallway, she caught a glimpse of him polishing his shoes. And when she looked at herself in the mirror, she pictured Mick pushing back her hair when he kissed her. All that time at Warlingham she hadn't even remembered his existence. But now she couldn't stop wondering about her first marriage. She'd recalled a few more facts, but what about the *feelings*? Had they been happy? Still in love? Was it disrespectful to Mick to remarry? Perhaps she would never know. But after a while she told herself firmly to put the past behind. She had another chance of happiness with Reggie. She needed to take it.

Reggie took Molly to her last recorded address to confirm his findings. They walked along Sydenham Road until they reached an area that seemed familiar. Molly stopped outside a house.

'That's the Clarks' house!' she exclaimed. 'They were our neighbours. They had an Anderson shelter in their garden. Jack and I used to go in it sometimes.' She walked further along the road, then paused, frowning. 'That's wrong,' she said, looking up at the new maisonette next door to the Clarks. 'That should be our house.' Behind the neat maisonette a ghost house hovered. Pebble-dashed walls. Old brown paint. Hollyhocks.

Realisation dawned. Molly buried her head inside Reggie's jacket. In the warm darkness she saw Jack in his gas mask, his dark-brown hair being squashed by the strap and his green eyes looking at her steadily through the glass. She remembered the smell of the mask too – a stale odour mixed with something medicinal.

'It's all right, Moll,' said Reggie, stroking her hair. 'You must've hurt your head badly when your house was bombed. Goodness knows how you found the strength to walk so far, though.' She'd been discovered a long way from Sydenham Road.

Molly slowly looked up. 'Dr Lee said my physical injuries were bad but the damage to my memory was more serious. He thought my brain had protected me from the shock of everything.'

'You must have a mighty good brain to protect you for all those years!'

But Molly didn't laugh. 'Dr Lee was certain Jack wouldn't have survived. But what if he did?'

'I don't know, Moll.'

Molly's grasp on Reggie's jacket tightened. She knew she had to let Mick go, but she wasn't prepared to lose Jack too. 'You found me, Reggie. Can you help me find out what happened to Jack? I need to know one way or the other.'

Reggie looked up at the sky. Molly heard him start to sigh, then hesitate. He seemed to speak very carefully. 'Maybe. But there's something *you* have to do first.'

'Go on.'

Reggie took Molly's other hand and kissed it. 'Plan that wedding!'

This time she did laugh.

Six weeks later, Molly stood on the town hall steps, squinting into the sun. She wore a navy-blue suit, a white headpiece pinned to her brown curls, and carried a small bunch of white carnations. Reggie stood smiling next to her in his Jamaican suit, now a little tighter-fitting, and a new pair of brown leather shoes.

Their guests were lined up on the steps behind them, ready for the group photo. Matron produced a Brownie camera to capture the scene. Molly had asked Dr Lee to stand beside her. Any attempt to search out relatives had ended in failure. And if she'd found some, would they have come? They might not have approved of her marrying a Jamaican. When she'd married Mick, it'd been Mum there next to her. She'd walked her up the aisle, tucking Molly's shaking hand into her own arm, reassuring her with her warmth and solidity. Mum had liked Mick. He made her laugh and she knew he adored Molly.

From time to time, though, she'd caught her frowning at the glass in Mick's hand. He'd liked a drink, had Mick.

Molly wondered what Dr Lee was thinking as he stood stiffly next to her, a grim smile on his face. She knew he had his reservations about the marriage. But together they'd show him. She could be happy with Reggie, she knew it. And besides, she was one of Dr Lee's great success stories, wasn't she?

At the last minute, Molly had invited Annie and Lucy from Warlingham. Annie still wore her grey plaits but had adorned them with a number of red roses, pushed in at strange angles, as a concession to the occasion. It must have been strange for her to leave the home where she'd lived for so long, even for an afternoon. Molly hadn't been sure how she'd cope at the wedding, not having been out for years. Rumour had it that Annie had witnessed her father murder her mother when she was thirteen, and hadn't been right since. She'd been taken into Warlingham in a terrible state. Over time, she'd grown calmer, but she refused to face the outside world. And the plaits, so strange on the head of an old woman, along with her youthful clothes, were evidence of her determination never to progress into adulthood. She was an elderly lady trapped in the body of a teenage girl, frozen at the point her life had fallen apart.

Lucy cowered behind her, clutching a small holdall and peering myopically at the crowd who'd paused in their Saturday-morning shopping to gawp at the strange gathering. Poor Lucy: had not the incessant duty of caring for infirm parents eroded any shred of self-confidence, and had two world wars not drastically pruned the stock of available men, she might have had a day like this too. Molly had been so lucky to have a second chance.

A couple of women in headscarves and gabardine macs were pointing at her and Reggie. One of them, carrying a large straw basket bulging with vegetables, tut-tutted loudly. Her neighbour shushed her, but kept staring. Molly looked away and smiled determinedly. Reggie was looking elsewhere, thank goodness.

Dr Lee had arranged for a couple of taxis to take them back to Warlingham, where Cook had laid on a bit of a spread ('Nothing fancy, mind, just a few savouries and a cake').

By the time the new Mr and Mrs Edwardes entered the dining room, all the staff and patients had assembled. Most cheered the couple loudly, and Matron took photos.

Reggie and Molly sat at the top table munching sandwiches and slices of pork pie. For a second Molly allowed herself to imagine Jack alongside them. He'd be sixteen by now. Would he have walked her up the aisle, smiling awkwardly in an ill-fitting suit, then polished off a huge plate of food, relieved that his duty was discharged? Or would he have stood up and made a speech? Leaned across to shake Reggie's hand, or sulked at her betrayal of his dad? She wondered again if she'd done the right thing. But this was no good. She shouldn't torment herself.

'Molly?' said Reggie. She looked up to see Cook wheeling in a trolley with a magnificent three-tiered wedding cake.

'Oh my,' said Molly, following Reggie over to the table. 'It's beautiful.' She looked down at the smooth white icing piped with neat rosettes and the plaster bride and groom perched on top. Both had white faces, and the groom's jacket was slightly chipped. Each layer of the cake was tied with pink satin ribbon. Molly moved forward to pick up the knife. 'It's a shame to spoil it.'

'Don't worry, my dear, you won't spoil it.' Cook put her hands round the top layer of the cake and tugged. The whole structure came away in her hands: it was made from cardboard and paste. 'The cake shop hired it out.' She beamed.

Underneath was a tiny sponge, the colour of fruit cake but without all the raisins and candied peel. 'Put a bit of gravy browning in it,' said Cook. 'Came up a treat.' It looked awful.

Molly suddenly remembered the cake she'd had at her first wedding. Her mother had steeped the fruit in brandy for days. She'd used best butter for the mix and proper icing on the top and round the sides. But Cook had done her best; she should be grateful.

'Thank you,' Molly said.

Reggie stepped forward, curling his hands round Molly's as she held the knife. 'You're very kind,' he added.

They both smiled into the camera as Matron clicked the button.

When Molly and Reggie walked down the drive, everyone stood on the steps to wave them off. She'd wondered about keeping her flowers to put on Jack's 'grave' in the Warlingham cemetery, but had changed her mind. Wouldn't that be another admission that he was dead? There was still a glimmer of hope. She didn't want to jinx it. In the end she'd thrown them over her shoulder. Annie had caught them and set about adding carnations to the roses now drooping out of her grey hair.

They were going to get the bus to New Addington. Dr Lee had persuaded the council that Molly was eligible for a prefab on account of her house being destroyed. It was up on Castle Hill, a single-storey building with a small garden plot, an indoor bathroom, a gas fridge, and even an ironing board that folded out from the wall. 'They call these prefabs *people's palaces*, you know,' Reggie had said when they first went to inspect it. 'Just the ticket for Princess Molly!' Molly clapped her hands. She couldn't wait to have her own home and live in it with Reggie. She thought back to when she'd first stayed at Mrs Croft's, feeling she didn't belong anywhere. Now she did. She had a home. And someone to share it with.

'We're not going straight back,' said Reggie. 'There's somewhere I want to take you first. We'll need to catch a different bus.'

'Oh?'

'Follow me.' Reggie winked at her and led her down Limpsfield Road.

By seven they were in Streatham. The bus had rumbled along through Purley and Thornton Heath, heading north towards London.

'Aren't we going the wrong way?' asked Molly as they'd crossed the railway line at Norbury. She'd been inspecting her wedding ring and looking out of the window at her reflection.

Strange they'd never found her old wedding ring. She couldn't imagine she'd stopped wearing it after Mick had died.

'Not for what I have in mind.' Reggie smiled mysteriously at her. 'Come on,' he said, as the bus chugged past Streatham Common in the gathering gloom. 'Our stop's soon.' Molly followed him down the stairs, smoothing her skirt and trying not to dirty her new white gloves on the metal rail.

They got off at the junction with Leigham Court Road. A few early-evening stragglers were making their way home, mingling with others heading out to cafés for a bite to eat.

'Hungry?' said Reggie.

'Not really. Still full of wedding cake.'

Reggie grimaced. 'I'll get you a proper one for our first anniversary.'

Molly squeezed his hand.

They walked past a newsagent's and a small dress shop with ghostly mannequins posing in its darkened window, before reaching a large concrete building with a lighted entrance. *The Locarno* it said over the top in large red neon letters.

'Here we are.' Reggie led her in.

Molly smelled cigarette smoke and perfume. A band was playing 'I Wanna Be Loved', and as she walked further in, she saw couples dancing on a brightly lit dance floor while people sat at tables in the room's shadowy fringes drinking and smoking. Most people were white, but there were quite a few coloured faces too.

'Oh my goodness,' said Molly.

Reggie grinned at her. 'Couldn't let the day go by without

215

a dance with my new wife. I'll get you a drink.' He motioned her to an empty table. 'And then we're going to celebrate properly.' Molly sat down, watching Reggie anxiously as he made his way over to the bar. Her ears had started to buzz. She quickly rammed her fists against them.

He came back with a martini glass for Molly, full of pale yellow liquid, and a pint of beer for himself.

'Cheers!' He chinked his glass against hers. She took a small sip and made a face.

She wondered if Reggie had seen her reaction, but he'd stood up again and was waving at a group of coloured men in suits making their way over to their table.

'Hope you don' mind, Moll. I met some friends at the bar. These guys were with me in the Clapham shelter. They all want to meet my lovely new wife.' He was drawing spare chairs from other tables, asking other occupants if they minded. Most shook their heads, but one man in a business suit scowled. Luckily Reggie didn't notice, too busy making introductions: 'Lester – my wife, Molly. Deelon – Molly. Major – meet my wife.'

Molly shook hands, wondering if she was going to have any time with her new husband. They all greeted her politely, but it was obvious it was Reggie they wanted to speak to. Clearly they had much to catch up on since he'd left the shelter. The men sat down. There was a lot of back-slapping and laughing. She shrank into her chair, gripping the stem of her glass. This wasn't the way she'd planned to start her new marriage. After her first wedding, she remembered she and Mick had gone to Cornwall for a few days. Deckchairs, ice creams. Sun in her eyes. Sand between her toes. The two of them alone at last. But it seemed she'd to share Reggie with everyone. And on her wedding night too. Was this how her marriage was going to be? Maybe she'd been too hasty, marrying someone from a different culture. But Reggie had seemed so strong, so keen to protect her. She'd thought it would be wonderful to have a husband who could look after her for the rest of her life. But how do I know he really wants me, she thought, when he seems to prefer being with his friends?

No one was speaking to her, so she turned to watch the band play. They were West Indian by the looks of it, in white jackets and black trousers. She could see a drummer, a guitar player, a tall man with a tambourine and another shorter, younger chap with a triangle. And a singer, of course, crooning into the microphone. All men. The sound was upbeat. As the musicians swayed on the stage, Molly found herself tapping her foot. The buzzing in her ears was still there but the music was much louder.

'"Hoop-Dee-Doo"!' Reggie was on his feet, pulling on Molly's hand. 'Let's have that dance, Moll.' Molly put down her glass then wondered where to stow her handbag. She wedged it between her chair and the table leg, feeling oddly light without it, and followed Reggie onto the dance floor.

For a moment, she stood awkwardly. Reggie seemed to be doing some complicated dance on his own. How on earth did he move like that? Then he grabbed her fingers with one hand and circled her waist with the other. His hips moved against hers, coaxing her into the dance until she relaxed to the rhythm. He closed his eyes and held her tightly.

217

*

By ten thirty, the table was covered in empty pint glasses. Only Molly's martini was still half full. She'd taken off her headdress in an attempt to ease the pain at her temples. It lay on the table like a limp bouquet. Reggie was taking ages at the bar, greeting yet more friends. And buying yet more drinks. Spending a fortune when they should be saving for furniture for the prefab.

Molly looked up as an unlikely figure meandered around the tables full of drinkers and smokers. He was wearing some sort of official uniform: a smart black suit with a white shirt and black tie, and a black cap with a badge on the front. A strip of medals was spread across his chest. Must be a war veteran, thought Molly. Clearly still proud to be seen in his uniform. But what on earth was he doing at the Locarno? The man had paused at a table. He had a pile of magazines in his hand and was passing one to a smartly dressed woman smoking a cheroot. She was nodding vaguely at him and smiling. He stayed to chat for a while, then moved on.

Molly watched the man until he approached her table.

'Good evening, ma'am,' he said, putting down his magazines. Molly glanced at the cover. *The War Cry*. 'Would you like to buy one?' the man asked.

Molly's hands went to her bag at her feet. 'I don't know. What's it about?'

'I'm a Salvation Army officer,' said the man. 'This is our magazine.' Now that he was in front of her, Molly realised that the words *Salvation Army* were on his hat. A vague memory came back to her: a park, a bandstand, a group of musicians wearing uniforms and playing brass instruments.

'What are you doing here?' Molly asked.

'Apart from selling these?' The man looked down at the magazines on the table. 'Having a chat to people. Seeing if there is anything I can do to help.'

'What kind of help?'

The man pulled out a chair next to her. 'May I?'

Molly nodded.

He sat down and leaned towards her. He had kind blue eyes in a baggy face. Molly imagined he must be in his fifties at least. 'Drink. Homelessness. Missing persons.'

'What do you mean, missing persons?'

The man took off his hat and placed it on the table, moving the pile of magazines to make room. 'We have a service to help reunite family members.'

Molly's stomach lurched. 'Can you look for anyone?' she whispered.

The man reached out to pat her hand. 'Have you lost someone yourself?'

'My son. We got separated during the war. I lost my memory so I couldn't go looking for him.'

The man's eyes were really very blue. 'How old is the lad?' he asked.

'Sixteen.'

The man removed his hand and picked up his hat. 'I'm sorry, my dear. We don't trace relatives under eighteen.'

Molly looked away, biting her lip.

'I tell you what, give it a couple of years then get in touch with us. We'll see what we can do.' He took a copy of *The War Cry* and put it in front of Molly. Automatically she felt for her handbag again. 'Have this on me,' he said. 'The address is on the back.' He tipped his hat to her, picked up his stock and ambled off to another table.

Molly picked the magazine up listlessly, folded it and put it into her handbag. Then she slumped against the back of the chair. Another light extinguished. Her body had fizzed with excitement throughout the wedding. Now it was as flat as stale lemonade.

After a while, she realised it was getting late.

'Reggie.' He was deep in conversation with Major. She tugged his sleeve. 'I'm worried about our bus. We need to go.'

'Course, Moll. Won't be long. Just one more thing I need to do.' He sauntered over to the band leader. The musicians were having a break, lolling against the piano with amber-filled glasses. Reggie spoke to them for a few minutes then returned, grinning. 'This is for you, Mrs Edwardes,' he told Molly, then he bounded back to the stage, took the proffered microphone and started to sing.

In Dublin's fair city, Where the girls are so pretty . . .

The band accompanied him quietly, a harmonious undertone to Reggie's strong, smoky voice. Gradually people put down their glasses and stopped talking.

I first set my eyes on sweet Molly Malone . . .

You could have heard a pin drop. Reggie looked across at her and smiled.

Molly smiled slowly back. And the drinkers, the dancers, the tables piled with empty glasses . . . all faded. It was just her and Reggie. His voice caressing her. His brown eyes full of tenderness.

Desire for her husband flooded her body. They would go home. Away from Reggie's friends, the endless rounds of drink, the gossipy groups of people. They would consummate their marriage; his strong body above hers, the half-remembered rhythms, her white hands clasping his brown back. She would feel safe at last. It would be perfect.

Except that a huge part of her was still missing.

Molly insisted on accompanying Reggie the next time he went to the town hall. He'd have gone on his own, like before, but Molly didn't want to stay in the house alone again. She was tired of sewing up holes in Reggie's socks, listening to the clock on the mantelpiece tick with irritating precision. She'd ended up drinking three cups of cocoa when he'd gone back to the records office, just so she could pace around the kitchen while the milk boiled, then felt even more sick than her nerves had made her to start with. At least this way she was doing something. Jack was her son. She should hear news of him at the same time as Reggie did.

A male records clerk greeted them. He had protruding ears and wore an off-white shirt with a beige sleeveless pullover that'd been darned with a slightly darker thread. He confirmed that Molly's house had been destroyed in the bombing raids on Croydon in 1941. That coincided with Molly's arrival at Warlingham. Reggie thanked the man and put his hand on Molly's elbow to guide her out of the door.

But she resisted. 'There's something else.' She had her handkerchief in her hand and was twisting it into a rope. 'We don't know whether my son died in the raid.'

'Name?' said the clerk.

'Jack Malloy,' whispered Molly.

'Why don't I look him up for you, love? Go and take a seat over there.'

Molly tried to smile. 'That would be so kind.' She followed Reggie over to a table and they both sat down. Her ears were buzzing loudly. She put her hands up to stop them and caught Reggie looking at her strangely. Did he have any idea what she was going through? He sat staring into space, tapping his foot on the floor.

Eventually the clerk called them over. Molly tried to read his expression. Was it encouraging?

'First of all, there's no record of a death.'

Molly slowly exhaled. 'So what could have happened?'

'I was coming to that. Any unaccompanied children would have been rounded up and brought here, to the town hall.' The clerk placed a large ledger on the desk and carefully turned over its yellow pages. 'Here we are.' He angled it so she and Reggie could see. 'We do have a record of a Jack Malloy, who was taken to Melchet House, near Romsey in Hampshire. But we have no more details. He doesn't seem to have been admitted to hospital, so there are no medical records. He might be the boy you are looking for.'

Molly put her hand to her chest. Tried to breathe. In . . . out . . . Why was it so hard? Slow down. Take in what the clerk had said. *Jack might be alive.* A memory flashed: Jack, walking to school in an overlarge blazer, turning the corner in a pool of sunlight. She blinked. That was the last time she'd seen him. The day of the bomb.

'Hampshire?' Reggie was asking.

'It's about sixty miles south-west of here. Out in the country. The lad was probably taken there to avoid the bombs. The Jerries didn't bother with the countryside much. Not like Croydon.' The clerk sucked in his breath.

Reggie muttered something in response, but Molly remained silent. *Don't get sidetracked talking about the war,* she thought. *Stay with Jack. Please.* A bubble of optimism was forming deep in her stomach. *Don't hope too much. It's too soon,* she told herself.

The clerk pulled his chair closer to the table. The sound juddered up Molly's spine. 'Anyway, Melchet House is where a boy called Jack Malloy was taken, but we've no idea what state he was in or whether he's still there. How old do you think he'd be now?'

'Sixteen.' Again Reggie did the talking. Molly tried to imagine a teenage Jack. Was he tall like Mick? Did he still have dark hair? The bubble of hope was still there.

'Well, all the best then.' The clerk closed his ledger with a thud and Reggie stood up and shook his hand. Molly didn't move. She wanted to find out more from the kind clerk. Perhaps she could ask him some more questions about Jack. But Reggie had taken her hand and was pulling her up. His arm tightened around her as they left the office. She wasn't sure she'd have made it otherwise.

But she couldn't stop talking once they got home. 'I *knew* it. Dr Lee was so adamant. But did he know all along? Surely he couldn't be that cruel. Perhaps he really suspected Jack had died and was trying to protect me. Or maybe he just couldn't be bothered to track him down. Whatever the reason, he's denied me all those years with my son. I'll never forgive him for that.

'But as soon as I remembered his name, something told me Jack was alive.' She just reached the sofa before her legs buckled. It was strange how weak her body felt when her mind was whirling. And now another thought. A good one. 'We can be a family. You, me and Jack. A new start for everyone.' She sat upright. 'We need to go to Melchet House as soon as we can.'

23

When John came in that night, Jack was at the dining room table doing his homework and Kathleen was standing by the stove in the kitchen, stirring something in a saucepan. Condensation fogged the windows and a strong smell permeated the room. Not unpleasant, but not particularly appetising either.

'Evening, sport.'

Jack looked up from a copy of *Hamlet*. 'Hello.'

'Dinner won't be long,' said Kathleen.

'Great, I'll have a quick drink first.' John opened the huge cream refrigerator and pulled out a Swan beer. Kathleen silently passed him a bottle opener and a glass.

He waved the glass away. 'Real men don't use glasses,' he said, winking at Jack, who smiled obligingly back. They'd got on better recently. After that awful business with his friend, Jack had withdrawn into himself even more. John suspected he thought about the lad a lot. Perhaps the poor kid even blamed himself. But lately he'd come out of his shell a bit. Kathleen was good at calming him down. Maybe Jack had finally accepted them as his mum and dad.

John went onto the veranda to savour his drink until the

meal was ready. He needed to contemplate how he was going to break the news to Kathleen. Best to bide his time until the moment was right.

It was cooler outside. He stood by the wooden rail, dimly aware of the Carter children playing next door. Nearby, sandgrinders buzzed in the parrot bushes, their distinctive voices rising to a crescendo then dying away. John shifted his gaze and was shocked by how overgrown the lawn was. Kathleen had been neglecting the garden recently. Probably too busy with Jack. Maybe he'd mow it at the weekend.

The minister had phoned earlier. They hadn't spoken for a while. He'd been surprised that day John had told him they'd taken on Jack permanently. Grown a bit tetchy too at the implied criticism of Bindoon. But now he was keen as mustard with a new plan. John hadn't liked it at first, but the minister had talked him round. John just hoped he'd persuade Kathleen that easily. A few more brownie points with the minister wouldn't go amiss.

He put the mouth of the bottle to his lips and drank, then tilted his head to catch the evening sun.

Ten minutes later, Kathleen placed three bowls of soup on the table.

John took up his spoon and scooped up some glutinous liquid containing lumps of unidentifiable origin. 'What's this, Kath?'

'Pumpkin soup,' was the prompt reply.

Jack ate his obediently, but John took one mouthful then spat it straight out.

'Stone the crows, woman. What are those lumps?'

Kathleen sniffed. 'Pearl barley. We've been told to use up reserve stock.'

'Over my dead body.' John snatched up his bowl and marched with it into the kitchen. He deposited it in the sink with a clatter.

'Don't waste good food, John.'

'I'm not eating that muck,' John replied. 'Growing boys need meat.' He winked at Jack again. This was playing into his hands. 'I think you need some help, Kath. You've a lot to do, looking after Jack and me as well as the house. Then you could manage your resources better and you wouldn't be feeding me rubbish like this.'

Kathleen looked at him steadily. 'I cope.'

'I know you do, darl, but wouldn't you like some more time to yourself?'

'What are you proposing?' Kathleen pointedly picked up her spoon and manoeuvred some of the offending liquid into her mouth.

John reached forward to realign his place mat. 'I was speaking to the minister earlier.'

'Oh yes?' Kathleen swallowed with visible difficulty.

'He wants us to take on an Abo girl. They're still bringing them out of Moore River, or Mogumber as we're s'posed to call it now, and getting them to work for white families. She'll be trained.'

'John – we don't need any more people in this house.'

'Of course we do. She can have the attic room. And she'll

take on all the chores you don't like.' John tipped back in his chair. 'Besides, a man of my standing ought to have a domestic.'

'So this is what it's about. That and keeping in with the minister.'

John rocked back with a thud. Why was it that Kathleen always saw through him? Best to bring the subject back to her. 'Surely you'd like a little more leisure? And more time for Jack, of course.' And me, he thought. A picture came into his mind of Jack drinking cocoa in bed when he was crook and of Kathleen running up and down the stairs with his meals. She'd never done that for her husband.

Kathleen sniffed and took a sip of water. 'What about her own folks?'

John had asked the minister that question himself. He repeated his reply: 'Most of the parents are crims or druggies. Taking the children gives them a chance. Eventually the race will die out and that'll be a good thing for Australia.'

'And aren't we supposed to breed the colour out of them?' asked Kathleen, raising an eyebrow. 'Marry the half-castes to white trash and not their own kind?'

John didn't answer. He was thinking of the blotting pad he'd doodled on during his conversation with the minister. It was only afterwards he realised he'd drawn a series of boxes on it, one inside another.

'Why do we use them as servants when they got here first?' asked Jack, who'd finished his soup.

John looked at him levelly. 'Abos are primitive, mate. That's why we need to take them on and train them. They ought to be grateful to us.'

Jack drew in his breath to ask another question, but a warning glance from Kathleen silenced him. 'Is there any more soup?' he said instead, and John saw Kathleen give him a grateful smile.

John laughed. 'Blimey, mate. You must be hungry.'

*

What with Christmas and the long spell of bad weather early in the new year, it was March before they could travel to Melchet. Reggie stared out of the bus window, watching the sprawl of suburbia give way to rural tranquillity. The sky was full of fast-moving clouds that seemed to turn the sun on and off like a light switch. The wind was skittish: tousling the treetops and sending the newborn lambs frisking round the fields in a frenzy. Blackthorn flowers fizzed in the hedgerows.

He'd learned not to look for bright skies each morning, but he'd never got used to the English cold. Here they were in early spring and the air was still freezing. He edged closer to Molly. Still looking out of the window, he reached for her and put his hand on her lap, then threaded her fingers with his own. Marriage was good. He'd been right to stay.

But would things change if they found Jack? Reggie remembered himself at that age. Riding a motorbike around his parents' farm, stealing eggs from the neighbours' hens and bananas from their tree. Posing bare-chested and watching the local girls squirm and giggle. He'd had a different chick each week until he'd come to England. But they'd been silly empty-headed girls in the main. He doubted if they'd given him a second thought once he'd left the island. Molly needed him. He wanted to help her find Jack, to see her anxious eyes light up with pleasure. But if they did, would she spend all her time caring for her son and ignore him? Would seeing Jack again bring back memories of Molly's first marriage and make her resent her second? It was risky. Yet she was Mrs Edwardes now. He should do his duty and help her track Jack down. He needed to stop thinking about himself and concentrate on making his wife happy.

He stared out of the window again, blinking at the blur beyond and trying to resist the soporific drone of the engine. He had no recollection of the last ten miles.

The bus dropped them off in Romsey and they got a taxi out to Melchet. Reggie was horrified by the cost – he could have bought several rounds of drinks for that. The driver deposited them in front of a large red-brick building with huge windows. It looked like a Victorian mansion Reggie had seen in a school textbook, although the chimneys were made from a different-coloured brick and seemed older. He could hear a low hum coming through a defiantly open window. It took him a moment to realise it was children's voices.

Molly stood for a minute looking at the old house, trying to imagine her son arriving alone; walking through the large oak doors. Her stomach clenched with apprehension and she massaged it absent-mindedly. Then she and Reggie walked up to the front door and rang the bell.

The door was opened by a nun with a smooth pink face and pale blue eyes. She listened intently to their enquiry, then motioned them in. The home, with its high ceilings and long, wide corridors, reminded Molly of Warlingham. Perhaps all institutions looked the same.

'I'll go and find Sister Constantia.' The nun clomped away in her black lace-up shoes, leaving Molly and Reggie sitting on a hard shiny bench in the entrance hall.

A door slammed in the distance, and Molly heard an advancing *tap-tap* sound. For a minute she was back on the ward, waiting in dread for Matron's visit. She shivered, and felt Reggie edge closer.

'You all right?'

'I keep feeling I'm back at Warlingham.'

Reggie's laugh echoed round the high hallway. 'You escape from the hospital. If Jack's here, he can escape too.'

Molly pictured herself showing Jack round the little prefab. Would he still let her tuck him into bed at night? Probably not, but she could cook for him. Boys of his age needed lots of protein. She pictured herself at the gleaming stove stirring a huge pot of beef stew, its meaty odour percolating through the kitchen, then effortlessly crisping up spam fritters in the pan. And didn't he used to like shepherd's pie? A cloud of buttery potato appeared; in her mind, Molly layered it carefully over the minced lamb, flicking it up with the fork the way

Jack liked it. He could have her meat rations. She'd gladly go without food herself. He'd realise she would do anything to make him happy – that she'd never have forgotten him if she hadn't been so ill. It was vital he knew that. But then a terrible thought darted in.

'What if he doesn't want to come back to us?' she asked Reggie.

'We'll cross that bridge when we come to it.'

The nun appeared. She was tall, with bony wrists protruding beneath the black sleeves of her habit.

Molly's shoes seemed to be wrapped in layers of cotton wool. They couldn't make contact with the floor.

'Mr and Mrs Edwardes?' When she shook Molly's hand, the nun's palm was cool and dry. Reggie was pulling at his ear lobe. Sister Constantia didn't offer to shake his hand, although she darted a crisp nod in his direction.

'How may I help you?' she asked.

'I think my son came here, during the war. His name is Jack.'

The nun's expression didn't change. 'We have had many boys of that name over the years. Especially during the war. Lots of comings and goings.' She looked weary, as though the strain of the evacuations had suddenly just caught up with her.

'But you kep' records?' Reggie said. 'His full name is Jack Malloy. He'd be almost seventeen by now. Is he still with you?'

Sister Constantia's lips were pressed together, her eyes expressionless.

'We don't have a child of that name and I'm afraid the records are no longer stored here. They are at the office in central London owned by our order. They may be able to help you. But you will have to make an appointment.' She sniffed. 'It would be unacceptable just to turn up.'

Molly's cheeks grew warm. It'd been her idea to arrive at Melchet unannounced. How stupid of her. She'd thought they'd find Jack straight away – that they'd be shown into a dormitory or refectory or something and he'd recognise her immediately. She'd imagined him running to her, throwing his arms around her. He'd be laughing and smiling and shaking hands with Reggie. They'd have helped him pack and then taken him home on the bus. The three of them would live together. Happily ever after.

But Jack wasn't in this quiet, chilly place. A bit of her was relieved. What would it have done to him to be ruled by Sister Constantia day in, day out? That woman didn't have an ounce of warmth in her, for all that she was a nun. The trusting expression on Jack's little face would have turned to bewilderment and fear. He would have hated going to bed without a cuddle or a story. And would anyone have applied witch hazel if his eczema got bad? Molly could see the sore, weeping skin on his skinny arm. She wiped her hand across her eyes. But if he wasn't at Melchet House, then where was he?

'I'm sorry you've had a wasted journey,' said Sister Constantia, smoothing her skirts. 'As I say, your best option is to contact our order's central office. It's in Marylebone.'

Marylebone. That was only a forty-minute train ride from home. To think they'd spent the best part of the day travelling down to Romsey. And they'd have to spend the rest of it getting back. Not to mention wasting a whole load of money they didn't have. Molly looked apologetically at Reggie, but his head was tipped back. He was gazing at the ornate ceiling. A nerve twitched in his neck.

She was about sixteen, liquid-limbed, with dark brown eyes and shiny black hair. A woman from the girls' home brought her, handing her over on the doorstep like a parcel. Kathleen reached out, smiling, and pulled her in, nodding her thanks to the woman, who hurriedly departed.

Kathleen found it hard to know how to treat Rosie. She'd longed for children for so long; she couldn't bear to regard her as just a hired help. But she knew she risked John's wrath if she accorded the girl the same status as Jack. Rosie looked a little thin; perhaps Kathleen would slip her some nourishing food when she could. Build her up a bit. She'd tried to make the attic room as comfortable as possible. John had given it a lick of paint, but it was Kathleen who'd hung the curtains and plumped up the pillows.

She offered Rosie a lamington and a glass of milk, which the girl ate and drank shyly. They sat at the kitchen table in silence for a while. In between sips and tiny mouthfuls, Rosie looked round the kitchen. Kathleen wondered how it appeared through her eyes. She seemed particularly transfixed by those three flying ducks on the wall. Probably never thought of birds as ornaments before. When she'd finished, Kathleen took her upstairs to see her room. She hoped she'd like it.

After Kathleen and Rosie had set off for the attic, Jack wandered into the kitchen from the dining room, where he'd been studying. He'd glimpsed Rosie through the half-open door but Kathleen had suggested he wait until later to meet her. 'Let me get to know her a little first. It'll be me she'll be working with; you won't have much to do with her.' Jack had caught a flash of dark hair and smooth skin, and a fleeting impression of gracefulness.

He sat at the kitchen table, in the chair Rosie had just vacated, listening to the two sets of receding footsteps, although Rosie's tread was much lighter than Kathleen's.

He wondered what difference the new occupant would make. Would a shared wariness of John draw them together? Perhaps he could help Rosie out sometimes. John had made it very clear that she was to be viewed as a servant. But what did that mean? They'd certainly not had servants in Croydon, and at Bindoon *they* were the servants. He wouldn't treat Rosie as the brothers had treated him. Perhaps he could be a friend to her. Although he'd have to be careful whenever John was around. But it would be nice to have a proper friend again. His heart still ached for Sam. He'd never known anyone he could talk to like he could Sam. They'd had such fun on the ship. And Sam had even made Bindoon bearable. Jack would never forget him. Or his promise to avenge his death.

He wrapped his hands around the tumbler Rosie had drunk from. Then looked at it closely. A perfect map of her lips, with their blurred contours, was fused into its edge. Jack pressed his own lips to the glass.

*

Molly and Reggie trudged down the drive, away from Melchet House. 'Sorry,' said Molly. 'I didn't think it would be like this.'

Reggie shrugged. 'I've seen some more of England, anyway. It's pretty round here.' He looked back at the lawns, turning gold in the late-afternoon sun, and the woods behind the house, luminous with green shoots. He took Molly's hand. 'We'll get in touch with Marylebone and go across as soon as I've been paid.'

They carried on, but stopped at a sudden cry. 'Please wait!'

Molly looked round. A different nun was hurrying after them. She had a round face, reddening with the effort of trying to catch them. A fluff of grey hair escaped from her headdress. When she got closer, Molly could see the deep wrinkles etched into the nun's skin. She caught the faint scent of peppermint.

'I heard you were looking for Jack Malloy.'

Molly froze.

The elderly nun led them over to a bench at the side of the gardens. 'I'm Sister Beatrice. And I think I might be able to help you.'

'You knew Jack?' Reggie asked.

'Oh yes. He was with us for about seven years.'

Molly sat down abruptly on the bench. *Seven years!* He'd been there all that time and Sister Constantia hadn't told her. She *must* have known. How could she be so cruel?

'He was a lovely lad,' the nun continued. 'I was very fond of your Jack.' She had a faraway look on her face. 'He used to sit on my lap and I'd tell him stories.'

Molly felt a heave of nausea. To think that all that time she'd been in a hospital bed, Jack had been in a dormitory bed. Only sixty miles away. He'd spent all those years with these childless women and not with her, his own mother. There were a hundred questions she wanted to ask, but most were too difficult to frame. 'What did he look like?' she finally said.

'He was small for his age, with dark brown hair and lovely green eyes.' Sister Beatrice looked at Molly. 'A bit like yours, dear. He was one of the quieter ones. Took a while to find his feet. He came here during the Blitz. I seem to remember he was sent here from Croydon.'

'Yes, that's right,' said Molly. She told him about the bomb and Warlingham. 'The authorities didn't know who I was, so they thought Jack was an orphan. He must have been sent here for safety.'

'He never thought he was an orphan,' the old woman murmured. 'Even though we told him you were missing, presumed dead, he was sure that somehow you'd find him.'

Reggie put his arm around Molly, steadying.

'He knew I was alive?'

The nun looked down at the bench, as if suddenly fascinated

by the grain of the wood. 'I'm afraid we persuaded him that you would have come to find him if you'd survived.'

Molly remembered herself in the hospital bed, staring at the photo of a young boy in a newspaper. 'I knew I'd lost something,' she whispered. 'I just could never find out what. My memory didn't work for a very long time.'

'That explains a lot. We made enquiries but couldn't track you down. When the opportunity came, we told Jack to forget the past and move on.'

'Opportunity?' Reggie sounded sharp.

'Yes.' Sister Beatrice blinked at him. 'A Christian Brother came to visit us a few years ago. He offered all the children the chance to go to Australia to build a new life there.'

'Australia?'

'Jack was excited about going . . . The sunshine . . . the horses . . . all that fresh fruit . . .'

'*Australia?*'

The nun nodded. 'We never dreamed you would turn up like this.'

Reggie looked from Molly to Sister Beatrice. 'What else can you tell us?'

'It must have been 1947,' said the sister. 'He went out on the SS *Asturias*, the first ship out after the war. I believe he was bound for an orphanage in Western Australia.'

'But surely someone in authority needed to give permission?' asked Molly.

The nun looked out across the garden. 'Orphans didn't have to have anyone's permission,' she murmured.

Molly thrust a hand against her ear. 'But he wasn't an orphan!'

'We didn't know that.' Sister Beatrice's voice was firmer now. 'As far as we were concerned, Jack had no parents. We did the best we could.'

Reggie stood up. 'You've been very helpful, Sister.' He shook the woman's hand. 'It's a lot for Molly to take in. We need to go home and think about what we do next.'

Molly tugged at his sleeve. 'But I want to know more.'

'The light's going.' Reggie tilted his head towards the shadows on the path. 'And we've got a long journey. I'm sure Sister Beatrice will talk to you again.'

The nun inclined her head. 'We have a telephone here now,' she said. 'Just put in a call to Melchet House and ask for me.'

'Did Jack leave any message?' asked Molly.

The nun started. 'Oh! Yes, he did tell me something I was to pass on if you ever came to look for him.' Her forehead creased. 'I'm sorry, it's been a few years and my memory's not what it was.'

Molly sagged against the hard wood.

'If it comes back, I promise I'll let you know.'

Reggie scribbled Warlingham's number on the back of a cigarette packet and handed it to Sister Beatrice. If she hadn't been so anxious, Molly would've laughed at the elderly nun clutching an empty box of Luckies.

'This is my work number,' he said. 'Ask for Mr Edwardes.'

The packet disappeared into a fold of the nun's habit. She inclined her head again, then made her way slowly back up the drive.

Molly fizzed with suppressed energy on the bus home. 'I can't believe he's alive! It would be wonderful news if he wasn't so far away. We must find out where he was sent, go out there ourselves and get him. I can't have him in Australia. It's the other side of the world. He's my son. He needs to be with me.'

Reggie's arm tightened round her. 'Molly, calm down.'

'We'll get a ticket and go out and search for him.'

'Moll, it's a huge amount of money. It took a day's pay to get to Romsey. How could we afford to travel to Australia? And there's no guarantee he'll still be there. What if we can't find him? What if he's moved on somewhere else and there are no records?'

'Don't say that. There must be records. We've got to track him down.' Molly bit her lip.

'You've been apart for a long time. He's been given a chance of a new life in Australia. A far better life than we can afford to give him. Do you really want to bring him back to all this?' He waved his hand around vaguely.

Molly turned away towards the window. She wiped at the condensation angrily. After all she'd been through, was she *still* not to meet her own child? How could Reggie say such things? Of course Jack would want to come home to his mum – wouldn't he?

But then again, if he was having such a wonderful time in Australia, maybe he wouldn't want to leave. What could she offer him in return for such an adventure? Perhaps if she really loved him she shouldn't take him away. But she couldn't bear to think of never seeing him again.

'We must find him,' she said, 'even if it's just to give him a choice.'

'You mustn't set your hopes too high.'

Molly banged her head back against the padded seat and closed her eyes.

A week later, they both had news. Molly was laying the table and humming to herself when Reggie came through the door. She turned to him, beaming.

'You first,' she said, after they'd both tried to speak at once.

'No, you.' Reggie shrugged off his coat and hung it up on the hook in the hall. His face was grim.

'You. I insist.'

'All right.' He sighed. 'But I'm afraid it ain't good, Moll.'

A fork clattered to the floor. 'What's happened?'

Reggie rubbed his forehead. 'I've made some enquiries. Apparently, even if we do track Jack down, the authorities won't let me into Australia. They've got rules out there as tight as their arses and they sure don't like niggers.'

For once Molly didn't tell him off for his language. She reached for the nearest chair and crumpled into it. 'We've got to find a way,' she said faintly.

'If we do manage to save enough money, you'll have to go alone.'

She put her head in her hands. Could she go all that way without Reggie? And what if it wasn't Jack after all? And even if it was, he might not want to see her.

There was another reason, too. When she looked up, she knew her cheeks were red. 'I can't, Reggie. That's my news.' She placed her hand on her stomach. 'I'm pregnant.'

Two weeks later, Molly sat beside Reggie on the Tube, swallowing down the nausea exacerbated by the jolting train. The smell of overheated bodies and the smoke-clogged air did nothing to help either. She took a shallow breath and looked up at the posters advertising the Ideal Home Exhibition, Coca-Cola and something called the Blue Travel Line. A glum line of passengers sat opposite, obscured by a wall of *Daily Telegraph*s and *Daily Mirror*s. How strange that almost all their legs were crossed in the same direction.

Reggie helped her off the train when it stuttered to a halt on the platform. They made their way to the escalators. He was all solicitude over her pregnancy. She wondered what he really thought about trying to find Jack when he had a child of his own on the way. What would she have done in his position? She swallowed down another surge of sickness and clutched his arm as she swayed on the moving staircase, longing for the moment when they emerged from the subterranean world and into the bright London street.

*

The Marylebone convent was mercifully cool. It reminded her a little of Romsey, with its polish-and-incense smell and its long, gleaming corridors. They walked into the mother superior's office together. Another middle-aged woman staring at them inscrutably beneath a starched white headdress. Soft, pale face, expressionless grey eyes behind severe metal glasses. Above her head a painting of a beatifically smiling Virgin Mary, her hair suffused with gold light.

'Thank you for making an appointment, Mrs Edwardes.' After a disapproving glance in Reggie's direction, her gaze remained firmly on Molly. 'So you are looking for your son, who you say is called . . .' a swift glance at a beige memo pad in front of her, 'Jack Malloy.'

'Yes,' confirmed Molly, her mouth suddenly dry. 'My first child . . . with my late husband. Mick.'

'Mick Malloy?' The look was sudden and sharp.

Molly nodded.

'So you are not the boy's father.' The nun finally turned to Reggie.

He shook his head.

'Then I'm afraid I'll have to ask you to leave the room.'

He glowered at her. 'If I must.'

Molly plucked at Reggie's jacket. 'I need you here.'

'It's okay, Moll,' he said. 'I'll be right outside. You can come and get me whenever you want.' He stood up and left, closing the door behind him.

The nun remained motionless during the exchange. 'Now, Mrs Edwardes. I have to tell you that although we do have a record of a Jack Malloy leaving Southampton for Australia in September 1947, we cannot confirm conclusively that he's your son.'

'One of the nuns at Melchet . . . Sister Beatrice . . .' faltered

Molly, 'she knew Jack from when he was there and she said he looked a lot like me.'

The mother superior raised a single unplucked eyebrow. 'I'm afraid that does not constitute evidence.'

Molly was aware how lame her words sounded in this severe, cell-like room. Yet in the garden at Melchet, full of flowers and hope, everything had seemed so positive.

The nun sighed. 'I don't know how much you know about the project . . .' she began.

'Moving kids to Australia after the war,' ventured Molly. 'The kids they thought no one wanted.' She could hear the bitterness in her voice.

Again the sharp look. 'Taking children out of homes and giving them the chance of a lifetime,' corrected the nun.

'Taking them away from their parents?' returned Molly.

The mother superior put her elbows on the desk and looked across unblinkingly. 'Mrs Edwardes, our records showed that both Jack Malloy's parents were dead.'

Molly's ears roared. 'Then your records are wrong. When Jack and I were separated, I *was* a widow. That part is true. It was assumed I'd been killed in the bomb attack, as no one could find me. But it was my memory I'd lost, not my life.'

'Hmm.' The nun's face was still expressionless. Not an ounce of pity. 'Well, we had to assume the information we had at the time was correct. Our policy was to offer all orphan children a passage to Australia.'

'But he wasn't an orphan!' shouted Molly. She stood up and a volt of dizziness hit her.

Reggie burst through the door. 'What's going on?'

The mother superior stood up too. 'I'm afraid I have to repeat my request for you to remain outside, Mr Edwardes.' She hadn't raised her voice, but her tone was full of iron.

Reggie turned to Molly. 'Are you all right?'

'Yes.' She flapped her hand weakly over her face. 'Yes, it's fine, Reg – go.'

Reggie departed reluctantly.

The nun resumed her seat. She rested her palms on the table and watched Molly.

'Jack Malloy, if he is your son, is having a wonderful life in Australia. Imagine him, outdoors in the fresh air and sunshine, riding, fishing, swimming in the river . . . having endless opportunities. What boy in his position wouldn't think himself in paradise?'

'But I just want to let him know I haven't forgotten him. That I think about him all the time . . .' She felt her eyes welling up. 'That I love him dearly.'

'Mrs Edwardes. It is not our policy to pass on contact details, and so much time has passed we would not know where he was now anyway. I simply cannot break with protocol. Even for you.' Her voice softened. 'Sometimes, my dear, we have to make the greater sacrifice. We have to put the children and their interests first.'

Molly glanced up at the picture of Mary above the nun's head. Mary lost *her* son, didn't she? How come they always showed her smiling? Why did artists and sculptors feel compelled to create a mask over the hurt?

245

'Let him go,' the mother superior continued. 'This boy may not be your missing son, but even if he is, he's made a new start. Any communication from you would only unsettle him. Concentrate on your new family now. That's the best you can do for Jack.' Molly hadn't told the nun she was pregnant, but she wondered if she had an inkling. Her hands went to her stomach. I'll never let this baby out of my sight, she thought.

She stood up. 'If Jack ever does get in touch, will you promise me you'll let me know?'

The nun bowed her head. 'Of course.'

When Molly joined Reggie in the corridor, she gave a tearful shake of her head in response to his enquiring expression.

'Take me home, Reg,' she said. They walked wearily out of the building.

24

Jack knocked on the door.

'Come in.' The careers officer sat in a cloud of pipe smoke, his whiskery cheeks and tweed jacket oddly incongruous at the school desk, as if he were an ageing pupil who'd been kept back year after year. 'Jack Sullivan?' Behind him was a series of hastily erected posters. *Your future in our hands*, read one; the caption on another was *How to stand out and get noticed*.

Jack sat down in front of the man. He glanced at the desk on which lay a piece of foolscap paper with his name on.

'Date of birth?'

'The twelfth of April 1936.' It was as good a date as any. The nuns had never celebrated Jack's birthday and there'd certainly been no mention of it at Bindoon. But John had one day claimed to have had some communication from England, and a few weeks later, Jack had come down to breakfast one day to find a pile of presents by his plate.

'Hmm,' said the man. 'Seventeen . . .' He firmed his lips as though Jack's age gave him particular cause for disapproval. 'You'll be doing your national service next year. One hundred and seventy-six days.'

'Yes, sir.' Jack didn't know how he felt about becoming a

Nasho. Might make him fitter and stronger. That could be useful. Other than that, it was just something to get through.

'And after that?'

Jack cleared his throat. 'I thought the law.' He'd been determined to enter the police force ever since he'd found out about Sam. There was no chance of him launching an investigation on his own. No one would believe the words of a young lad. He needed to get qualified before he could do anything. But when he'd mentioned it to John, he'd told him to aim higher. Typical John. Having a lawyer in the family would give him more status than a cop. But maybe he was right. It'd take longer to train, but perhaps this was a more powerful way of looking into Sam's death. And he'd be more likely to make his own decisions as a lawyer. He'd had enough of carrying out someone else's orders.

The man's next glance was more positive. 'An admirable profession. Four years at university. Perth'll be fine. The University of Western Australia.' He scrawled something across the paper. 'Good luck, Sullivan.'

Jack got to his feet, realising the interview was over.

*

All Molly could do was count . . .

One, two, three, four as the pain marched round the walls.

One, two as it pulsed from ceiling to floor.

One, two, three as it zigzagged across the room and back again.

'You're doing well,' said a calm female voice. A white cap loomed into view. 'Use the facepiece when it's bad, dear.' A rubber contraption was thrust into her hands, like a gas mask. For a few seconds she imagined she was back in the Blitz, and strained her ears, briefly immune to the pain, but no, all she could hear were hospital noises: the hum of machinery, the soft tread of shoes, and, far off, a baby's cry. In a few hours she'd be a mother again. She'd have a baby in her arms. Hers and Reggie's. She lowered her chin and grimaced through another contraction.

After a while, the waves came too fast to be counted. Their rhythm was lost. Just a relentless onslaught of pain. Molly threw herself across the bed, trying to escape.

'Come on now, Mrs Edwardes.' The serene voice spoke again. 'That won't do baby any good. Try to lie still.' Molly did as she was told, glancing across at the young nurse. She had a shiny face and dark-blonde hair pushed back into the paper-stiff white cap. She stroked Molly's hand. 'Do you remember last time?'

Molly had told them she'd had another child, although she barely remembered Jack's birth. 'That was long ago,' she said, and winced, both from the pain and the reminder. 'If he's still alive, my son will be seventeen by now.'

'Gosh, that's a big gap.' The girl hurried forward as Molly gave a long, low groan and thrust her hand out for more gas and air.

Eventually came a new rhythm. She marked it with staccato breaths and an intuitive need to submit to the primitive down-ward force.

'You're doing well,' said the nurse again. Molly could feel the battle being won as she fought off the attacks of pain. 'Nearly there now . . .'

A fumble, a slapping sound, then an indignant cry. She looked down with surprise and relief. At last it was over.

'What is it?' she asked.

A second's hesitation, then, 'Congratulations, Mrs Edwardes, you have a baby girl.' A warm, slippery weight was pressed into her arms.

Molly smiled. A daughter. 'We're calling her Susan,' she said.

The baby was beautiful. Her skin was darkest caramel, a gorgeous mixture of Molly and Reggie's tones. She had his nose, and despite the vernix covering her head like a lace cap, his black wiry hair was clearly visible. She was perfect. Molly smoothed the creases on the plump little wrists, so deep it looked as though she had elastic bands round them. Susan was making little sneezing and snuffling noises and struggling to open her eyes.

But why hadn't the nurses admired her? Surely they could see how beautiful she was. They were folding towels and writing up their notes in silence. Was Susan all right?

'Is anything wrong?' Molly asked hoarsely. Her throat was so dry. And that gas mask had made her feel sick.

One of the nurses shook her head. Yet Molly was sure a look passed between them. She sighed. It must be Susan's colour. She hoped other people would be more tolerant of her beautiful baby, otherwise life was going to be very hard for her.

Outside the ward, Reggie had an uneasy wait with a line of other fidgeting husbands. All those white hands: tapping, scratching, clenching, flexing. Reggie's were the only black ones in the row. By the time he was called in to see Molly, he was surprised they hadn't turned white with worry.

Once he'd heard a scream and thought it was Molly. He'd hammered on the door, demanding to be let in, but Matron had turned him away.

'Stay outside with the other fathers-to-be,' she'd said, looking at him disapprovingly. 'I don't know how you do things where you come from, but in England husbands wait outside. We'll summon you when your wife and child are ready to see you.'

Reggie had returned to his seat and taken out his cigarettes, rigid with frustration. A bit of red string was wrapped round the packet. He went to flick it away, then stopped. It wasn't rubbish. It was something Mudda had sent him when he'd written to tell her Molly was expecting. *It'll run duppy, son. I tied it round your wrist when you were born and I'd like you to use it for your own child.* She'd held onto it all these years. Maybe it *had* protected him from evil: he'd been kept safe during the war and again on the *Windrush*. Perhaps it had led him to Molly. It could do no harm. He would put it on the baby in Mudda's honour. In the other pocket was a small black bible she'd given him too. Jamaican mothers put them in cribs to keep the baby safe. Reggie started to turn the tissue-thin pages. Wasn't it supposed to be left open at a psalm? Before he found his place, Matron appeared again.

'Mr Edwardes?' She seemed to be looking at a spot past his right ear. 'You have a baby daughter. You may see her and your wife now.'

Reggie stood up, scattering his cigarettes onto the floor. He bent to retrieve them and return them to his pocket. But without him noticing, the red string had disappeared into the dust under his seat.

Reggie was utterly smitten with his daughter. 'She's the best of us both, Moll,' he declared, holding her carefully between his large brown hands. Susan squinted up at him, her dark eyes trying to focus on his features. He stroked her chin carefully and she opened her little mouth. Reggie leaned forward to savour her warm baby fragrance.

'You're a gorgeous little lady. A real princess, like your mother.'

Molly looked across at them both. If I had a camera, she thought, I'd take a photograph of them and treasure it always. Instead she stared hard at her husband and daughter, trying to imprint the picture on the pages of her memory so she would never lose this moment.

Reggie continued to talk to Susan, and Molly leaned back against the pillows. It'd been a difficult labour. Although she didn't consciously remember giving birth to Jack, a few blurred recollections filtered through, like an old fuzzy newsreel. She remembered a searing pain in her back and her belly. She could vaguely picture the same white starched caps and hear the gentle female voices. And that of a stern doctor. Yet even he had sounded triumphant when he called out, 'It's a boy!' She remembered Mick too, afterwards, a trembling glass of beer in his hand to wet the baby's head. Women said you forgot childbirth but it all came back when you went through it again. Oh yes. But at least this time things would be easier. Molly wouldn't have to look after this baby on her own as she'd had to do with Jack for a time. Please God, Susan's dad was here to stay.

Reggie went home to dig a hole for the afterbirth and cord, intending to plant a tree for Susan there later, but when he returned for them, the hospital informed him they'd been incinerated. What strange traditions they had in England. He'd wandered round the prefab at a loss for what to do. There must be some way he could celebrate. It had crossed his mind to ask one of the other fathers out for a drink, but none of them had spoken to him. Apart from the run-in with Matron, the only conversation he'd had was with a yardie orderly when they'd briefly reminisced about Jamrock, as all her countrymen called Jamaica.

Nothing else for it. He'd hopped on a bus down to the Locarno. The place was as busy as when he'd taken Molly there on their wedding night. What an evening that'd been. He made his way round the dance floor, towards the tables on the far side. There were his brethren: Lester, Deelon and Major – all sitting at the same table as a year ago, as if they'd never left.

'I'm a fadda!' Reggie announced.

Major got him the first drink: Reggie didn't have to buy another the whole night. It was only the next morning, after the aspirin had cleared his head, that he realised he'd lost the red string. Perhaps, he told himself, in an attempt to be philosophical, it was just an old superstition. But something nagged at him deep down. His mother wasn't well educated, but she was wise. She must have thought the string was important. It couldn't have been easy for her to compose an accompanying note in her childlike scrawl, painstakingly copy down the address Reggie had sent, then trudge down to the old post office at Crofts Hill, waiting in line with folk who wanted to know the reason her son hadn't visited her in years and fend off questions as to why he'd married a white woman when there were plenty of lovely Jamaican girls back home.

Poor Mudda, with her strange old ways. Reggie swallowed down his guilt and uneasiness. Maybe he'd send her a photo of Susan to make up for his neglect. When he had time.

After a few days, they brought Susan home. They'd splashed out on a taxi from the hospital, as Molly was worried about her catching cold on the bus. Reggie made Molly put her feet up with a cup of tea while he carried his daughter around the prefab, introducing her to her new home. 'Here's the kitchen. Here's Mudda and Dada's room. This is where you're going to sleep.' He looked overjoyed to be holding her. Matron had had so many strict rules, he'd been wary of even picking her up in the hospital.

She slept by their bed so that Molly could watch her face, translucent in the moonlight. At the first cry she'd lift her carefully from the empty drawer that served as a cradle and put her to her breast, almost before Susan had woken up. Then she would watch her tiny mouth, surprisingly strong, pull and suck while her miniature hand pressed up against Molly's chest. Sometimes Molly felt Reggie smiling at them in the darkness of the womb-like room. And the walls lost their daytime rigidity and cocooned them all.

The milestones brought back more memories – first smile, first tooth, first whole night's sleep. Sometimes, half awake, she would hold her mewling daughter and imagine it was Jack she cuddled. She sang the songs she'd sung him and whispered the same endearments, remembering his bright eyes seeking hers before they drooped in sleep. She knew instinctively what Susan wanted: which cry said hunger and which meant she was tired. Had Jack taught her that? His baby presence stayed with her, shadowing Susan; providing memories and comfort. Yet haunting her too.

The pregnancy had sapped Molly's health and energy. 'As soon as you've had the baby, we'll get some help with our search, Moll. We'll find him. Just you see.' And Molly had smiled, although privately she'd wondered if Reggie had any idea how parenthood would change things.

She often thought of Jack when she sat nursing Susan, particularly during the two o'clock feed when the house was silent and it seemed like they were the only creatures awake in the world. How were his new parents treating him? In spite of only having him for five years, Molly knew Jack was bright. He could read and write at four, and he was forever asking questions. Perhaps he'd been allowed to stay on at school in Australia. Was he, even now, slipping into the clothes some other woman had bought him? Did she make sure he ate properly? Hug him when he was upset? Or help him with his homework? Had she marked his height on the back of the kitchen door as he grew up? Did Jack used to say *look at me, Mummy* to her as he had with Molly? Did she tell him she loved him?

When Molly's imagination tortured her, she tried to focus on the past. As a baby, Jack had been quiet much of the time but with an insistent cry when he wanted something. She thought of him as a toddler too, running through the house on his stout little legs, holding Mick's hand, or once putting his finger on the end of Mick's cigarette before letting out a wail of outrage. Sometimes when she stood over Susan's bed, listening to her gurgling and admiring her starfish fingers, she saw the ghost of Jack at a similar age. She would catch her breath at the memory.

Pictures came to her mind: bending over the kitchen table with Jack doing a jigsaw; Mick carrying Jack upstairs when he'd fallen asleep on the floor; and after Mick had died, she and Jack dancing to Glenn Miller on the wireless. Before the bomb that had ripped them apart. Jack was a frozen child, forever trapped in her mind in his five-year-old body. Molly could no more imagine him at eighteen than she could fly.

Part Four

1955–1958

25

Rosie dragged the battered cardboard box down the drive, grimacing at the weary scraping sound. It smelled horrible. Empty cans sat on top of flaccid vegetable peelings, tea leaves and bits of gristle. Sullivan rubbish. The remains of yet another meal she'd prepared and served. For a second she wondered what her mum would have thought of all this skivvying she did. There'd been plenty of chores at home: sweeping, washing, cooking, but they'd shared them. She and Alkira had hauled the dirty clothes down to the river, scrubbing the garments on stones to clean them, or foraged in the bush for *woorines*, always making sure they left some of the yam in the ground so that it grew back again for others to enjoy. Mum had done most of the cooking and cleaning and Cobar and Darel had done the heavy work – hunting, chopping up firewood, building shelters. But here it was all down to Rosie. She wondered how Mum was managing on her own. A sudden image of her mother sitting outside their house, crying, came into her mind and she snapped it off forcibly. It was too painful to remember her family.

There'd been a bin shortage that year. Perth had run out of sheet iron after the war so Kathleen hadn't been able to buy a new bin when John'd thrown out the broken old one. Stuff had to be put in boxes and piled up instead. Rosie still had several to collect and then all the housework to do. She stopped to wipe her forehead. Kathleen kept her busy. But she could be kind too, often giving her extra food and even a few old clothes. Not like *warra wirrin* John. He treated her more like a slave than a servant. Rosie spat into the rubbish, wishing it were John's tea, then smirked at the frothy globule glistening on top of the garbage as though a spittlebug had squirted there.

An old lipstick case gleamed from the depths of the box. She thrust in a hand, wincing as the warm mulch squelched between her fingers, and drew out the case with a flourish. Carefully she twisted off the top, noticing with satisfaction that a slick of crimson still greased the bottom. She inserted her little finger into the case, scraping some of the red waxy substance under her nail, and smeared it tentatively over her lips. Then she arched her back and raised her face to the sun, allowing its warmth to bathe her skin for a moment before stiffening in surprise as the front door slammed shut. It was Jack, striding towards her with a pile of books under his arm and a college scarf, already streaked with sweat, knotted round his neck.

'G'day, Rosie.'

She looked up at him, conscious of her red-stained mouth.

But Jack didn't seem to notice. 'Isn't it your afternoon off today?' he asked, looking down at the ground.

'Yes.' Rosie wondered what he had in mind.

'Great. If I wag lectures, would you like to go to Kings Park? I could do with a break from all that studying.'

Rosie glanced nervously at the house, but no one peered out of the windows and the front door remained closed. 'I'd like that.'

'Good. Shall I meet you by the main gates at two?'

Rosie loved it when Jack smiled. She nodded, then bent over the rubbish box again as he walked quickly off down the road, whistling.

Rosie glanced sideways at his departing back. She could trust Jack. They'd become friends over time; thrown together by shared wariness of John, although Jack was treated a lot better than her on account of him being a *wadjela*. She often wondered why he never brought girls home. He seemed to prefer her company. But they were older now. Was it safe to go to the park with him? Some boys were like *gympie gympies*, those plants with beautiful heart-shaped leaves that delivered a deadly poison when touched. But not Jack, surely.

Like her, he had lost a mother. He hadn't told her much about his first mum, but it was enough to make her feel for him. She understood his loss more than most, and although he put a brave face on things, as she did, she felt as though the sadness in both their pasts created a bond between them.

A thinly whistled tune drifted back to her and she pictured his face as he'd looked at her earlier: open, eager. He felt that bond too. She'd be safe with Jack.

*

Rosie got to Kings Park first. She peered through the black metallic gates at the people ambling around the botanical gardens. A mother in a wide-brimmed straw hat pushed a pram in which perched a small child who leaned sideways towards the flower bed, brushing the plant heads with his fingers and scattering petals. Two elderly ladies pointing out shrubs to each other stopped and stared. The mother jerked the pram away.

A family group followed: a couple with a toddler in between them holding their hands. Every few seconds the parents swung the child off the ground, its excited laughter drifting back to Rosie.

It had been a hot day, and the sprinklers were on. From her viewpoint behind the gates, Rosie saw shimmering rainbows in the jets of water arcing into the blue sky. They washed the stale air and made the grass smell sweet. Nearer by, a flock of ringnecks pecked at the wet turf, ready to pounce on any worms that came to the surface.

The sound of pounding feet made her turn.

Jack was running towards the gates, grinning at her. 'Sorry, got held up.' He was panting slightly. 'Shall we go in?' He pulled back the gate and motioned Rosie ahead of him.

She walked quickly. She'd never liked the formal part of Kings Park. The garish arrangements of gerberas, nemesia and linaria; the circular beds that looked like Kathleen's gaudy dinner plates; the smartly dressed people, all of whom seemed to be staring at them. She put her head down.

'You all right?' Jack was striding confidently past the elderly women, seemingly unaware that they'd found a new object of disapproval. 'It's lovely here, isn't it?'

Rosie didn't reply. Out of the corner of her eye she caught a park keeper bearing down on them.

'Rosie?'

'Folk round here don't like to see us together.' Another couple were staring at them, talking in low voices.

'Well, folk can mind their own business.'

Rosie glanced behind her. The disapproving people, the rigid railings, the manicured lawns were closing in on her. She needed open space to breathe. 'Let's go to the bush.' She quickened her step. Beyond the formal gardens lay the wild area, behind Mount Eliza, where the blue hills of the Darling Ranges bruised the horizon. That was Noongar territory. Mooro Katta, they used to call it. The *gubba* garden planners hadn't meddled that far. And they would be less likely to meet people there.

'Okay.'

Rosie didn't pause until the lush grass had turned to dry stubble and the paintbox colours faded to pale green and ochre. When they looked back, the park keeper was a tiny dot, the other people nowhere to be seen.

Rosie took off her shoes and wriggled her toes on the hot ground. That was better. Jack raised an eyebrow at her.

She tucked the shoes behind a balga. 'I need to feel the earth under my feet. It's safer that way.' She made a mark in front of the shrub so she would find them on the way back.

'Safer! When you could step on a scorpion or a dugite at any moment?'

'Nah! Don't judge me by your soft ways.' Teasing Jack made her feel less like a maid, more like a friend. She led the way, pausing after a while to point out gecko tracks like tiny handprints cut through by a long wavy line. Further on was a mound of slimy brown pellets: *koomak* scat. She stood on tiptoe, squinting up into a leafy gum tree, and saw a loose bundle of straw-coloured sticks balanced on a branch. Yes, that was his nest.

'What are you looking at?' Jack was standing close to her, shielding his eyes against the sunlight, still strong despite the trees.

'A *koomak* nest. You'd call it a possum.'

'I can't see a possum.'

Rosie laughed. 'You won't see one at this time of day. They're night creatures. They'll be hiding somewhere.'

'How do you know all this stuff?'

She could feel Jack's admiration growing but wasn't sure she deserved it. Every one of her people understood the bush. Her brothers had learned how to track almost before they could walk. 'If I didn't know about it, it would be like not knowing about my left arm.'

'I wish I'd grown up here. There are so many things I don't understand.'

'Don't say that. You must know English stuff.'

Jack wrinkled his forehead. 'I remember making acorn pipes in the woods at the orphanage.'

'Acorn pipes?'

'Yes, at Melchet there were oak trees everywhere. In the

autumn, if you took the really big acorns out of their holders, you were left with the dry cups with a stalk on the end, like miniature pipes. We used to stuff them with dried leaves and pretend to smoke them in the woods where the nuns never tracked us down.'

Rosie tried to imagine Jack as a little boy. She shut her eyes and saw him: thin-limbed, with bright eyes and choco-late-brown hair. 'What were the nuns like?'

'Some were cruel.' Jack grabbed a low-slung branch that Rosie had swept aside, before it sprang back at him. He released the branch once he was safely past, then stood deep in thought.

'But you had friends there, didn't you?' Rosie didn't like to think of Jack being lonely. He'd told her about Molly but said little about the orphanage.

Jack described Bert, how he'd been kind at Melchet but turned nasty on the boat. And at Bindoon.

Rosie drew a circle in the ground with her toe. Jack hadn't mentioned anything about Bindoon before. She wondered what it'd been like.

'Were you happy there?'

'Happy?' Jack laughed, but it wasn't a good laugh. 'I hated it. I was so relieved to get away to the Sullivans. The brothers were appalling.' He blinked a couple of times, and Rosie wondered what picture he was seeing in his head. He yanked at a banksia branch until it snapped. 'I got out, but my best friend died there.'

Rosie looked at him in horror. 'What happened?'

Jack hurled the branch away into the undergrowth. 'He was

killed in an accident. Supposedly. That's why I want to become a lawyer, to find out.'

'Good for you.'

'Anyway, let's not talk about the past,' said Jack. 'Lead on!'

Rosie glanced at him in sympathy, then set off again down the track.

As they picked up the pace, Rosie was vaguely conscious of tufts of spinifex brushing her ankles through the sandy soil, but Jack didn't seem to notice. He was marching straight ahead with a set look on his face. Poor Jack, she thought. How terrible to lose his friend like that. No wonder he had a score to settle.

A parrot screeched in the distance, but Jack probably wasn't aware of it or, nearer at hand, the *chir-p, chir-p* of a cockatoo. Rosie stopped to see if she could spot the noisy bird nestling in a eucalyptus. She tipped back her head to scan the branches.

At first she was so absorbed in her search, she thought the sharp cry had come from within the tree. Even through the leaves the sun was dazzling; she shielded her eyes to see better.

But then Jack screamed her name.

Instantly she was on her knees beside him, scrutinising the dust. A spike-limbed spider, a bright splash of crimson on its shiny fat tummy, was scuttling away. 'Redback,' she said, wincing.

'Bugger!' said Jack. 'I can't believe I was that careless.' He looked down at his calf, already red and starting to swell. 'I haven't brought anything with me. I need some aspirin and ice quickly. Might even have to go to hospital.'

'Nah,' said Rosie. 'You'll be all right. But you mustn't move. Otherwise the venom will spread.' She put her arm round Jack's shoulders and steered him to a nearby boab before making him sit down, easing his back against its solid trunk.

Jack's face was white. 'Shouldn't you be sucking it out or something?'

Rosie shook her head. 'You'll be fine. Just do as I say.' She settled herself next to him and put her hand to his chest. Once the galloping pulse had slowed, she spoke again.

'You'll feel better after an hour. I promise.'

'I can't sit here for an hour.' Jack looked pale, and a few tears of sweat gleamed on his forehead.

'Yes you can, I'll talk to you.'

Jack sighed sharply and looked away. Rosie waited until his body relaxed, until he turned back to her and leaned in close.

Her skin prickled. She'd never been this near to Jack before. When she nestled her head on his shoulder, he didn't pull away. 'I'll tell you a Dreaming,' she said.

'What?'

'It's a story of how places came about.'

'Places like Kings Park?'

'Yes.' Rosie picked up a stick from the ground. She leaned forward, trying to keep the rest of her body still, so as not to lose the contact with Jack, then started to draw patterns in the dirt. They echoed in her mind: shadowy shapes swirling, dissolving and re-forming. 'It was made by the Wagyl.' She made the stick zigzag backwards and forwards, then repeated the movement beside the first set of marks. Then she drew some shapes in between the lines. She made the drawing pointed at one end and round at the other. 'That's the Wagyl.'

Jack was watching her more intently now. 'It's a snake!'

'Yes, a Dreamtime snake. It made the Swan river, and the Canning.'

'It must have been very big.'

'Huge.' Rosie was still working on the drawing, adding fangs and eyes. 'But not as big as the Rainbow Serpent who made the universe. Him murry big.' The Noongar expression escaped before she'd realised. The Sullivans insisted she spoke only 'proper English'. She had to be so careful with them. Yet her guard had slipped with Jack.

He hadn't seemed to notice. 'So what did else did the Wagyl make?'

'The Darling Scarp. He had a great big body.' Rosie mimed his actions on the ground with her hands. 'He slithered over the land, whipping up hills with his tail and pressing down gullies with his weight.' Her fingers were moving all the time, creating shapes. 'Some of the gullies filled with water and made rivers, but when he stopped for a rest he made big, big holes that the rain watered and they became lakes and bays. As he moved, some of his scales scraped off and became forests and woods. And his scat . . .' Rosie pushed the dust into heaps, 'created piles of rocks. Sacred sites.'

'Wow.' Jack looked fascinated. He seemed to have forgotten the pain in his ankle. 'Is the Wagyl still alive?'

'Oh yes, he lives deep underground. Beneath the springs of Lake Monger.'

'Could you find him?'

'No.' Rosie frowned. 'I think he's asleep.'

'I'm not surprised after all that hard work.'

Rosie looked at Jack steadily. He'd better not be teasing her. But his expression was genuine. She shrugged and nodded.

Jack felt his calf and winced. The skin was stretched tightly. It looked hot.

'It needs a bit longer,' said Rosie. 'Just be patient.'

Jack grimaced.

'Let's keep talking,' she said. It would take his mind off the pain.

Jack leaned back. 'Tell me about your family,' he said, after a bit.

Rosie hadn't been prepared for that. She'd enjoyed telling Jack about the Dreaming, but this was a harder subject. She started to scratch around in the dust again. When she eventually spoke, she was conscious how lifeless her voice sounded. Best just to give the facts quickly.

'I was born in Narrogin. Mum was a full-blood but Dad wasn't. He was lighter-skinned, not Aboriginal. He was in the army, off serving his country. There was just Mum and us kids at home. When Mum went to the shop the Welfare came and grabbed us. The boys were sent to the Wandering Mission and Alkira and I ended up at Moore River.' She picked up a piece of boab bark and started to break it into pieces, trying to suppress the memory of her sister's cries. 'I'm two years older than Alkira, so I was the first to go. I haven't seen her since I started at the Sullivans'.'

Jack took the bark pieces from her and placed them on the ground. Then he covered her fingers with his own. 'I know how that feels,' he said. 'I didn't have any brothers and sisters but I still miss my mum.'

The warmth from Jack's hands crept through her body. Rosie swallowed. 'Maybe one day I'll get back to the settlement. See if I can look up Alkira, although she might have gone out to a family by now. I don't know if I'll ever see Cobar and Darel again. Mum must be tearing her hair out. I just hope Dad survived.' She blinked several times. She mustn't cry. Not after she'd held back the tears for so long. The only way to survive was to keep busy. And not think.

When the sound of manic laughter echoed through the bush, they both started. Rosie imagined for a second it was the Welfare people come back to gloat. Then she caught a flash of sapphire deep inside a tree.

Jack had spotted it too. 'Aha! A kookaburra!'

'Yeah, he's laughing at you.' Rosie forced a grin. 'Can't believe you know so little about the bush.'

Jack pulled her hair playfully, then rose shakily to his feet.

'Come on, Rosie-Posie. I'm feeling better and it's getting late. We ought to go back.'

Jack had glanced at his watch, but Rosie was watching the huge red sun sinking low in the sky and listening to the whisperings from the shadows beneath the eucalyptus trees. She looked at Jack in alarm.

'Oh no, Mrs Sullivan will kill me.'

26

Molly sat at the table in the neat little prefab kitchen, a thin blue sheet of paper in front of her. Several similar pieces were scrunched up in the bin by her feet.

Susan was in bed and Reggie was at the club, as usual. She'd intended to do a bit of mending while she listened to *The Archers*, but something made her go to the drawer and take out the airmail paper she'd stowed there ages ago. She'd wanted to write to Jack then, but Reggie had persuaded her they needed to hear back from the Sally Army first. So she'd waited until Jack was eighteen to contact them, only to find out he'd left Bindoon with a private couple. Then, once she'd had Susan, there never seemed to be any time, with all the feeding and washing. And she was always too exhausted to concentrate. But Susan was a little easier now, and with Reggie at the club, she finally had some time to herself. Tonight, she was absolutely determined that she would write the letter.

The Calor Gas stove hissed beside her feet. She'd moved it into the kitchen as the lino was so cold. Behind the cheerful green-checked curtains, the rain pitter-pattered against the window. She hoped Reggie would take care driving home. They hadn't had the Zodiac for long.

He'd used up all money they'd put by on the car. 'We'll start saving for Australia after that,' he'd said. 'I must have some wheels now, though. I'm never out in time to catch the last bus, and it'll be cheaper to get a car in the long run than all those taxis. And besides, we can use it to take Susan to the seaside at weekends.' He knew he'd get her with that one. Always Susan. Never Jack. But how could she argue with giving their own child a better life?

She'd been so patient. She'd waited for months to see if the Salvation Army could track Jack down or if, by a miracle, he had contacted Sister Beatrice. And every so often Reggie would try the British Embassy to see if they could do anything. But the answer was always the same. It seemed as though all trace of Jack had vanished. Reggie assured her she just had to be patient. He was getting a few spots at the Locarno now. People loved his voice and there was starting to be a demand for Jamaican music. 'Times are changing, Moll,' he'd said. 'We'll keep pestering those Aussies and those stiff-necked nuns and one day we'll get there. And we'll keep saving, too. I'll set some money aside from what the Locarno pays me. We'll have that air fare before you know it.'

Molly had nodded, although privately she'd doubted it. It would cost an enormous amount. Far more than they could ever afford. Sometimes she felt that everything was stacked against them. She hadn't worked since Susan had arrived, and although Reggie was making good money at the club on top of his Warlingham salary, there was seldom much left over. Things always came along that needed paying for.

Like the car. Sometimes the longing and vexation made her feel she was back under the care of Dr Lee. Thank goodness she had Susan to look after; without her she'd have gone demented.

But she had to do something. She decided to write to Jack care of Bindoon to see if the Christian Brothers would forward the letter. It was worth a try.

Molly hadn't told Reggie, but when she'd taken Susan to the clinic for her diphtheria vaccination, she'd not used the extra money he'd given her to pop into Lyons afterwards for a bun and a drink. She'd taken the Tube to Marylebone to visit the convent head office instead. There she'd pleaded with the clerk at the desk to give her an address for Bindoon. Thankfully Susan had looked suitably woebegone after her jab, and that, combined with the genuine tears Molly had shed while telling her tale, was sufficient to engage the clerk's sympathy.

'Here you are,' he'd said, passing a slip of paper over the counter to her. 'Not a word, mind. It's more than my job's worth.'

'Thanks,' said Molly. 'I'm really grateful.'

'Good luck!' the clerk had said, winking at her.

She'd smiled at him before turning the pram round ready to leave. She knew there was only a slim chance of a letter reaching Jack, but at least she was taking control at last.

Dear Jack, Molly wrote. She'd experimented with *Dear Son,* and that was what she really wanted to write, but decided not to force the issue early on. It might antagonise him. *You will be surprised to hear from me after all these years. Please don't throw this away.* She had a horror of that. Jack not giving her a chance to explain. *You must consider me a very bad mother. Or did you think I was dead? I was badly injured in the bomb attack that destroyed our house in the war. I was taken to hospital in Warlingham, not far from where we lived. I got better but had lost my memory. I was in hospital for several years. No one could tell me who I was or what had happened to me. So many records had been destroyed in the war. I didn't even know my name, let alone that I had a son. Please understand, Jack. I just had no idea.*

Molly put the top of the pen between her teeth. What kind of young man was Jack? Was he sensitive and kind? Would he be reading her letter carefully, perhaps wiping away a tear when he realised how she'd suffered, or would he be tight-lipped with anger and on the verge of tearing up the paper? She had to keep him reading.

Eventually I started to get better. I left Warlingham and got married. Probably best not to say too much about Reggie. Jack might have become as intolerant as other Australians were said to be.

Molly strained her ears. Was that a sound from upstairs? Susan had had a few nightmares lately. She put down her pen, tiptoed up and opened the door to Susan's room. She was sitting up in bed, her hair sticking out like a brush.

'Come on, little lady,' whispered Molly. 'You've just had a bad dream.' She picked her up for a cuddle, rocking her backwards and forwards in her arms. But she was still thinking of

276

the letter as she did so. It was so important to get it right. Every word had to be perfect.

Susan became heavy; she'd fallen asleep again. Molly laid her gently in her cot and she turned over without a word. She probably wouldn't wake until the morning.

Molly had often tried to see Jack in Susan when she'd been tiny, but she could never detect any similarities. After a while, she'd given up. Susan was a new person, she told herself, not the reincarnation of her first child. She'd a right to be herself.

She read over the letter again. It wasn't faultless, but it was the best so far. If she tore up another attempt she'd never get it done before Reggie returned. And Susan always got her up at the crack of dawn. She'd better keep going.

I'd always felt strange whenever I saw pictures of young lads in the papers but never knew why. I managed to get a little job in a dress shop. One day a lady came in with a young boy she called Jack. That was the trigger. I finally remembered I was a mother. I remembered you.

Should she tell Jack about the 'grave' at Warlingham? It might upset him if he realised how easily she'd been persuaded he was dead. She'd still been recovering then, though. And Dr Lee and Reggie had gone along with it. No, better to tell him the lengths she'd gone to in trying to track him down – as well as convince him of the obstacles in her way.

I tried very hard to find you, I really did. Reggie, my husband, managed to discover you'd been sent down to Hampshire after the attack. You were in a children's home there – Melchet House – do you recall it? Molly could still picture the elderly nun who'd told them Jack had been a child migrant. *We went there to take you home*

277

but Sister Beatrice told us you'd gone to Australia. She wondered whether Jack remembered Sister Beatrice. Another woman who'd tried to be his mother. She massaged her forehead. Why couldn't he have his real mother? She hated the thought of other women looking after him. Sometimes she felt gnawed by jealousy.

I was horrified. Reggie and I weren't wealthy. We still aren't. We couldn't afford to go to Australia. Then the baby came along. You have a younger sister called Susan.

She glanced at the clock. Eleven thirty. She stretched, then went to get some water, reading over the letter again as she sipped from the glass.

I hope you are having a nice life, Jack. It must be wonderful to be under sunny skies all day long. I expect you are very tanned. You always looked like your dad. Do write and tell me what you're up to. To think of you, a Croydon boy, over in Australia. I bet you can do all sorts now. Do you have lots of friends? How are you getting on at work? He must have a job by now. Molly wondered what he did. I mustn't ask too many questions, she thought. Men hate that. And Jack was a man now. Just one more question, though. The really important one.

Did you think I was dead? Is that why you went to Australia? Or did you know I was alive but wanted to get away from your cruel mother? Was that a bit too strong? She couldn't cross it out. Jack would still read it. Perhaps if she put down the words she feared were in his head, then they wouldn't be. She'd always been a good mother to him. But could he remember that? She wanted him to know she still could be.

278

Write to me as soon as you get this. We could try to send you some money for a ticket. It would be much easier for you to come to England than for us to go out to you. Please do think about it. I miss you so much. And I really am so very sorry.

She leaned back in the chair. How should she end the letter? It had to be right. In the end, she compromised:

Your loving mother, Molly.

She read it through once more and nodded to herself. Then she put it into a blue envelope with dark blue and red stripes round the edge. She copied the address carefully, wrote 'Please forward' across the top and slipped it into her handbag. She'd take it to the post office when she took Susan out in the pram tomorrow.

As she rubbed cold cream into her face in the steamed-up bathroom mirror, Molly decided not to tell Reggie she'd written to Jack. She knew he wanted to be the one to track him down for her. He was always trying to make her happy. But he was so busy working, and besides, if Jack didn't reply – and in her heart of hearts she didn't really expect him to – then Reggie would be none the wiser.

She wandered into the bedroom and climbed under the brown-and-white counterpane, pulling it up to her chin to keep herself warm. By the time Reggie came in, she was fast asleep.

*

As soon as John left for work that morning, Kathleen opened her underwear drawer. She rifled through the nylon roll-ups and bullet bras, even the old rayon girdles that she really should throw out, until her fingers scrabbled against the hard cover of her diary. Since she'd caught John reading it all those years ago, it had stayed safe in its hiding place. She'd known John would never look there. Mind you, she hadn't recorded her feelings in it for a long time now. Not since Jack had arrived.

She turned to the chart at the back, removed a pencil from her bedside drawer and struck through another square. Eighty-eight days. Nearly halfway through now. She sucked the end of the pencil. The waiting was hard, really hard, but somehow the ticking-off of dates made it bearable.

Something about that precise record-keeping made her think of Mr Brownlow. She wondered if he still performed that old bobbing movement when he met people. He'd come out of retirement to help the war effort by managing the finance office at the convent, but that was long ago now. He was doubtless sitting in an old chair smoking his pipe and checking his household accounts. And what of Mavis? Kathleen had kept up with her for a bit. Met her for the odd cup of tea at that nice café in Highgate. But since they'd taken on Jack, she'd been too busy and had let the friendship drift. She felt guilty really. Perhaps Mavis was married by now, with children of her own. In her mind, Kathleen put her in a colourful floral dress and an apron, presiding over a bright-eyed brood sitting round the breakfast table, her disastrous time as a nun and the unhappy days at the convent a distant memory. Every woman deserved to be a mother.

She tucked the diary away and started to get dressed. The

clattering in the kitchen suggested Rosie had started her morning's chores. Poor Rosie. She missed Jack too. Kathleen knew about their friendship. The secretive glances when John was reading the paper. The low rasp of whispered conversation she heard from the attic stairs when she dashed up to her bedroom to retrieve a handkerchief. A rising arpeggio of laughter, instantly suppressed. She didn't mind them being friends. They were entitled to happiness. But she hoped the friendship wasn't becoming something more. She'd warned them more than once that John would be incandescent if they became boyfriend and girlfriend. He'd never tolerate his precious white son being with an Aboriginal girl. And sometimes, when she'd seen Rosie and Jack looking like a couple, she'd diverted John's attention to protect them. As far as she knew, Jack hadn't had a girlfriend. No one he wanted to bring home anyway. Perhaps he'd meet someone at Swanbourne.

She trudged down the stairs. The noises from the kitchen came at her through a thick fog. The hall was empty, its beeswaxed air stagnant. She stood by the front door and fixed her eyes on the mailbox, willing a letter from Jack to fly through its clamped metal mouth. But it remained closed.

She went into the lounge room and looked around. The cushions were symmetrically positioned on the sofa. She had long since conceded that battle, although John still inspected them from time to time.

She ran her finger along the top of the photo frames. No dust. Rosie was a good worker. Kathleen had taught her well.

But it was almost disappointing not to have any housework to do. Perhaps she could start doing a keep-fit class again. It would give her a focus, and the physical exhaustion might help her sleep better.

She looked at the pictures. Apart from the wedding photo of her and John, they were all of Jack: in his school uniform, holding up a rugby ball that day he'd scored the winning try; with John on the beach. She adjusted the latest one a fraction to see it better. She hadn't wanted John to photograph Jack in his Nasho uniform, but he had insisted. John was delighted about Jack being called up. 'It'll make a man of him,' he said.

And in many ways he had been right. When Jack had come home on leave after the first month of national service, he was taller, broader, more confident. Almost as though he'd gone from being a boy to a man overnight. Rosie couldn't stop looking at him. Kathleen had had to give her a warning glance or John would have picked something up.

Her husband had spent hours talking to Jack about training manoeuvres, even though he'd never seen combat himself. He'd been so keen on Jack joining the army. 'You remember that time the Japs attacked Darwin, Kath? We were unprepared. Fifteen months it took us to muster sufficient forces. Can't afford to risk that again. Not with all this stuff with the Russkies going on.'

Kathleen was just glad the Korean War was over. Jack wouldn't need to go overseas. And so far he'd barely left training camp. Maybe John was right. Perhaps national service would make him into a man. As long as he came back safe.

Only eighty-eight days to go. In less than three months, Jack would be returned to her.

When John came in from work that evening, he collected the post from the hall table, where Kathleen had left it, and wandered into the kitchen. Rosie was there, fixing supper. It looked like chook. Good.

'Get us a tea, Rosie. I'll be on the veranda.' It was pleasant to have a maid in the house. Fitting for someone of his status. Good to keep the minister's approval too. At first he'd had a bit of a jolt whenever he saw the Aboriginal figure, but after a while he'd learned to pretend she was part of the furniture. If he ignored her most of the time, it was fine.

He wandered outside to read his mail. Kathleen hadn't appeared. Perhaps she was upstairs freshening up. It was pleasing that she still made an effort for him, even though she'd looked a bit crook of late. Missing Jack probably.

He sorted through the pile. A couple of bills. Some official-looking envelope from the ministry. A subscription reminder. And a bluey. He picked it up. It was for Jack. The original destination, *Bindoon Boys Town*, had been scratched out and their own address written beside it in neat copperplate. The letter shook in John's hands. Thank goodness Jack was away. It would have been catastrophic if Kathleen had given it to him. Or Jack had found it. He turned the envelope over. It was a British address. Someone called Mrs Molly Edwardes, who lived in Croydon.

John's stomach lurched. Molly? Wasn't that Jack's mother's name? The document he had safely locked away in his office drawer listed her as Molly Malloy. Perhaps she'd remarried. At any rate, she was trying to communicate with Jack. She must have found out he was alive and in Australia.

John wiped a film of sweat from his forehead. If Jack knew his mother wasn't dead, it would unsettle him horribly. He'd want to do something starkers like fly to England to meet up with her. Abandon his education. Abandon them. No, Kathleen had grown so fond of him. He had too if truth be known. He couldn't jeopardise either of them. He must tell the brothers not to forward any more letters. Once Jack had returned from Swanbourne, he might easily intercept them. Or Kathleen, come to that. Thank God she hadn't looked at it.

John went back to Bindoon from time to time. He could pick up the letters then. He toyed with asking the brothers to throw them away, or writing back to this woman himself and telling her Jack was dead. But she still might want to come out to investigate. Better to say nothing and let her assume he had moved on.

He flashed a rare smile at Rosie as she brought out his tea. She rattled the cup in surprise as she placed it on the ground next to him as he'd instructed, then departed for the kitchen.

John took a quick slurp, then pushed a finger under the flap of the letter and opened it at the crease. He read quickly.

Dear Jack, You will be surprised to hear from me after all these years . . .

284

He looked over his shoulder at a slight noise. Just a curtain blowing. Still no Kathleen. He placed the letter under the others and carried them into his study. It was gloomy after the bright glare on the veranda and had a closed-in smell to it. The key to his desk drawer was in his jacket pocket. He retrieved it and opened the drawer quickly, then slid the letter inside.

'Hello, John.' He whipped round, trying to assume a calm expression. Kathleen was standing by the door in her navy spotted frock.

'Evening, Kath. Pile of bills here. I'll pay them later.' He stood up and motioned her out. 'You look nice. What's for supper? I'm starving.'

Thank goodness she hadn't seen the letter. He'd pop back later and lock the drawer. Then hide the key where she'd never find it.

27

Still no news. Molly checked the mat every morning, hoping against hope to find a blue airmail letter there with unfamiliar writing on it, but none had ever come.

They were playing Elvis on the radio as usual. Molly perched Susan on her hip and hummed along to 'Love Me Tender'. It seemed to have been Susan's favourite song ever since she'd turned two. Molly had never been good at remembering words; well, not since the war anyway. Susan took her thumb out of her mouth and squinted up at her. Molly supported the little girl's back and held her arm out as if about to waltz. Susan had been out of sorts all day, but dancing seemed to pacify her. She giggled, then started as another voice joined the one on the radio for the second verse. Word perfect. Reggie was brushing his feet on the mat, singing loudly with his arms outstretched like an opera singer.

Molly laughed. 'Why're you home so early?'

'Can't a man leave work before the end of the day to see his beautiful wife and daughter?'

Molly put Susan down and wound her arms round Reggie. He smelled of tea and autumn air. 'Well, I'm sure he can. But it's not like you.'

Reggie hugged her quickly, then stepped back. Suddenly he looked serious.

'I just had a feeling I needed to be home.' He shrugged. 'Can't say why.'

'Well, I'm glad you're here.' Molly sat down and lifted Susan onto her lap, stroking her back absent-mindedly. 'Susan's been a nuisance all day. She keeps crying at nothing. I haven't been able to get on with a thing. It would be nice to have some help.'

Reggie pressed his palm to Susan's forehead. 'Hmm. She does seem a bit hot.' Molly kissed the back of her daughter's neck, inhaling her sweet still-baby smell, then tightened her grip on the plump little tummy as Susan squirmed.

Reggie reached out to take her. 'I'll play with her for a bit while you get on.'

'Thanks.' Molly stood up and took the iron out of the cupboard, ready to heat up. Then she traipsed upstairs to fetch the clothes from the airer over the bath. At least she'd be able to do the ironing.

She set up the board, and started on Reggie's shirts, watching the two of them playing as she pressed out the creases in a sleeve. Susan liked nothing better than to open cupboards and explore their contents. Molly had put all the precious stuff out of her reach, but it didn't stop her investigating. She found a set of Bakelite cups and took them out. Reggie helped her build them into a tower. But as soon as he knocked it down, Susan started to cry. That wasn't like her: she normally laughed. Reggie picked her up and cuddled her, then sang to her quietly until she was soothed. Molly carried on with the ironing.

By the time they put her to bed, Susan seemed a little better. She snuggled up to her teddy and was asleep before Molly had finished her bedtime story. Molly stood for a moment watching her face in the moonlight, her daughter's dark lashes casting spidery lines on her cheeks, her pale pink mouth slightly open, her chest rising and falling peacefully. Then she tiptoed out.

'I think she'll be fine,' she said as she came back into the lounge.

Reggie handed her a cup of tea. 'Let's hope so.'

Molly took a sip, then yawned. 'D'you know, I think I'll go up in a minute. I'm pretty tired myself.'

Reggie smiled at her, then raised his own cup to his lips. 'I'll just finish this, then I'll join you. It'll do us good to get an early night.' He lay back in his chair and closed his eyes, still clutching his tea.

Despite her tiredness, Molly struggled to fall asleep. When she finally nodded off, she had a strange dream. It was hot. Dust in her throat; the smell of wet earth and wood fires. A large green plant dying in her hands. Where was the shade? The water? Her heart hammering. Feet pacing. Stumbling. She had to save it. Then a loud wail.

'Wha' issit?' she muttered as Reggie groaned beside her. The wail sounded again, nearer this time, and small fingers plucked at her nightdress. 'Jack?' She opened her eyes. Susan. What on earth had made her think it was Jack? Perhaps her dream had been about him. Molly lifted her daughter in beside her, half registering the hot little body. But Reggie was awake now, pulling himself up the bed and looking at Susan.

'You all right, precious?'

Susan shook her head, then screamed in pain. Molly sat up and felt her forehead. 'She's definitely got a temperature.'

'I'll get her a drink.'

'No, it's worse than that.' Susan was holding her throat, and tears glazed her eyes. 'She's really sick,' said Molly. Susan understood the words and gave a rasping cry. Molly put her hands over the little girl's ears and turned to Reggie. 'What if it's polio?' she whispered. 'Dick Warren, the butcher's delivery lad, woke up with a sore throat and a fever. He's in an iron lung now. Reggie, I'm frightened. It can all happen so quickly.' There'd been a polio outbreak in New Addington that summer. The council had closed the library, the swimming pool and the community centre. Everyone knew someone who'd caught the disease. Parents were often seen anxiously feeling their children's foreheads, and Molly had spent the last few weeks dreading that Susan would be next.

Reggie jerked upright and snapped on the bedside lamp. Susan flinched and Molly looked anxiously at Reggie, but by now he was out of bed and dressing. 'I'll run to the phone and call an ambulance,' he shouted over his shoulder.

'An ambulance?'

'I'm not takin' no risks, Moll.'

Molly nodded, but already Reggie was racing down the stairs. She put a palm to Susan's head and stroked her damp black hair, which sprang back as she did so. Then she leaned over and inhaled its warmth. 'Dada will make it right, darlin', don't you worry.' But Susan's eyes were heavy and she didn't respond.

By the time Reggie returned, Susan was asleep again, a dead weight on Molly's chest, and her arms were aching with the effort of holding her.

'They're on their way,' Reggie said. Molly's ears were buzzing again. They hadn't done that for a long time. Reggie pulled a battered carpet bag from the top of the cupboard, its florid patterns muted with dust. He stuffed it with Susan's clothes, sliding them off shelves and pulling them from hangers. Molly watched, too numb with fear to tell him he was packing far too much.

They waited. Reggie paced up and down the room as though measuring its dimensions while Molly lay motionless on the bed, listening to the ragged breaths rattle through Susan's tiny chest. Somewhere in the house a clock was ticking. Reggie had lit the Calor Gas stove and it hissed and spluttered. A whiff of paraffin tainted the air.

At last Molly heard a bell clanging in the distance, followed by the low shush of brakes and a smack of doors. Reggie stopped pacing and rushed to let them in. Then the sound of boots clattering up the stairs, and two ambulance men appeared. Molly relinquished Susan, slack as a doll, and watched in terror as her small body disappeared beneath an armoury of medical instruments before being wrapped in a blanket and carried downstairs. She and Reggie followed shakily.

A few minutes later, they were huddled in the ambulance talking quietly so Susan couldn't hear, although the roar of the vehicle easily drowned out their voices.

'Maybe it's just a bad cold,' ventured Molly, trying to push back the fear in her head.

Reggie smiled thinly at her. 'Mebbe, Moll.' The ambulance men had refused to give a diagnosis. They were too busy checking and probing. 'I think we're right to be cautious, though. You can't take no risks when there's an epidemic. She could easily have picked something up.'

Terror inched up Molly's spine. She'd already lost one child. It was war and bureaucracy that had separated her from Jack, not disease. But that did little to reassure her.

The ambulance raced past Coombe Road's stately parades of shops, down Duppas Hill and then right into Purley Way, traffic scattering or freezing at its insistent bell. They drew up in front of a large building. The heavy back doors of the ambulance opened and Susan was carried out on her stretcher. Molly watched, momentarily transfixed by the words *Waddon Fever Hospital* above the entrance, then scuttled after the ambulance men with Reggie, half registering the sharp antiseptic smell, mixed with something fetid, that permeated the corridors. They sped along polished floors lined with gurneys, and steel shelves piled high with white linen. Every so often a nurse in a starched cap hurried by, some of them darting curious glances at Reggie.

At last they reached the children's wing. Susan was carried through a wooden door that swung shut as they approached.

Molly went to push it open but a disapproving face appeared in the glass porthole. A finger wagged at her, and when she returned a puzzled look, a stern figure emerged.

'I'm Sister. Can I help you?' She had a large face above a dark-blue uniform.

'Yes, ma'am,' replied Reggie. 'We've come to see our daughter. She just been admitted.'

The woman stared at them, pursing her lips at Reggie. 'This is an isolation ward. *Outsiders* are not allowed.'

'But we're her parents. She's only two!' Molly heard the tremor in her own voice.

'You'll be able to look at her through the glass and a doctor will come and speak to you soon.' Sister turned on her heel and re-entered the ward, her shoes clattering away.

Molly peered through the round window at rows and rows of prone children in little beds, some enveloped by long metal tunnels with only their heads emerging: iron lungs. She shivered. What if Susan were to join them?

They sat on a polished bench near the door. Molly picked at a thread on her sleeve. Leaning forward, his head in his hands, Reggie tapped a nervous rhythm with his foot.

'I should have found that string,' he muttered.

'What?'

'The red string. Mudda sent it over to put in Susan's crib when she was born. It was suppose to bring her luck, but I lost it. Mebbe that why she sick now.' His English was slipping, as it always did when he was anxious.

Molly thought that was just superstition, but perhaps they

292

needed to do something to give them hope. 'Do you think we should pray?' She didn't know if she believed in God any more, not since she lost Jack. But where else could she go for a miracle?

Reggie put his arm round her shaking shoulders. 'Let's wait for diagnosis first.'

Eventually a white-coated doctor appeared. He approached Reggie and Molly, a hand outstretched, and they both stood up. His scrutiny was less overt than the sister's had been, but he still looked at Reggie curiously.

'Mr and Mrs Edwardes.' It was a statement, not a question. 'I'm Dr Knight. I'll be keeping an eye on young Susan.' The jolly words fell through the stale air. White stubble powdered the doctor's chin and jowls. His eyes looked dull.

'Is it polio?' Molly whispered.

'We think it might be. At the moment she's breathing on her own, but her muscles have been spasming and she seems to have difficulty swallowing.'

Molly gripped her handbag. 'She had a sore throat this morning. And a headache.' She couldn't believe she'd just thought Susan was being a nuisance yesterday. Why on earth hadn't she realised she was ill?

'We'll know more after twenty-four hours. You did well to summon an ambulance. Time is of the essence in these cases.'

'So what do we do now, Doctor?' said Reggie.

Dr Knight put his hands in the pockets of his white coat. 'You go home and look after your other children.'

'We have no other children,' Reggie said.

Molly drew in her breath sharply.

'Then go home and get some rest,' the doctor advised.

Molly slumped at the kitchen table, watching Reggie make several attempts to roll a cigarette before he threw the Rizla in the bin in disgust.

'Why did you tell the doctor we had no other children?'

Reggie sat down. He leaned his head on his arms and looked at her through red-rimmed eyes. 'He meant at home, Moll. I've told you we'll find Jack as soon as we can. But I don' know how you can be thinking about him when Susan is strugglin' for her life.'

Molly pressed one hand to her ear. She spoke slowly and quietly. 'I've lost one child and I might be about to lose another. But I won't give up either without a fight.'

Reggie reached forward to pick up Susan's jumper from the table. It was one Molly had knitted herself. He pressed it to his face.

Molly heard a choking sob.

28

It surprised Jack how much he missed Rosie during his national service. There were WRAAC girls at Swanbourne, of course, with their tight uniforms and bright smiles. He and Scotty took a couple out one evening, Raylene and Jenny. Several rounds of Swan bitters and a few gins later, he had a pleasurably long kiss with Raylene outside the base, before she had to rush back, hastily adjusting her uniform. But she was posted to Adelaide a couple of days later so nothing came of their flirtation. And he was only going through the motions really. It was still Rosie he saw when he closed his eyes at night, and her voice he heard if he woke up in the still small hours.

As soon as his spell as a Nasho had finished, he was keen to get back to Highgate. Initially, after a long, dusty journey in an old truck, and a welcome-home meal with John and Kathleen, all he'd wanted was a bath and bed. He'd caught glimpses of Rosie in the kitchen, although they hadn't managed a proper reunion.

But the next morning, when Jack opened his bedroom door, he heard a creak from the attic and realised with pleasure that Rosie must be in her room. He was conscious of the Sullivans talking loudly downstairs in the kitchen. Good. At last he'd be able to speak to Rosie without being heard. He tiptoed up the rickety staircase, avoiding the steps likely to protest the most.

Rosie seemed equally keen to speak to him. She appeared at the door, still in her maid's uniform and clutching a hair-brush. 'Jack!' Her voice was low, to avoid being overheard, but it was warm with happiness.

Jack hugged her. 'I've missed you.' He stepped back to take in her changed appearance. 'You've grown.' He could have bitten his lip at that. It was the kind of thing old women said. But they didn't mean it in the way he had. Rosie was a bit taller, it was true. But she'd also filled out. Her chest strained against her white overall and her hips fitted snugly into the black skirt. Jack swallowed drily.

'I've missed you too. D'you want to come to the Coolbaroo tonight?' Rosie whispered. 'Namatjira's gonna be there.'

Jack hadn't a clue who Namatjira was. 'Yeah, okay. Sure. Will you be allowed out?'

'The curfew's over, remember. Aboriginals don't have to be in by nine any more, thank God.' Rosie darted a quick look downstairs. 'You head out at eight. I'll meet you by the Manchester Unity at half past.'

'Great. I'll shine up my winklepickers!'

Rosie flashed him a quick smile, then went on down.

Jack returned to his own room. He lingered in front of the mirror, surveying the floppy fringe and preppy clothes: the chinos, navy blazer and white polo shirt. He'd have to get rid of those. He'd never danced with Rosie before. It'd be worth dressing up for. Maybe he'd get hold of some Brylcreem to slick back his hair, and try out that leather jacket he'd bought at the market. Kathleen would have a fit if she saw it. Probably accuse him of robbing a bank to buy it. But at least he'd gained some muscles since he'd been in the army, lost that awful thinness that had plagued him for so long and put on a few pounds. He took a step closer and curled his lip at his reflection. Perfect. All that practice in front of the dunny mirror had paid off.

Even before he'd crossed Birdwood Park, Jack could feel the beat. It pulsed from the ground, throbbing through the soles of his shoes: 'Rockin' Through the Rye'. He was looking forward to bopping with Rosie. It was good to be wearing his own clothes. All his life he'd worn a uniform: hand-me-downs at the orphanage, an itchy navy suit on the ship, rags at Bindoon, Kathleen's choices when he'd first got to Perth and green army-issue for his national service. Even his high-school gear felt like a costume. And next he'd be in lawyer's silks. But tonight he was his own man.

He reached the plane trees on the other side of the park and turned into Bulwer before crossing into William Street. The noise was increasing all the time, and he could see the queue of people waiting to get into the Manchester. Most of them were his age or a little older, some couples but also groups of lads and girls talking and laughing. There were lots of Abos and a good many whites too. Jack was surprised by the mix. It wasn't a sight he saw much in Perth, with its policy of strict segregation; nor had he encountered it at Swanbourne, since Aboriginals were exempt from national service.

He walked down the queue. How on earth would he find Rosie in that lot? A couple of times he thought it was her, but when he approached, a different girl turned round. Once a white guy with ox-like shoulders accused him of pushing in and he backed off. But eventually there she was. Out of her maid's uniform, wearing high heels and a pale yellow dress, she looked as glamorous as a film star. She'd straightened her dark hair; it shone under the street lamps and her warm skin glowed. She'd done something with her eyes too. They looked deeper and darker than usual. Jack felt a shiver of desire. He couldn't believe he'd mistaken those ordinary girls for Rosie. Yet she looked so different at the Sullivans', dishevelled from the heat or grubby from hauling rubbish or beating rugs. He whistled loudly.

'Jack. You came!'

'Wouldn't miss it.' He put his hand on her shoulder. 'You look very . . . clean.' The minute the words were out, he knew he'd blundered. The word *stunning* had been in his head but he hadn't wanted to overwhelm her. She probably would have laughed anyway. But *clean*? Whatever was he thinking of? Rosie made a face and pulled him into the queue. Jack grinned back. Perhaps he was forgiven.

They joined the centipede of people advancing up the street. As they approached the club, Jack saw a sign hanging above the door: *The Coolbaroo Club*, in swirly orange letters. Underneath

298

was a picture of a magpie, its monochrome plumage gleaming. *Eat, drink, dance and be happy*, it commanded.

Inside, the busy, colourful room reminded Jack of a kaleidoscope he'd had at Croydon, when he'd lived with his mum, its bright patterns effortlessly dissolving and re-forming. Most of the girls were in wide-skirted dresses, like Rosie, and a few of the boys wore black leather and denim. Some men wore shirts, braces and fedoras. Others were dressed in sports jackets, straight trousers and thin ties. It didn't seem to matter what you wore.

'That's Ronnie Kickett,' said Rosie, pointing to the drummer.

'He's good. And who's the singer?'

'Gladys Bropho.'

Jack looked at the tall woman, sheathed in red, pouring liquid notes into the microphone. 'She's good too.'

'Let's get a drink.' Rosie led Jack over to a long table at the side of the room, covered in a turquoise cloth, where bottles of Tizer, Passiona and Creaming Soda were laid out.

'No sly grog?' asked Jack as they queued to pay.

'No, sir!' replied Rosie. 'Don't want to be busted by the police. So no smokin', no drinkin'!'

It was nice to see clearly round the room instead of having to peer through a fug of smoke like at most clubs Jack knew. The walls were a dark cream colour, and low lamps on the tables threw out a lemon glow. Someone had strung a line of jewel-coloured lights along the wall, giving the room a festive air. Besides the drummer and the singer, there were other percussionists on stage. And a woodwind player who danced so smoothly with his saxophone they looked like a couple.

Rosie didn't seem to notice some of the Aboriginal men around the room looking at them. She was an attractive girl, men were bound to stare, but Jack realised they included him in their scrutiny too. He shifted in his chair, thinking of the magpie sign outside the entrance to the Coolbaroo, symbolising black and white together. An admirable attitude. But perhaps not one all Aboriginal men subscribed to. Especially when the whites were pinching their girls.

Rosie and Jack downed their drinks, then Jack held out his hand. 'Dance?' Might as well be hung for a sheep as a lamb.

'I'd love to.' Rosie followed him onto the glassy dance floor and they jived to 'Ready Teddy' and 'Shake, Rattle and Roll' until Rosie collapsed in giggles at Jack's awkward movements. For a second he had a fleeting memory of dancing with his mother. Rosie had the same dark hair and liquid grace he sensed Molly had had. He wondered if they'd have got on. Would she have accepted Rosie if he'd taken her home? Rosie was so beautiful. He felt sure his mother would have grown to like her, even if she'd been suspicious at first of her colour.

Later, they sat on red velvet chairs at the edge of the room, sipping amber soda.

'This is really cool,' said Jack, wiping his mouth. No one had done anything more threatening than stare at him in the last half-hour. Bopping with Rosie had relaxed him. It was good to have a reason to touch her, despite the disturbingly strong feelings of arousal it caused. 'It's much more fun than any other dances.'

'That's because you've never been to a real dance before, just those dull things with white folks. We're not like you lot with sticks up your backsides!'

Jack laughed. Rosie was a much better dancer than him. It was strange, seeing her so confident in her own environment. She was in the background at the Sullivans', a shadowy figure glimpsed dusting in the lounge or hanging out washing in the garden. She took her meals in the kitchen on her own, while Jack sat with Kathleen and John in the dining room at the mahogany table Rosie polished each day. John would test her by checking if he could see his reflection in it. A single smudge and Rosie would be instructed to do it again. Poor girl. Jack had been treated worse at Bindoon, but at least he'd not been there long. Rosie would be at the Sullivans' for the rest of her working life, unless someone rescued her.

The nine o'clock curfew might have been abolished, but Aboriginals still weren't allowed across town. He knew Rosie sometimes had to walk an extra five miles to avoid the prohibited area that her race was banned from entering. And on the rare occasions she met other Aboriginal maids also running errands, they weren't allowed to speak their own language. No wonder she loved the Coolbaroo so much. John would be down on him like a ton of bricks if he found Jack trying to include Rosie in their activities. Even talking to her was forbidden. Yet Jack had had to rely on Rosie completely that day the redback got him in Kings Park. If she hadn't stopped him from moving, the venom could have circulated round his body and killed him.

He looked around. This was Rosie's territory. Even though whites were supposedly welcomed, it was still an Aboriginal club. Imagining the Sullivans finding him there made his gut tighten. Yet John and Kathleen would never come to this area of town. Nor would their friends. He and Rosie should be safe.

'I'm glad you brought me here,' he said. 'It's good to see coloureds and whites together.'

Rosie raised an eyebrow. 'Perhaps folk think you've brought along your servant.'

'I never treat you like that.' Jack scratched at some dry skin on the inside of his arm.

'No. You ignore me most of the time.'

'I have to. You know John'd go mad if he thought we were friends.'

'Of course you have to keep in with him.'

Jack couldn't tell if she was mocking him or not. 'I do until I qualify, Rosie. Once I'm earning real money, I can leave and get a place of my own.' He blinked away an unbidden vision of him and Rosie alone in the duplex he would rent. Lying on his new bed, her head snuggled into his chest. Or kissing . . . He suppressed the dangerous image. Far too risky to contemplate. He coughed. 'Until then, yes, I do need to keep in with them. And besides, they *have* been good to me. They treat me like a son.' He tugged at his collar. He knew the Sullivans loved him, were proud of him. He'd tried so hard to be the son they wanted. But he'd never stopped wishing it was Mum who'd asked about his day, or stroked his hair when he was sick. Would he ever believe he was Jack Sullivan and not secretly call himself Jack Malloy?

Rosie snorted. 'They certainly don't treat me like a daughter.'

'Why would they? You work for them.'

Rosie leaned forward and her raven hair swung across her face. 'We've both come from children's homes and lost our families. How come I'm the servant and you're the favoured son?'

'I didn't make the rules.'

'But you do obey them.'

'I've told you. Just until I'm qualified.' Jack didn't want to upset Rosie. He knew he was lucky. He owed the Sullivans so much, and he certainly didn't want to disappoint them. He could easily still be at Bindoon facing God knows what horrors. Or dead, like Sam. But it was hard for Rosie, seeing the Sullivans favouring him and ignoring her – except when there was work to be done. And she was right, they did have similar backgrounds. In many ways it wasn't fair. But it was the way things were. At least as long as they were under John Sullivan's roof.

He took another swig of his drink and looked round the room. Suddenly it was almost unbearable to sit so close to Rosie. To breathe her perfume. Watch her toss her hair back. The band had shuffled to the front of the stage and were starting to play 'Blueberry Hill', one of his favourites. 'Let's dance again,' he said. This was a quieter number. He'd be able to hold Rosie, stroke her hair, whisper in her ear. Maybe show her how much she meant to him. As long as he didn't let himself get too aroused.

He got to his feet and Rosie followed suit, a little more slowly. But as he put his arms around her, and she looked up at him, he saw the tenderness in her eyes, and felt the beat of her heart when he pulled her close. For once she wasn't teasing him or making fun of his dancing. Maybe that had just been to hide her feelings. But she wasn't attempting to hide them now. And Jack felt a little surge of pleasure to see the clear affection on her face. He'd realised for a while how strongly he felt for Rosie. Dare he hope she felt the same way too?

But just as he was beginning to enjoy the music, and the pleasure of being so close to Rosie, the band disappeared.

'What's going on?' he asked.

Rosie led him to two chairs near the stage. 'It's time for the Corroboree.'

'The what?'

'Proper dancing!' Rosie sat down.

Jack swallowed. 'Am I expected to join in?'

Rosie laughed. 'Absolutely not. You just watch. With me.'

Jack took his place beside her.

Although the last band had been Aboriginal, their instruments were familiar: saxophone, drum, trumpet, the tunes mainly from the top ten. But this lot were different. The easy swing and rock sounds were replaced by something atavistic and tribal. Rosie named the instruments for him: didgeridoo . . . clapsticks . . . gumleaf. A series of stark paintings was screened across the back of the stage, of haggard brown mountains that bulged and gouged their way down to pewter lakes; white-barked trees with feathery branches; purple shadows and turquoise skies.

The room turned raw and something pulsed deep in Jack's body. He glanced at Rosie's face. She must feel so cut off from her people at the Sullivans'. At least he was with his own race. He reached for her hand and held it. No one would disapprove of that here. She didn't try to pull away.

'Here come the dancers,' she whispered. There was the sound of feet stamping in unison as a procession of Aboriginal men and women entered, crouched low, lost in the music. Their faces and arms were daubed white and the men were bare-chested. None of them wore shoes. They moved with the same ease Jack had admired in Rosie, yet their dance couldn't have been more different from their own attempts to jive and swing.

'We've been doing this dance for thousands of years,' said Rosie, a rapt expression on her face. Jack wished she'd look at him like that. In this vibrant place he felt an outsider in more ways than one.

An older man came on stage carrying a painted wooden slat, about a foot long and two inches wide.

'What's that?' Jack whispered.

The man began to whirl the slat round in a circle on a length of cord. It made an urgent sound that vibrated through

Jack's skin and into his very bones. He started and Rosie stared at him.

'Sorry, it reminds me of something.'

'From Bindoon?'

'No.' Jack cleared his throat. 'Long before that. The noise of bombs before they drop. I'd forgotten how they sounded.'

Rosie squeezed his hand and nodded towards the man on stage. 'White men call it a bullroarer,' she said.

'And isn't it?'

'Well, there were no bulls in Australia!'

'So what do you call it?'

Rosie put her finger to her lips. 'It's secret-sacred. Only my people know its real name.'

'Oh go on, you can tell me.' Jack pinched her lightly on the arm. 'Rosie-Posie?'

'Ow! No, I can't. And don't make fun of me. Or my people. I don't mock your traditions.'

Jack turned back to the dancers, wondering if he had any traditions.

The compère came on stage and invited Namatjira to join him. He walked up the steps, a thick-set, serious man with a tangle of dark hair. The crowd roared and whooped.

'They were Namatjira's paintings we saw at the beginning,' murmured Rosie.

'Are his paintings for sale? Would you like one?'

Rosie laughed. 'I would, but Kathleen'd have to add a nought to my wages. They're worth a fortune!'

'Really?' Jack had quite liked the paintings, but they were

hardly Constable. 'I think I'd rather see the real scenes in the outback.'

'Me too. Maybe we can go upcountry one day.'

Jack smiled at Rosie. She must miss the outback. And her family. 'Maybe we will. It would be nice to go somewhere other than Kings Park.' And to be alone with Rosie.

'You'll find redbacks to bite you wherever you go!' Rosie mimed a spider walking up Jack's arm.

Jack shivered, then grabbed her hand again. 'Well, I'll just have to take you with me, won't I?'

Namatjira made a speech about Aboriginal rights, and then someone from the club presented him with a life membership. The artist hung around on stage for a while afterwards, signing autographs. Jack could see Rosie was tempted to go up, but she held back, probably for his sake. He didn't try to persuade her, although he wondered afterwards if he should have done. She'd precious little opportunity to enjoy her culture. He squeezed her hand and received a sad smile in return. 'I'd like to have got his autograph for Mum,' she said. 'She loves Namatjira's paintings. But what would be the point? I'm never going to see her again.'

Jack stroked Rosie's face with his other hand. 'Never give up hope,' he said.

Rosie swallowed and nodded.

When the dance was over, they walked back through the dark streets, enjoying the coolness and the faint scent of eucalyptus. They stopped at the end of the street to say goodbye. It wouldn't do for them to turn up at the Sullivans' together. Jack put an arm round Rosie and pointed up at the night sky. It was a deep navy, underlit with a milky glow by the lights of Perth.

'That's the Southern Cross,' he said, looking at the blazing shape overhead. John had pointed it out to him once and taught him to distinguish it from the Diamond Cross to its right and the False Cross further on.

Rosie nodded, then gasped. 'The emu!' she said, pointing near the Southern Cross.

Jack followed her gaze but couldn't see a thing. 'Can you show me? John never told me about that one.'

'Well he wouldn't. Only my people know about the emu in the sky.' She reached up and gently tilted Jack's face. Her eyes were dreamy. 'When we see them there, we know they've begun their courtship dances and soon there will be eggs to collect.' She darted a glance at Jack.

Jack wondered what she meant. It was nice to stand this close to her again, though.

Rosie was looking back up at the sky, with a trance-like expression. 'The shape changes as the year goes on. Later on, the emu's legs will vanish. That's when the male emu sits on the eggs to incubate them. When we only see the body, we know the emu is looking after us, keeping everything safe.'

'That's beautiful,' said Jack.

Rosie nodded, then collected herself. 'I'd better go in, it's getting late.'

Jack reluctantly let her go. He wondered if he should have tried to kiss her. And whether she'd have let him.

He watched her slip in through the back door, her body briefly silhouetted against the glass panel, then he reached for a packet of Chesterfields in his pocket and lit up. He blew a plume of smoke into the darkness as he thought about the Corroboree. He'd never seen Rosie so animated as when she'd watched her people dance. She really was lovely.

He tipped his head back again to look at the space where Rosie had pointed out the emu. Perhaps it was a sign for them too. He knew Rosie was fond of him; he could see it in her eyes. And he wanted to look after her too – just like the emu. But how could it ever work with the way things were at the Sullivans'? John would go mad. And Jack couldn't risk upsetting him when he still needed their support. Better that he and Rosie stay as friends for now. Although he couldn't imagine a future without her.

He took another drag of his cigarette. He could barely remember the northern stars. Wasn't there something called Orion? And the Plough? What he *could* remember was looking up with his mother and her telling him that beyond the stars was heaven – where his dad and grandparents were. Was she with them now? In heaven? But that was above England, in a different part of the sky. Could she even see him where she was? His throat prickled at the thought of her being in the wrong bit of heaven. Ridiculous. He wiped his eyes with the back of his hand. She wasn't floating around in the ether; she was probably blasted to bits under a ton of rubble in a British bombsite. But he wished with all his heart she could have known about Rosie.

He ground the cigarette stub under his heel and headed back to the house, his mind rehearsing a version of his evening for the Sullivans.

Through the tiny skylight in her attic bedroom, Rosie was also looking up at the constellations. She remembered her mother first pointing out the emu in the sky to her when she was small. Once it appeared each March, she, Alkira, Cobar and Darel would be sent off to search for the eggs that the emu's appearance heralded. When they'd brought them home, her mother would pierce them to suck out the fluid, then dry the shells. Then they would all sit around painting stories on them.

Sometimes Rosie felt like that hard, empty shell. Her core was missing. And who knew what story she would ever be able to paint? She wished her mother were here now. How would she advise her to treat Jack? They'd been friends for so long. She'd loved dancing with him at the Coolbaroo. It felt wonderful to be so close. But they could never have a relationship; if the Sullivans found out, they might send her packing and then she wouldn't see Jack at all.

Her heart ached for Jack whenever he spoke about his mother, or the brothers' cruelty. She longed to hold him and make it all right. But that could never be. Perhaps it was better to stay friends rather than wish for more. That was all she could ever hope for. She'd grow old working for the Sullivans, rarely have a life beyond their walls, probably never see her family again.

But at least she would still see Jack. She'd have to be content with that.

Part Five

1959–1962

29

Jack had known Kathleen would fuss, and he was right. She'd already ironed his shirt twice, and she'd phoned the University of Western Australia weeks ago to find out the colour of his hood (royal purple) so she could buy him a matching tie. Normally he'd have baulked at all this nonsense, but he reckoned it was a big day for her. Any mum would have been proud at her son's graduation.

It wasn't just Kathleen fussing either. John had set his alarm for an hour earlier than normal, purely so that he could polish everyone's shoes himself, rather than leaving them for Rosie. What was it with older people's obsession with gleaming footwear? Anyone would have thought John had been in the army during the war, he had such a military pride in his appearance. It reminded Jack of his national service year: endless kit inspections; the sergeant major barking that he needed to see his reflection in each of their boots; hours spent pressing his uniform and polishing the buttons. He suppressed a distant memory of the Piccaninny paste at Melchet, a black face on the lid. No wonder he couldn't bear to go near an iron or a tin of shoe polish. It probably wouldn't do him any harm to look smart today, though. He knew there'd be endless photos and that the choice ones would be placed on the windowsill for Kathleen to dust and admire, along with all the others she'd taken over the years. Might as well look his best. Besides, he'd have to get used to all that formal wear once he was a lawyer.

As Jack climbed into the Holden, conscious of his new suit pulling at his shoulders, he glanced up at the windows of the house. He half wanted Rosie to see him in his finery, but she didn't look out. She hadn't appeared earlier when John was yelling from the living room that they needed to hurry up and Kathleen was calling down from the bedroom that she wasn't going to rush her make-up on Jack's big day. He wondered where she was. He'd be bound to see her later. He'd tell her all about it then.

Jack left John and Kathleen at the entrance to the Winthrop Hall, squabbling about where the best seats were. He'd be sitting on the stage with the others, under the huge grey organ pipes that ran along the back like a dense line of gum trees. He hoped the ceremony wouldn't drag on too long.

A woman from the academic dress company, with a Marilyn Monroe hairstyle and halitosis, helped him put on his gown. Jack clenched his hands to stop himself pushing her out of the way. It wasn't just her breath; he still didn't like being touched by strangers. Even now, Brother Cartwright's fat fingers could still flash into his mind. When the woman loomed up a third time to fiddle with his tie, he backed off.

'I'll be fine, thanks.' He strode over to a mirror.

'Looking good,' said a voice behind him. He could see her in the glass. Peggy Arnold: long legs, pale face, dark-blonde hair. They'd been in the same faculty for three years. She hung around with the other preppy types. Jack always assumed she considered herself a cut above him and his mates.

He turned round and stepped to one side. 'You look nice too.'

'Thanks.' She swirled her gown in front of the mirror. It seemed to be made from a different cloth to his. Perhaps her rich parents had bought it for her. 'Shame we won't be sitting together – I'm A and you're S!'

'Yes.' They'd been told they had to sit alphabetically across the stage. That was the problem with alphabetical order – he'd be between Ronald Saunders, with his rugby player thighs, and tubby Charlie Symons, who was prone to sweating. Jack would be lucky not to get squashed, and then Kathleen would moan about the creases in his gown. 'Never mind.'

'Have you got anything lined up for next year?' Peggy was still admiring herself, so the comment was thrown over her shoulder.

Jack cleared his throat. 'I've decided against advocacy. I feel stupid enough in this gown, let alone having to wear a wig all day.'

Peggy laughed. 'You do look a bit awkward.'

Great. That did a lot for his confidence. 'I'm sure *you'll* do well in court, though.' She really was preening herself.

She turned round and smirked at him. 'Well, thank goodness

for the backroom boys. Someone has to pore over all those statutes and judgements.'

Jack put up a hand to steady his mortar board and tried to push the wretched tassel out of the way. Peggy seemed to be hanging around for something. What did she want?

'You going to the ball later?'

That was it. 'I might look in for a bit.' He thought he ought to go for a while, and it would spare him from the Sullivans' inevitable post-mortem.

'Well, save a dance for me, honey.' Peggy strutted off towards the hall, throwing a glance back at him.

Jack stared after her. For a second he wondered what it would be like to lead Peggy around the dance floor. They would look good together. Both tall, fair – and soon to be lawyers. How John and Kathleen would love it if he arrived at dinner with a future barrister on his arm.

The organ struck up with a pompous fanfare Jack didn't recognise as he made his way to his seat with the others. He felt so conspicuous on stage. Best to stare straight ahead, try not to fidget, and wait for his name to be called. The As and Bs were already lining up. Peggy Arnold gave him a wink as she caught his eye. She sauntered across the stage, paused briefly to beam into the audience, then shook the chancellor's hand. Everyone was looking at her.

Somewhere out there were John and Kathleen. John would be grinning widely, shiny shoes perfectly aligned on the floor, Kathleen would be scrabbling in her bag for a handkerchief. For a second he fantasised about Molly being in the audience, getting to her feet and cheering as he crossed the floor, or waving frantically to attract his attention. She'd have been a fish out of water. He'd have pretended to be embarrassed but been secretly pleased at her obvious pride. His throat tightened. She'd never know how far he'd come.

They'd reached the Rs now. Jack felt a little hop in his gut as the noise from the audience swelled and billowed. One of his legs had gone numb. It tingled as he made his way to the side of the stage, trying not to limp.

'Jack Sullivan.' He felt a jolt, even now, when the announcer didn't call out 'Jack Malloy'. He took a deep breath.

The chancellor was a huge padded figure, decked out like some modern-day Thomas More in a red velvet gown and bonnet. His palm was warm, his smile warmer still. How did he manage to make Jack feel as though he was the first person he'd greeted when he'd already shaken hundreds of hands? 'Well done, young man.'

'Thank you, sir.' Jack remembered to smile in response before setting off again to the safety of the far side of the stage, clutching his certificate. The drum roll inside his chest settled to a slower beat, then faded.

Despite his impatience with the pomp and ceremony, Jack still felt a rush of triumph when he glanced down at the thick embossed paper. Who'd have thought a scared little boy from a children's home would ever become a law graduate? He had the Sullivans to thank. Though they drove him mad at times, they'd believed in him. Would his real mother have been capable of that?

For a second he wondered whether Sam would have gone to university, had he lived. He'd certainly been clever enough. And determined. What fatal throw of the dice had secured Jack a place at law school and Sam a Bindoon grave? Would he ever get over the guilt of escaping the Boys Town and leaving Sam behind? He gripped the certificate more tightly and a crease knifed across it. This was for both of them, him and Sam, and the fledgling friendship that had never had the chance to develop. It was for Sam that he'd studied law. Now, finally, he could find out what had really happened to him. And expose those bloody brothers once and for all.

Afterwards, Jack posed by a stiff board of fake books, a failed attempt to give the illusion of a library. He held a dummy scroll in his left hand and grinned until his jaws ached. Kathleen hovered behind the photographer, blowing her nose, while John scanned the room, probably looking to see who could witness his moment of triumph.

Jack had intended to hang around with some of his graduating friends, but the Sullivans had other plans. They'd booked the table at the Palace Hotel for six o'clock, rather than later, as he'd hoped.

'Come on, sport.' John clapped him on the back. 'Take your hat and gown back and we'll go and celebrate.' Jack did as he was told, but wondered if he might go to the faculty ball after all. It would give him an excuse to escape after the meal and he'd be able to meet up with his mates then. He followed John and Kathleen out to the car.

John pressed open a gilt-and-glass door at the side of the large hall and ushered Jack and Kathleen into the restaurant. Jack had never been anywhere this smart before. John must be really pushing the boat out. Some old-fashioned music was playing and the maroon carpet was deep enough to swallow his feet. Staff in white uniforms moved around discreetly. Jack smelled something overpowering: a combination of flowers and expensive food. He was starving. A smiling waiter approached.

'Sullivan,' said John, and they were led to a small table covered in a starched cloth and a complicated configuration of cutlery. Jack nearly fell over as a hovering waiter pulled out his chair just as he was about to sit down. John caught his eye and winked as the same waiter ostentatiously shook out his napkin and placed it reverently on his lap.

The waiter handed John the wine list, but he waved it away. 'Your best champagne, please.' Jack cringed at the loudness of his voice, calculated no doubt to carry across the room. He slouched a little in his chair until Kathleen frowned at him.

Oil paintings, surely copies, adorned the walls, and self-consciously romantic music oozed out of the loudspeakers hidden behind potted plants. Jack decided not to comment. Kathleen and John had invested a lot of money in his education. This kind of thing was important to them. And besides, the food should be good.

When the champagne arrived, John stood up. Praying that

he wasn't about to give a speech, Jack looked round the restaurant, pleased to find people were too busy eating to have noticed.

'This is a great moment for us all,' proclaimed John. Now people *were* turning round. Jack's cheeks burned. He shrank into his seat and buried his head in the menu. 'And a huge success for the child migrant scheme. The education and opportunities you've received in Australia have been second to none. Who knows where you'd have ended up if we hadn't rescued you.'

Yeah, from bloody Bindoon, thought Jack. Not England. Jack had often wondered how much the Sullivans knew about the brothers' cruelty. Ever since that day Kathleen had asked him if he'd been beaten, and he'd nodded his assent, the subject had remained closed. It was a stone no one wanted to turn over. John had never discussed life at the Boys Town, but then why should he? Bindoon had been a stepping stone on his career path and he didn't want it to wobble. And Jack had buried too many memories under the stone ever to want to raise it again.

John raised his glass, and Kathleen stood up. 'To our son – the hotshot lawyer!' They chinked their drinks together.

Jack didn't join them in the toast, just took a sip of his champagne. It was cold and gassy, a kind of sophisticated pale, dry Tizer, although John wouldn't have liked it described that way.

'I'm not a lawyer yet,' he said quietly as John and Kathleen sat down.

'Yeah, but you will be. We'll soon be able to watch you in court.'

Jack frowned. 'I've told you. I won't be in court now I'm not going to be a barrister.'

John straightened a knife that had moved half an inch out of line. A muscle pulsed in his jaw. 'Remind me again, sport.'

'From September I'll be an articled clerk.'

Kathleen took another sip. Her face was a bit pink. 'I'm glad you'll be at Martin and Rowan. Elsie used them when Howard left her and she said they're very good.'

Jack hadn't a clue who Elsie and Howard were, but at least Kathleen seemed to think he was doing the right thing. 'Thanks for all your support.' He included John in his smile. 'Now I'll finally be able to look into Sam's death.'

John choked into his champagne. 'Sam?'

Jack looked John in the eye. 'Yes, Sam,' he said firmly. How dare John say Sam's name as though he'd forgotten who he was? He knew bloody well what Sam had meant to him. And if he couldn't see how Sam's death had haunted him over the years, then he was either more stupid than Jack had thought, or deliberately ignoring the signs.

Perhaps he should have waited until after the meal. But he had to tell them sometime.

'It's what made me go into the law in the first place. Something was wrong about the way Sam died. Now I'll be in a position to investigate.'

John set his glass down very deliberately. 'Stay away from Bindoon, mate. I don't want you meddling.' His voice was mild, but Jack recognised the force behind it.

He shrugged his shoulders. 'It's what lawyers do. Put right wrongs.'

John loosened his tie. 'Take any other case, but not this one. Too close to home.'

Beside him, Kathleen was fussing with her cutlery. 'Please, Jack.'

He didn't want to spoil the meal. A waiter had arrived with three bowls of mushroom soup and a basket of rolls. He served them all slowly. The soup glistened and the bread smelled freshly baked. Jack's stomach growled. Guess he didn't need to have this conversation now. But he wasn't going to be told what to do. This was too important. Sam should never have been at Bindoon in the first place. Instead of receiving the welcoming care of a family, he'd been driven into the violent hands of strangers. Jack wouldn't rest until he'd found out what had really happened to his best mate – 'shipmates', they'd called themselves on the boat. He'd just be sure not to confide in John about it in future.

He picked up his spoon and scooped up some of the thick, creamy liquid from his bowl. 'We'll discuss this later,' he said.

'Good man,' replied John, buttering a bread roll energetically.

Jack went home with John and Kathleen to freshen up before going back to the Winthrop. Still no sign of Rosie. Perhaps she was in her room, like Cinderella, longing to go to the ball. He'd have much preferred having her with him. He cast a wistful look over at his jeans and leather jacket, wishing he didn't have to stay in his formal wear for the dance. He'd have to get used to dressing this way at work: three-piece suits were the order of the day. At least he'd be able to smoke a few Chesterfields outside.

John had lent him the Holden for the evening, and Jack drove down Mounts Bay Road with all the windows open, enjoying the stiff breeze coming off the sea. His carefully Brylcreemed hair was all ruffled; he'd see to it later. He'd spent most of the day spruced up. At least now he could relax.

When he returned to the hall, magically divested of chairs and adorned with festive banners and balloons, Scotty and Greg were standing by the entrance, their lit cigarettes glowing in the darkness. They fell short of hugs, but slapped each other's backs enthusiastically.

'Now for the good part,' proclaimed Scotty.

Jack took out his packet of cigarettes and approached Greg for a light. 'If you call dancing the good part.' Ever since he'd started attending the Corroboree with Rosie, all that time ago, he'd found all-white dances insipid. 'Want a beer?' he asked the others, and the three wandered inside.

While Jack was queuing up at the bar, he felt something digging into his back. He turned round.

'What about that dance, Sullivan?' It was Peggy.

Jack hadn't even paid for the beers yet. 'Sorry, I'm just having a drink with Scotty and Greg.'

Greg winked at him. 'That's fine, Jacko. I'll get these. Have a bop with lovely Peggy here and you can join us later.'

Peggy beamed. Jack had no choice but to relinquish his place in the queue and lead her out onto the dance floor. But he threw a scowl over his shoulder at Greg as he did so. Greg just laughed.

It wasn't even a bop – more of a waltz, seeing how slowly the band played. He was surprised no one had fallen asleep with boredom. He led Peggy round, trying not to look too inadequate.

'This is nice,' she murmured, her face pressed into his shoulder. She was wearing a sort of red, floaty garment and something sparkled at her throat. Her hair was piled up on top of her head – it made her ears look a bit big.

'How come you're so keen to dance with me? You've barely talked to me in three years.'

Peggy put her head to one side and smiled at him coyly. 'You're the one that got away. I reckoned if I didn't make a move tonight, I might not see you again. It was now or never.'

'I'm not a prize, you know,' said Jack.

Peggy patted her hair.

It was strange dancing with another girl. Peggy was a catch, no doubt about it. Dating her would make Jack's life a lot easier. He thought he'd heard once that her father was a judge. Her family could certainly help him up the legal career ladder a lot quicker than he'd manage on his own.

But as he guided her around the dance floor, he tried to suppress the memory of the Abo band playing 'Shake, Rattle and Roll'. And the vision of a girl with raven hair and laughing brown eyes giggling and twirling in front of him.

30

Molly stood up, rubbing her back. Another evening spent writing to Jack. Another letter that would doubtless be lost or ignored. It was hard to keep on torturing herself like this. It had been years since she'd written that first letter.

She'd been to see Dr Lee when she was in the family way again, to see if he could help her contact Jack, but he'd advised her to stop writing. Perhaps he'd been right. She had two beautiful children now. She should concentrate on them. Jack had never replied. He obviously didn't want to get in touch. Either that or the letters had never got to him. Whichever way, it was a lost cause.

Just one more letter and then she'd give up. She wondered whether she should put in a photo. That nice one taken on Brighton beach earlier in the summer might help Jack to see the family he still belonged to. She opened the drawer and started to rummage. Eventually she found the picture she wanted. Reggie had borrowed a box Brownie for the day and taken a few snaps. This was just the three of them. Susan in that dratted caliper as usual. Molly wondered if she'd ever see Susan limp without wondering what might have been. Would she have been a good runner? Won races at sports day? Performed that Stroll dance the kids were all doing?

She was so glad she'd had another child. It had been a difficult pregnancy but absolutely worth it for the arrival of a perfect little boy at the end of it. Peter. Molly had lost Jack, allowed Susan to get polio. Peter was her last chance to get things right before she was too old to have children.

She was wearing her favourite lilac seersucker blouse in the photo and her hair was blowing in the wind. What would Jack think of her? She must look so much older than he remembered. If his new mother were young and glamorous, Molly would look old and dowdy in comparison.

The picture was a little overexposed, so Susan and Peter could just have been suntanned. Reggie hadn't set the snap up well. There was a big gap to Molly's left.

I've enclosed a photo so you can see us all. Please don't think that just because I have two more children there isn't room for you. Look, you could easily have been standing next to me. I think about you every day.

She massaged her back again and read the letter through. It was almost certainly pointless since Jack was probably never going to read it, but she didn't like him to think his old mum couldn't put a decent letter together. She framed the last sentence in her mind, moved words around a bit, took a deep breath, and wrote.

If I don't hear from you this time, I'll give up. Maybe you've moved on and never got my letters. Or maybe you just want to leave the past behind. If that's the case, I'll accept once and for all that you don't want to know me. I don't blame you. Have a good life, Jack. You deserve it.

Then she signed her name: *As ever, your loving mother, Molly.*

*

Jack read through the document meticulously. It was long, and there were dozens of subsections to be checked. He'd given the matter a lot of thought and decided this was the best way to do it. He didn't want to wait years to buy a car. Goodness knows, he'd waited long enough already. All those evenings when he'd had to seek John's permission to borrow the Holden to take Peggy out. All those times John had let him down with a last-minute meeting at the ministry. Too many nights out forfeited. Too much freedom lost.

The paperwork all seemed in order. Plenty of his friends had used hire purchase without apparent problems, but he had to be sure. He scanned the last paragraph, then pulled out a pen from his blazer pocket, nodding at the salesman, who turned back from the window, a professional smile pinned in place.

Jack smiled in return. He signed his name neatly. Finally, his own car. Not given or lent but bought through hard work and careful saving. His real mother would have been so proud of him.

'Thank you, Mr Sullivan,' said the salesman. His voice had a slightly nasal quality. He must have worked hard to avoid sounding as though he was whining. 'I'm sure you won't regret this.'

Jack shook the proffered hand. 'Let's hope not.'

He followed the man out of the showroom and into the parking area where the Ford Falcon was waiting. It was as fab as he'd remembered: pale blue with a lightning stripe of white down the sides. There were aerials front and back, and the cone-shaped red rear lights protruded from their sockets like lipstick tops. A model of a falcon was fixed across the bonnet. He peered inside: one long bench seat in grey quilted leather, a thin white steering wheel and soft charcoal-coloured carpets on the floor. He and Peggy could have a blast in this, although it was Rosie who would ride in it first.

By noon he'd arrived at the corner of Vincent Street, where Rosie was waiting as planned. She'd done something new with her hair. It looked all puffed up. The style suited her.

He pulled up alongside her and wound down the window. 'Hey, gorgeous.'

Rosie feigned a pout and climbed in. 'Nice wheels.'

'What have you done with your hair?'

Rosie patted the back of her head. 'Backcombed it. D'you like it?'

Jack whistled and Rosie gave him a playful punch, then sank down in her seat, grinning.

They drove onto the Kwinana Freeway and Jack opened up the throttle. Rosie wound down the window and stuck her head out.

'You'll ruin your hair!'

She pulled it back in and made a face at him. 'I forgot.'

'Oh well. You'll have to change it anyway, before Kathleen sees you. Where did you tell them you'd gone?'

'To the market. Better pick up some veggies on the way back.'

'Okay. We'll go via Canning Vale.'

'Thanks.' Rosie smoothed her fingers over the leather seat, then brushed the dashboard admiringly. 'So where are you going to go now you've got your own motor?'

Jack frowned. 'I promised myself I'd go up to Bindoon the minute I could. See what I can find out about Sam.'

He felt Rosie watching him. 'That won't be easy.'

'I wrote to the brothers a while ago, but they didn't reply. I think I'll just have to turn up unannounced – launch a surprise attack.'

Rosie pulled down the passenger visor and looked at herself in the mirror.

'It'd give me moral support if you came with me.'

'How can I?'

'You'd have to tell Kathleen that Perth has run out of veggies and you need to go out of town for them.'

'It's not funny, you know. You might've got your freedom, but I'm still at Kathleen's beck and call.' Rosie turned to look out of the window at the acacias and paperbarks flashing by. There were tuarts too, as well as the odd velvet bush. 'Besides, the brothers would love me turning up!'

'Maybe just come with me for the journey then.'

'I'll think about it. But what about Peggy?'

Jack frowned. 'She won't mind.' Jack hadn't told Peggy about his and Rosie's friendship. She thought Rosie was a servant. Peggy didn't know anything about his past either; she just seemed quite impressed that his father worked at the ministry. Best to let her think that. John and Kathleen certainly wouldn't let on. And John's connections, alongside Peggy's, might help with his legal career.

He fiddled with the radio control. He wasn't being deliberately deceitful with Peggy. He had to succeed in the law for Sam's sake. The more clout he had behind him, the more likely he was to find out what had really happened. The ends justified the means, didn't they?

A crackling sound issued from the radio. It rose to a pitch, then faded.

'Let me do it.' Rosie turned the knob until some music oozed out. It was Ray Charles: 'Hit the Road, Jack'. Rosie giggled. 'They're playing your song.'

Jack grinned.

They sang along for a bit, then Jack stopped. 'The Sullivans are off to some ministerial function on Saturday. It's an all-day thing. Probably well into the evening too. We'll go then. I'll help you catch up with your chores.'

'It's a deal.' Rosie looked a bit flushed.

Jack turned the radio up and they resumed their singing.

The further he drove up the Great Northern Highway, the more Jack's gut contracted. By the time they were on the outskirts of Bindoon, it felt like a pack of boy scouts had been practising knots with his innards. His chest was starting to hurt too. He let out a long breath. Rosie reached out and touched his hand lightly.

'Thanks.' He was glad he'd brought her with him, even though it had meant an anxious morning waiting for the Sullivans to leave.

The car rattled down the long dirt track. Jack had to stop a couple of times to open and close the stock gates that barred the road. The farmland and paddocks looked just the same: bleak and barren, with only the odd ruined building to break up the landscape. Small dots in the distance suggested that boys still worked on the farm. Why on earth hadn't someone closed this place down? He glanced up at the statue on the hill. Jesus. Silhouetted against the sky, staring implacably across the valley.

They drove up the tree-lined drive.

'What are those?' Rosie pointed out a series of stone constructions, set on rocks. They hadn't been there in Jack's day. But he knew what they were.

'The stations of the cross.'

'The what?'

Jack changed to a lower gear. He'd forgotten how steep the hill was. 'Jesus's last journey. They're supposed to mark the stages of his suffering. The boys must have built them after I left.'

'*Whose* suffering?' Rosie's tone was ironic.

Jack grunted. He wondered if Sam had helped build them; hauling the stones with calloused hands that bled from the knuckles, knees burning from the lime as he mixed up cement. Brother Cartwright used to refer to the boys as God's little soldiers. But Jack had been a soldier, on his national service, and it'd been a breeze compared to the hell of Bindoon.

'So what's the plan?' Rosie tucked a strand of hair behind her ear. No backcombing today.

'I'll park up here and then go into the main building.' Jack glanced at the watch on his suntanned wrist. It almost blinded him with the bright light reflected from the sun pouring in through the window.

'Then what?'

'I suppose I'll find out if any of the brothers are still around from when I was here. It's been over twelve years now.' Jack shuddered as he brought the Falcon to a halt at the side of the low Italianate building.

Rosie got out and stretched.

'I'd like you with me,' said Jack. He wanted to take hold of her arm – to give him courage and to show the brothers that someone cared about him – but he knew how judgemental they were. Rosie was right. It wouldn't do his cause any good if she came too.

'We agreed, remember,' she said. Then shivered. 'Besides, there are *warra wirrin* here.'

'*Warra* what?'

'Bad spirits.' Rosie looked around her with a scowl, then touched Jack's arm. 'I'm worried what this will do to you.'

'Save your worrying for kids like Sam.' Jack kicked a stray stone down the path. 'I wonder what became of the others.'

'Time you found out.' Rosie held out her hand. 'Give me the keys, Jack. I'll be rooting for you here.'

Jack climbed the stone staircase to the huge front door and lifted and released a large iron ring. A metallic sound reverberated through the hallway. Jack bit his lip.

Eventually an elderly man in a long black gown flung open the door and stood blinking at Jack from the gloom of the hall. One of his eyelids drooped and his bald head was covered in age spots.

'Yes?'

Jack's mouth was almost too dry to speak, but he had to sound confident. He moistened his lips. 'I'm Jack Malloy.' No point in calling himself Sullivan. 'I used to be one of the boys here. I'd like to see Brother McBride if possible.' He hesitated. 'Or Brother Cartwright.' The memory of Brother Cartwright's fleshy fingers encircling his own as he milked the cows bored into Jack's brain.

The man pushed the door back and turned without a word, leaving Jack standing outside. He heard the brother's footsteps receding, then the sound of an internal door opening and shutting. The silence surged back, bringing with it the faint smell of boiled mutton. Nothing had changed there. That was probably the poor boys' supper.

The footsteps returned. Two lots this time. An even older brother accompanied the original one. Short, stocky, pugnacious-looking. More suited to a boxing ring than a seminary. Brother McBride. Jack would have recognised him anywhere.

'I don't know if you remember me. I'm Jack Malloy.'

Brother McBride peered at him through watery eyes.

Jack made a small movement forward. It was important he was allowed in. 'I wrote to you a while ago but didn't get a reply.'

The brother made no response.

'May I come in?'

He shrugged, almost imperceptibly, then shuffled off down the hall. Jack followed.

He was aware of the ornate surroundings, little changed since his day. The high ceilings, oil paintings and gleaming wood. The odour of polish and meat fat.

Brother McBride led him into a small room with white-washed walls. A large dark-wood crucifix hung beside the window. The air smelled faintly of incense. Jack perched on a hard stool while Brother McBride seated himself in a green velvet armchair, tucked his hands into the sleeves of his gown and waited. Clearly he wasn't going to make this easy for Jack.

Jack cleared his throat. 'I was here with a boy called Sam Becker. He died about ten years ago.' He paused deliberately. 'He was Jewish.' Jack had long wondered if Sam's religion had had something to do with his death.

The brother stared at him unblinkingly. No mileage there then.

Jack was aware of his own voice. It sounded thin. 'Perhaps you could tell me how he died.'

The brother extracted one hand and picked at a loose thread on the arm of his chair. 'It was a long time ago,' he said. 'An accident. Becker was working on the construction of one of the dormitory blocks. He fell from the scaffold. His head struck a rock and he was killed straight away.' He might as well have been reading out a laundry list, such was the tone of his voice.

Jack's anger rose but he kept his voice steady. 'It's hard to imagine that something like that happened in broad daylight,' he said, glancing at the man mildly. It was important he appear innocuous or Brother McBride would never give him the information he wanted. 'It seems strange. Sam was so safety-conscious. He wasn't a daredevil.'

No response. Did Brother McBride have a shred of humanity?

'I'm a lawyer,' said Jack. If he worded this carefully, maybe he could imply he'd been assigned this as a case. Frighten the old bastard into disclosing more. 'May I see the paperwork?'

The brother rubbed the side of his nose. 'We no longer have records from that period.'

'Someone must have documents relating to the incident. The police would, surely.'

Brother McBride was picking at the armchair again. 'There's no point in going to the police. I've told you, it was an accident.'

There was a sharp pain in Jack's jaw. He realised he'd clenched his teeth with the effort of suppressing the fury bubbling up inside.

He silently pressed his knuckles into the stool. The angry boy inside him wanted to punch Brother McBride again and again until his bulbous nose spurted blood, and black bruises stained his face. He wanted to see him shaking and sobbing and gasping for breath. He wanted to maim McBride so badly that every time the nasty little man closed his eyes, the scene would replay, causing him to spend the rest of his life jumping at shadows.

But the lawyer in him resisted the child. He couldn't risk his career before it had started. Bindoon had given him brawn but it hadn't robbed him of a brain. Besides, you didn't fight violence with violence. You fought it with cunning.

He breathed deeply and stood up, clamping his arms to his sides with difficulty. He kept his tone mild and deferential. 'Then can you direct me towards Sam's grave? I'd like to pay my respects while I'm here.'

The brother pointed out of the window. 'Go round to the back of the building, then strike out diagonally to your right. The cemetery's about half a mile down there.'

Jack left the room without speaking.

He collected Rosie on the way and filled her in on the visit. As they hurried past the ornamental gardens, where plants wilted in the early-afternoon heat, Jack felt exhausted. He didn't know why he'd expected to get anything from this. Brother McBride had been a bully in his day; why did he think things might have changed? He knew from his law studies that criminal tendencies tended to remain with people for life. Yet he'd still hoped the brother might have reformed in his absence.

The walk did little to calm him and Jack was still angry by the time they came to a scrubby patch of land with a few overgrown graves. 'Cemetery' was far too grand a word for it. He swiped at some bridal creepers that had wound their way across a headstone. It wasn't Sam's. He found that in the corner of the small plot. *Samuel Becker*, it said in small plain letters. *1935–1949. Rest in peace.*

Jack briefly surveyed the neglected grave before tearing at the long grass and capeweed, scratching his nails on the hard stone. Then he picked up a piece of flint and hurled it into the undergrowth. *Rest in bloody peace.* What peace was there for a boy who'd been ravaged and beaten? Neglected and half starved. Treated like an animal. Whose bright hopes had been snuffed out along with his life by the very people who should have protected him.

'Stop it.' Rosie wrapped her arms round his shoulders and he realised he was shaking. 'This isn't doing any good.'

Jack shrugged her off. He had to do something. He strode into the undergrowth, bashing away thick leaves and kicking at woody stems. Eventually he found the flint, half buried in the red soil. He returned, panting, to Sam's grave and placed it on top of the headstone.

'Now what are you doing?' Rosie stared at him.

Jack batted away a fly that was hovering near his face. 'It's what Jewish people do to honour their dead. I read about it somewhere.'

'But you're not Jewish.'

'No, but Sam was. This is a mark of respect.'

Rosie sat back and crossed her legs.

Jack knelt down beside her, waiting for the blood to stop pounding in his ears. Eventually other sounds drifted in. A faint scraping noise suggested work going on in the distance. Nearby was the whine of mozzies and the hum of bees. He touched Rosie's cheek briefly and she smiled. He wished his twelve-year-old self had known that he'd be back at Bindoon all these years later with a beautiful girl: happy, successful and secure. For a second, a young boy hovered at the edge of his consciousness, with bare bleeding feet and tattered clothes, his ruddy face smeared with dirt and his hands covered in blisters. Pining for his mother, but trying to be a man. And grateful to the older, stronger friend who rarely left his side. He pulled Rosie to her feet and they trudged back to the car.

'So where now?' asked Rosie as Jack manoeuvred the Falcon down the drive.

He couldn't leave Bindoon fast enough. It was only because of Sam that he'd come back at all. There must be a way to find out what had really happened to his friend. He refused to let it rest here. 'We're going to the police station.'

'Even though the brother warned you not to?'

Jack gripped the steering wheel. '*Especially* as the brother warned me not to.'

Rosie threw her head back, punched her fist into the air and whooped.

31

As they walked from the car, the sun seared the top of Jack's head and the pavement scalded his feet, even through his shoes. But the thoughts that whirled round his brain were even hotter. He couldn't order them like a lawyer should. Instead he wanted to ram his fist into the wall of the police station, rip up files and reports, obliterate all the filth and lies and sheer bloody smugness to finally get to the truth.

But as they entered the building, there was a shock of chilly air. Jack breathed it in and the coolness calmed his mind. His legs still felt hollow and his heart still pounded, but at least he was beginning to think more clearly. He told the desk sergeant he wanted to speak to someone about a historical death at the Boys Town. He and Rosie were shown into a small room with beige paint on the walls and a wide dark-wood table at one end. They sat on wooden chairs listening to the distant clatter of a typewriter. Jack tipped his head back. An old grey cobweb stretched, hammock-like, across the corner of the room. Above it, inexplicably, was a single blood-red fingerprint.

Eventually a tall man appeared in the doorway, in a blue shirt with sweat stains under the armpits. He shook hands with Jack, motioning to him to sit down. His eyes switched to Rosie but he didn't acknowledge her. 'Can the girl wait outside?'

'No, she can't.' Jack suppressed another surge of anger.

'Then how can I help *you*?' His words were addressed solely to Jack.

Jack placed his palms on the table. He was furious with the man's rudeness to Rosie but he had to focus on the main task. 'I've come to find out about a death in 1949. Samuel Becker. He lived at the Boys Town.'

'But that was twelve years ago. And what has this to do with you?'

'I'm a Perth lawyer,' replied Jack, conscious that his voice sounded gruff. He leaned forward slightly. 'But I'm also a former child migrant. I spent a short time at the Boys Town. Sam was my friend.'

The policeman pushed his glasses further up his nose but the gesture did nothing to hide the sharp glance he'd given Jack. 'I'll see what I can do.' He walked out of the room, leaving the door ajar. Jack looked at Rosie, who shrugged her shoulders. Jack drummed his fingers on the desk.

The officer returned carrying a cream-coloured file. He sat down heavily at the table, opened the file and rifled through it. Then he ran his finger down the final page until he came to some underlined type. 'Death by misadventure.' He looked up. 'Everything's in order.'

'Is there a doctor's report?'

The policeman rummaged through the pages again. 'Yes.'

'May I have the doctor's name and address? I'd like to speak to him.'

'Dr Munro is dead.' The policeman examined his nails.

'Then may I see the report?'

The policeman closed the file. 'You may not. It's confidential.'

Jack leaned forward. 'I have reason to suspect malpractice at the Boys Town. Samuel Becker was Jewish. I think that had something to do with his death.'

The policeman stood up. 'The brothers do wonderful work in our community. Their reputation is beyond reproach. I will not have ex *boys*,' he sneered at Jack as he said this, 'meddling in their affairs. Now kindly stop wasting my time.'

Jack took Rosie's hand. The man noticed and glared at them.

Resentment at the policeman's attitude, to both Sam *and* Rosie, charged through Jack. 'I will be taking this further,' he said as they left the room. Even to his own ears, his voice was full of iron.

'You realise that policeman *gubba* was lying, don't you?' said Rosie, outside the police station.

'He said the case was in order.'

Rosie sniffed. 'I was watching his eyes. Shifty. Sure sign of a liar. And he kept looking at his nails. He definitely had something to hide. Could spot it a mile off.'

'So how do we prove it?' Jack opened the car door for Rosie then climbed into the driver's seat.

'Well, my people would use a Dreaming to track down the evildoer and then we'd spear him. That would be the end of it. Your people drag things out for far too long.' She tipped down the sun visor and patted her hair in the mirror.

Jack laughed bitterly. 'That may be the case, Rosie, but lawyers have to go through the proper channels.'

Rosie shrugged.

Jack drove back down the Great Northern Highway in silence. He was furious with himself for not doing more. He hadn't expected much support from the brothers. No surprises there. But the police . . . Surely they had a duty to investigate an allegation? Despite his comment to Rosie, being a lawyer hadn't helped him much. Perhaps he should act off his own bat: write to anyone and everyone who might have some influence. There must be something. He gripped the wheel tighter, composing letters in his head to newspapers and embassies. He needed to get to the bottom of this, if only for his own satisfaction.

But there was nothing more to be done today. Rosie needed to get back. He couldn't risk a row with the Sullivans on top of everything else. He remembered when Rosie had been late returning from Kings Park, all those years ago. John had been furious with her. And he hadn't even known she'd been with Jack.

It had been then, when they'd met up in Kings Park, that Rosie had told Jack about her family. She must miss them dreadfully. He swallowed. They'd both lost their mothers. Were both haunted by their memories. Sometimes he wondered whether his sadness was as much for Rosie as for himself.

Rosie's skirt had ridden up a little when she'd got into the car, and unusually, she'd failed to tug it down. Jack glanced across at her smooth thighs, then turned back to the road, swallowing. A thin line of sweat trickled down the side of his head. The Falcon surged as he put his foot on the accelerator. Suddenly Peggy's pale legs lost their appeal. Her prissy ways had begun to annoy him anyway. In spite of the frustrations of the day, he'd enjoyed being with Rosie again. Her company felt natural; he didn't have to be on his guard all the time like he did with Peggy, worrying that he'd let something slip about England and his real mother. She certainly wouldn't understand his past like Rosie did.

When she'd knelt beside him at Sam's grave, he'd felt Rosie's warm breath on his neck, smelled her sweet fragrance. But he hadn't allowed himself to be distracted. This had been for Sam, not Rosie. His self-control hadn't achieved anything, though. Perhaps he'd have been better concentrating on her.

He drove over Upper Swan Bridge, faintly aware of the low sun turning the river gold. On the far side, they'd be almost level with the tops of the gum trees, their leaves transformed to bottle green by the gathering dusk. It felt as though they were moving from one world to another.

He glanced at Rosie again, noticing how her face glowed in the mellow light. The road was straight and the car took very little steering. A lay-by was coming up on the left. Jack signalled and pulled in. The Falcon purred to a halt.

He turned to face her. 'Thanks for coming with me today. It meant a lot.'

Rosie smiled. 'I'm glad I could be with you.' She fiddled with a strand of hair. 'I still don't understand why you didn't take Peggy, though.'

Jack swallowed. 'Peggy doesn't know me like you do.'

'Maybe not, but she's your girlfriend,' replied Rosie drily.

Jack sighed. 'I guess I only took Peggy out because I thought she might be able to help with my career.' He felt his cheeks burn. It sounded terrible when he said it like that. 'I need to be the best lawyer I can be if I'm to expose those brothers and honour my pledge to Sam.'

Rosie sniffed.

'But I realised today that I don't feel the same way about Peggy as I do about you. She and I were never friends. I'd already made up my mind to break things off with her. Even when I'm with her, it's you I'm always thinking about.' The truth was, he found it almost impossible to be intimate with Peggy. She always made the first moves physically. But whenever she touched him, Brother Cartwright's fat fingers would sidle into his mind, even though Peggy was nothing like him. It was only with Rosie that Jack ever felt at ease. And it was strange: when he was with Rosie, he never thought of Brother Cartwright at all.

Rosie sniffed again, but this time looked slightly more mollified.

Jack took her hand. 'But I need to know how you feel.'

Rosie looked out of the window. 'You know I like you, Jack,' she said softly. 'But we can never be together whilst we're both living at the Sullivans'.' When she turned back to look at him, it was hard to read her expression. 'And I don't want to harm your career.'

'I know.' Jack squeezed her hand. 'Trust me, Rosie. There must be a way through this. I don't want to hurt you.'

Rosie nodded sadly.

'But now I really must get home, or you'll be in trouble.' Already the sun was sliding towards the horizon. 'We'll talk about this later, when there's more time.'

'Okay.' Rosie's voice was subdued.

Jack restarted the engine and drove back through the Perth twilight. He and Rosie had something special together. More than the bond they felt from losing their families. They'd always been friends, but both of them knew deep down that it was turning into something more. Jack couldn't imagine life without Rosie and he sensed she felt the same..

It *was* complicated, though. The Sullivans would never countenance their relationship. He couldn't date Rosie as he could Peggy. But he'd been kidding himself all along with Peggy. He needed to see her and let her down gently. Then he could talk to Rosie. But, he reminded himself, this trip had been about Sam. And that was where his priorities must lie.

32

Mr Martin was a mild man. He opened doors for people, shut them softly, and spoke in a measured voice without ever shouting. His expression was always benign, whatever the circumstances.

Except today.

Today he slammed open the door to his office and barked Jack's name: 'Sullivan! In here!'

Every head lifted.

Jack lurched to his feet, knocking over a cup of tea that he didn't dare pause to mop up. He stumbled towards the office. Mr Martin stood by the open door, his face red and his dark eyebrows close together. Jack followed him in.

His boss strode round to the front of his desk, without asking Jack to sit down, and brandished a sheaf of papers at him. 'What in God's name have you done?'

Jack swallowed. He could see the Martin & Rowan heading on each letter. Although he wasn't close enough to read them, he could guess who they were addressed to: *The West Australian*, ABC News, the British Embassy, the Western Australian parliament.

And each one was signed by the same person: Jack Sullivan.

He swallowed again. 'How did you get them?' Best defence was attack.

'Never you mind how I got them. What the hell did you think you were doing writing to all these agencies using our address?'

'I thought it would have more clout.'

'More *clout*? Did you have a *locus standi* for any of this?'

'No, sir.'

'Did I authorise them? Or anyone else from the office?'

'No, sir.'

'Then what the hell did you think you were doing?' Mr Martin sat down heavily on his chair and slammed the papers down in front of him. His eyes still bored into Jack's face.

Jack sat down too, even though he hadn't been asked. He spread his palms on the desk. 'My friend Sam died at Bindoon in mysterious circumstances. I've talked to the brothers and the police, but everyone's clammed up. I needed to find a way to pursue this more formally.'

'Then go through the official channels. Don't drag us into it.' Mr Martin thumped the papers.

'I've tried. My adoptive father works for the Ministry of Immigration, but he's warned me off the case too. I didn't know what else to do.'

Mr Martin sighed. 'Why didn't you ask me, Jack?'

Jack tried to scratch his arm through the sleeve of his jacket. 'I'm sorry. I know I should have. But I'm just so tired of being fobbed off. Bashing my head against a brick wall. Every time I ask someone official, they dodge the issue. I seem to be the only person trying to do something. In the end, I took a risk. Thought the legal letters might jolt them into responding.' He looked down at the purple carpet. 'I didn't think they'd come back to you.'

'Clearly not.' Mr Martin still looked furious.

'Sir, please tell me how they got into your hands.'

Mr Martin smoothed the edge of his moustache. 'They came from the Ministry of Immigration. Must have been tipped-off who you were writing to. Seems like you've made enemies in high places.'

'I thought so.' Jack cleared his throat. 'There're young kids at Bindoon being made to work from dawn to dusk in bare feet. The brothers whipped us.' Even now he couldn't bear to let on about the other stuff.

Mr Martin didn't speak.

Jack gripped the edge of the desk. 'Sam's death wasn't an accident. Someone should close that place down. We were supposed to be white stock, the shining youth of England, come to help Australia in its hour of need. Instead we were treated worse than animals.'

'Okay, Jack. I know you've had a bad time. But this isn't the way to go about it.'

'Then what do I do?' Jack knew he was being unprofessional shouting like this. But the fury was bubbling up inside him again. He'd tried so hard. For Sam. For the other lads. For himself. Why wouldn't anyone listen?

Mr Martin sighed. 'I don't know. It seems like someone's covering this up at the highest level. We don't have a mandate to investigate, and if none of the agencies you've contacted will cooperate, then it really is a dead end.'

Jack rubbed his jaw. 'I can't give up. But I'm sorry I dragged Martin and Rowan into this.'

'I'm sorry too, Jack. You could have been struck off. But I don't want to lose you. Apart from this moment of madness, you've done well here. I wish you luck in your quest.' Mr Martin stood up, tore the letters down the middle and threw them in the bin.

Jack left the room on shaky legs. The matter was on hold for now.

But he *would* avenge Sam's death. And he *would* get justice for all the brothers' victims, past and present, himself included.

Even if it took the rest of his life.

*

Reggie lolled on the brown nylon sofa, a child under either arm. Susan had taken off her caliper and tucked it out of sight, her legs curled up underneath her on the cushion. Peter had his thumb in his mouth and was stroking Reggie's hair.

'Hey, don' do that, Peter. I've told you before.'

Peter reached across and stroked Susan's hair instead.

'Ow!'

Molly popped her head around the kitchen door. 'Stop it, both of you. Reggie – control your children, please.' She came into the room, removing her apron as she did so, then flopped down on an armchair and picked up a ball of wool from the floor.

'I *am*.' Reggie shook Susan and Peter's shoulders gently. 'Enough, you two. Come on, it'll be starting soon.' He moved forward, dislodging both children, and twiddled a button on the front of the small wood-clad television. There was a humming sound and a fuzzy picture appeared. Reggie repositioned the aerial. The snowstorm was replaced by the ATV symbol, followed by a series of stars. Then the screen was lit up with popping fireworks. He turned up the volume and the familiar theme tune blared into the room. The children sat back contentedly. Apart from the noises from the television, the only sounds came from Peter, still sucking his thumb, and the clack of Molly's knitting needles.

They always watched the first half of *Sunday Night at the London Palladium* together. It was their favourite. Reggie had forbidden *The Black and White Minstrel Show*, so it was the only programme they saw as a family, although the children were allowed to look at *Blue Peter* at teatime if they'd been good.

The show opened with some dancing girls. Their sparkly swimming costumes and high-kicking legs prompted a sniff from behind the knitting. Then Bruce Forsyth bounded on and introduced a magic act. Susan and Peter were entranced. When Adam Faith appeared, singing 'Lonesome', they all joined in.

'When are you going to sing at the Palladium, Daddy?' asked Susan.

Reggie laughed. 'Soon I hope, princess.'

Molly looked up from counting stitches. 'That would boost our savings.'

Reggie winced. He still hadn't put much money by. The television rental cost quite a bit, but he needed to watch these sorts of programmes for research. It was important to find out what people were singing, how they stood, how they danced. Mind you, he could do a lot better than that wooden Faith, who didn't seem to be able to sing and move at the same time. If Reggie were on the stage, he would *command* it. He puffed out his chest, imagining himself at the Palladium, then pulled it in as he remembered he'd meant to think about making more money.

He was still working at Warlingham, but he did fewer shifts now that he'd taken on more singing work. A new place had recently opened in Croydon, the Fairfield Halls, and they'd offered him a regular gig as a backing singer. If he played his cards right, he'd be centre stage before he knew it. Derrick Morgan and Prince Buster were making Jamaican music fashionable in Britain. There was big money to be made. That would please Molly.

He glanced over at his wife. She was engrossed in her knitting, a dark blue jumper with a red train motif for Peter. Did she look pale? He thought she'd seemed listless of late. He wondered if anything was wrong. He had the night off tonight. He'd make the cocoa for a change and tell her to put her feet up. That was the way.

After a bit more dancing, a comic magician came on and made them all laugh. Afterwards a young girl sang 'Bless this

353

House', which had Molly dabbing at her eyes. But Cliff Richard had star billing. When the first notes of 'The Young Ones' started, Reggie pulled Molly to her feet, sending the needles flying, and twirled her round while Susan and Peter clapped. But afterwards, Molly crumpled in her chair, clutching her stomach and wincing.

'You all right, Moll?'

She gave him a watery smile. 'Yes, fine. Just a bit puffed, that's all.'

Reggie went back to the television. The programme was nearly over.

'Right, you two.' He gave his children a gentle push. 'Upstairs and ready for bed. Susan, you have school tomorrow.'

'Do we have to?' whined Susan. 'I want to see them all waving at the end.'

'You know you can't,' said Molly. 'Come on, kiss your mum goodnight before you go.'

Susan and Peter dawdled up the stairs while Molly disappeared into the kitchen. Reggie heard the sound of a cupboard door opening and closing and then a tap running. He shuffled his head against the sofa, trying to find a soft spot between the lumps. The news was coming on. He had to turn it up because of the clattering from the next room. Eventually Molly returned with his cocoa and a glass of water for herself. She picked up her knitting again, and sat down next to him on the sofa. Damn. He'd forgotten *he'd* intended to get the cocoa.

He meant to ask her again if she was all right, but was

354

sidetracked by a news item. 'Says here they're laying a cable, Moll.'

Molly looked up. 'Oh?'

'S'called compact or somethin'. Anyway, it's goin' all the way to Australia.'

'Australia?' The sound of knitting stopped.

'Yeah. You'll be able to phone Jack soon.'

Molly passed her hand over her eyes. 'You've got it wrong. I don't want to contact Jack any more.'

'Why ever not?'

Molly wouldn't look at him. If anything, she was even paler now. 'I've been writing to him for years. Sending letters to the Boys Town and asking the brothers to forward them. I didn't tell you at the time as I thought you might be cross. Anyway, it doesn't matter. He never replied. He doesn't want to see me. Probably thinks I abandoned him and can't forgive me.' Her long-drawn-out sigh seemed to pierce his heart.

He put his arm round her. 'You don' know that.'

'It must be that. Either that or the photo I sent him.'

'What photo?'

She rubbed at her left ear. 'Me and the kids. It was that one you took on the beach last summer with Lester's Brownie. Maybe he disapproves of their colour. Or he thinks I've tried to replace him – even though I told him I hadn't. I don't know.'

Reggie turned his head away. All these months of work, rushing from Warlingham to the Locarno, and she'd never told him. They could've had some holidays with the money

355

they'd saved for travelling to Australia, he thought, forgetting that they'd spent a good deal of it on the car and the television. He might have given up the Warlingham job and devoted more time to music. Who knows, he could have been famous by now. Why the hell had she kept it a secret all this time, making him feel guilty, while it had been her who'd let him down?

He took his arm away and turned to remonstrate with her, but her eyes were glassy. She really didn't look well.

His anger turned back to pity. 'I'm sorry,' he said.

'I'm sorry too. I should have told you. I didn't want you to know at the time but I should have said something when I didn't hear back. It's been eating me up for years, knowing my own son doesn't want me.'

'Now you don' know that.' He pulled her close again. 'If he hasn't written back, maybe he never got the letters in the first place. You said you asked them to forward them. P'raps they forgot. Why don't you try once more?'

'No. My mind's made up. I'm not putting myself through that again. Susan and Peter are enough for me.' She pulled herself up with an effort and Reggie made to hug her, but she moved away.

'I'm going up to bed.'

Reggie stretched out on the sofa and tipped back his head. He'd had no idea all this was going on with Molly and he didn't know how to fix things. There had to be a way. But he was damned if he could think of one right now.

33

Jack opened his eyes and straightened his legs under the covers. Saturday. Bliss. He could turn over and doze if he wanted, or prop himself up on the pillows and read all morning. The day stretched before him like a clean beach: fresh and full of promise.

It was still a novelty, being on his own. There'd always been someone with him: first Mum; then the boys at Melchet; Tom, Bert and Mattie on the ship; his fellow Bindoon inmates, the other Nashos on service, Kathleen and John.

He strained his ears. There were some distant traffic sounds and the occasional cry of a child from further down the block. But no one fighting, no one shouting at him to get up, or even politely knocking on his door with some daft question or other. His own place. Solitude. He'd waited all his life to have mornings like this one.

When he had first moved out of the Sullivans' house, Kathleen had kept popping round with meals. At first Jack had been resentful, but when Rosie told him how sad and lonely Kathleen was without him, his heart softened. 'You're welcome any time,' he told her, swallowing down the lump in his throat when her eyes had glazed with tears. He'd given her a key so she could pop a casserole in the oven for him if he was working late. And if she ever needed a bolthole from John, she knew she could go there. He knew Kathleen adored him and he'd grown to love her too over the years. There was room in his heart for two mothers.

He wondered what Rosie was doing today. Kathleen had a lot more labour-saving devices now, like the new washing machine and the electric vacuum cleaner, so there was less heavy work. And of course, Rosie had claimed that Jack moving out had lightened her load still further. 'None of your *noorti* rubbish to clean up now,' she'd teased, flicking a duster at him. Jack had laughed. Kathleen had always forbidden Rosie to set foot in his room. He'd cleaned up his own *noorti* rubbish, although he'd often suspected Kathleen's intervention when he'd returned from school to find his belongings moved and a distinct smell of polish in the air. At least all that was over now.

He felt sorry for Kathleen. She'd held onto him as long as she could, but in the end even she had acknowledged he needed his independence.

Jack's stomach felt empty, but he didn't want to move. Perhaps he'd bring his bowl of cornflakes back to bed with him, another luxury. And if he spilled milk on the covers, no one would nag him.

He opened the fridge: a block of butter, a white-bearded tomato that had rolled to the back, and a bottle of milk, its neck clogged with yellow cream. He sniffed it. Not great, but worth risking. The packet of cornflakes was sitting on top of the fridge where he'd left it the night before. Come to think of it, he'd had rather a lot of cornflakes lately. But they filled him up and there must be some vitamins in them. They'd had wheat flakes during the war, he and Mum. He remembered eating them under the table with her when the air raids were on. Although cornflakes were different, nicer even, they still took him back to that time.

Having used the last clean bowl for his breakfast, he decided to tackle the pile of washing-up that had mounted over the week. He'd enjoyed having a cooked breakfast each morning, but now he discovered that dried-on egg yolk had the consistency of concrete. And it took ages to scrape off the sticky dark-orange mess the baked beans left behind. There were five cups of tea, all half drunk, surfaced with varying amounts of scum. Kathleen would be horrified. He never had 'instant food' at the Sullivans'. 'You're a growing boy, you need proper meals,' she'd said. He'd taken for granted the fish pies and treacle tarts, roast chicken and jam roly-poly. Rosie had learned to make them for him once she'd taken over from Kathleen in the kitchen. He'd never realised how time-consuming cooking was or what a mess it made. And that was just for basic food.

Once the washing-up was done, Jack wandered round the living room collecting discarded clothes and putting them down, then staring out of the window. He picked up the paperback copy of *Oliver Twist* from the sideboard. He'd hoped reading the classics would make up for the gaps in his education, but Oliver's adventures held no appeal for him today.

The clock's ticking echoed through the room. The still air smothered him like a blanket. Perhaps he needed some company after all.

He'd pop round to the Sullivans'. He hadn't visited for a bit. Maybe Rosie could be lured away for the afternoon. And Kathleen would be delighted to see him. John too, probably, although he'd show it differently. Jack picked up his coat and let himself out.

The duplex, at Mount Lawley, was only about a mile away from Highgate, one of the reasons Jack had rented it. The neighbourhood was nondescript: blocks of cream-coloured buildings, mostly housing Perth workers like Jack, a few bungalows sitting smugly on well-watered lawns, and a sprawl of suburban dwellings. There was the odd café and a couple of grocery shops – and the Astor cinema, of course, on the corner of Beaufort Street and Walcott. He'd taken Rosie there once. They'd sat at the back where no one could look at them and watched *To Kill a Mockingbird* with Gregory Peck as Atticus. Jack had been so inspired by the lawyer's integrity, he hadn't heard Rosie crying quietly beside him. It was only when she let out an audible sob at Tom Robinson's shooting that Jack had turned to her and held her hand.

'Things are changing, Rosie,' he'd said as they left the building, ignoring the curious stares. 'Look at the civil rights movement in America. The blacks there have had enough. Kennedy's taking them seriously. It's only a matter of time before Australia goes the same way. You'll see.'

'Maybe,' Rosie had replied, with a slight grimace. 'But someone is goin' to have to tell Mister Sullivan that.'

Jack turned into Grosvenor Road. He'd lived there for fourteen years, yet it was as though he was seeing it for the first time: the evenly dotted acacias; the neat green squares of grass – some more kempt than others; the Fords and Holdens gleaming in the drives. On the corner, a middle-aged woman with a tight grey perm was pruning roses while her corpulent husband cleaned their car. Further down, an elderly lady chatted over the fence with her equally elderly neighbour. They wore almost identical cream blouses, mirroring each other as though the fence was a line of symmetry. Jack realised how safe and staid the road's inhabitants looked, compared to the younger population in his block. He thought of Dan next door who played 'She Loves You' all day long until Jack was hearing it in his sleep, and the young couple at the end of the corridor who left the block on identical motorcycles each day wearing matching black leathers. He'd even been invited to a few parties.

He walked up the path and knocked on the door. He didn't like to use his key now that he no longer lived there, even though Kathleen had insisted he keep it. Rosie answered, her eyes widening at the sight of him. She ushered him into the lounge, where the Sullivans were sitting on the green sofa sharing a copy of *The West Australian*. There were two cups of tea on the low oak table and the remains of a plate of Anzac biscuits.

'What a lovely surprise,' said Kathleen, discarding the newspaper.

John got up and stepped forward to shake Jack's hand. 'Good to see you, old sport. This'll make your mum's day.'

Jack smiled at him.

'Are you staying for lunch?' asked Kathleen, as she gave him a tight hug then pushed a wisp of hair out of her eyes. 'We've got plenty, haven't we, Rosie?'

'Yes, ma'am.' Rosie's eyes were downcast. She seemed to have shrunk into the shadows.

'Come on in and grab a beer then,' said John, leading the way. Jack followed him onto the veranda, leaving Kathleen to rush upstairs and change and Rosie to return to the kitchen.

Jack had forgotten how nice cottage pie could taste. Especially followed by Kathleen's famous apple crumble and custard.

'How's work?' asked John, sipping his second beer. He reached forward to straighten a fork that had dared to slip out of line on the table.

'Still going well. Mr Martin's really taken me under his wing. Told me he's grooming me for promotion.' Jack straightened his tie.

John patted Jack's back forcefully. 'See that, Kath? Our boy's headed for the top.'

'Hardly that. But I'm doing okay.'

Even after all this time, neither of them mentioned Bindoon. Or Sam.

'Coffee, Jack?' said Kathleen.

'Please.'

Kathleen beckoned to Rosie, who cleared the plates then

brought in a tray of coffee and a small jug of milk. Her arm pressed up against Jack's as she handed him his cup. His mouth twitched with the effort of not turning to her and smiling. Her touch sent a charge through his body.

'Let's take these onto the veranda,' said Kathleen. 'It's such a lovely day.'

'You go ahead,' said Jack. 'I'll just use the bathroom.'

He made sure the Sullivans were seated before he popped his head round the kitchen door.

Rosie was standing by the sink, her hands immersed in suds. She was wearing her black-and-white maid's uniform and her hair shone in the sunlight that drenched the room. Jack tiptoed up and put his arms round her waist, pressing his face into her back. It was warm and firm, the silky fabric stretching across her taut muscles. When she turned round to face him, he kissed her, breathing in the faint scent of apples on her lips.

'I've missed you.'

'Me too.'

He kissed her again and reached up to stroke her hair. She was so beautiful. He was glad he'd thrown over Peggy for her. Even if they did still have to meet in secret.

They both jumped at the sudden crash behind them.

'What the hell d'you think you're doing?' The words sounded slow and thick. Rosie stiffened in his arms and Jack buried his head briefly in her shoulder. After all these years of stealth, he'd finally blown it.

He turned to face John.

If the situation hadn't been so serious, it would have been almost comical. John's face was changing from white to red as though someone was pressing a switch. He had a coffee cup in his hand. The saucer was in pieces on the floor.

'So now that you've left the house, you think you can come back and grope the maid, is that it?'

All Jack had to do was say yes. He'd get a telling-off for sure, and John would make a few coarse comments about keeping it in his trousers and finding a girl of his own race. But after a while, that would be that. He knew how John thought.

He'd stepped away from Rosie but he could feel her looking at him. He didn't dare return her glance, but he knew what her expression would be. If he shrugged off the incident, as common sense demanded, it would be to deny her. He loved this girl. He knew she loved him too. She was too precious to write off as a cheap tart. He had to come clean. And after all this time it would be almost a relief to do so.

He looked steadily at John. 'No, that's not it. Rosie and I are engaged.'

He heard Rosie's sharp intake of breath but didn't take his eyes off John's face. To look away would be seen as a sign of weakness, and he couldn't risk that.

'Engaged! You bloody idiot!'

John's shout brought Kathleen in, her mouth already open in horror at the scene.

'What on earth's going on?'

'This dumbass thinks he wants to marry the maid.'

'Is this true, Jack?' Kathleen's shock was even harder to bear than John's incandescence.

'We've been in love for a while.'

'So that's why you wanted to move out. So you could conduct your grubby affair on your own patch.' John's face was purple now.

'No, it's not. I wouldn't treat Rosie like that.'

'Jack?' Kathleen's hand was on his shoulder. 'Tell me this isn't true.'

Jack stayed silent.

'Don't do this to us. Not after all we've given you.'

'I'm sorry, Kathleen. I wouldn't hurt you for the world . . . but I really love Rosie.'

'*You!*' John marched up to Rosie as though to hit her, and she ducked. But it wasn't violence he intended. 'You scheming bitch! Go and pack your bags. I'll give you a week's wages.'

Rosie didn't move.

Jack went to stand beside her, putting his arm around her rigid shoulders.

'It's okay. I mean what I say. We'll get married. You can live with me at the duplex as my wife. There's nothing John can do.'

He shouldn't have said that.

John's anger leapt at him from across the room. 'I rescued you from Bindoon.' Every word was a shout. Even through his horror, Jack registered 'rescued'. So John did know how things were there. 'I made you my son. Poured money into your education. Brought you up to be a lawyer . . .' Jack didn't mention that the law had been his choice, 'so you could marry this bloody boong from the back of Bourke. Are you mad? You'll be turned out of the firm, shunned by everyone you know. And your children . . .' John visibly shuddered, 'will be half-caste. It's dis-gust-ing. *You're* dis-gust-ing.' He pounded a fist on the worktop in time with the syllables.

Jack drew a deep breath. 'Rosie means far more to me than any job.'

Kathleen gave a choking sob.

John stepped forward, his fists bunched. Jack stood his ground. Let John hit him if it made him feel better. It wouldn't do his cause any good.

But John's hand didn't connect. Suddenly it was his own chest he was pounding. Little gasps were coming out of his mouth and his face was greasy with sweat. He sank slowly to his knees.

'*John!*' Kathleen rushed towards him; her fingers scrabbled at the button on his collar. But John didn't move. Jack realised afterwards that he was probably already dead before he hit the floor.

Afterwards, Kathleen was mute with shock. Rosie was sobbing, while Jack was trying to keep his hands steady long enough to dial 000.

Medics confirmed the fatal heart attack. They asked if John had experienced any warning signs, but Kathleen shook her head. Just the mild indigestion a man his age could expect, especially after the rich ministerial dinners he ate on a regular basis. He'd given up playing rugby a few years ago, pleading fear of injury, and had gained weight as a result.

But no one mentioned the terrible shock of Jack's apparent betrayal of all John held dear. Jack wondered if Kathleen would ever forgive him.

The days blurred with visits: undertakers followed the medics, then friends and colleagues from the department. Kathleen greeted them all white-faced and frozen-lipped. When Jack looked back on that time, he felt as though he'd been pulled into a vortex.

Kathleen let him arrange the funeral. She had a few requests for hymns and readings but left the rest to Jack, seemingly wanting to spend as little time with him as possible. She stood beside him in the church, stick-thin in a black suit and pillbox hat, but refused to let him take her arm or accept his offer of a handkerchief.

The obituaries were effusive: John had been a much-respected executive who'd worked tirelessly for the Department of Immigration. His contributions to the White Australia movement were admirable; he'd played a major part in securing child migrants at such a crucial time in the nation's history. He'd even adopted one of his own – a laudable gesture – and had been a key player in the operation to reduce the indigenous population.

Even Jack started to believe the eulogies despite being all too aware of John's less desirable side. Turning a blind eye to the brothers' cruelty; trying to prevent him from investigating

Sam's death; never acknowledging that Rosie had been torn away from her family. Yet what he'd said on that fateful afternoon had been true in part: John *had* rescued him. He *had* given him opportunities beyond his wildest dreams. Jack would always be grateful for that. And although he'd always feel guilty for his role in John's death, a little part of him was relieved that it would now be easier to find out what had happened to Sam.

Jack moved back into Grosvenor Road for a bit, while Rosie took his place at the duplex. People were tolerant there, and seeing them both together would be too much for Kathleen.

'But how can you be so sure I *am* prepared to marry you?' Rosie had asked him, hands on hips and eyebrows arched. 'Surely you'd be much better off with Prissy Peggy?'

Jack shuddered. Rosie sometimes pretended to be jealous, but he knew she trusted him deep down. 'Okay, I'll leave you behind with Kathleen then. You can grow old together.'

Rosie screwed up her face in horror. 'All right. Where's the ring?'

Jack laughed. 'On its way. In the meantime, you can live the high life over in Mount Lawley.'

'Guess I can always pretend to be the maid if anyone asks what I'm doing there.'

'Well, I suppose you'll be getting used to your future home.' Jack earned enough now to give Rosie some housekeeping money to compensate for her loss of wages. Kathleen didn't comment on her absence.

Jack was overjoyed that he'd chosen warm, loving Rosie over cool, ambitious Peggy. There was no contest. Never had been. Rosie was his girl. He'd brave anything to have her by his side.

34

Molly rubbed rouge into her cheeks in the bathroom mirror. Her face was so pale these days. At least some semblance of health could be scraped from the little pot of red cream. She rummaged in the back of the cabinet to find her winter foundation. She'd read in a magazine that if you dotted a lighter colour under your eyes, it would cover up the dark circles. She patted the foundation in gently, then stepped back to check her reflection from the other side of the room. Better, yes. But tiredness still tugged at her eyes, the skin above them wrinkled like crêpe bandages. She was constantly exhausted, asleep by the time Reggie came home from the Locarno. Yet it was she who was up first for the children whilst he dozed on in the morning. Sometimes she wondered whether they were ever in the bed at the same time.

She'd run out of lipstick, but she smeared a little more of the rouge onto her mouth. The other women were bound to look glamorous. She didn't want to show Reggie up. But even getting ready drained her. There was still a little puddle of lily-of-the-valley perfume left in her scent bottle. She dabbed it behind her ears, then popped her head round the door of the children's room to check if Susan was ready after her nap.

If the child was to be up late, as Reggie had insisted, she needed to rest first.

Susan was sitting on her bed putting on the leg brace. Molly had made her do it up herself once she was old enough. She knew from her time at Warlingham how easy it was to let people do things for you. And how important it was to be independent. But Susan would always limp. All her life.

Molly had tried to blot out the memory of all those little bodies trapped in the iron lungs that hissed like snakes. Children should run, chase balls, swim in rivers, climb trees, not be incarcerated. Though Susan would never play like other children, at least she wasn't in a metal box.

Molly had gone up to the hospital most days when Susan was ill, despite not being allowed to visit her as she was in the family way with Peter. Matron wouldn't even let Susan have Winnie, her favourite teddy bear. Molly left little letters at the gate lodge filled with pictures and rows of xxxx's, so she knew her mummy still cared. Deep in her bones she still felt the pain of those months away from the daughter she'd nearly lost, along with the ache for the son she'd almost given up hope of ever seeing again.

'Moll-y! Sus-an! You ready?' Reggie shouted.

'Just coming.' Molly beckoned to Susan. 'Hurry up. Dada's waiting.'

Susan followed her haltingly down the stairs. She'd tied her dark curls back with a red ribbon and her brown eyes were huge with excitement.

Old Mrs North from next door was leaning back on Molly's

armchair, her plump lisle-clad legs stretched out in front of her. Peter was lying on the carpet constructing a lorry from Meccano pieces, and barely looked up as Molly kissed him goodbye.

'Another half an hour, then Peter needs to be in bed,' Molly said.

'Right you are, dearie.' One of Mrs North's chins wobbled her agreement.

'Thanks so much. I'm ever so grateful.'

Mrs North smiled, a little arc appearing between heavy jowls. 'Always a pleasure. Peter and I get on just fine, don't we?'

Peter nodded, lining up two of the hole-punched bars of metal ready to push through the bolt.

As soon as he saw Molly and Susan, Reggie made a low bow. 'Your carriage awaits, my ladies.'

'Are we going in the car?' Susan asked.

'No, I've book' a taxi,' replied Reggie. 'Save you the long walk from the car park.'

Molly pursed her lips. Money was like liquid in Reggie's hands. He even raided Susan's piggy bank sometimes.

Once the taxi drew up outside the Locarno, Reggie ushered them in. Children weren't normally allowed at the club, but Susan was to stand in the wings to watch Reggie, whilst Molly sat in the audience. She dreaded being at a table on her own, having to buy her own drink, remembering to take little sips so it would last all evening, and trying to ignore the curious stares from all those confident women and flashy men.

After the warm-up act, Reggie came on and sang 'Catch a Falling Star'. Molly had forgotten how smooth and warm his voice sounded. It sent little pulses deep into her body. When the crowd clapped and roared at the end, Reggie, with his bright smile, looked more alive than she'd seen him for a long time. He squinted into the darkness until he found her, and gave her a wink. Molly squirmed with pleasure. What with looking after Susan and Peter and the ever-present concern for Jack, she sometimes forgot she was also a wife. Reggie was lovely. Perhaps she should treasure him more. It was just that she was always so tired.

People were shouting and stamping their feet. They wanted Reggie to sing again.

But instead he darted into the wings and returned carrying Susan in his arms. A murmur travelled round the room.

Reggie carried her up to the microphone and the crowd quietened. Some of the women said, 'Ahh . . .' and a man with brilliantined hair shouted, 'Hello, little lady,' causing people to laugh. Reggie turned back to the band and tilted his head. Behind him, Deelon started to play his guitar softly; Lester had swapped his drumsticks for brushes, which made a quiet shushing noise.

Reggie spoke into the microphone. 'This is my little girl, Susie. It's long past her bedtime. I've let her stay up as a special treat. But I'm goin' to sing her a lullaby now. It's one my mother used to sing to me back home. I've had to change the words a bit.' He pulled a funny face and the audience giggled.

Molly thought Susan looked a bit cross. She'd be furious

with her dad for treating her like a baby. Reggie was holding her like a baby too. Susan was probably dying to wriggle, but she just closed her eyes and snuggled into his arms. Molly swallowed.

Reggie sang, very quietly: *When you're not with me and I'm feeling blue, I like to close my eyes and think of you.* No one made a sound. Molly could feel people straining to hear in the darkness. *Hush little baby, don't you cry, Dada sing Jamaican lullaby.*

Reggie's voice was all husky. He rocked Susan gently as he sang. She was almost asleep when he finished.

Molly wiped her face with her hanky. She'd forgotten all about her foundation.

35

A month after the funeral, Kathleen asked Jack to help sort out John's things.

'I'll give most of his clothes to the Salvos.' The frost was still in her voice. 'Unless you want anything?'

Jack shook his head.

Kathleen handed him a pile of suits and shirts, which he stuffed into boxes. Jack thought how the clothes reflected John's life: the discreet office apparel; the evening finery; the showy sportswear. Somewhere amongst those bundles was the suit he had worn to Bindoon when he'd first met Jack; the swimming trunks he'd displayed on the beach that Christmas when he'd taught him to play rugby; maybe even the old suit from his wedding to Kathleen. And the casual slacks and jumper that had clothed him that day he'd walked into the kitchen to an unplanned confrontation.

Eventually the clothes were packed and lined up in the hall ready for collection.

'Just in time,' said Kathleen. 'The Salvos said they'd come this afternoon.'

Jack nodded, rubbing his back.

Kathleen turned to go into the kitchen, then stopped. She

burrowed inside her apron pocket and drew out a key. 'By the way, I found this in one of John's suits. D'you recognise it?'

Jack took it from her and held it up to the light. It was tiny, a little tarnished. He frowned. 'Can't be a door key. Too small. Suitcase?'

Kathleen shook her head. 'All the suitcase keys are in my bedside drawer.' She paused for a second, then grabbed the key from Jack. '*Drawer!*' She ran into John's study.

It didn't open straight away. Kathleen rattled the key in the lock, then drew it out and reinserted it straighter. When she tugged at the wooden knob, the desk drawer shot out. She thrust in her hand, pulled out a stack of papers, then dropped down onto the carpet to read them. They looked like work documents.

'Most of these will need to go back to the ministry,' she said, pushing a strand of hair out of her eyes. 'Some of them I'll file away. The remainder can be binned.'

'I'll help you.' Jack joined her on the floor, listening to her running commentary as she held up the files and letters: 'Rubbish . . . keep . . . return . . . return . . . rubbish . . . keep.' He dragged the waste-paper bin from under John's desk and maintained pace with her, jettisoning or filing the material as instructed. After a while he became conscious of a lack of sound and movement. He looked up. Kathleen had sat back on her heels and was reading a flimsy pale-blue sheet.

'What's the matter?' He couldn't fathom her expression.

She passed the airmail letter to him; he glanced at it quickly, then sharpened his attention. *Dear Jack, You will be surprised to hear from me after all these years . . .*

His stomach swooped.

Mum.

He read to the end without speaking, then snatched up the other letters from the pile and read them quickly. They'd been filed in date order and were increasingly desperate in tone – until one dated December 1960, which ended: *If I don't hear from you this time, I'll give up. Maybe you've moved on and never got my letters. Or maybe you just want to leave the past behind. If that's the case, I'll accept once and for all that you don't want to know me. I don't blame you. Have a good life, Jack. You deserve it.*

A photo had fluttered out of the last letter. An older Mum but still with long curly hair and bright eyes. And a child either side of her. Jack heard a guttering noise come from his mouth.

'Jack?' Kathleen was ashen.

He stood up. His whole body was shuddering. Kathleen rose to put an arm round him, but he shrugged her off.

Kathleen looked him in the eye for the first time in weeks. 'I'm so sorry. I'd no idea John was hoarding all this stuff.' She pulled at the edges of her cardigan until she'd wrapped it across her chest.

Jack strode over to John's desk and kicked at the still open drawer, which jerked on its runners. He yanked at it until it careered out of the desk, then hurled it against the wall.

Kathleen ran out of the room.

*

'Bloody John,' Jack said to Rosie later, back at the duplex. He was pacing up and down whilst Rosie sat on the grey sofa.

Rosie picked up one of the turquoise cushions. She'd insisted on buying them, claiming the sofa was dull. 'Perhaps he thought he was protecting you.'

'*Protecting* me? Allowing me to think my mum was dead when all this time she'd been desperate to get in touch?' He thumped the door frame.

Rosie threw down the cushion. 'Careful! Maybe he was helping you to feel you belonged?'

Jack started to pace again. 'Why did I have to belong? I had a mother in England! I could have gone back to her.'

Rosie stood up and put an arm round him. 'But your birth mother was poor, wasn't she? She could never have given you the things the Sullivans gave you.'

Jack pulled away from her. 'She wouldn't have had such high ambitions for me either. Sometimes I thought I'd suffocate under the weight of their expectations.'

'I know.' Rosie led him gently to the sofa and drew him onto it. 'But if you hadn't been at the Sullivans', you wouldn't have met me.'

'S'pose not.' Jack put his arm round her. He thought back to the last time he'd hugged Kathleen. Her shoulders had felt bony compared to Rosie's. Perhaps he shouldn't take his anger out on Kathleen. She'd been deceived too.

'And we can visit Molly after we're married.'

Jack's first reaction had been to rush over to England straight away. It was vital his mother knew he'd never forgotten her. It wasn't that he hadn't cared about her. He'd been told she was *dead*! But perhaps it was better to wait. Once they were man and wife, it would be much easier for Rosie to go with him.

He sat up, dislodging her. 'How *dare* John deprive me of all those years when I could have seen my mother?'

'But how would you have got to England? John would never have paid for you, and you've only recently earned your own money.'

Jack swallowed drily. 'But I could have written. Told her all the things I wanted her to know. That I can play rugby, that I've done my national service, gone to uni . . .'

Rosie sniffed.

'. . . met a beautiful girl.'

She smoothed down her skirt. 'You can still tell her those things when you meet her.' She put her hand on his knee and squeezed it.

Jack covered her fingers with his own. Rosie had been more physically affectionate since John died. And since Jack had made their wedding announcement. He had always desired her, but it was also hard to blank out the memory of Brother Cartwright's probing fingers. They came into his mind now, fleshy, greasy. He shuddered. 'If I hadn't gone to Australia, I wouldn't have met Brother Cartwright.'

Rosie shifted in her seat. 'But the other boys would. And no one would have protected them.'

'No one protected *me*! Living in poverty with my mother

would have been infinitely better than working myself to the bone to help build bloody Bindoon. And fending off the bloody brothers!'

'I know. What they did to you all was terrible. But if you'd gone to England, you wouldn't have become a lawyer. This way you can get revenge for all of them – if that's what you want to do.'

'I haven't had much success yet.'

'But you will. I know you. You won't give up. However long it takes.'

Jack rammed his fist against his chest. 'I certainly won't. I'll honour my promise to Sam.'

'And anyway . . .' Rosie touched his cheek; he hadn't realised it was wet, 'perhaps it was better your mother didn't know what you were going through.'

Jack pulled from his pocket the picture Molly had sent. Her grinning between two sprogs. 'No, she was getting on with her life. Marrying some chap, having kids.'

'You'll be able to meet your half-brother and -sister when we go to England.'

'I'm not sure I want to.'

Rosie raised an eyebrow.

'Two plump cuckoos who've basked in my mother's affection all these years?' Jack scratched furiously at the skin inside his elbow. The site of his childhood eczema still itched when he got upset. So whilst he'd been trying to come to terms with the fact that his mother was dead, she'd gone on to have other children. *His* mother had nursed and cherished another boy and girl. *His* mother had sung to them, read to them, stroked their hair, hugged them. Had loved them as much as she had him. Maybe more.

'But she was constantly trying to contact you. Look at all those letters. It wasn't her fault John hid them.'

'No.' Jack slumped back in his seat. 'Bloody, bloody John.'

Rosie leaned back with him. 'Why don't you write to her now? You're good with words. Tell her how you feel.'

Jack got to his feet. 'There's some airmail paper around somewhere from when I wrote to the British Embassy.' He prowled round the room, flinging open cupboard doors and snatching at drawer handles.

Rosie stood up too. 'Tell her we'll come and see her as soon as we're married.'

'Of course.' Jack shoved back a strand of hair that had flopped onto his forehead.

Rosie turned to go into the kitchen. 'And be thankful you *can* be in touch with your mother. I'd give anything to have my family at our wedding.'

Jack shot a glance at Rosie. Poor girl. All this fuss about *his* mother; he'd forgotten how much she must miss hers. He found the paper at last and sat down thoughtfully to write to Molly.

Jack went back to Grosvenor Road that night. Rosie had calmed him down, as she always did, and he needed to sort things out with Kathleen.

He found her in the kitchen, dispiritedly chopping up apples. She didn't turn round as he came into the room.

'I'm sorry, Kathleen.' He put a palm on her back.

The chopping continued, a bit more slowly.

'You weren't to blame.'

She laid down her knife and turned to face him. Her hair looked lank; her eyes dull.

Jack put an arm round her and steered her towards the veranda.

'I need to finish this apple crumble.'

'A whole apple crumble. Just for you?'

Kathleen shrugged. 'Old habits die hard.'

'It can wait.' Jack pressed her gently into a chair, then drew the other wooden seat close to her. 'Finding Molly's letters has been a terrible shock. I really believed she was dead when John showed me that official document.' He didn't mention the tiny flame of hope that had never quite gone out.

Kathleen delved into the sleeve of her cardigan. 'I was as much in the dark as you were.' She drew out her handkerchief and blew her nose.

'I know. Rosie told me off for treating you so badly.'

Kathleen sniffed. 'She's a good girl. But she's my maid. You went behind my back. Both of you.'

Jack spread his fingers across his knee. 'I would have told you, but I was too wary of John's reaction. With good reason, as it turned out.'

'The shock killed him, Jack.'

'That was the final straw, yes. But so did the drink, the big meals, the lack of exercise . . .'

Kathleen gave a juddering sigh and looked away from him, across the garden. A myna bird was perched on the back fence, scooping his head in little darting movements.

Jack cleared his throat. 'Rosie and I really want you to come to our wedding.'

Kathleen didn't move.

'Kathleen?'

Her eyes were still on the bird, which had fluffed out its feathers and was chirping in a staccato rhythm.

Jack reached into his pocket and pulled out a thick white envelope. He laid it on Kathleen's lap. 'Here's your invitation. We can't force you to come.' He stood up. 'But I really want my mother at the church when I get married.'

She didn't touch the envelope. 'I'm not sure, Jack. I need to think about this.'

Jack dropped a kiss on her head and left her, still staring out into the garden.

The next few weeks were hectic. So many people to see: the vicar, the organist, the tailor. All alongside his work at Martin & Rowan. But no amount of busyness could hide the fact that Kathleen hadn't given him a decision. She changed the subject whenever he mentioned the wedding.

A few days before they were due to get married, Jack popped into the duplex to tell Rosie he was going on a road trip. 'I want to put the Falcon through its paces.'

'What, *now*?'

'I just need to get out of Perth.'

'Can I come?' Rosie was holding up a mirror and trying out different hairstyles.

'Not this time. We'll go on lots of trips after we're married, but this one I have to do alone.'

'And you'll be gone overnight?' She twisted her hair at the back and pinned it on top of her head.

'I need to put the miles in.'

'How do I know you're not visiting some girl upcountry?' She let her hair fall loose again.

Jack grabbed the mirror off her. 'Oh for goodness' sake, I'd have had to acquire her pretty rapidly. I've never been away before, have I?'

'No-o.'

Rosie always reacted badly when he left her. He could certainly identify with that fear of being abandoned. Yet he needed to put her off the scent. This mission was for her but she mustn't find out yet. 'Don't Aboriginal men go walkabout before they get married?' he asked casually.

'Yes, they do. To prove themselves in the bush. But that goes on for six months! If you disappear for that long, you'll come back to find me married to someone else.'

'It's just a two-day walkabout. You won't find someone to put up with you that quickly.'

She wagged a finger. 'Okay. But no girls.'

Jack returned the mirror. 'Absolutely no girls. This one is more than enough for me to handle.'

*

The next day, Jack slung an overnight bag onto the back seat of the Falcon. He drove north-east out of the city, following the course of the Swan as it meandered inland, through fertile valleys dotted with dusty green sheoak trees and towering flooded gums. The road steepened as it wound up the Darling Scarp, and Jack remembered Rosie's tale of the Wagyl all those years ago, when he'd got bitten by the redback in Kings Park.

He was doing this for Rosie. But telling her the purpose of his journey would only get her hopes up. Better to bear her suspicion that he'd got a girl somewhere, even though the notion was ridiculous, than risk her disappointment if he came back with nothing. He gripped the steering wheel. He was still hammering on every door he could think of to find out how Sam had died, but even now no one would give him an inch; with this mission he *had* to be successful.

When he reached the Great Northern Highway, he opened up the throttle. You could drive for miles here without seeing another car, and that suited Jack's mood. This was the route to Bindoon, and although he had no intention of stopping, he still felt a lurch of dread when he saw road signs pointing to the Boys Town. It wasn't until he was safely on the Moora road that he felt himself relax.

By early evening he'd reached his destination. He climbed out of the car and stretched his arms to ease the stiffness. In front of him were some low ramshackle buildings surrounded by a cluster of tall marri trees. He walked purposefully towards a small whitewashed chapel, and the meeting he'd arranged a few days earlier.

On the day of the ceremony, Kathleen sat for a long time at her dressing table. Eventually she leaned forward and smeared on a little rouge from the small pot in front of her. No need to pinch her cheeks these days. Was that too much? Didn't want to be accused of being a merry widow. She damped it down with some powder from her compact.

At first she'd been almost surprised to see her face staring back at her when she looked in the mirror. Since John died, she'd felt sheathed in bandages, like an Egyptian mummy. They wrapped round her feet, stopping her from feeling the ground; they encased her head, numbing her thoughts; they enveloped her limbs so no one could touch her, and she couldn't feel anybody either. There was even a thin layer over her face, her eyes, her ears so the world looked fuzzy and sounds filtered in as though from a long way off. Did all widows feel like this?

The word *widow* was a strange one. It sounded a bit like window, but that helped you to see out; being a widow only made you see in. Into your head, where disturbing thoughts echoed night and day.

She rummaged in her drawer for that Elizabeth Arden lipstick. John had said it suited her.

She'd hated John's domineering ways, his lack of understanding. But she'd realised over the years that much of that was to do with their inability to have a child. Once Jack had come along, John had changed. He taught Jack rugby moves, helped him patiently with his homework, endlessly explained Australian politics over the dinner table.

But Kathleen couldn't forget the sad faces of the boys at Bindoon. It'd been the brothers, not John, who'd ill-treated those lads. But John had known what went on and done nothing to stop it. He'd been too in awe of the minister, too keen on his own standing, his own promotion, to intervene.

Yet Kathleen knew she hadn't done anything either. She'd realised the boys were victims too, but had kept her silence so she could keep Jack.

They were both to blame.

She feathered her eyebrows with a little brown pencil, then checked in the mirror again. She didn't want to overdo things, yet it was strange to have no one to criticise her. 'Look like a hooker, Kath,' John had said to her one day when she'd tried to lengthen her eyes with kohl like Audrey Hepburn. She'd hastily wiped it off.

She retrieved the kohl stick from the back of her drawer, where she'd shoved it that day. Hiding things in drawers. She and John had done a lot of that. Her diary. His private documents. Kathleen's hands shook at the memory of those letters from Jack's mother.

She leaned forward again. Damn John. She *would* do her eyes. Once her hands were steady.

For some reason the man from William Street on VJ night came into her head. She'd thought of him from time to time. Wondered if things would have been different if she'd had an affair with him, or even left John. But then there'd have been no Jack. And she still might not have had a child of her own.

She applied the eyeliner, then reached for the little pillbox hat she'd bought yesterday from Ahern's, when she'd finally decided to accept the invitation. It had a veil she could slip over the top half of her face. Might be useful if the kohl ran. One last look in the mirror. She didn't look too gaunt in her peacock-blue tunic. She'd lent Rosie the old shantung silk wedding dress she'd once put aside for a daughter.

Jack was at the door in his new suit. 'The car's here.'

Kathleen swallowed. 'Let's go.' She took her son's arm and they set off together to his wedding.

Two days after the formal service at St Alban's, Rosie, Jack and Kathleen went to Kings Park for a Noongar ceremony. Rosie had told Jack he had to light a ceremonial fire to open a doorway for their ancestors who'd passed on. As he held the flickering taper, Jack sent up a silent prayer of thanks that Molly was alive and well. He'd kept her letters under his pillow, as a child would do. After a while he knew the words by heart. Just as well, as his tears had blurred the ink.

He'd written and rewritten his reply to her so many times. But in the end he'd decided it wasn't fair on Kathleen to send a letter too soon, in case Molly decided to fly out for the ceremony. So he'd dropped the blue envelope into a postbox as he left Perth for his road trip. Letters still took weeks to get to England. By the time Molly received it, he and Rosie would be safely married.

When the fire died down, a swirling smoke rose from the ashes. Jack watched Rosie's face as four ghostly figures walked towards them, appearing as if through mist. A middle-aged woman with a careworn face and greying hair, flanked by two boys in traditional Noongar dress and a girl a little younger than Rosie. Not ancestors. Real-life flesh-and-blood.

Rosie screamed. 'I don't believe it!' Then she ran towards the figures. 'Mum . . . Alkira . . . Cobar . . . Darel.'

Jack blinked back the tears. This time he'd succeeded. 'My wedding present, Mrs Sullivan.' At first he'd hated the thought of Rosie taking the name he so associated with John. But Rosie knew him as Jack Sullivan, so in the end they'd agreed it would be their married name.

He'd driven up to Mogumber on his road trip and used all his legal powers to track down Rosie's family. Then gone all the way to Narrogin to collect them. They'd stayed at a boarding house in town until the wedding.

Jack touched Rosie's arm. 'No girl should have to get married without her family there to support her.'

And no boy either, he thought.

I'm married, Mum. Me. Scrawny little Jack Malloy, a husband.

How he wished he still had *that* name.

36

By the time Molly went to the doctor's, even her bones were aching.

'Why on earth didn't you come sooner?' Dr Cole glowered at her over his glasses.

'Would you have been able to cure me?'

The doctor averted his gaze. 'We could have given you something for the pain.'

Molly shifted in her seat. 'Aspirin takes the edge off it.'

He pulled a small pad towards him and scrawled across the top sheet. 'We'll have to wait for the results of the tests, but in the meantime I can certainly give you something stronger than aspirin.'

'Thank you.' She was aware how thin her voice sounded. She took the prescription, slipped it into the pocket of her checked woollen coat and stumbled out of the surgery.

As she sat on the bus home, wincing at every bump and judder, she wondered how to break the news to Reggie. He'd be angry she'd gone to the doctor's by bus when he could have driven her there and accompanied her to the appointment. But he'd be even more furious when he found out how she'd hidden the symptoms all these months. She could hear his voice now: *Why the hell didn't you tell me, Moll? What am I, a mind-reader?* And how would she answer? That the physical pain distracted her from the mental anguish of knowing that Jack didn't want to meet her; that she'd never see her firstborn son again.

In the meantime, Susan and Peter were growing up. This was both solace and gall. Molly was a much older mother second time around. One time she'd stood at the gates as the children had tumbled out of school and heard Peter's friend shout that his grandmother was waiting for him. Peter had hugged her but released her more quickly than usual. Molly knew that was only the start. Soon he'd beg to be allowed to walk home on his own, and when Susan was old enough to see boys, she'd find excuses not to introduce them to Molly. No such problem with the ever-youthful Reggie, of course. Perhaps it was easier just to slip away and let them all cope without her.

She leaned back against the worn nylon headrest of the bus. This was the pain talking, she knew it. And despair at the inevitable.

When Molly let herself into the house, Reggie was already home. She pulled out a chair and joined him at the kitchen table.

'Cup of tea?' He'd stood up to kiss her and was already reaching for the kettle.

'That would be nice.' She eased off her shoes and stretched her legs out, watching her husband with eyes she knew looked exhausted. Was it her imagination, or had Reggie slipped something into his pocket? She'd learned from experience it was no use asking. He'd tell her in his own good time.

Reggie poured boiling water into the pot, swilling it round as Molly had shown him all those years ago. Then he tipped it out, spooned in some ground leaves from the packet and added more water, releasing the distinctive fragrance. She watched listlessly as he set out the cups and walked over to the fridge. He was letting the tea steep, keeping himself busy with milk and sugar until the time was right to pour. Molly smiled to herself. She'd taught him well.

As she predicted, by the time he'd handed her a steaming cup and joined her at the table with his own, he was ready to divulge his secret.

'I've got some news,' he said.

'So have I, but you go first.' This game again. She was glad of a reprieve, however short-lived. Why would she be eager to drop the bombshell that would shatter her husband's world?

But Reg had a bombshell of his own. He pulled a flat shape from his pocket. It was a blue airmail envelope. Strange. She'd anticipated a bill and a confession, or even, thinking more positively, the long-awaited agent's letter, but he looked too anxious for that.

'This came this morning. It has an Australian postmark.'

Molly put her hand to her chest to suppress the jolt from her heart. 'It must be about Jack,' she whispered. Her ears roared.

'I didn't like to open it while you were out, but I'll do it now. Just in case it's bad news.' Reggie was looking at her in that way he'd started to recently. Like she was one of his patients from Warlingham.

Molly reached across. 'I'll do it.' She took the flimsy paper with shaking fingers, eased up the flap and read it silently. Then she picked up her teacup and hurled it against the wall.

'Molly! What is it?'

'How could this happen to me now?' She watched the brown liquid trickle down the paintwork.

'What? What's happen'? Tell me. What does it say?' Reggie was on his feet: pale, shaking.

Molly finally met his eyes. 'It's all so hopeless.'

'Please, you've got to talk to me.'

'It's from Jack,' she said wearily. 'He's coming to England to see me.'

'But – that's wonderful!'

Molly could hardly drag the words out. 'It would be wonderful. It would be the most wonderful thing ever.' She picked up her teaspoon mindlessly, then stared at it. She couldn't remember what it was for.

'Moll?' Reggie prompted gently.

She threw the spoon down. 'How can it be that the day I find out my son has tracked me down and is finally coming to see me after all these years . . .' she didn't even bother trying to disguise the bitterness, 'is the day I discover I won't live long enough to meet him?'

37

Kathleen dusted the photograph, then repositioned it carefully. She couldn't believe how well her wedding dress had fitted Rosie. It had never occurred to her before how similar she and Rosie were in size. Kathleen had never expected to relate to Rosie as a wife like herself. Perhaps Pete Seeger was right. When Jack had moved back in, he'd endlessly played 'To Everything There is a Season' on the record player.

The first thing Kathleen did after she lost John was to get rid of those hideous ducks on the kitchen wall. She'd stood on a chair and prised them off one by one. She'd bought some new paint and covered over the pale marks they'd left behind, before distempering the rest of the walls in the same colour. But she didn't change anything else.

She missed John more than she'd expected. The emptiness reminded her of wartime, before Jack's arrival, when John was working long days at the ministry. Perhaps she should look for a job again, despite John's government pension leaving her well provided for. But there might be grandchildren to occupy her soon, assuming Jack and Rosie didn't stay in England to bring up a family. She couldn't bear the thought of Molly robbing her of that joy, although, God knew, the other woman deserved her time with her son.

*

Reggie pulled back the curtains. Another grey day. Molly had slept fitfully. He'd been awake most of the night, attuned to her every breath. When it was low and even, he could feel the tension seeping out of his body. When it rasped or paused he'd stop breathing himself, waiting for the next rhythm to start, and relaxing again as it did. All of life boiled down to this, he thought: the ins and outs that marked our existence. Molly had breathed their children into this world, held them as they took their first gasps; he planned to be with her when she took her last.

She had replied to Jack's letter, saying how excited she'd be to see him again, yet she hadn't told him she was ill. She was hungry for his visit but worried that time and illness had changed her too markedly from the pretty young mother he'd known. Jack had been vague about timings. Reggie would have to find some way to phone him in Australia if he didn't get in touch soon.

Reggie climbed out of bed and stood up, anxious not to disturb Molly. His back was stiff from where he'd lain rigid in the night. He stretched awkwardly, his shoulders creaking, then stumbled into the kitchen to make his first tea of the day.

Molly would need to go into hospital soon. Dr Cole had

left the decision about when it should happen up to them. Reggie would have kept her at home until the end, but it wasn't fair on Susan and Peter. They'd seen too much of their mother's slow decline: the tightening skin, the thinning hair, the jutting bones. Reggie's grandmother had died painfully, and he still carried the memory of her suffering. He needed to protect them – and Molly – from the last indignities of death, with its stale odours and harsh sounds. Let them preserve their memories now, before the horrors became too vivid.

As he poured the milk into his teacup, *the English way*, he realised his hands were shaking.

*

Rosie laid the items out on the bed: a thick turtleneck sweater in burnt orange; a pale-green chunky-knit cardigan; a purple skinny-rib. They were going to mainland Europe first, then on to England. Rosie had imagined Jack would want to fly straight to see his birth mother, but he'd been suddenly reluctant. She couldn't work out why he was delaying after all this time. He'd gone to so much trouble to track down *her* mother; how come he didn't want to see his? All he kept saying was how cold it would be. Anyone would have thought they were going to the North Pole. Still, it was nice to have some new clothes. She'd dashed into Perth to buy the jumpers; they'd ceremoniously burned her maid's uniform before the wedding. She just hoped everything would fit into her suitcase.

England. She expected the cold, and rain too, of course. The grey streets, the men in bowler hats and suits, and the women all looking like Queen Elizabeth. Would people be able to understand her when she spoke? What would they think of an Aboriginal girl walking into their shops, visiting their restaurants? She slapped a pair of checked woollen slacks down on the bed. She mustn't think like that.

*

Peter knelt on Susan's bunk and scrabbled his fingers along the windowsill until they connected with the cool, ridged surface of the shell. He pressed it to his ear. Yes, the sea sound was still there, like someone breathing loudly. The other noises in the room, the ticking clock and the pattering of the rain hitting the window, disappeared. His world was the world of the shell.

That day on the beach had been the last time they'd all gone out together. He and Susan had had donkey rides. They'd bounced up and down on the donkeys' warm backs while Dad took photos. Susan's donkey had been slower than his. Afterwards they'd walked along the beach to find Mum. He'd found the shell on the way, half covered by a piece of slimy seaweed. He hadn't wanted to touch the seaweed, but Dad laughed at him and dangled it in his face.

'Don't be so fraidy fraidy,' he said. Sometimes Dad used these funny words. 'People will think you're a maama man!' Peter hadn't known what a maama man was, but Dad hadn't said it in a nice way.

'I'm not a maama man,' Peter had replied. 'I'm a dada man!' For some reason Dad had bent over at that, wheezing and cackling. He hadn't made a noise like that for a long time. Peter had run back to Mum to show her the shell.

Perhaps he'd take it to the hospital to cheer her up.

*

Jack hadn't wanted Kathleen to drop them off at the airport in case it got too upsetting for her, but in the end she was pretty good. She left the engine running while she opened up the boot for their cases, then hugged both Jack and Rosie quickly. The next thing Jack knew, the Holden's tail lights were disappearing down the slip road.

'That could have been worse,' he said to Rosie.

Rosie picked up her case, grimacing at the weight. 'Didn't you see her crying?'

'No. Was that why she wouldn't stay?'

'Honestly!' She put the case down. 'You did let her know the name of our hotel, didn't you?'

Jack frowned. 'I'm not sure.'

'You'll have to get in touch later. Now do something useful and find a porter.'

Jack put down his own case and did as he was told. He hoped he and Rosie would be okay on the plane. It was a big adventure for them both. They'd cross the Indian Ocean a lot quicker than the *Asturias* had done all those years ago. But it wasn't the journey that worried him. It was the destination.

Now that they were leaving Australia, he realised he wasn't ready to meet Mum yet; the prospect was too huge, too daunting. He was glad they were going to Paris first. He'd promised Rosie a honeymoon. Surely it wasn't selfish to enjoy the first heady days of marriage in such a romantic city? There was plenty of time to see Molly after that.

*

Sometimes, when the pain woke Molly, she imagined she was back at Warlingham. Hospital noises never really changed. Still the clatter of bedpans and the squeak of trolleys; the soft murmurings of the night-shift nurses, the inhuman whir of machines.

The smells were similar too. A whiff of disinfectant or urine could transport her back to those times more powerfully than any sound, although these days subtler scents had replaced the unmistakable reek of carbolic and bleach.

She lay back against the pillows. Maybe Jack would come soon. She hadn't planned for him to see her like this. In her dreams she was always young and glamorous, the mother he'd known as a child, not this frail woman in a decaying body. Would he still recognise her? She'd recognise him. She knew she would.

Molly closed her eyes and dozed. The vision appeared again. In front of her were huge black iron railings. A bit like the ones Dr Lee had ordered to be cut down at Warlingham. Only one stretch had remained in the park, to remind them of when the hospital had been a prison. But this wasn't Warlingham. Huge rolls of mist swirled around the gate, but there was no smooth green lawn, no flower beds. Just a shadowy figure in the distance. She peered closer. The figure smiled encouragingly. It was a bit like the boy she'd once seen when Dr Lee was trying to convince her Jack was dead. But this figure was taller. Jack would be twenty-six now. Could it be him?

Molly took hold of the railings and shook them. No response. Shook them harder. She needed to get out. The sun was hot on her back; she knew brightness and comfort lay behind her. But she wouldn't turn. Not yet.

'Jack!' she shouted, the voice coming from deep within. It was her soul crying. 'Let me go to him! He's mine.'

The figure moved closer.

She grasped the gates with both hands, her nails digging into her palms where she wrapped them round the metal struts; rocked them until she'd no strength left. But it was only herself she was rocking; the gates didn't move.

*

Kathleen was surprised to hear the strange voice on the phone. What with the crackling line and his accent, it was hard to work out what he was saying.

'Who are you?'

'I'm Jack's stepfather, ma'am.'

'You don't sound English.'

'I'm Jamaican. English Jamaican now . . . May I speak to Jack, please?'

'Jack? No, he's on his honeymoon. I didn't realise Jack's mother had . . . er . . . that she was married.' Had Jack told her? Of course he must have. Best hope Molly's husband thought he hadn't. Didn't want him thinking she condemned miscegenation. Not everyone thought like John. 'His hotel . . . Hang on . . . I must have it here somewhere.' She went to put the phone down to search, then remembered. 'I'm sorry . . . I don't think he gave it to me. He's in Paris. Can you track him down? . . . Oh dear. I'm terribly sorry . . . Yes, of course, when he gets in touch, I'll tell him to contact you straight away . . . Yes, he has your address. The one on your wife's letters? He knows it . . . I do hope he'll make it in time . . . Thank you. Goodbye.'

Kathleen managed to replace the phone on its cradle before her legs buckled from shock.

*

The sensation that wouldn't go away started in maths. Susan was copying down some sums Mrs Turner had written on the board in her sharp writing when her stomach plummeted. She'd been looking out of the window earlier, wondering as usual about Jack and when her exciting older brother was going to visit, when she suddenly thought how difficult it must have been for Mum, trying to look after her and Peter while Jack was missing. Perhaps Mum had felt guilty all this time.

401

'Are you all right?' asked Alison Lucas, who sat next to her.

'Not really.' Susan put down her pencil.

'Wassup?'

'I don't know.' Susan didn't mean to snap.

'All right. I only asked.' Alison half turned away from her to sharpen her pencil in the inkwell, even though they weren't supposed to, but Susan knew she was only pretending to be busy.

She needed to find a peace offering or Alison would be huffy all day. But this feeling wasn't easy to describe.

'It feels like there's a big hole inside me.'

Alison turned back towards her. 'I've got an apple in my bag if you're hungry. You might be able to put your desk lid up and eat a bit.'

'It's not that,' Susan replied, then added hastily, 'but thanks anyway.' She pressed her fingers to her stomach and kneaded it. 'It's more of an empty, sick feeling.'

Mrs Turner was wandering round the room checking on their sums. Her pupils thought she was geometry personified: her body like an isosceles triangle with a little head and wide hips, and her arms bent at right angles. Susan lowered her head over her book, noticing Alison doing the same. She hoped Alison would keep quiet for a while. She couldn't make her understand what this feeling was, she didn't understand it herself, but she knew it had something to do with Mum. She made the decision quickly. 'I think I'm going to throw up,' she whispered.

Alison's hand shot up. 'Miss.' Mrs Turner swept towards them. 'Susan Edwardes is going to be sick.'

Mrs Turner was at her desk in a jiffy, laying her palm against Susan's forehead. 'Okay, quickly, child. Off to sickbay.' Susan scraped back her chair and limped out of the room.

But she didn't go to sickbay. She hobbled along the corridor, out of the double doors at the end, across the quad and into the field. She and Alison had spotted a loose plank in the top fence the other day when they were up there during break reading a battered copy of *Jackie* that Alison had filched from her older sister.

Susan managed to cross the field without anyone shouting at her to stop, despite the awkward gait that was so instantly recognisable. She reached the top fence that ran like a rigid grey curtain around the edge of the grass and tapped it carefully to locate the spot. A minute later, she pushed the wobbly panel to one side and squeezed through the gap, shifting it back afterwards to hide her tracks. Then she limped off down Glynn Avenue to the bus stop.

Susan had been to hospitals before, of course. Memories of the Waddon Fever Hospital had never left her: the gramophone in the corner of the ward playing *Vilia, O Vilia! The witch of the wood* again and again; metallic-tasting milk with no sugar from a chipped enamel mug; Mum's letters with their little drawings and kisses; the feeling of being trapped in metal . . .

She'd gone to Roehampton as a day patient with Mum whenever she'd had to have a new brace fitted, but she'd never been to St Helier. She'd known to take the 157 bus. Lucy Phillips had visited her dad there once and taken that route

403

from school. The bus dropped Susan in Wrythe Lane, only a few yards from the hospital. Easy.

No one stopped her walking down the corridors. Mum was in C5. She'd heard Dad mention it. She followed the signs and there was Mum, turned on her side on a metal bed covered with a thin pink blanket. She was asleep, so Susan sat on the chair by the bed, watching until she woke up. Mum's face looked like one of those Egyptian mummies when they peeled back the bandages: all yellow and shrunken. Surely this strange figure couldn't really be her mother? But when the figure stirred, Susan was relieved to see Mum's familiar green eyes looking at her, even if they were cloudier than she remembered.

'Hello, Mum.'

'Susan.' Mum's lips framed the word.

'I'm sorry, I know I wasn't supposed to come – Dad said children aren't allowed – but I had to see you.'

Mum's thin fingers plucked at the blanket. She didn't speak.

'Mum . . .' How was Susan to express it, this thing that had been eating her up all morning? She took Mum's hand and felt the slightest pressure on her own. No more than a twitch, really. Her emotions surged. 'I just wanted to tell you you're the best mother in the world.'

Mum's face was jerking. Susan looked round for a nurse. Was she having some sort of fit? Mum half turned her head towards the bedside cabinet. Perhaps that was what she meant. Susan went across and opened it. Her fingers fumbled over the surface until they encountered a hard metal shape. She drew it out. It was the photo Dad had taken of her and Peter on the beach the day they'd ridden the donkeys. She held it up to show Mum, and Mum motioned to her to bring it nearer, right up to her face. Then she reached forward and pressed her lips to Susan's image.

'Excuse me. You'll have to go; this isn't visiting time, you know. And besides, we do not permit children on the wards.' The tall nurse loomed over them. A lock of greasy hair had escaped from her hat and hung like a pendulum over her eyes.

'I'm sorry,' Susan said. She'd hoped to stay longer, but at least she'd told Mum what a good mother she was. Just in case Mum was worried she wasn't.

The nurse sniffed. 'Say a quick goodbye and then off you go.'

Susan looked back at Mum. Mum's cheeks were wet and she was still holding the photo. Susan planted a kiss on her head. 'Bye, Mum. I love you.'

'I love you too.' The first words Mum had spoken. And the best.

*

Rosie gripped the wooden rail with one hand and clutched Jack's arm with the other. Then she leaned out, trying to keep her upper body as far away as possible from the brown metal. From the ground the construction had looked like a giant with his legs astride. From the top it gave her a view of the world she'd never imagined. In the plane, things had been too far away; she'd grown tired of the miles of ocean and the tiny

405

jumbles of fields and houses. In the end Jack had made her swap seats as she'd spent too long asleep beside the window. But here it was different: the treetops looked like green fur and the fountains spouted like tiny waterfalls. She could see buildings with domed roofs and cars like rectangular beads in a long necklace. The ground pulsed with life. And she, like a circling buzzard, could see it all.

'What do you think?' said Jack.

'I think this is the closest I'll come to being a bird.'

'I bet you didn't think you'd see this for real.'

'I didn't know about it, so how could I? Besides, Uluru is much bigger. And it's been there since the beginning of time.'

'You've got a point. It's an interesting perspective, though.'

'Makes you realise how small we all are.' She'd thought that on the plane. How people became invisible once you were up in the sky. Here, men and women were toy-like, as if their hopes and dreams and worries didn't exist. Or if they did, as if she could solve them with a wave of her hand.

'Which way's England?'

'Um . . .' Jack wheeled round, then pointed. 'That way, I think.'

Rosie stood on tiptoe, facing the direction Jack had shown her, and closed her eyes. Her hand clasped his. She let the sun fall on her face and the breeze stir her hair. Her spirit wandered free, exploring winding paths and labyrinths, travelling up and down, near and far until it caught the dream. The dream whirled in the darkness. She felt it buffet her mind and stir her body.

She was flying over the landscape, tracing the course of the river as it snaked through the brown earth. She swooped low over patchwork fields dotted with tiny cows and sheep, and soared over towns studded with grey roofs. Lakes shimmered below her and she watched ribbon-like roads carrying long lines of cars.

A current of air carried her upwards; she rode on its balmy breath as it spiralled higher through layers of heat and light until the sea was a wrinkled mirror beneath her. She glided across it until greeted by stern white cliffs and a baize of more fields. Then she was swooping low, low again until she could see the separate colours of the buildings, the children in a school playground, the women hanging out washing in their tiny green yards.

Then lower still, towards a sprawling concrete building with myriad small windows. One of them was open; she flew in, darting along long corridors, past doorways leading into cave-like rooms, before she turned into one and hovered over the narrow metal beds surrounded by blue curtains. The last bed drew her in: an old woman lay sleeping in a white dress, her grey curls spread out across the pillow, her mouth slightly open. A thin snake of plastic burrowed into her arm.

Rosie's eyes snapped open. 'We've got to go to England now,' she said. 'Your mother needs you.'

*

Rosie and Jack dropped their cases off at the New Addington Hotel and Jack asked the receptionist to call them a taxi. He gave the address that had appeared at the top of Mum's letters in her careful writing.

As the taxi sped through the streets, he looked out of the window. He wondered if he might recognise any roads or buildings from his childhood town, but either the post-war reconstruction of Croydon had changed it too dramatically or the years in Australia had wiped it from his memory, as nothing was familiar. Rosie was looking out of the other window. She wore a purple jumper and a grey skirt. Thankfully she'd taken his advice about dressing warmly. Her beautiful tawny skin was beginning to look pinched and matt.

Jack scratched at a rough patch of skin on his hand. Annoying that his eczema had come back again. He hoped their children wouldn't inherit it.

The taxi rumbled to a halt.

''Ere we are, guv.' The driver threw the words over his shoulder. Jack had forgotten how people spoke over here, kind of rough and friendly at the same time. He scrambled out, then held the door open for Rosie. 'That'll be three pounds ten.'

Jack handed the driver a crisp ten-pound note, one of several he'd collected from the R&I before they set off. The man tutted and deposited a huge amount of change in Jack's palm. Damn. He'd be rattling like a train when he greeted his mother.

'Stop,' shouted Rosie. The taxi driver was just about to drive off. 'Can you wait for a minute, just in case the person isn't in?'

The driver nodded.

Jack's throat was tight. He tried to moisten his lips, but his tongue was too dry. He looked at Rosie, but she was staring at the small house in front of them. It was very different to Kathleen and John's place. He gave her a reassuring smile and knocked on the door.

A tall black man answered. This couldn't be right. Jack must have got the wrong address. 'I beg your pardon, sir. I was looking for a Mrs Molly Edwardes.'

'Jack. Thank God.'

Jack stepped back, thunderstruck. 'Yes, but . . . who are you?'

'I'm Reggie. The man who loves your mother.'

Jack's heart lurched.

'We're wasting time,' said Rosie. 'Aren't we?'

Reggie looked at her as though he'd just realised she was there. 'You're right,' he said. 'She's in St Helier Hospital. I'll drive you there.'

Jack dismissed the taxi and he and Rosie climbed into Reggie's car. As he drove through the grey streets, Reggie spoke to Jack. 'It all happened so quickly. I tried to contact you, but your . . .' He paused, searching for the right word. 'Er, Mrs Sullivan said you'd gone to France. Thank God you got the message.'

'We didn't,' said Jack. How selfish of him, deliberately forgetting to give Kathleen their address in order to protect their privacy. And how cowardly to dawdle in France when he should have come straight to England. Thank goodness Rosie had sensed Molly was ill. 'My wife suggested we came.' He scratched frantically at the inside of his elbow and felt Rosie's sharp glance. 'Is she very ill, my mother?' Even now it seemed strange to say the words.

Reggie nodded. Then he turned away abruptly and looked straight ahead.

Once at the hospital, Reggie dropped Jack and Rosie at the entrance and went to park the car.

'Ward C5,' he shouted out of the window.

They hurried along a cool corridor with a high domed ceiling, dark wooden doors appearing every few yards. The blood thumping in Jack's ears sounded louder than their footsteps. He was finding it hard to breathe.

'There's a sign to C block,' Rosie said. They turned right down a long passageway. 'C4 . . .' They passed a pair of double doors behind which was a blur of nurses and patients. 'Here it is.' Another set of doors. They pushed their way in.

Jack scanned the room. Ten beds. Elderly women in pastel bed jackets with grey perms or straight greasy hair. Of course, Mum was old now, wasn't she? He walked slowly down the beds, noting the names: Mrs E. Green, Miss Marlow, Mrs Bednow . . . What was he looking for? Malloy? No, *Edwardes*, that was it. Eventually he found it, scrawled across the chart clipped to a metal rail. But instead of seeing Mum, all he encountered was an empty bed, its pristine sheets and blankets as flat as if they'd never been occupied.

'We're too late,' he whispered. He buried his head in Rosie's shoulder, numb with shock.

Rosie pulled him away gently. 'Things may not be as you think,' she said. 'Let's ask the nurse. An important-looking figure in a stiff uniform was bearing down on them.

Jack couldn't move; couldn't speak.

Rosie did it for him. 'Excuse me. We're looking for a Mrs Molly Edwardes. We expected to find her here.'

'She's been moved,' the nurse informed them, staring at Rosie. 'C6. Down the corridor and to your left.'

'Thanks.' Rosie grabbed Jack's hand. His legs regained their solidity. They ran together, their footsteps pounding, until they reached the new ward.

The years contracted. Jack was a young boy again, terrified as he returned home from school, looking for a house and a mother that the war had stolen.

'Mummy!' he'd called on that terrible day when the bomb had dropped. It was the word that spilled from him again as he saw the frail figure in the bed.

The figure struggled up. Mum stretched out thin arms that shook with effort. 'I'm here, Jack.' She pulled him close in a tight embrace, like she used to when he was frightened during the raids.

Jack caught the faintest scent of lily of the valley. He felt safer and sadder than he had in twenty-one years. 'I'm here, Mum,' he said. 'I'm here.'

Epilogue

16 November 2009

Jack rubs his eyes. It's been a long flight for the three of them from Perth to Canberra. But he wouldn't have missed this day for the world. He's worked for so long to achieve justice. Parliament House is packed. Filled with people like him from all over Australia. He glimpses a heavy-set man, his lips pressed together as though to muzzle all emotion. And a woman with short cropped hair and eye bags like hammocks, her expression the embodiment of sadness. He looks around and catches Rosie's eye. She gives him an encouraging smile.

In the end, Kathleen was too frail to come with them. Jack visited her in the nursing home the day before the flight.

'Apologies?' she murmured, her blue eyes for once unclouded, as she lay in bed, a slight figure, in the neat little room.

Jack pressed her hand. 'The Australian and British prime ministers are apologising to the child migrants. The governments are claiming responsibility.'

Kathleen sighed. 'Governments, yes . . . but people too.' Her voice was slow and heavy.

Jack leaned forward, across the garish quilt. 'D'you mean John?'

She swallowed. 'He paid his due.'

'Yes.'

Kathleen was struggling to sit up. 'What about me?'

Jack rearranged the pillow to support her. 'You only did what he told you. You did your best.'

Kathleen's mouth trembled.

Jack clearly hadn't said enough to reassure her. He wiped the back of his hand across his face. Ridiculous he could still get upset after all this time. 'Kathleen. You have been the most wonderful mother. And grandmother. No one could have done any more.' The matron of the care home had warned him Kathleen's heart wasn't strong. It was important he told her these things now.

As her grateful smile lit her face, Jack had a sudden memory of the lovely young woman she'd once been, the woman so eager to raise a child that she'd invited a motherless boy into her home. And loved him dearly for the rest of her life.

There's a sudden hush as Kevin Rudd makes his way onto the platform. The prime minister fiddles with the lectern, stares out into the crowd, then speaks into the silence:

'We acknowledge the particular pain of children shipped to Australia as child migrants – robbed of your families, robbed of your homeland, regarded not as innocent children but instead as a source of child labour.

'To those of you who were told you were orphans, brought

414

here without your parents' knowledge or consent, we acknowledge the lies you were told, the lies told to your mothers and fathers, and the pain these lies have caused for a lifetime.

'To those of you separated on the dockside from your brothers and sisters; taken alone and unprotected to the most remote parts of a foreign land – we acknowledge today that the laws of our nation failed you.

'And for this we are deeply sorry.'

Jack bows his head to hide the tears in his eyes. Beside Rosie, Sam's sister, with copper hair and sunglasses pushed up on top of her head, is shuddering like someone who's been crying for a long time. Long after Sam died, she suddenly got in touch, wanting to see her brother's grave for herself. Jack picked her up at Perth airport and drove her to Bindoon so she could put her own stones alongside the ones he had placed there all those years ago. She was horrified by the manner of Sam's death. It is only right that she has returned today to hear the apology too.

Jack never did find out whether Sam's death was really murder or just a terrible accident. Even his finely honed legal skills weren't able to penetrate the closed ranks presented by the brothers and the police. The guilt still haunts him from time to time. But he has honoured Sam in the best way he can, by living life to the full. And it means a lot to him that Sam's sister is here for the apology.

But Jack has played his part in the campaign to expose the truth about the child migrants, just as he vowed he would. In the end, he tracked down a British organisation and helped them investigate what had happened at Bindoon. The world finally knows the untold story of all those innocent children.

Sam's grave is well tended now, and he and Rosie visit often, with their children and grandchildren. They fly to England each year to see Reggie, Susan and Peter too.

'This is for you, Mum,' he whispers. 'And for you, Sam.'

And Rosie, his still beautiful Rosie, squeezes his hand.

24 February 2010

Reggie reaches out a gnarled finger to turn on the radio. This has been an age coming and he doesn't want to miss it. He stares up at the old photo of Molly on the mantelpiece and wishes for the thousandth time that she was still here, particularly now.

'And now we go live to the Houses of Parliament, where Gordon Brown is speaking,' says the announcer's voice. Reggie sits up straight and listens to the gravelly Scots burr.

'To all those former child migrants and their families, to those here with us today and those across the world – to each and every one – I say today that we are truly sorry. They were let down.

'We are sorry that they were allowed to be sent away at the time they were most vulnerable. We are sorry that instead of caring for them, this country turned its back, and we are sorry that the voices of these children were not always heard and their cries for help not always heeded.

'We are sorry that it has taken so long for this important day to come, and for the full and unconditional apology that is justly deserved to be given.'

Reggie looks again at Molly's photo on the mantelpiece. At her dark curly hair and her laughing green eyes. At her fragile face that he still longs to cup in his hands and to kiss until he's extinguished the pain of all those years separated from her firstborn child.

Then he raises a cup of tea, made the way Molly taught him all those years ago, in salute to her picture.

Author's Note

Back in 2010, I was in the kitchen, performing some desultory domestic task and listening idly to the Radio 4 news, when an item stopped me in my tracks. The then prime minister, Gordon Brown, was apologising to a group of ex child migrants to Australia on behalf of a British government that had allowed them to be sent there decades before. The children had been told their parents were dead when many were in fact still alive. My first thought was what a shocking account. My second was what a powerful story it would make.

I had been searching for a while for a subject on which to base a novel, and this event excited both my pity and my imagination. I came across the book *Oranges and Sunshine* (formerly *Empty Cradles*) by Margaret Humphries, and that provided more in-depth information on the child migrants' stories. There is an excellent film based on the book, starring Emily Watson (also called *Oranges and Sunshine*).

Orphans of the Empire by Alan Gill gave me the historical context to this heart-wrenching story. I discovered that Britain has a long history of 'exporting' human stock to Australia. It began with convicts in the eighteenth century, when the first penal colonies were established, and ended with child migrants in the late 1960s, when the changing social attitudes of a more enlightened age finally ended it. It's estimated that 150,000 children were sent to Australia and countries of the Empire in total, around 10,000 since 1947. Far from experiencing the wonderful life they were promised, they were sent to live in harsh conditions, were poorly educated, submitted to hard labour and sometimes abused. Britain is one of the few countries in the world to export its young in this way.

It took forty-three years for the apologies to come. The full transcripts of the respective speeches of Kevin Rudd and Gordon Brown are available online: https://tinyurl.com/kevinruddapology, and https://tinyurl.com/gordonbrown-apology.

But I realised books could only tell me so much. I needed to speak to some of the people who had been through this experience. An advert I placed in an Australian newsletter led me to Joan Thorpe, now in her nineties, who had gone out on the SS *Asturias* as a young nanny in 1947. We exchanged emails and spoke on the phone. Many of the details of Jack's crossing were provided by Joan.

Betty Tredinnick, who lived near Croydon, where her shopkeeper father kept his excess stock of fireworks under her bed for the duration of the Blitz, supplied some of the details of wartime life in England, as did John and Pauline Montgomery. Pauline's memories of being incarcerated in the Waddon Fever Hospital as a child provided the background for Susan's frightening hospitalisation for polio.

I was shocked to discover that the removal of Aboriginal

children from their families by the Australian federal and state government agencies and church missions, under an act of parliament, was also happening at this time. Hundreds of them, known as the 'stolen generation', were taken between 1905 and 1969, although in some places mixed-race children were still being taken into the 1970s. Apparently it was thought that this would encourage Aboriginal people to 'die out'. This practice is the subject of the film *Rabbit-Proof Fence*, starring Kenneth Branagh. On 13 February 2008, Kevin Rudd also apologised to 'the indigenous peoples of this land, the oldest continuing cultures in human history'.

My research took me to newspaper articles, websites and personal accounts, each revealing different stories about child migrants, and each deepening my sympathy and sense of outrage. I have Jack being 'rescued' by the Sullivans because I think it makes for a more complex and ultimately uplifting story. Fiction writers are allowed to do that! He doesn't escape unscathed, though, and although his experience at Bindoon is mercifully short, it is still damaging.

I'm very conscious that there were others who weren't so lucky, whose lives were horribly and irrevocably scarred by their experience. Of course, this novel cannot make up for their terrible past, but I hope it plays a small part in a future that brings them justice.

Acknowledgements

So many people have helped me write this story. Some were with me every step of the journey, others kept me company for short stretches when I needed some specialist help. I am grateful to every one of them for their kindness and time. I've tried to keep a list as I've gone along but if I have missed anyone off, I apologise. It's down to my lack of organisation, not my ingratitude!

England

Anne Williams, my wonderful agent, for her acumen and support.

Sherise Hobbs, my lovely editor at Headline, for her wise insights. Also Emily Gowers and Jane Selley for their perceptive help.

Stephanie Norgate and Jane Rusbridge for their amazing generosity, time and very much valued advice.

Lucy Flannery for her enthusiasm and expertise.

Jacqui Pack for her patience and wonderful eye for detail. Kate Lee for her encouragement and help.

My great teachers and workshop colleagues at the University of Chichester for their support: Dave Swann, Karen Stevens,

Stephen Mollett, Jac Cattaneo, Mel Whipman, Paul Newton-Palmer, Glen Brown, Richard Buxton, Morgaine Davidson, Hannah Radcliffe, Gina Challen, Kate Tym, Jordan Williams, Alex Churchill-Fabian, Miranda Lethbridge, Raine Geoghegan, Corrina O'Beirne.

My 'bookclub girls' for their kind interest and for being my beta readers: Alex Burn, Anne Hudson and Julia Arthurs.

Jude Thompson, Judith Hepper, Brigid Fayers, Ben Greenhalgh and Jenny Alexander, more early readers, who gave such useful feedback.

Sue Greenhalgh, Nicola Kingsley, Libby Morgan and Barbara Murray for their interest and encouragement.

Betty Tredinnick, Pauline and John Montgomery for sharing their helpful memories of Croydon during and after World War Two.

Lily and Kay Stewart for linguistic help!

Australia

The late Lynn and Laurie Champniss for their help with Perth geography, flora and fauna. I'm so sorry they won't be able to see the novel they showed such interest in.

Ross Isles, bushwalker, for kindly checking the scene in Kings Park.

Catherine Parry, Admin. and Technical Assistant Kings Park Perth, for her expert knowledge of flowers of the 1950's.

The amazing Joan Thorpe (nee Mapson) for all those helpful emails, and for believing in me for so long.

Michael Tubbs for talking me through his experiences of emigrating to Australia.

Phillipa White, Frankie Atkinson and Bernadette Bowey Hills for their kind help.

The wonderful journalist at *The West Australian* (whose contact details I have sadly lost) for being so generous with her time and advice.

Read on for an extract of
Gill Thompson's heartrending novel

THE CHILD ON PLATFORM ONE

Prologue

Eva had already scraped back the piano stool and was about to slide the music books into her bag when Professor Novotny lifted a hand to delay her.

'Just one more minute, my dear.' His thin finger pointed skywards, in imitation of the number. 'I have a piece I would like you to take home.'

While the professor rifled through the tottering pile of manuscripts on top of the piano, Eva cast a glance at the wooden clock on the wall. Four thirty. She hoped this wouldn't take long. Already the conservatoire rehearsal room was gloomier than when the lesson had started, shadows stretching across the floor. *Come on. Come on.* She placed her fingertips on the yellow keys, allowing the cool ivory to calm her.

'Ah, here it is.' Professor Novotny was wheezing from the effort of finding the score. 'Hector Berlioz. It's a villanelle from *Les Nuits d'Été*. One of his lesser-known pieces.' He switched on the overhead light and the room brightened.

'A villan . . . ella?' Despite her anxiety about the time, Eva was intrigued. She stood up as her teacher gestured for her to relinquish her place at the keyboard and positioned herself to the side of the piano, ready to watch Professor Novotny play.

'Yes. A secular Italian song.' The professor sat down on the padded piano stool with a thump. 'This one is a celebration of spring and new love. Perfect piece for a young girl.' He reached for the round black glasses on a cord round his neck, put them on as though preparing to play, then removed them again. The glasses swung loose on their moorings. 'There's to be a concert at the Rudolfinum next year, a tribute to Berlioz's work. I thought you could perform the villanelle as your first public solo.'

Eva drew an indignant breath, but the professor flapped his hand at her.

'Those children's competitions don't count.'

Those *children's competitions*! She straightened her back. Hadn't she won every one? Even the prestigious Dvořák Prize for Young Talent. A memory of lifting the heavy metal cup and hearing a crescendo of applause flashed into her mind.

The professor propped the folded pages of music against the metal prongs of the rest. 'I'll play you a bit. Please turn the page for me.' The glasses were perched in position.

Eva took up her place behind her teacher, trying to remain still; it would be rude to appear impatient. But inside her head she was begging Professor Novotny to play only a few bars. She knew he worked her so hard because he was proud of her, and she was keen to be the best she could, but the ornate hands of the clock showed twenty to five now. Today of all days she couldn't afford to be late.

'Listen. You'll hear the lovers wandering through the woods to gather wild strawberries.'

Eva flushed at the word 'lovers'. Sometimes Professor Novotny spoke to her as though she was older than sixteen. But as he started to play, she did indeed hear the light, tripping sound of footsteps, and felt the freshness of the spring breeze on her face.

She peered over the professor's shoulder. Beneath his tapered fingers, the printed notes skittering across the manuscript became an airy melody. Teasing, joyful. Eva had always seen notes as people. The rows of joined quavers – the short notes – were gangly lines of boys sporting over-large football boots at the end of their thin legs; or a straight band of dancers performing the Lúčnica, in black shoes, with their arms linked. The single crotchets – twice as long as quavers, – were teachers, ramrod straight in front of a class. And the long minims were powerful generals, commanding their army's attention by their stillness. But if Eva were a note, she'd be a really long one: a breve, strong and alone, surrounded by space and silence.

The professor finished playing with a flourish, then handed her the score. 'Homework. Start tonight.' The notes hovered in the air before the spring promise of the tune was smothered by the advancing autumn dusk. The sun must be even lower now. Eva's stomach clenched. An allegro beat started up in her head.

She thrust the manuscript into her bag, then put on her coat. 'Thank you, Professor Novotny, I'll be sure to practise.'

'Make sure you do. I want to hear you play it perfectly at your next lesson.'

'Of course.' Eva's hand was on the doorknob, its polished surface greasy under her fingers. She darted another look at the clock. Nearly five. This villanelle had claimed even more time than she'd realised. She'd have to run like a wolf dog.

'Goodbye, my dear.'

'Goodbye, Professor Novotny. And thank you for the lesson.'

The professor bowed, the overhead light he'd snapped on earlier illuminating his bald head. Eva made her escape.

She ran through the darkening streets with the music bag clamped under her arm, her chest burning, her breath ragged. Yet in spite of her urgency, Berlioz's melody still skipped through her head, and she tuned her footsteps to the chords pressed out by Professor Novotny's liver-spotted hands. She was running through the woods with her lover, away from the stifling confines of the city, her senses alive to the sound of the birds and the sweet-sharp perfume of the strawberries. She could feel the boy's breath on her cheek, his mouth on her lips, perhaps – if her face hadn't already been red, she'd have blushed – his body pressed against hers. Only the pungent smell of coffee seeping out from under the door of the Kotva reminded her where she was. As she darted past the café, shadowy shapes lifted cups to their lips, gesticulated in conversation, or blew plumes of smoke from Stuyvesants whose tips glowed red in the gloom. How lovely to linger at the table with friends rather than having to rush home for the curfew.

Eva glanced up at the sinking sun. Mutti would have finished the chores by now, the challah already baked and resting on the lacy cloth, its plumply plaited crust shining with egg wash and oozing a fresh bread smell. She would have put on her grey dress, wrapped the gauzy scarf around her hair and gone downstairs to light the candles, whose silver holders gleamed from the polish that she'd given them earlier.

Abba, in his shiny black suit and prayer shawl, would have filled the Kiddush cup with sweet wine, his lips rehearsing the blessing for daughters that he'd speak later with his warm hands resting on Eva's head:

May you be like Sarah, Rebecca, Rachel and Leah.
May God bless you and guard you.
May God show you favour and be gracious to you.
May God show you kindness and grant you peace.

If Abba had fathered sons, he'd have asked God to make them like Ephraim and Menashe, two brothers who lived in harmony. But there'd been no sons. Only Eva. A beloved only child.

A mist was rising from the surface of the Vltava, and Eva inhaled the wet air as she sped along the pavement. She couldn't risk stopping to cough properly, so she tried to clear her throat in shallow breaths whilst running. She wasn't used to going so fast. Most days her lesson ended on time, so she walked to the Josefov via well-lit streets. But with sunset approaching, the quickest route home was through the cemetery.

An animated mosso beat pulsed through her. Should she risk it? Perhaps the gates closed at curfew. Mutti had told her again and again to stick to the main roads. They'd be full of people on their way home from work. Longer but safe. Yet Eva paused on the pavement to peer at the winding path through the tombs. The ancient stones were crammed together as if the graves had been hastily dug, not placed in ordered rows like a modern cemetery. Wind threaded through the trees, causing the branches to shiver. To stifle the jump of her heart, she imagined she was performing at the Rudolfinum on a gleaming black Steinway, to a shadowy audience awed to silence by her playing.

She placed her palm against one of the dark metal gates and it yielded slowly. Perhaps it was a sign she should go through the cemetery. She could make up for some lost time this way.

Trying to rekindle Berlioz's melody, to renew the thrills of spring and blot out the fears of autumn, she crept through the gate. The dew had already fallen and the leaves were damp underfoot. Creepers clung to her stockings and she had to kick her feet out to dislodge them. It would be foolish to run; the gravestones were too crowded, the path too meandering. But she hastened her steps, her senses alert for danger.

Inside the cemetery, tall horse chestnuts and sycamores diffused the low sun's rays. Gravestones loomed either side of the path, inscribed with old symbols and ancient lettering. Abba had told her once that some of the graves held as many as ten bodies, all piled on top of each other to conserve space. In spite of her serge coat, Eva shivered.

She was halfway through when she heard the thud of boots, a harsh laugh, a sharp cough.

She froze. 'Who's there?'

No reply, but beyond the shadowy stones she caught a glimpse of biscuit-coloured cloth. Blood pounded affrettando in her ears.

'Who's there?' she asked again. Her voice sounded hoarse.

A uniformed figure stepped out from behind a tree. A youth, maybe late teens, with a sweep of blond hair across his forehead.

'What have we here: a young lady?' His tone was leering, mocking.

Eva pulled her coat tighter, trying to ignore the gallop of her heart.

Another youth stepped forward. Then another. She wheeled round. Two more came up behind her. She was surrounded by five young soldiers, all wearing red armbands.

Was this what Mutti had feared when she'd warned her not to go into the cemetery? Eva had nodded solemnly at the time, but in her head she'd dismissed her mother's advice. All parents said things like that, didn't they? Of course she was careful. Although recently, even Eva had felt uncomfortable at the sight of German boys standing on street corners muttering to each other and pointing at passers-by. Those Hitler Youth seemed to be everywhere these days.

Surrounded by a ring of menacing young men in their distinctive uniforms, she wished desperately that she'd heeded Mutti's words and ignored her lateness. Saliva pooled in her mouth, her throat too dry to swallow.

The first youth advanced towards her. 'Don't be frightened, pretty girl.'

Eva stood her ground, trying not to show her fear. But when she opened her mouth to shout for help, the boy reached forward and slapped his palm against her lips.

Eva darted terrified glances at the other boys.

The pressure of the youth's fingers slackened, but he kept his hand close to her mouth, in case she tried to cry out again.

She clenched her fists.

'Such beautiful clothes,' he murmured, dropping his hand to stroke her coat. Eva couldn't stop herself flinching. Or inhaling his sour breath.

Slowly he undid her grey buttons.

The other boys were watching, waiting.

'Hold her arms.'

Eva struggled as the youth tried to take off her coat. But the boy behind her grabbed her wrists, until the garment was yanked off her and tossed onto the ground.

The youth reached forward again. He touched Eva's cheek softly, then ran his finger under her chin, around her neck and down to the dent of her throat. He carefully edged up a section of the gold chain she always wore. She found herself mesmerised, in spite of her fear.

'What a nice necklace.' It was almost a whisper.

Did he want to steal it? Eva reached down and hooked her own finger under the thin metal links, pulling the whole chain out from under her collar so he could see the gold star on the end, the star that usually lay hidden under her blouse.

The boy gently removed it from her grasp, prising her fingers open one by one, and held the star up to the fading light.

The chain tightened against the back of Eva's neck. She muted a protest at the pain.

'How interesting.' The boy's eyes were on her face, but his words were addressed to his companions, who jeered and laughed.

The spell was broken. The boy let the pendant go abruptly. 'She's not for me.' His expression hardened and he shoved

Eva away. 'All yours, Otto.' He turned round and gestured to the smallest of the youths to come forward.

Eva let out a long-held breath as silently as she could. Dare she flee? The first boy had his back to her now; perhaps this was her chance. She lowered her head to charge through the gap.

But as the smaller boy was shoved forward by his mocking companions, their circle tightened to prevent his escape, blocking Eva's too.

The lad approached her. He was slight, with hair so blond it was almost white and eyelashes so fair they were nearly invisible.

If he had been on his own, Eva could have defended herself. She was no coward. She'd have kicked and punched and spat until the boy released her. But surrounded by a leering wall of soldiers, she had no chance. She reached behind her, fingers scrabbling against the top of a gravestone, searching for a weapon. But if there'd been any stones placed along the rim, they'd long since vanished.

'Come on, Otto, not scared, are you?' The first youth, who'd retreated to become part of the wall, goaded the lad who was now standing in front of Eva.

'Yes, come on, Otto, our balls are freezing.'

The boy laughed, the strangely eerie cackle betraying his nervousness.

Although the youths spoke German, Eva understood them perfectly. All the families in the Josefov spoke German at home. Her stomach tightened and her breath rasped in the cold air.

'Please don't hurt me, my parents are waiting.' Her voice

came out thin, reedy. Why couldn't she make herself sound threatening? Perhaps she could appeal to the boy's sense of honour. He seemed hesitant; maybe she could persuade him. If he realised how important it was for her to get home, he might leave her alone.

But as the other youths catcalled and whooped, making strange gestures with their hands, the boy responded to their raucous taunts. His eyes narrowed and his mouth pressed into a threatening line. He hawked up a gob of phlegm and spat on her. She let the slime trickle down her cheek, too terrified to wipe it off.

He yanked at her pendant and it broke immediately, the chain abandoned to the autumn leaves. A whoop went up from the group.

A different youth tore off her blouse in one violent movement. Another cheer.

Then they were all mauling her, ripping her skirt and stockings in a frenzy, their straining, sweating faces contorting in the moonlight, the air thick with their beery stench. And at the same time they were singing some ugly drinking song that had them bellowing out loud, flat notes in a terrible cacophony.

Eva wrapped her arms tight across her chest, desperately protecting her cream camisole. But someone wrenched her hands away and stripped it off her, the delicate fabric that Mutti had hand-sewn tearing under his fingers.

She was thrust backwards and pushed down onto her own coat, her head thumping against the soft lining.

Then the boys came at her again.

*

438

Afterwards, it was an owl that first penetrated her consciousness, hooting mournfully through the cold air. Her fingers dug into the wet earth; she inhaled the musty odour of leaves. But the animal reek of her own blood was still there. She curled her bruised body into a ball, trying to shut out the black miasma and the memory of the boy's nervous laugh.

The time for the Shabbat blessing had long since passed. Eva's anxious parents would be presiding over an empty table, asking themselves again and again where their devoted daughter could have got to, when she knew that all good Jews must be indoors by nightfall, on this most sacred of evenings.

From the darkest place came
a journey of hope

The
Child *on*
Platform
One

Inspired by
heartrending
true events

GILL THOMPSON

**Inspired by the real-life escape of thousands of
Jewish children from Nazi-occupied Europe on
the *Kindertransport* trains to London.**

Prague 1939. Young mother Eva has a secret from her past.
When the Nazis invade, Eva knows the only way to keep
her daughter Miriam safe is to send her away – even if it
means never seeing her again. But when Eva is taken to a
concentration camp, her secret is at risk of being exposed.

In London, Pamela volunteers to help find places for the
Jewish children arrived from Europe. Befriending one
unclaimed little girl, Pamela brings her home. It is only
when her young son enlists in the RAF that Pamela realises
how easily her own world could come crashing down.

**Two mothers must ask an unthinkable question:
will they ever be reunited with their beloved children?**